# The Tundra Diary: A Didactic Alaskan Novel

Roman Acleaf

# DEDICATION

This novel is dedicated to the late Dr. Ralph Lewis. He never let mediocre curriculum, or mediocre students, get in the way of excellent instruction and, in doing so, inspired a generation of redneck jocks sitting in the back row with their baseball cap brims pulled down and their cowboy boots propped up to be something more than just cannon fodder, underpaid labor, and good breeding stock.

# CONTENTS

# ACKNOWLEDGEMENTS

First and foremost I would like to thank my Alaskan Parents; SL and KL of Wasilla. I never would have made it that first year without you. I would also like to thank my many editors and contributors; RK, CS, CL, JM, DB, DP, JR, and all of you who asked to remain completely anonymous. I'm sure that all of you had your moments of, "Really? You need this proofread by tomorrow? Really?" Your efforts did not go unnoticed nor unappreciated. Finally I would like to thank my parents who might not have always believed in what I was doing, but always believed in me as a person nonetheless, and supported me anyway.

# CHAPTER ONE

Rays of sunlight shot across the ridge of the Chugach Mountains and pierced the 40-foot high windows of Ted Stevens Anchorage International Airport's "C" terminal. I tried to block them with my arm, then my baseball cap, and finally wrapped my head in the black sweatshirt I had used as an improvised pillow to keep my head off of the coarse poly-nylon-hair-dandruff-lint-dust-crumb-microbe blended commercial grade carpet. A few minutes later I removed the sweatshirt-cum-hijab and replaced it with my baseball cap, then dug out my Maui Jim's sunglasses and thrust them upon my face. Eyes puffy, mouth dry, lifeless hair matted down under a baseball cap, and slightly hung-over; coupled with the audacity to wear sunglasses indoors at four in the morning. I wondered if this was what Lindsay Lohan felt like on her way to rehab, or what Amy Winehouse felt like on her way from rehab, or what Robert Downey Jr. felt like for most of the 1990's.

I made my way to the gate for my next flight and evaluated my motivations as interpreted by the elements highlighted in the opening stanza of *Walden*.

Why was I going to the woods or, more accurately, the tundra? Why had I chosen to abandon my split-level end-unit with stainless steel appliances and laminate flooring (in enviable proximity to both Chipotle *and* Panera) in favor of a small village above the Arctic Circle?

Did I want to live deliberately, to front only the essential facts of life? Yes; my life had continued to become more complicated, despite my best efforts to simplify it. Every year I had more documents, accounts, usernames, passwords, and dates to keep track

1

of. My life had filled up like one giant kitchen junk drawer with twist ties and rubber bands and expired coupons for half-off one when you buy any two on a Wednesday after 7:00 p.m., mingled into a nebula of paper and plastic and foil, rough and smooth and sticky and slippery all at the same time; which obscured the really useful items like a flashlight and my extra keys.

Would I learn what the tundra had to teach? Most likely, although I couldn't imagine what that would be. Maybe I would learn to hunt caribou or sew fur mittens or ride a dogsled, even build an igloo. I looked forward to seeing the Northern Lights. That for sure was going to be cool.

I left the secure area, grabbed a venti mocha, went downstairs, and arrived at the gate for Frontier Flying Service without a second security check. At 6:30 I presented my ticket and was directed outside to a twin engine plane about the size of a stretch limo. No metal detector, no x-ray machine, no latex covered fingers to examine my waistline; just out the door, feet in shoes and loose change in pockets, straight to the plane. I figured that the lack of security before less than a dozen passengers boarded a small commuter plane was either a lone example of common sense by the TSA or a simple oversight that the entire population of Alaska had effectively conspired to keep secret. As improbable as either option was, the second theory had a better chance of being true.

The passenger door of the plane was rotated downward and had small steps built into it. An extended family of Native people tried to encourage their matriarch up the stairs and into the aircraft. She wore a lightweight, thigh-length, pullover-style smock over her t-shirt and jeans. It was made of brightly colored cotton-twill, in a floral pattern, trimmed extensively with ribbon.

After several false starts and much manual assistance she made her way up and through the door. She was quickly followed by the rest of her brood which consisted mostly of school age children with the same taste in styles and accessories found anywhere else in America, namely jeans (paradoxically two sizes too small for the girls and four sizes too large for the boys) and hooded sweatshirts. All of the girls had thick, slick, jet-black hair pulled back in a ponytail that fell well below their shoulders and all of the boys' heads had obviously been shaved within the past week. Each and every one carried their provisions, at least two bottles of soda and several candy bars, in a Wal-Mart bag.

I boarded last and crouched down the aisle until I found two empty seats in the same row. I strapped my pack into one and myself into the other. In front of me was a seat pocket for the inflight magazine, but no magazine; just a laminated card of emergency instructions and an air sickness bag joined together by a wad of discarded gum. I figured that was advantageous since if a person needed one of those items, they would probably soon need the other.

The engines roared to life and the plane rolled across the taxiway. Out on the runway it picked up speed and became buoyant as the wheels left the ground and retracted beneath the wings. I peered over the top of my James Michener novel and noticed my fellow travelers either shuffled-searched-clicked-tapped through their iPods if they were under the age of twenty-five, or slept with their heads against the bulkhead and their hands buried deep in their pockets if they were over twenty-five.

About thirty minutes into the flight a voice came over the speaker. I only caught fragments but I did hear, "Side... McKinley....." I had been a mountain junkie since birth and not only wanted to see Mount McKinley since I learned of its existence, but climb it as the sun, repelled by the frosty armor that concealed its foundation, pushed against my skin. This was my mountain, my Mecca, Mount MeccaKinley, and today was my Haj, if only visually and from five-thousand feet above. As my fellow passengers stirred only enough to shift their feet or retrieve another snack I focused all of my attention, physically and spiritually, through the twelve-inch Plexiglas oval beside my shoulder and peered intensely at the landscape below.

Pristine white and translucent blue not just folded about each other but... creased; like the crisp lines of a Marine Corps uniform, or a stealth fighter, or an Origami swan. Smooth and precise; as if Euclid had placed them upon a template by Frank Lloyd Wright before da Vinci, inspired by Beethoven directed by von Karajan, caressed it with his brushes. Perfect, only better. Perfection with an umlaut. The ultra-precise creases crossed and collided then crested into ridges and plunged into valleys; full of grace and free of friction. Peak after peak after peak converged infinitely until a defined ridge like the dorsal fin of some mammoth terra-fish breached the prismatic apices, then arched earthward again.

As the grand peaks gave way to lesser peaks the translucent blue dissipated and the pristine white frayed into streaks of uninspired gray. The angular granite bowed into more conical and curved shapes before it became infested once again with the detritus of foliage. I knew then that my personal zenith of all things mountain-esque had just been eclipsed, perhaps irrevocably.

The whir of the propellers scaled back to a deeper whump and thrum note as the plane pitched slightly and descended into Fairbanks. From above it looked very similar to Billings, Montana or any other city of the Upper Great Plains; many roads crossed at perfect right angles to one another and the landscape was covered in tan, brown, a tree, more tan, more brown, another tree, and the compact squiggle of a river.

The plane glided softly down to the runway then maneuvered to a smooth stop alongside the terminal. When the pilot came out of the cockpit and opened the hatch-like door the matriarch rose from her seat and made her way toward the front of the plane; one white, Velcro-fastened, sneaker shuffle at a time. I unbuckled my backpack from the seat and followed the twenty-first century Hansel and Gretel style trail of strewn wrappers, bottles, and Wal-Mart bags that marked the way to the door.

Inside I found my luggage piled on an abandoned cart.

I had brought the entire luggage ensemble that I owned; my backpack, a recently inherited leather garment bag worth more than any garment I had ever placed in it, an extra-large Realtree Woodland camouflage Cabela's duffel bag purchased in 1997 (1997 having been a big year for Realtree Woodland camouflage) that I had trimmed out and accessorized with silver duct tape accents, and a large rolling suitcase a former girlfriend once coerced me to purchase (under threat of abstinence) because she was mortified at the notion of arriving in Baltimore accompanied by someone carrying an extra-large Realtree Woodland camouflage Cabela's duffel bag.

With my pack on my back, my garment bag slung over one shoulder, and my hands filled with my suitcase and duffel bag I ventured forth like some destitute version of Indiana Jones. I walked east, then west, and within three minutes I had explored the entire Fairbanks International Airport. However, I questioned its international credentials since it had neither a baggage carousel nor any type of fast food restaurant. Worse yet it had only one bar which, due to oversight or overly zealous puritans, was located on the second floor beyond the security check point. With my culinary needs unmet I vowed to someday lobby for legislation that would require all airports to have alcohol available in areas open to the general public.

I retraced my steps to the ticket counters but did not see one for the airline I had a reservation with. I approached the lone agent and asked her where the William's Air Service counter was. She pleasantly availed me of the type of tacit information that is never printed in brochures, guidebooks, or websites, but should be.

"They're located on University Avenue," she half-sang.

"Where's that?" I asked.

"On the other side of the runway."

"Is there a shuttle?"

"No, unfortunately, most people take a taxi," she said with a sympathetic tone. "But you could call them and see if they have anyone available to come pick you up. Would you like me to write their number down for you?"

I thanked her and pinched the stationery between my thumb and forefinger then dialed my iPhone and after seven rings a woman answered, "William's."

"I just arrived over at the airport, the main airport, and I am supposed to be on your two o'clock flight to Iqsaiqsiq (Ick-suh-ick-sick). I was wondering if someone could come over and pick me up."

"We picking up buy pass in free's at noon. Might-could pick you up if you want to wait until then. Just wait at the west end where the fence comes to the end of the building."

"Thank you," I said, without clarification of exactly what type of Alaskan euphemism, "Picking up buy pass in free's," was. I pressed my thumb over the red bar on the glass screen. When the main screen reappeared I went to my NFL app to download the previous night's game. A message informed me that I needed to connect to Wi-Fi before I could load the file. I checked my settings and found that no Wi-Fi networks were available, private or public. No fast food, only one bar, and no Wi-Fi. International airport my ass.

Outside I fetched my Michener novel and a Clif bar then settled back to feed both body and soul as I basked in the perfectly still seventy-eight degree air suspended beneath Interior Alaska's unconstrained sky.

At noon I wedged the empty wrapper between pages ninety-six and ninety-seven and put the novel away, certain that the next truck would be my ride. No truck came. At 12:20 I decided to call again.

"William's Air Service," came the woman's voice.

"I have a reservation for the two o'clock flight to Iqsaiqsiq, and I was told that someone would pick me up over here at the main airport while 'Picking up buy pass in free's.'" (A term I was still vaguely suspicious of, and therefore did not feel comfortable enough to change between active and passive voice or past and present tense.)

"Oh, we never pick up buy pass in free's (there was that term again, albeit slightly modified), so bring taxi, or you can wait until Friday if you cheap." She quickly added, "I jokes," and giggled.

I approached the next taxi cab along the curb and after I told him my destination he said, "Park service or school district?"

"Pardon me?" I asked.

"You're headed to William's, so you're headed to The Bush. You could be a state trooper, but they usually have the local police pick them up. You haven't asked me where the polar bears are, so you're not a tourist. You don't have a rifle case or the type that scientists use to carry all of their instruments, so you're not a guide or biologist. That only leaves the park service or the school district." His amethyst-shaded eye locked on me from beneath a bushy eyebrow.

I wondered if all Alaskans were as perceptive as he, or if all outsiders were as conspicuous as I; in either case I appreciated his skill. "School district," I told him.

As we made a series of left-handed turns the driver dispensed his wisdom. "The Bush is a whole 'nother world. They've got their own way of doing things out there. Almost like a foreign country. And their own language. It's like that book from the nineties 'Men Are on the Moon and Women Are on Uranus' or whatever the hell it was. They use the same words, but the words have different meanings than they usually do, or at least different than the way we mean them. Like they will say 'I go store.' 'Go' could mean they *are going* right now, or it could mean they *will be going* later, or it could mean they *have gone* there at one time. It just depends on what else they happen to be talking about when they say it."

The driver whipped the taxi into the parking lot with a final hard left and I asked him, "You probably know the answer to a question that has bothered me all morning. What does pick up buy pass in free's mean?"

"Bypass is the bulk mail, like parcel post, which means it's cheap for the customer; but hardly pays for itself, it's not nearly as profitable as passengers and local freight. The airlines are required to carry it anyway, which they do only as a last resort and only if they have a full load of it all going to the same place. It's the mail that 'bypasses' the post office and goes directly to one specific village. It's a losing deal for the airlines, might cost them five or six hundred dollars to operate the plane but they're only getting paid a hundred bucks or something to haul the freight, so they drag their feet as much as possible until the postal service tells them that they absolutely have to deliver it or else pay a fine."

I offered him a twenty dollar bill to cover the $16.25 fare. He peeled back singles for my change but I waived my hand once from left to right. "Keep it. What is free's?"

"Freeze is food that is frozen, which is the best way to transport food in Alaska since it may take a full day to get all the way out to the villages and most planes don't have any type of refrigeration. Besides, people in the village like TV dinners and ice cream just like everybody else so a lot of that gets sent out too. It's the exact opposite of bypass as far as freight goes. Airlines get to set their own price for freeze, usually two or three dollars a pound, so they *love* to haul freeze. If they carry just two-hundred pounds of freeze with their bypass they can actually break even, or if they carry five-hundred pounds of freeze that's like a thousand dollars profit."

The driver picked up my duffel bag and suitcase and headed for the terminal. I trailed behind him with my backpack and garment bag and followed his lead when he placed them down in a pile at the base of the ticket counter. "Good luck," he said and fled before I could thank him.

I faced the counter and was greeted by the thickest, darkest set of bangs that floated over an acne strewn face filled with remnants of partially rotted teeth. "Good morning," she said. It was the same voice I had heard over the phone and it belonged to a Native woman in her thirties.

"I have a reservation for Iqsaiqsiq," I said.

"Bags." She pointed to a scale as she retrieved a calculator from beneath the counter.

I placed my suitcase on first, forty-four pounds. I replaced the suitcase with my duffel bag and watched the needle move up to forty-seven pounds. My garment bag came in at an even thirty-five pounds and my backpack was twenty-nine pounds. The ticket agent combined the figures on the calculator then asked, "How much you weigh?"

"Two-hundred twenty pounds." I didn't understand why this information was pertinent unless the airline wanted to deter most of the women I knew from ever flying on an airplane again.

"Your name?"

"Ken Shosatori."

She pulled out a Tupperware box similar to one my mom has kept recipes in since the Reagan administration and found a triplicated form identical to the one she had filled out previously. She transferred the figures from the first form on to the new one, and said, "One-hundred fifteen."

I assumed that was my flight number, or ticket number, or some other set of three digits used to identify me.

"How you pay?" she asked.

"I already paid when I made my reservation," I said.

"Bags is over forty pounds. You gots pay dollar for every pound over forty."

That made the $20 a bag Alaska Airlines charged seem downright charitable. I offered up my Visa card and made a mental note to significantly reduce the size of my wardrobe.

She tore off the top page of the form and handed it to me along with my credit card. "Flight leaves at five so be back by four."

"I thought the flight left at two?" I inquired.

"No, busy today. So flight leaves at five."

I retrieved my backpack from the pile and found a seat across from a tall, gangly man with thick, wavy, copper hair; kind of a masculine version of Conan O'Brien, but with Jay Leno's chin. His attire was part REI, part Tractor Supply Company; mocha-toned fleece vest, green long sleeve shirt, ultra-thick brown leather belt, tan Carhartt canvas work pants, and dull chocolate brown XtraTuf boots. As I dug the Michener novel out of my backpack he semi-growled, "Michener huh? You read his latest?"

"Latest?" I thought. The guy's dead; if he has a book based on his most recent journey *that* would be an epic novel. When I raised my eyes I saw that he held the very book to which he had referred, *Matecumbe*. "No I haven't," I said.

He leaned across with hand extended. "Roby, I'm the principal in Aciq (Awe-chick). I heard you up at the counter. You're going to Iqsaiqsiq? What do you teach?"

I began to wonder if I had "TEACHER" written across my forehead or a note in the shape of a little red school house pinned to my chest with my name and bus number on it. "Ken Shosatori. Math. High school math."

"First time in Alaska?" he asked, as he read details from my manners and appearance I had unintentionally posted more prominently on myself than on Facebook.

"Yep," I said.

"I started in Ciaciqiq (Chee-uh-chick-ick) seven years ago then got the principal gig in Aciq last year. Iqsaiqsiq is the roughest village, but not as bad as everybody says. That incident with the principal was several years ago. Besides, ever since the shooting there's been a trooper stationed there full time so things should start getting better."

Rough? Incident? Shooting? These words had not come up during my interview. Granted I had not thought to ask how many rounds students fire on an annual basis, or what the most recent body count was, but I hadn't really thought I had reason to. I hadn't applied to teach in a juvenile detention center, or some depressed inner-city ghetto, I was headed to the wilderness of Alaska; part *Grizzly Adams*, part *Little House on the Prairie*, with a dash of *Northern Exposure* on the side. This new information begged my next question, "What shooting?"

Roby rolled his eyes up as he did some mental arithmetic. "Last Christmas break, probably January, I think." He spilled some coffee on his hand and wiped it on his pants where their dark cream color and stoutly woven texture dissipated it effortlessly and invisibly.

"What exactly do you mean by rough?" I asked.

"The kids are pretty outspoken. They like to tell teachers things like, 'Your breath stinks' or 'Those clothes make you look fat.' Most people get sucked into it, and that just makes it all the more miserable for them. Be fair, firm, and consistent. Don't let them know what gets to you, and don't lose your cool. Ever." Roby leaned back against the red molded plastic chair.

"What happened with the principal?" I had to ask.

"Ancient history, none of the students involved are even in school anymore. Don't dwell on it. If something like that happens again, it will be in some other village." He cut the air with his flattened right hand as if to indicate "stay" to a blackjack dealer. It implied that there would be no more discussion of that topic.

"Why'd you choose Alaska?" Roby asked.

"When I started teaching I had almost thirty students in every class because the district had a policy that limited class sizes to thirty students. Then the limit was changed to thirty-five as a so-called-temporary measure to deal with a so-called-unexpected increase in enrollment and I had thirty-five students in every class. Last year the bond measure failed and all I heard was; 'we're going to have to cut teachers next year, we're going to have to cut teachers next year.' Eventually nobody actually got fired, but the maximum class size was supposed to be moved up to forty *and* the district was going to require teachers to pay $250 a month toward their health insurance premiums. No job security, reduced benefits, and not enough time to spend any one-on-one time with students; on top of the ten hour days, weekends grading papers, occasional f-bombs or middle fingers and what's the point? I could have skipped college and been a welder or a prison guard. During lunch one day my friend Dan, who grew up in Fairbanks, said 'Why don't you try teaching in Alaska? They pay really well, your medical is completely covered, and you don't have to pay for supplies out of your own pocket.'"

"Yep." Roby drawled. "And if you put in twenty years your medical is free when you retire. Plus, the Arctic Circle School District is the highest paying school district in the United States. As soon as you get to your classroom make a list of anything you want; microscopes, colored pencils, a DVD player, even rugs and chairs and lamps. If you feel it would help students, just order it."

Roby produced a can of Copenhagen from his vest pocket. He pried the lid up with his thumb, rolled it back with his middle finger, took a pinch of snuff between his thumb and forefinger, held his bottom lip down with his pinky, placed the pinch along his gum line, rolled the lid back on the can, and dropped it back in his pocket; all with such effortless dexterity it would have made David Blaine jealous.

"Here're some things I wish someone had told me early on. First, these kids thrive on routine. They revere and admire it. If you decide to do one page a day, then always do one page. If you decide to do two, then always do two. Don't try to double-down because it's the end of the quarter or cut your lesson in half because it's Friday. Second, write down the schedule on the board in the same order every day; topic, concepts, page numbers, materials, whatever. Most of these kids' brains are beehives of anxiety and if they have one less thing to obsess over it will make their lives easier, and that will make your life easier. Don't expect them to read it, some of them may not be able to, but write it down for them anyway just so they have a pattern they can follow."

Roby spat into the now empty cup and continued. "Third, you may have heard people say 'Don't smile until Christmas,' or 'Don't smile until Easter.' Well, don't ever let these kids see you smile. Be polite, but never smile."

I felt like I had just been given the freshman survival guide, or better yet the prison survival guide. The Arctic Circle version of, "Don't drop the soap, don't be a snitch, and get yourself a shank so nobody tries to punk you out."

Roby spit in the cup again. "At least you don't have to do the milk run today."

"What's that?" I asked, "I just learned about bypass and freeze. My guess is it doesn't involve any actual milk, or even much running."

Roby enlightened me. "A milk run is where the plane makes several stops. Typically this flight goes from here to Aciq, to Ciaciqiq, to Iqsaiqsiq, then stops in Klaciq (claw-chick) on its way back down. Any opportunity the airlines have to pick up a passenger, they will. A typical milk run would probably take four hours to weave all the way up to Iqsaiqsiq. Straight through it'll take two."

A person walked in through the door on the runway side of the building, followed by another, then another, and then another, all of them Native in appearance. Each dialed the phone in turn and made the same request, "Got taxi? William's, yeah, yeah, okay," then followed the shaft of sunlight that streamed through the front door. A few minutes later the squeal of a loose fan belt or under-nourished steering pump approached, the gravel crunched and crumbled, and a car door closed. Every few minutes the process repeated like a tidal flow of taxi's that surged in, ceased momentarily, and retreated.

A mustached white man of massive girth and loose features entered. He wore a "William's Air Service" baseball cap, sweat stained into a halo around the rim and faded to a uniform shade of pink except for a red band arched across the apex from ear to ear. Roby nodded to him then said, "No chance of getting get weathered out today, Banzai Bill flies in anything."

Roby's words reminded of something a crew chief on a CH-46 had once told me, "Guys that will fly *in* anything eventually fly *into* something." Those words stuck in my head like elevator music for the next twenty minutes.

Banzai Bill addressed a thin Native man headed in the direction of the runway access door. "Moses, put seven-hundred pounds of fuel in the two-oh-seven along with the rest of the bypass from yesterday, and four seats." Moses nodded and walked out.

When Moses reentered Banzai Bill called out, "Aciq!"

Roby rose to his feet as he dug the Copenhagen out from beneath his lip with his tongue. Most of the snuff he spat out made its way into the Styrofoam cup pressed at the base of his prominent Jay Leno-esque chin. The rest drifted down in flakes and blended with the surface of his mocha-toned fleece vest. A wardrobe that appeared unsoiled even after exposure to coffee and tobacco, this man was a genius. It made me wonder what fabrics, tones, and textures were equally as impervious to marinara and merlot.

Roby gave my hand the signature squeeze, double-pump, release familiar on used car lots across the country and offered me one last tip before I left orientation and stepped into general population. "For reasons you'll soon realize, the Bush is a tougher place to teach than South Central L.A. or inner-city Detroit. Remember; routine and consistency. Never validate their effect on you, positive or negative, disappointment or exhilaration. Not smiling is just as important as not yelling in front of these kids. Lastly, when you have a day where *everybody* craps in your lap, repeat this mantra: Come what may, May will come."

"Thank you." I didn't know what else to add to such a dire forecast. "Best of luck to you. Best of luck to all of us I guess."

"Better to be lucky than good."

Two similarly attired people met Roby and Banzai Bill at the door to form an octopod of perfectly matched leggings and footwear as they approached a jalopy of a plane about the size of a compact station wagon.

Roby negotiated the single step welded beneath the door and slithered his legs in behind him. The single propeller spun and the plane bobbed as it rotated in place on an invisible axis. Roby's stoic face peered back at me, a finger from each hand pointed directly at his flattened lips.

I took on Michener once again until my weary eyes could no longer scan the densely worded passages. Eventually my head drooped, my eyes fell shut, my hands loosened, and the book slid from my fingers. I retrieved it from the floor and curled up between the two mated chairs.

I was startled awake by the clang of an aluminum-cased logbook flopped on the counter. Banzai Bill clomped around for a few minutes then asked, "You headed to Iqsaiqsiq?"

"Yes." I said.

"Let's go."

As we approached the Subaru with wings I reflected that I had left Seattle on an aircraft with two jet engines, left Anchorage on an aircraft with two propellers, and was now about to board an aircraft with one propeller. If this regression continued the next aircraft would be either a hot air balloon or a hang-glider.

The plane had only two seats; front left, and front right. I settled into the right seat and saw that the back of the plane was filled with the United Nations of Pepsi products. Perched alongside this veritable soda-mid, almost as an afterthought, were my duffel bag, garment bag, and suitcase. A cargo net was ratcheted taut across all of it.

Banzai Bill's headphones aligned perfectly with the sanguine band across the top of his baseball cap. He pushed a button on the instrument panel and the propeller transformed from a stationary blade to a wavy haze that filled the cabin with a dull whir of high-pitched static. Laboriously the plane began to roll down the runway like a semi-truck going up a steep grade until it picked up enough speed to have merged into the left lane of I-5. Finally it peeled away from the ground, marginally at first, then more and more dramatically until all I could see was blue sky.

By the time we leveled off the landscape was largely indiscernible. There were no roads or power lines, or large swaths cut and aligned into rectangles. Occasionally there was a dissonant accumulation of perfect rectangles clumped abstractly. The only trees were the ones that crowded the riverbanks, which meandered like ribbons in the wind and wove back upon themselves in grand oxbows.

Soon the auburn and sage landscape stretched upward, as if tugged at by the sky, until it disappeared completely into thick stratus clouds at the horizon. From my vantage point the clouds could have rested directly on the surface, or hovered several thousand feet above it. I had no bearing save for the altimeter. The cloudscape droned on, an appropriate visual compliment to the monotonous whir of the engine.

Sometime later I stirred from my sleep as the plane traveled in figure-eights that made my body heavier on one side, and then the other. I glimpsed the earth's flesh where clouds wore thin into gauzy wisps of condensation. The first peeks were inconspicuous patches of hardpan soil and some random shipping containers in dull shades of dusty basketball orange, pear-peel green, and concrete grey.

Banzai Bill poked me in the shoulder and tapped a handle in the upper-left corner of the windshield then pointed to a similar handle in the upper-right corner of the windshield. I reached for it as the plane rolled to the left and the clouds sucked in the left wing. My right hand clamped around the handle like a Chinook salmon on a fly and my left hand mated itself promiscuously with some nameless, metal bracket under the seat.

The sky over my right shoulder faded to white as the entire plane was engulfed by the pervasive vapor. Eventually the vapor dispersed and structural components within three or four feet of the windows became visible again as beads of moisture migrated up the windshield. Banzai Bill took this as a good omen and leveled out the wings. We dropped away from the white layer above and neared a mélange of brown soil and short green stalks that stretched endlessly below.

Straight ahead two parallel rows of lights, spread maybe sixty feet apart, blazed like a hundred paparazzi assembled to meet us.

Banzai Bill turned some knobs and discs and with innate effortlessness settled the plane without a hint of tire squeal or jolt. The engine dropped several octaves from the pitched whir to a rapid glub-glub-glub-glub. We made a semi-circle at the end of the runway and backtracked to an area where two identical, white, four-door, Ford trucks waited.

Banzai Bill shut off the engine, took off his headset, opened his door and swung his rubber-encased calves out then hopped down to the surface. He immediately lit a cigarette that flicked to and fro like a conductor's wand on his lips as he said, "You can let go now."

I released the handle and unbound the bracket, then opened the door and slid down until my Merrell boots slapped against the loose gravel.

# CHAPTER TWO

A man with a ponytail and dark blue coveralls approached. Three-fourths of his face was covered by a beard and moustache and the open space that remained was occluded by a pair of halcyon-tinged safety glasses, save for the peach toned tip of his nose. "You Ken?" he asked, and received my luggage from the pilot.

"Yes." I took my garment bag and backpack from him.

"I'm John Sledson, head of maintenance. We got you put up at the quad-plex. I've got a set of keys for you." I followed him to the truck and we heaved the bags into it. "You want to go straight home or stop by the school first?"

"Home please." I noticed that the other truck had backed up to the plane's cargo doors and a flurry of hands handed case after case of soda into it. "I guess I came on the same plane as the annual soda delivery."

"Annual?" said John, "Try *daily*."

As we passed houses I noticed that they were not the quaint collection of cabins I had expected to find in Alaska but more like the world's northernmost trailer park; a repository of double-wide, vinyl-sided, shallow-roofed prefabrication plotted within a grid of gravel lanes and power lines. Each boasted a collection of snowmobiles in various states of disrepair deposited around the front entry in place of the traditional pink flamingos and garden gnomes found in lower 48 trailer parks. A few of the houses had two boats in front of them; one was a typical aluminum hulled skiff while the other was a wood-framed job covered with what looked like some type of white canvas. Interestingly, every other house had a gray trash can and a yellow recyclables can in front of it. I never would have guessed that there would be a recycling program in a little place like this.

John stopped the truck at the first intersection and pointed straight ahead to the largest building in town; an overly tall, yet not quite two-story, brown building with yellow trim and almost no windows. "That's the school right there." Like all of the buildings in town, it was raised about four feet off of the ground on a series of posts. He turned the truck left and headed down the road past the customary double-wides to a building heretofore unimaginable, yet immediately identifiable. The building wasn't double-wide, it was triple-wide, and double-tall. It was an Appalachian McMansion, the envy of every hillbilly from Virginia to West Virginia. John stopped the truck in front of it.

I stepped out and grinned, half out of disbelief for the ingenious feat of engineering, and wondered what they would think of next; a double-necked banjo so Jimmie Page can play Bluegrass? Not even Jeff Foxworthy could have dreamt up this one. "If your double-wide has an upstairs…" I imagined him saying.

We carried the bags across a series of wooden pallets that bridged the path from the gravel road to the front steps, which were made from a serrated steel mesh similar to a giant cheese-grater, then up to a six-by-ten foot porch made from similar material. The pallets apparently kept occupants and visitors from having to step into the soggy mud produced by the not-so-permanent permafrost. I realized then why Roby, Banzai Bill, and John all wore the same signature XtraTuf boots.

John said, "Your apartment is on the top floor, right hand side," descended the steps, crossed the pallets, and drove away.

I stepped from the shared front porch into the shared front foyer. I had just enough time to get a glimpse of the hallway to my left, the stairs to my right, and the mezzanine above before the door slammed shut. My four bags and left foot hovered somewhere between the first and second step. I re-opened the door and placed my suitcase against it then tried each switch on the wall. None of them had any effect.

A man exited from a door directly to the left of the front door. He was a little like Danny DeVito, but with thick gray hair and large wire rim glasses. He spoke with a rural, southern drawl. "How you doin'? I'm Cornell Coalman." He stuck out his hand and I shook it.

"Pretty good. Ken Shosatori."

Cornell shook his head. "No power or water yet Bud. Supposed to be set up by Monday though. All last year all they talked about was how we was gonna have a new water system put in this summer, and here we are still usin' honey-buckets and waitin' on the water tru-uck. Wuh-ell, I'll hold this door open down here for ya until you get up the stairs Bud."

"Much appreciated," I said as I gathered my bags and headed up the stairs

I may not have known about bypass, freeze, or milk-runs, but I did know what a honey-bucket was from my time in the forest service. It was a metal can with a toilet seat attached to the top and lined with either plastic bags or a smaller plastic bucket. When people were done with their business they emptied them into some type of group receptacle. It was my guess that the large yellow trash cans were the group receptacle. Iqsaiqsiq was not at the forefront of municipal services, as I had thought, but the backend.

I reached the top of the stairs and waved to Cornell as he ducked back into his apartment, then I opened the door to mine.

My foot landed on typical, Grade-B, vinyl. To my right was a self-asserted living room with a couch and a chair arranged beneath two narrow windows. At the far end of the living room was an open door through which I could see a bed, night stand, and lamp. To my left were four chairs and a large oval table. Along the inner wall was a counter top flanked by a refrigerator and a stove. At the far end of the counter top past the stove was a door that led to what I assumed was the bathroom. I made my way into the bedroom to unpack my bags.

First I emptied my garment bag, which contained all of my teacher clothes. Every male teacher owns at least two and as many as twelve pairs of Dockers casual pants, the majority of which are in khaki, and I had filled my quota; two khaki, two blue, and one brown. The greatest upside to Dockers is that if they are removed from the dryer and hung on a hanger quickly, within at least one quarter of a football game or ten laps of NASCAR, they don't need to be ironed. This low care aspect of Dockers was important to me since I lacked an iron as well as a trained operator for such a device, and if I were fortunate enough to find a trained operator in the middle-of-nowhere-Alaska I wasn't going to waste those talents on ironing, especially since

17

past operators I had known became prone to headaches and narcolepsy. To match my khaki, blue, and brown Dockers I had various shades of green, blue, and brown shirts in both short-sleeve polo and long-sleeve twill. For more formal duties like basketball game chaperone or bake sale supervisor I had a few ties, all received as gifts and all portrayed some species of fish. I wondered if any human had ever actually worn-out a neck tie.

I threw the garment bag under the bed and moved on to my suitcase. Every male teacher also owns at least two, sometimes three if he is really fashion conscious, pairs of non-athletic shoes. One is formal, expensive and well-crafted, intended to be shined and polished weekly. He tells himself and others that these are his everyday shoes, proper and professional to match his demeanor and the dignity of his profession. The other is more casual with a full set of laces and a one-piece molded rubber sole, perhaps a rounded toe and extra arch support. He tells himself that he will keep these in the bottom drawer of his desk and only slip them on after the last bell has rung and the students have gone home, or maybe on a Friday when he is assured that no parents or administrators will visit. In practice the formal shoes get worn until 3:01 on the first day of school at which time they switch places in the bottom drawer with the more casual shoes that become the adornment of choice except for the monthly awards ceremony and the bi-annual performance evaluation. I placed both pairs along with my athletic shoes on the closet floor and spread all of my socks, underwear, and T-shirts across the shelf.

Further down in my suitcase were three king-size, heavier-than-average flannel top sheets. They could be folded around any mattress from twin to king size, serve as top sheets on an equally broad range of mattresses provided they were tucked in far enough, and double-layered to serve as blankets. In a pinch they also made decent table cloths. I once used one as an improvised bathrobe, but after it had arm holes it was never quite the same. I also unpacked several bath sheets. Not bath towels but bath sheets, a distinction I had discerned around the age of 30. Bath sheets are larger and better at protean tasks such as curtains or a post-bath sarong. At the very bottom of my suitcase was a nylon bag about the size of two loaves of bread that contained my down sleeping bag and a plastic box about nine inches square and two inches thick with a lockable hasp. Inside was my Beretta 92FS pistol. I spread the sheets out on the bed and put the box on the shelf under the bath sheets.

I returned to the kitchen to unpack my duffel bag which contained Clif bars, powdered Gatorade, freeze-dried dinners and a few utensils.

Clif bars, usually eaten in transit and accompanied by a venti mocha, had been my primary source of morning energy for the last three years. I filled a series of drawers next to the refrigerator with them.

I had always found Gatorade easy to sip regardless of temperature, mood, illness, or previous over-consumption of alcoholic beverages because it could be ingested without further disruption to an already compromised gastro-intestinal process. There are no better post-bachelor party friends than soft cotton, cool porcelain, and a quart of freshly mixed lemon-lime. I stacked the canisters on top of the refrigerator along with my Nalgene bottles.

The freeze-dried entrees were labeled as two-person meals in the same way Smart Cars are marketed as two-person vehicles; only if one of the people is a child and the other is anorexic. One meal was just about perfect for me provided it was accompanied by some type of baked good or, as a last resort, a vegetable. I laid them out in the cupboard nearest the stove along with my non-stick sauce pans and microwave-safe bowls.

With my luggage unpacked I settled into bed with Michener. Before I turned a page my eyes were closed and the book was on my chest.

It was light outside, more accurately it was *still* light outside, when I heard the rapid metallic "kaputtputt-putt, kaputtputt-putt" of four-stroke engines and the screech of gravel as rubber slid across it. I looked out my window. Two streets over a trio of red Honda four-wheelers raced and evaded each other. In addition to the operator, one person rode on the seat behind them while two more rode side-saddle on the rear rack. Sometimes a fifth person rode on the front rack as well. Eventually they all pulled up to a house and ran inside. I checked my iPhone and noticed it was 2:52 a.m. Twenty minutes later, as my eyelids became comfortably resettled, I heard an engine start, then another, and then another. They revved and screeched for about ten minutes. The pattern continued, ten minutes on, twenty minutes off, until I eventually put on my headphones and wrapped my head, swami-style, in a bath sheet to drown out the noise.

My alarm went off at 6:00 a.m. and I quickly gathered a fresh one of everything along with a towel and my shaving kit plus, since I preferred to light candles instead of curse darkness, my headlamp to navigate the darkened hallway.

Out on the front porch I looked across the endless plain of dew-laden grass and felt the cool damp air penetrate my clothing. It didn't feel at all like it was my first summer morning in the Arctic. It felt more like a thousand winter evenings on the deck of my parent's home at the Washington Coast where I would nurse a cup of coffee or a bottle of beer after dinner as the collected elements of a storm waited to catalyze. But it wasn't my parent's home. It was mine, at least for the next nine months.

Even before 7:00 a.m., children were on the swings and monkey bars in front of the school. As I approached, they all ran up with a singular chorus. "Hi teacher, hi teacher! What's your name? What's your name?"

"Mr. Shosatori."

"Whose teacher are you? Yeah, whose teacher are you? What grade you teach? You teach fourth grade?"

"I teach high school math."

"You know Mitch? Mitch gots dog. It named Gobi. You see Mitch? You see Gobi?"

"No I haven't met Mitch. I don't know where Gobi is."

"Gobi can play dead," said the smallest of the boys who was maybe kindergarten age.

The children then proceeded to shoot each other with their thumb and forefinger. "Bang," one would say, and another would lie down on the gravel and close their eyes. Seconds later the one on the ground would get up and shoot at another kid.

It was all very Shakespeare-in-the-playground, or maybe Shakespeare-in-the-arctic. Either way I saw my opportunity for a curtain call.

I tried my collection of keys at the front door until I found one that worked. Inside the foyer were hallways to my left and right, as well as a larger one straight ahead. Instinct told me that the larger hallway led to the gym, and where there was a gym there was a locker room with showers. I again went through a process of elimination with my keys at the gym and locker room doors. After my shower I dressed and walked back to the front of the school.

A plaque to the right of the main entrance designated rooms from Kindergarten to sixth grade. A plaque to the left designated the office, library, and "Secondary" classrooms. I passed the office, library, and science room on my way to the room with "Math" emblazoned on the door. I unlocked the door after only two keys, flipped a switch, and entered.

Six tables stacked high with boxes formed an island in the center of the room. Beyond that was a tall slender window. To my right were a teacher's desk and a filing cabinet, and further still was a white board. To my left, across the back wall, were eight computers fenced in by a row of chairs stacked two high.

The first box contained something I had never seen in my previous years of teaching, something I had assumed was only a myth like Sasquatch or the Loch Ness monster: Brand, new, books. Complete sets of twenty-one including the annotated teachers editions and supplementary PDF's on CD-ROM. I had spent substantial portions of my short teaching career photocopying, scanning, downloading, and *inventing* texts; as well as swapping teachers editions around like a non-custodial parent to correct assignments and create lesson plans. I meditated on this moment of Zen.

The next four boxes also contained new books, one set for each section I would be teaching. The final box contained notebooks, pencils, protractors, rulers, and graph paper.

"Finding everything you'll need for a successful year Mr. Shosatori?" A voice bellowed from behind me.

I turned and saw a compact, mature version of Don Draper in his early fifties. He wore a white, French-collared shirt and a shimmering emerald tie held in place by a sterling pin at the top and a pearl dot in the middle. "I've got all new books," I said with an unveiled smile, "Every place else I've worked the books seemed to magically appear ten years old and (I wanted to say, "Beaten to shit," but thought better of it) quite worn."

"Just one of the benefits of the Arctic Circle School District." He stepped forward and extended his hand. "Emory Atkinson, we spoke on the phone."

After the grasp, double-pump, release I remembered the name and now the voice. He was the principal, but had not been present at my interview which had consisted of meeting with the personnel manager for twenty minutes in a cubicle at the Tacoma job fair. About a month later Principal Atkinson called, asked about my experiences with effective classroom management and cross-cultural communications, then faxed me a contract I was required to sign and

FedEx back the same day. It was also his first year in Iqsaiqsiq after two decades with the Kenai Peninsula Borough School District.

"Nice to finally meet you in person," I said.

"Same. Did you get the agenda I emailed about the staff meeting?" Principal Atkinson inquired.

"No, I haven't been online since I left Seattle Wednesday night."

"I'll bring you a copy. We're meeting in the library at eight-thirty. See you then."

"Eight-thirty, got it."

Principal Atkinson vanished as precipitously as he had appeared and I returned to my boxes. I arranged my room to the maxims my mentor imparted to me my first year: The further the teacher's desk is from the door, the less likely things are to disappear from it. Always have a workspace near the board to keep papers on. Always have an unassigned desk to send students that need to be separated. Occlude the window somehow so it cannot be looked directly into or out of.

Just a few ticks short of 8:30 I hustled the ten steps to the library.

The library consisted of a regular classroom with bookshelves along three and a half walls, the final half was covered by a whiteboard and a large plasma screen mounted on a wheeled cart. Six child-sized tables, each with four child-sized chairs, were staggered down the middle of the room. Atop each table were four copies of the agenda set out equidistantly at three, six, nine, and twelve o'clock along the edges. The agenda was Times New Roman script in a twelve point font and impeccably outlined in perfect APA style: Roman numeral, capital letter, Arabic numeral, lower-case letter, parenthesized Arabic numeral. "Welcome," was the first heading, followed by the sub-heading, "Expectations."

Principal Atkinson began his presentation. "Welcome to the first staff meeting of the year. I'd like to begin with some expectations." He had a PowerPoint presentation of his agenda on the plasma screen. "We start on time, we end on time. Glad to see everybody made it here early today, let's try to maintain that tradition for the rest of the year especially as we return from our nine thirty break, lunch is being flown in from Igloo Italiano in Aciq courtesy of the school board. We'll break for lunch at noon as you can see on the agenda…" Principal Atkinson's voice began to drone as he followed the agenda, with his PowerPoint of the agenda, which outlined the schedule listed on the agenda.

Eventually we went through introductions; first teachers (none of whom were Native) then support staff (most of whom were Native) and finally the Alaska State Trooper who lived in our village. "I'm Senior Trooper Jeremy Stanisauvlauvski and, it's not a coincidence, Jennifer Stanisauvlauvski, the secretary, is my wife. Just as she said you may call her Miss Jenn, I usually go by Trooper Stan. Don't feel bad if you mispronounce my last name, I was in the fourth grade before I could do it correctly myself, so Trooper Stan is fine.

"I try to be here in the school at least a few hours every day and I'm usually in the village at all times unless I have to guard or transport a prisoner." Trooper Stan cut the air alternately with each hand and pointed in various directions as he spoke. "Mr. Atkinson is going to talk about his policy in dealing with emergencies here at the school, but I want you all to know that ninety-five percent of the time I'm here in the village, and even if I'm off-duty, I'm still on call."

Principal Atkinson stood back up. "One of the things they stressed at the administrators in-service was the district policy concerning the removal of students from classrooms. Teachers are not to use physical force on students, except in cases of immediate physical danger. Teachers are not to use physical force to bring students into or remove students from the building, classrooms, or their seats. If a student refuses to enter or refuses to leave your classroom after you have instructed them to do so the first step is to call Trooper Stanisauvlauvski. If Trooper Stanisauvlauvski is unavailable, then I will deal with the student. If I am not available, then Mr. Dowe will be acting as principal and he will remove the student. No one else should ever use force on a student. Likewise, no student is allowed to grab, push, shove, or hit a teacher. If that happens, then the student will be suspended. Any questions before we head to break?"

"What if the student is damaging property, pushing things off desks, tearing things off of the wall?" Brenda Bortund, the fifth and sixth grade teacher, asked.

"Tell them to stop." Principal Atkinson responded. "If they don't, then call the office and either Trooper Stanisauvlauvski or myself will come down to remove the student. Anything else? No? I have nine twenty-seven by my watch. We will take a break and see everyone ready to go again at nine forty-five. Dismissed."

Fifteen backs arched and fifteen mouths yawned as thirty arms stretched out to their full extension. A woman with coils of blond hair draped over her high, prominent cheek bones approached my table. She was Joanne Sledson, the kindergarten teacher, and, with three whole years under her belt, Iqsaiqsiq's senior most staff member. She was also the wife of John, the head maintenance man. "I've got something in my room I need help with, can you give me a hand?" she asked.

"Sure," I said.

I followed her down to what had to be the kindergarten room: pictures of animals attached to the walls, stuffed animals piled in a corner, plastic animals in boxes. Every corner of the room had a set of letters, numbers, shapes, and colors in it. There was also a couch, which I thought was odd but dismissed as something unique to kindergarten. Joanne picked up a Costco sized jar of Jelly Belly's from her desk, poured out a handful for herself, and offered it to me. "If you ever want privacy around here, just mention that work is involved and people will stay as far away from you as possible."

We sat on the couch and passed around the Jelly Bellys as we chatted about what had brought us to Alaska.

Joanne had come up from Illinois to Anchorage one summer to run in the annual Mayor's Marathon. Over a pitcher of beer at Anchorage's landmark restaurant Humpy's she met John, a heavy equipment operator born and raised in Juneau. A few months later he adorned her left hand with a two-carat diamond ring. She had substitute taught in Anchorage while John rotated back and forth to the oil field every two weeks. Eventually they wanted to be someplace where they could both earn good money as well as be home every night, which Iqsaiqsiq allowed them to do. They planned to semi-retire at age forty-five. As we headed back to the library I made a mental note that a two-carat diamond is comparable in size to about one and a half Jelly Bellys.

# CHAPTER THREE

Back in the library we sat down to watch the plasma screen whereupon the Superintendent, a kind of Donald Trump knock-off with reading glasses that incessantly migrated down his sweat-sheened nose, espoused the virtues of "strategic goals" and "mission statements" aligned with "proficiency benchmarks" and "performance mandates" which we were implored to "enthusiastically pursue" and "rigorously engage" in order to help students "integrate the ideals of excellence" and "collaborate for achievement."

A member of the school board, Native and in his early fifties, took the podium and delivered a speech that was less nebulous, more genuine, and, thankfully, much shorter. Whereas the Superintendent had used language that was equal parts political, corporate, and academic; the school board member spoke in tones that wavered between a Greenpeace organizer and a caller to NPR. He shared the "community's vision" and "cultural heritage" which "valued" and "understood" the "traditional language" and "spiritual beliefs" that led to "healthy individuals."

As the camera panned back and swept to the right it focused in on a woman in a brightly-colored pullover smock similar to the one worn by the elderly woman on the plane. After a little confusion she began to speak. "Bet tee uh eek uh look uh. Meek taw, tock ah lock ah tock, ick…" Captions began to appear in black blocks along the bottom of the screen:

My name is Betty Iqaluq. I was born in 1941 in the village of
Aciq. My parents were Zipporah Iqaluq and Ezra Iqaluq. When
I was growing up there were no schools in the village. No
school, no television, no phone, no electricity. We learned by
watching, by being around people and doing the same things
they did. I wore only animal skins until my twelfth birthday…

She had a pretty cool story. It was bucolic, but with authentic
representations of the harshness of life in the pre-modern Arctic. She
explained the culture shock when she first visited Fairbanks in her early
twenties and was exposed to soda pop, toothbrushes, telephones, and
elevators; all things that even the poorest rural people in Western-
Anglicized-Contemporary-Industrial-Society experience before their
fifth birthday. She didn't bemoan a diet solely of animal flesh or
winters spent on the wood plank floor of a sod house, but she didn't
romanticize it either. It had all just happened, good or bad; without
intention, malice, resentment, or reflection.
    When Betty Iqaluq (Ick-uh-look) left the stage there was a
pregnant pause as the majority of the audience in Aciq got up and left
the room while we waited for another presenter. Eventually the room
cleared and the camera focused in on a Native woman in her mid-
forties on the stage.
    "*Qaniq (*Kuh-nick*) Itpitch (*It-pitch*)*! Hello, I am Terri Bowen-
Skeen and I am the Native Language and Cultural Education
Coordinator. I was born here in Aciq and I was in the first graduating
class after the Aciq School was built in 1985. Go Tundra Wolves! I
attended college and lived in Fairbanks for three years where I met my
husband Lars Skeen before moving back to Aciq, so I have an
awareness of the differences between common social norms and those
that are unique to the Inupiat." She paced back and forth across the
stage, but stopped at times to emphasize a sentence.
    "Inupiat are tolerant. We accept people who are different than
us and expect them to do the same. We try to avoid conflict. If you ask
someone, 'Do you mind if I sit here?' and they don't want you to sit
there, they will not tell you 'no,' they will just not acknowledge you at
all. Likewise, if someone does something you don't approve of, just
ignore them. When you tell someone, 'That's wrong,' it's like you are
saying there is something wrong with them. This is why if you ask,
'What sound does the letter 'm' make?' and a student answers, 'Ruh,
ruh, ruh,' all the other students will say, 'Ruh,' even if they know it's

wrong, because it could cause a conflict. That's also why if you ask, 'Who likes hamburgers?' and vote by raising hands, either none will raise their hand or everyone will. It is of greater consequence to be different than to be wrong.

"Inupiat are humble. We teach our children not to draw attention to themselves, which is why they are reluctant to raise their hands or speak up. It is considered very rude to single yourself out or to single other people out. In fifth grade I went to school wearing a new pink shirt. My teacher said, 'Terri, that's the prettiest shirt I have ever seen.' I felt bad because I'd let someone notice me so much. I know now that my teacher was trying to be nice and give me a compliment but it made me very uncomfortable because Inupiat just don't say things like that to each other. I know that teachers are told to positively reinforce students and say, 'Good job!' but our children don't appreciate that kind of attention.

"Inupiat cooperate with one another. There is no hierarchal structure in our society. We have elders who are revered for their wisdom and experience, but we do not have chiefs. We value the opinions of children equally as much as adults, and those of strangers as much as our friends and family. Burdens are shared equally, as are the rewards. In our history survival has only been possible through working together. To facilitate this cooperation it is important that we avoid conflict." She closed with, "We appreciate you being here and working with us to make our communities stronger and healthier and preparing our children for a successful future."

Principal Atkinson turned off the videoconferencing system as the camera panned out and Terri Bowen-Skeen stepped down from the stage. "A few housekeeping items before we break for lunch, then you can have the afternoon to get ready for Monday." He flipped over the pages of a yellow legal pad and circled or drew lines through certain words. "If any of your personal groceries are in the school refrigerator or freezer, have them out by the end of the day. I'm not going to pursue this any further, but now that I have made everyone aware of the policy I expect it to be followed. If the school kitchen continues to be used by teachers, I will speak with them individually. If necessary I'll have maintenance rekey the locks." He was about to move on to his second item, but a spindly, liver spotted hand thrust itself into the air.

"Mr. Atkinson," said Emma Rudd, the Social Studies teacher.

"Yes Miss Rudd?" replied Principal Atkinson.

"Mr. Atkinson, I have been cooking in the kitchen and keeping my freeze in there because there isn't any electricity or running water over at the quad-plex. Can those of us in the quad-plex use the school kitchen until that gets fixed?"

"I have been assured me that those issues will be remedied quickly. In the meantime, please remove your food from the school kitchen."

"But if the electricity isn't on by tonight, where should I keep my freeze?"

"That's a question you're going to have to find an answer to yourself. I'm required to make you aware of the policy; only school food is to be kept in the kitchen, so if food is in there that is not school food it needs to be removed."

"Well, when I was in Vitus Cove, we were allowed to use the school kitchen as long as it was after school hours and we kept it clean for the next day. There are two freezers, can't we designate a few shelves for the staff in one of them just until the power is fixed at the quad-plex?"

"I don't set the policies, the school board does. If you want an exception to the policy you'll have to ask them for it. I can't give it to you."

A man's voice piped up from near the front of the room, "You can bring it over to my place Emma," said Nick Dowe, the science teacher. His head was mostly bald with the remainder shaved flush on the sides and back to match the top. His skin and features showed the wear of decades spent outdoors and his thick arms and fingers looked more like they belonged around a steel cable or lead pipe than the Lustrous Chrome Cross pen that he held.

"Thank you Mr. Dowe," said Emma.

"Next topic," began Principal Atkinson. "I need to have a copy of your classroom rules submitted to me by email before you leave today. I will return it to you with any comments or suggestions by Sunday evening. During your prep time on Monday morning I expect you to make copies of the amended version. Submit one to me, post one on each side of your classroom door, and send a copy home with each of your students."

"How, how many copies should we make?" This time the voice belonged to Mitch Forman, the jack-of-all-trades-master-of-none secondary teacher formally and appropriately referred to as a generalist.

Principal Atkinson counted them off on his fingers, "One for me, one for the outside of your classroom door, and one for the inside of your classroom door. That's three." He held up three fingers. "And then enough to give each of your students a copy. You probably have each student more than once during the day, but just be sure they each get at least one."

"How many... how do, how will, how do I know how many students I have?"

"Check your class lists Mr. Forman."

Nick Dowe's gruff voice rumbled from across the room, "Fifty Mitch, just run off fifty and you'll be fine."

Principal Atkinson continued, "That concludes my meeting points. Any comments, questions, suggestions?"

"I got wuuun," drawled Cornell, who taught language arts. "What are we gonna do about soda and headphones in the clazz-room?"

"What do you mean by that Mr. Coalman?" replied Principal Atkinson.

"Wuh-elll," began Cornell, "Last year we had quite a few prob-lums with stu-dents wearin' headphones and listenin' to mew-zack during clazz. We also had a prob-lum with stu-dents drinkin' soda in clazz. I'd like to see a rule where we just don't allow those things in the school at all. No good ever comes of them. They aren't necessary and I get tired uh fightin' 'bout it all day."

"If you would like to ban those items in your classroom, then that is fine Mr. Coalman. I'll support you on that."

"How about we ban them from the whole school? Just tell kids to leave them at home. Otherwise it's 'I gotta take these to my locker' or, 'I wanna go get mine from my locker.' Can y'all just make a rule so that we don't have to deal with them at all?"

"Unless something is a health or safety issue, I don't like to make a blanket policy on it from the top down. If teachers individually want to allow or ban something from their individual classrooms, that's fine, but I prefer to give teachers as much discretion on those issues as possible."

"If we all as teachers agree on banning them, could we set a blanket policy on it then?"

"I think if all the teachers agreed on not allowing them, it would be a great disincentive toward students bringing them to school. And again, I will support any teacher who wants to ban them from their individual classroom. We as a staff have relatively broad authority to require students to behave in a way that is conducive to learning. But in order for me to make a proclamation as principal, an activity must either directly hamper my ability to function as principal, or be based on my direct experience with an individual student." Principal Atkinson tapped the podium with a pen as he ended the sentence.

"All right then," said Cornell as he ran his fingers back through his thick, gray hair.

Belle Coalman, the first and second grade teacher, asked, "What about language?"

"In what sense, Mrs. Coalman?" asked Principal Atkinson.

"The students don't seem to have any sense of appropriateness. Last year, walking around the halls, why, it was like an R rated moo-vie; fifth graders, tenth graders, it didn't matter if Elders or little children were around or anything. They used the most horrific language and if we correct them they only get worse."

"This is how I suggest you handle misbehavior such as that. First time, ask them not to do the behavior. Second time, warn them that if the behavior continues they will be given a referral to me. Third time, fill out the referral form and send them to the office. I will speak to them and either return them to class or hold them until the end of the class period. Repeat offenders will receive detention and I'll work my way up from there."

"Anything else?" asked Principal Atkinson. "Okay, I'll be in my office for the remainder of the day if you have any questions. Don't forget to supply me with a copy of your classroom rules before you leave today. Pizza and drinks are set up on the table in the hallway. Help yourself and let's capitalize on this opportunity to maximize the successfulness of this work day."

Metal chair legs slid across the carpet and papers where gathered in hands. As I passed the front of the room Nick had his hand on Cornell's shoulder and said something about, "Best efforts."

I scooped up a few slices of pizza and joined the rest of the staff on the benches in the foyer. Joanne asked Belle, "How's Roger doing?"

"Pretty wuh-ell I guezz, he and Margaret have a place in Whittier but I think they spend November and December in New Mexico with thuh-air daugh-tur," said Belle.

"Who's Roger, did he used to teach here?" asked Emma.

"Yes, he and his wife Margaret," said Joanne. "Last year someone used a chainsaw to cut the posts away from the front porch of the quad-plex over the summer, probably for firewood to go camping, and the only access for the first two weeks of school was by a ladder. Roger fell off one morning and spent six months doing physical therapy in Anchorage. Margaret tried to get excused for family leave but the district said she couldn't since he was in the hospital full time and didn't need her assistance. She quit and in retaliation the district got her teaching license suspended for breach of contract and threatened to do the same thing to him if he didn't return and finish out the rest of the school year. He came back in March but called in sick four days a week. They sued the school district and eventually got about $500,000 out of the deal plus his medical expenses."

"So instead of letting his wife take *unpaid* leave for six months and bringing both of them back for the rest of the year, maybe even several years, the district paid out a settlement equivalent to the salaries of five teachers to a guy who basically showed up in the classroom a total of fifteen days? What was the district thinking?" Brenda Bortund, the fifth and sixth grade teacher, asked.

"Thuh-ay wuh-urn't," Belle drawled.

"Or…" Joanne started, "They didn't think Margaret would go through with leaving in the middle of the year, but she called their bluff. Most of the people on the school board and at the district office in Aciq believe that just because this is the highest paying school district in America no sane person would leave. They fail to realize just how far out and isolated we are here. Aciq is a hub, so it gets at least two flights every day, is only an hour away from Fairbanks, has a video rental store and two restaurants, and the schools have enough aides that if the principal, or the secretary, or a teacher is gone for a week it isn't a massive hardship in the same way that it is out here in the villages."

Joanne wiped some sauce from her lips and continued. "Once the sun sets for the last time all it takes is one little glitch to move the needle on someone's suck-meter from 'tolerable' to 'intolerable.' Maybe it's the TV going out, or the internet, or the washing machine. Maybe it's news about a dying relative, or a friend in crisis, or just the realization that day-to-day life is ten times easier everywhere else. In Margaret's case it was not being with her husband, and when the needle of a person's suck-meter gets pegged that far to one side the rewards and consequences are no longer visible."

"That's sure an inspirational story," said Ben Bortund, the third and fourth grade teacher, with a smirk.

"Well it happens in the Bush," said Emma. "One Monday morning in Vitus Cove a teacher went out on maternity leave and before her replacement arrived the principal left for a conference. Tuesday the stove went out and we used welding torches from the shop to heat soup for lunch. The power plant manager was on a bender, nobody could find him, and the electricity for the entire village went out. The school had a generator so we were able to keep the school open, but teachers were living in their classrooms. Wednesday morning we had a parent show up at the school drunk and swear at us for sending her son home from community recreation Tuesday night because he was using profanity. Finally, Thursday morning the sewer system backed up and that's when one of the high school teachers put on his coat and walked out the door. He went home, packed his suitcase, and walked out to the airstrip. He got on the only plane that came in that day and sent an email a week later saying anybody who wanted the stuff he had left behind could have it."

Emma added, "I don't blame him for leaving, it was a tough haul. But I would never do that because it makes it that much harder for the teachers left behind. He did lose his teaching license for breaking contract though. I think he's going to law school now."

"How d'y'all feel about this soda and headphone situation?" asked Cornell.

"I never allowed them in my room the twenty years I was in Vitus Cove," said Emma. "I don't see them as having any benefit and I probably won't allow them here."

I threw my two cents in. "The last school I worked in had a tough policy about soda school-wide for nutritional reasons. Headphones have always been a challenge, but I think it's pretty obvious a student cannot listen to music and a presentation at the same time. Fact is, students who listened to headphones were generally lower performing. I had a rule that was kind of like, 'As long as it doesn't cause a problem, it's okay.' If it caused a problem, the privilege was lost."

Nick said, "I can go for or against, but I think we should have one policy across the board. In the end it's about consistency. I prefer not allowing them for the reasons Cornell mentioned, but I don't want to fight it if it's half and half."

"Where's that uh-thuh guy, Muh-itch?" drawled Cornell.

"I think he's out walking his dog," said Emma.

I returned to my room where Ben had methodically connected and updated the eight computers located across the back wall. Ben was originally a software developer and new to teaching while his wife Brenda had been a teacher in Iowa before they came to Iqsaiqsiq. I had heard something in passing about how they had both lost their jobs weeks apart and were now underwater on their mortgage. They were only a few years out of college and by far the youngest people on staff.

"Hey Ken. I'll show you the login information you need and how to access the curriculum server." Ben said.

I watched intently and took notes as he guided me through the dots, slashes, and underscores necessary to navigate my district email account and online grade book as well as the instructional software.

Ben and Brenda were two of the six new staff members along with Principal Atkinson, Emma, Mitch, and myself. I did some quick math in my head and calculated that between the ten teachers and the principle, six new staff members meant that the school had had greater than a fifty percent turnover rate from the previous year, not counting the midyear vacancies. I had never known of a typical Lower 48 school where turnover even began to approach fifty percent. The typical rate was somewhere between three to five percent, and anytime a school edged into the double-digits warning bells went off, meetings were called and experts were brought in.

"Here's the list of websites blocked by the district." Ben handed me a piece of paper.

I perused the list which began with the usual culprits: Pandora, MySpace, Facebook, MTV.com, and HBO.com. It also had some surprising additions: ESPN.com, pepsi.com, arcticcat.com, smithandwesson.com. "What's wrong with ESPN dot com?" I asked.

"They do live streaming through their website. It takes up too much bandwidth, so the district blocks it."

"What if I'm doing a unit on statistics or percentages?"

"Try CNN dot com slash sports."

"Why's Pepsi dot com blocked?"

"Unhealthy."

"Arctic cat dot com?"

"No educational value."

"Smith and Wesson dot com?"

"Oooh, guns. Dangerous."

"You mean in *the* state with *the* highest per capita gun ownership in the nation, the school district is afraid kids may be incited to violence by looking at a gun website?"

"Since the district gets federal money they have to block anything that might tick off the feds."

"So what is open?"

"The New York Times, Anchorage Daily News, NPR, most things with a dot EDU and everything with a dot GOV. I couldn't believe the list myself when I saw it. I'm going to get internet at home for sure."

"How much is that?"

"Eighty a month for dial up on top of the sixty-five a month for the landline."

"It looks like I'm sticking with Netflix through the mail and yelling out my window to the neighbors."

"That, or two soup cans and a piece of string."

As Ben left my room I wondered if he had received any of the same admonitions I had, if his initial impressions of the village were the same as or different than mine. I wondered if he knew the story about the principal, or that there even was a story about the principal. Would he be smiling or straight-faced when he met his students? Would he be the first one to bail, or the last, and would that be before or after I left? Even if those questions were answered it wouldn't help me through the next seven days which comprised the most crucial week of the school year.

I poured through my class lists and assembled books, worksheets, and supplies for each student. A little after five o'clock I decide to check out the store and maybe pick up some toilet paper and paper towels.

The playground cleared like a bar before a fight and I found myself corralled by children aged six to twelve. "Where you go? Where you go?" they said.

"I am going to the store." I answered.

"You gotta *dollar?*" asked one of the younger boys of the group. He drew out the word dollar as if it had four o's and three l's.

"I've got lots of dollars" I replied.

"You gotta *dollar?*" He leaned forward with his head this time.

"Yes," I said.

A girl maybe a year older stepped in as the interpreter. "He means you gotta dollar he can *borrow?*" She placed the same elongated emphasis on borrow as the boy had placed on dollar.

"Nope. None to lend today," I said.

"What you get?" another child asked.

"I don't know yet. It depends on what they have" I said.

"You might-could get soda. They got soda at store. And chips. You like soda and chips? I like soda and chips," said a boy as he pointed his thumbs at his chest.

"Maybe," I said.

I had reached the serrated metal stairs that went up to the metal-grated front porch of the store and as I stepped up them a child stopped and lagged behind on either side, as if that step was their own. Finally there were only two children from the gaggle still beside me when I reached the door and I realized they were also the two largest, the rest set out in a hierarchy commensurate with age.

The store, like the school and most of the houses, had a small room that separated the front door from another front door. Two circular, brown faces peered in through the slit of mesh-reinforced glass in the outermost door.

The interior of the store blended the Spartan décor and unimaginative product presentation of a Costco with the limited selection and price-gouging of a 7-11. The area I had entered was the genesis for an aisle that reached past an open counter and a check-out lane to the back of the store. I walked down this first aisle which had a refrigerated case against the outermost wall and shelves on the opposite side. The refrigerated case contained pint and liter sized bottles of soda pop, sport drinks, and juices and the Weight Watcher's nightmare shelves across from it contained the Rainbow Coalition of chips in every flavor and design imaginable; straight, wavy, strips, sticks, curls, cheese, nacho cheese, nacho ranch, habanero, jalapeno, salt, pepper, salt and pepper, salt and vinegar, and sea salt and cracked peppercorn. Beyond the chips laid all of the chocolate (bar as well as other forms), gum, and candy. One small section was reserved for peanuts, raisins, and apparently any dust that settled there.

The refrigerated items made a transition from sugar-based liquids to dairy items and lunch meat. Cheese, yogurt, bologna, hotdogs, eggs, and other products that I never bought were available. There weren't any typical gallon or half-gallon containers of milk, only quarts marked at $2.99 each, which translated to about $12.00 a gallon.

The end of the first aisle intersected a freezer case that stretched the entire length of the back wall. It contained all of the typical items; Banquet fried chicken, Totino's pizzas, Cool Whip, Marie Callendar's pies, Green Giant vegetables, Ore-Ida potatoes, hamburger, steaks, popsicles, and ice cream. I picked out a Swanson's Hungry Man chicken fried steak dinner with corn. The price, $9.00, was written across the front in black Sharpie.

I walked past the pop aisle, or more accurately the pop alley. The shelves had been removed and twelve-can packs of pop lined each side, piled directly on the floor; no six-packs, no twenty-four packs, and definitely no bottles. The aisle was segregated more definitively than the Antebellum South; Pepsi products and their kin on the right, Coke and it's scions to the left. The next aisle contained a few basic staples, as well as canned fruits and vegetables, but the majority of it was diapers and baby food.

The final aisle contained all of the inedible products. There were several types of oil for cars, boats, chainsaws, and snowmobiles as well as a modest quantity of clothes from socks to bras to jeans and even some sweatshirts with the name Iqsaiqsiq printed across the front. There were seven boxes of black and gray Nike Air Max running shoes in sizes 8, 8.5, and 9. Similarly there were four red and white Columbia Sportswear Bugaboo parkas; one each in small, medium, large, and extra-large. This was where I found a sixteen pack of Brawny paper towels and thirty-six rolls of Charmin bath tissue.

I made my way back to the front of the store and hoisted the paper towels, toilet paper and TV dinner on to the counter. Behind the counter under lock and key were the five most prized items in the village: cigarettes, batteries, spark plugs, DVD movies, and ammunition.

"Afternoon," said a gangly African-American man in his twenties with a smoothly shaved and buffed scalp. His nametag read, "Ty."

"Things comin' together over at the school?" he asked.

"Yeah." By now I had conceded the fact that I screamed, "School teacher," in some unconscious way.

"What's your sentence, I mean subject, over there."

"Math."

"I was always good at math. Enjoyed it. Hypotenuse of the angle and all that."

I charged the $54.00 to my Visa card and exited with the conspicuous tokens of deforestation. I was immediately swarmed by my hoard of groupies.

"You get any soda?" asked a voice from the lower steps.

"No, just paper towels and toilet paper."

Immediately about half the crowd dissipated and fled back to the playground as I stepped down the metal steps to the gravel road.

"Gaw-lee," said the oldest of the girls, "So much tissues you got!"

The oldest boy, one of the two whose nose and forehead had been pressed against the slit of mesh-reinforced glass, said, "You must gotta *anuq* (ah-nuck) really bad. You gotta *anuq*?"

"What's that?" I asked, although I could infer exactly what he meant.

"You know…" and as he said it he squatted a little bit, he leaned back over his heels and made a "Thhhdddddd" sound. This performance made the girls giggle into their hands while the boys imitated the posture and sound just as all the children had with the play-dead routine earlier.

"No, I don't have to lean back and make funny noises," I said.

"No, no, that's not what I mean," said the boy, "I mean you have to 'Thhhdddd' and make poop come out your butt?" This sent the other five or so kids into a tither, sort of an apprentice level Beavis and Butthead, "poo-oop… (giggle, snicker)… your butt!"

I really didn't have a good answer for the kid so I said, "No. Why? Do you?"

"No. I never." Said the instigator.

The throng now turned on the instigator. "Solomon's gotta poop. Solomon's gotta poop. Thhhddddd-thhhddd, Solomon. Solomon go *anuq*!"

Solomon ran to the nearest swing and pulled himself back and forth as he stood on it, then the rest of the kids imbued the playground like water drawn into a sponge. Despite the near constant and complete occupancy of the playground I had yet to see a local adult except for the clerk at the store and those that worked at the school.

I deposited the paper items in my room then went into the work room to microwave my meal.

Cornell came into the work room. "Hey Bud, watcha got there? Looks good, looks good. Say about this headphones and soda thing, have you given that any-more thuh-ought?

"You've been here the longest. Tell me why you're banning them."

"Wuh-ell, as far as soda goes, these kids don't just have one soda a day or even one soda a class. They'll come in with a," he mimed out a small box with his hands, "Case a pop and just sit there. Glug, glug, glug, then open another. Plus I think it's a part a what gets these kids all wound up and of course it gets spilled and argued about and whatnot. As for headphones, they can't have them without listening to them. Last year I tried, you know, lettin'em keep'em, but not use'em. Next thing you know they were up around their ears. Or they wanted to listen while they read, but it's not Mozart or Lawrence Welk, it's, 'Thumb-thumb-thumb, boom-boom-boom,' and they still don't get their work done."

I said, "I can respect that."

"All right then, I'll see you in the mornin'. Say do you know if they have the power on at the house yet?"

"No, I don't."

Cornell left and I finished my tray then returned to my room to type and photocopy into the night. The sun had finally dropped just below the horizon and I checked my watch. It read 11:38. I put down the yearbook and class list for my seating chart, threw on my backpack, and headed out the door.

I made my way into the still unlit foyer, up the stairs to my still waterless apartment, and retreated to my room as the four-stroke symphony of Honda engines vacillated from bass beat to treble hum. I put in my earbuds, wrapped my head swami-style in a gray bath sheet, and lie down upon the mattress in my sanctum.

# CHAPTER FOUR

I woke before six o'clock and headed to school. The gym lights were already on. Inside Joanne pedaled furiously on a spin bike as a big pool of sweat gathered beneath it. I took a shower and returned to my classroom to prepare. Emma came in shortly thereafter and the gravel lodged in the soles of her XtraTuf boots tapped the linoleum as she passed by. She returned, in tennis shoes, and asked me how I felt.

"I feel like the last two days have just been a treadmill of novelty, with no signs of stopping," I said.

"Oh yes, the Bush is very exciting. Challenging, but highly rewarding. There's just this level of autonomy that exists in Alaska, this spirit that says it doesn't matter if you're sixteen or sixty; if you want to make something happen, you can make it happen." Emma shook her fist in rah-rah fashion. "Whether it's building your own house or running your own business. Time and money are still factors but there isn't a lot of interference from laws or regulations and the quest for expansion is in the blood of Alaskans."

I shared how I came to be in Alaska and Emma explained how she had come up right out of college twenty plus years ago to work in a cannery at a place called Vitus Cove out in the southwest corner of the state. When the season ended she took a job as the school cook; which included the use of a one room cabin, with no plumbing and only a woodstove for heat, as part of her compensation. A few years later she received her teaching certificate and became a teacher there. There was mention of a son who studied at Stanford, but no mention of a husband.

"Would you like some tea?" she asked.

"If you're having some, sure," I said.

Fifteen minutes later Emma called me down to her room. It had the same dimensions as mine but was packed with many more things. Rows of desks faced the front of the room while tables lined the wall. Across the back of the room was a keyboard flanked by acoustic guitars and, just like Joanne's room, a couch. She had motivational posters about "reaching beyond" and "finding within." Where she ran out of room on the walls she plastered things to the ceiling.

"You have really put a lot of effort into this Emma, it looks great." I told her.

"Thank you, Ken. Stay a teacher long enough and this kind of stuff just grows on you I guess."

As we supped our tea Emma said, "Ken, may I offer you some advice?"

"Sure."

"I know that this is your first year in a village and I want you to be aware of something if you aren't already. The children in these villages have many needs that go unmet at home, physical and emotional. The school is their base, the one thing that remains constant, and they look to it for support. I guess what I would suggest, or ask on their behalf, is that you show them some extra patience and if need be some support outside your normal role. In Vitus Cove it paid huge dividends for the teachers who got involved instead of shutting themselves away in their houses."

"Support outside the normal role in what way?"

"I, for example, usually allow students to stay in my room after school as long as I am there anyway. Maybe once a month I'll host a movie and cook a good meal on a Saturday. If I see a child who needs some socks or a sweater or a toothbrush I will find a way to get it."

Before going to Afghanistan, I would have balked at such a suggestion. To me it was part of what was wrong with the American education system, this idea of school as babysitter and social service provider. But since then I had seen the difference just one act of kindness, like the Pringles sent to me via the USO from some anonymous source, could make and the twelve months that I humped the twenty-two pound M249 Squad Automatic Weapon across Sawtalo Sar Mountain had bolstered my appetite for humanity. I also knew that teachers, especially older, single, female teachers, were known to overextend this role or recruit others so that they might shrug this burden away from themselves. Instead of telling Emma yes or no I said, "I can respect that."

"Oh good then. Let's see how this first week goes and we can start planning the first event."

As we finished our tea, Emma, like all mothers, shared her exhilaration over her son's aptitude for both art and academics. She also spoke at length about the sparkling waters of Vitus Cove and how the community had taken her in as one of their own. Although she obviously admired both, at times it was difficult to discern which one she was more enamored with; her son, or Vitus Cove.

I checked my personal as well as school email and responded to my personal emails with a generic quip about the little airplane and the "pre-fab-ulous" manufactured quad-plex's lack of electricity and water. My school email contained an invite from Nick for a Pilot Bread and tuna spread buffet in his room at noon.

I analyzed the student's past performance and test scores. Of the forty-six students assigned to me in grades seven through twelve there were zero Above Proficient, nine Proficient, sixteen Below Proficient, and twenty-one Far Below Proficient. Even in Seattle it was common to have about a fifty-fifty split between Proficient and Below Proficient, but the complete lack of any Above Proficient scores and almost half of the scores being Far Below Proficient were profound anomalies.

In my experience, two factors played the largest part for students who scored Far Below Proficient; reading level and attendance. It appeared that of the twenty-one students in the Far Below Proficient category, fourteen had been absent more than fifty percent of the time, in four cases it appeared as if students had shown up maybe half of the first quarter then came back only for the three days of testing and vanished for the rest of the year. All twenty-one were Below Proficient or Far Below Proficient in reading. The attendance issue was beyond my control, but I had faith that I could increase their reading comprehension, at least as it pertained to math, if I focused on math vocabulary.

Even before I got to Nick's room I could hear Emma's blissful cadence as she recounted the various encounters she had had with parents and students during her years in Vitus Cove. Nick, Brenda, Emma, and Ben sat around a folding table upon which sat a large bowl of tuna salad, a pitcher of juice, stacks of paper plates and cups, and a blue, rectangular box with a picture of a sailor boy and the words "Pilot Bread" on it. Inside the box were round crackers about four inches in diameter. I spread some tuna salad on one of the disc-like crackers while Brenda poured me a cup of juice.

"Well, I hope you're right Emma but things don't usually work out that way around here," Nick said.

"Oh, certainly not at first. But as the year progresses and the students see those teachers that have their best interests at heart, they eventually soften up," Emma replied, then shared another story of how she had taken in an elementary student in Vitus Cove who had been effectively abandoned when his parents left "for an overnight" and were gone for two weeks.

Nick asked about the alcohol situation in Vitus Cove and Emma said that it was damp (which meant that alcohol could be imported and possessed but not bought or sold), and except for the occasional rowdy weekend, especially around dividend time, or the occasional high school party it really hadn't been a problem.

"Even though this village is supposed to be dry (which meant that alcohol in all forms was prohibited at all times), there's almost always booze comin' in. There aren't a lot of people passed out in public but you will see the empties and sometimes you can just watch the whole village circle the drain day after day until the supply runs out. Yeah, the worst is dividend time, but actually any time there is money available, like payday, it gets sideways. I mean, more sideways than usual that is." Nick wiped a non-existent dribble from his chin.

Brenda asked what Nick meant by "sideways" and Nick went on to describe items thrown or broken in the classroom or hallway, profanity which, "Even after twenty years of serving on submarines still shocks me," kids asleep at their desks or in any quiet corner they could find, and fights between, mostly, elementary students. He said that for some odd reason the high school students didn't seem to fight each other.

Whether it was optimism, naiveté, or just plain denial, I didn't ask if what Nick had just described fell into the usual category or more category of sideways.

"You know what happened to the principal a few years ago, don't you?" asked Nick.

I could tell by the looks on their faces that Ben, Brenda, and Emma had no clue. I remained silent.

Nick began, "Past the gym where the back door is there used to be a fire extinguisher mounted to the wall. Some high school boys were down there spraying each other with it. Ditching class, messing around, you know."

Nick took a hard gulp from his cup and continued. "The principal went down and told them to knock it off and get back to class or some such thing. It never was known exactly which kids left and which kids stayed but in the end the principal got whacked in the head with the fire extinguisher. Repeatedly. He was left unconscious in a pool of blood with the fire extinguisher lying next to him. Nobody found him until the next class period when the bell rang. The health aide came to the school, cleaned off the blood, put a bandage on his head and said, 'Take him to the airport and put him on the five o'clock flight to Fairbanks.'

"One of the other teachers had the presence of mind to say, 'This man is unconscious with a head wound and most likely a skull fracture, he can't just be belted into a seat and sent out. He needs a medevac.' In the end the Troopers came out with a helicopter and at least put him on a stretcher with oxygen and took him to Fairbanks. The helicopter landed at the Fairbanks hospital and the doctor said, 'We can't help him here. Take him to the Air Force base. They will fly him to the trauma center in Seattle because that's his only hope.' The guy was in a coma for weeks and had to learn how to eat, walk, and talk all over again. He didn't remember anything that happened that day, not even coming to school."

"What happened to the kids that did it?" asked Ben.

"Nothing. The Troopers could never determine who actually hit him with the fire extinguisher, or even how many kids were involved. They found two different sets of fingerprints on the fire extinguisher, but that wasn't enough to prove the assault so the Troopers charged them with 'Tampering with emergency equipment,' which they were convicted of as juveniles but never spent a day in jail for. The parents were still ticked-off that their kids got in trouble at all."

Emma gasped.

"As soon as the trial was over the school board had all of the fire extinguishers removed from all the hallways in every school in the district as a preventative measure."

"Prevent what? Future beatings or future convictions?" asked Ben.

Emma winced and Nick peered over the edge of his paper cup with a look that said, "Not funny pal," while Brenda chuckled clandestinely and I remained silent.

There was some idle chat about freeze, the post office, winter clothing, and the store, as well as plans and options for getting in and out of the village at Christmas time. Nick also repeated how Margaret was replaced mid-year as well as ten different secondary teachers; and that only he and Cornell remained at the end of the year.

"There are only five secondary teachers. How could ten quit? Especially if you and Cornell are still here?" asked Brenda.

Nick explained. "We started with five, including myself and Cornell. The math teacher left halfway through the first day. The social studies teacher quit in the middle of dividend season, as did the math teachers replacement. Before the end of the first quarter they were both gone. No grades reported or anything. The generalist stuck it out until after Christmas break, then at least had the decency to give two weeks' notice and wait for a replacement. His replacement was replaced himself in February. From then on it remained stable, but Cornell and I are the only ones that accepted contracts to return."

I thanked Nick for lunch and he prodded me to take several Pilot Bread cracker sandwiches, or crack-wiches, with me.

I researched the curriculum manual and located all of the math-related terms for each section I was assigned to teach (seventh grade, eighth grade, algebra one, algebra two, and geometry). There were one hundred thirty-six terms and twenty-three formulas spread across the five sections and I began to create word searches, posters, and mnemonic devices for each one. Every couple hours as necessary I walked to the bathroom, chomped another Pilot Bread crack-wich, and cranked away for another couple hours.

On one excursion I came across a very large Saint Bernard. He didn't move or look at anything in particular, he just stood in the middle of the foyer. Then he turned his head toward me and began to gallop. I took a wild guess, pointed at him, and said, "Bang."

His legs stiffened in mid-air and his body flopped on to the tile, eyes closed and motionless. I stepped around him and went into the bathroom impressed by the dog's authentic theatrical talent.

As I exited the bathroom I found him still motionless with his eyes closed. I said, "Gobi, hey Gobi, hey buddy," but received no response. "Gobi up? Gobi! Up!" Still nothing. I snapped my fingers. I clapped my hands. I petted his head, shook his foot, poked him in the neck, and lifted his eyelid. Nothing. Finally I gave him the same treatment I used to give my nephews, and occasionally roommates, which was to walk away; eventually they would have to either get food in or let food out, and when that time came they would move. Let sleeping, or acting, dogs lie as they say.

More than an hour later, about seven o'clock, Emma walked by my door and jested, "Don't work too hard, Ken. You don't want to have to walk home in the dark."

"Good night Emma," I said as the click-tap, click-tap of her Xtra Tuffs faded down the hallway.

Click-tap, Click-tap. Emma's gravel-logged Neoprene soles approached again. "Ken," she said, "Have you seen Mitch?"

"Not since the staff meeting yesterday."

"Well, his dogs out here in the hallway and it won't move."

I looked up at her and raised my hand in the air with my forefinger extended and wiggled my thumb. "The dog plays dead if you point at it and say, 'Bang.'"

Emma went into a rant about how much of an animal lover she herself was, especially for the dogs of Vitus Cove, and how much of a clod Mitch was because he had brought his dog in the school, especially since he didn't watch it.

I was only twelve hours through a thirty-six hour project so I listened calmly, nodded, and said, "I can respect that."

Emma wished me well once again and click-tapped down the hall.

Later I walked to the bathroom for what I hoped would be the last visit of the evening and passed by Mitch's room. Through the narrow, vertical window I saw Mitch reclined in his Herman Miller Aeron chair as he read some papers. His computer was open to Cabela's web page on tents and tarps. The door was closed so I knocked lightly on the metal door frame. He scattered his papers upward and held on to the armrests for dear life. As soon as his feet were back in contact with the ground he sprung up and came to the door and answered it with, "Yes?"

"Hey Mitch, just dropping in to say, 'What's up?'"

"Oh. Yes. Yes, yes, yes." He tapped the air and squinted. "What was your name again?"

"Ken Shosatori."

"Ken. Ken, Ken, Ken. I've got to write that down." He looked around, I assumed for a writing implement, on the various table and counter tops; all of which were covered with some type of paper, folder, book, manual, computer disc, power cord, or food container. He wore one of the Iqsaiqsiq sweatshirts from the store, swim trunks, wool socks, and Teva sandals. His salt-and-pepper hair was pulled back into a stub of a ponytail held by a rubber band.

"Looks like you're getting it in gear for the year in here," I said.

Mitch raised his arms above his head and waved his hands. "Trying to. Trying to."

"This is my first gig here in the Bush, how about you?"

"First? First, Bush? No. No, no, no. I've been in and out of Alaska since 1979. I was in Cooper's Bay the first year they had a school. Helped build it over the summer, and the next fall when it opened they needed a teacher so I stuck around and taught there a few years. Then I was out in the Aleutians. Denali. The Yukon. Kodiak. I've been down in New Mexico the last six years at a Bureau of Indian Affairs school."

"You must like it out here then?"

"Out? Out, here? Yes. Yes, yes, yes. I could never teach…" he waved his hand toward the south end of the building, "In that thing they call civilization. Nope. This is where it's at. This is the real world. These people love me. We are kindred spirits. We understand each other and that's why I've been so successful out here for so long. Most teachers have a hard time out here. They try to urbanize and whitewash these kids, make them into fascist cogs, and the kids rebel against that. But not me, I get along just fine with these Bush kids."

"Right on. How do you get your dog up after he plays dead?"

Mitch had moved beyond the desktops and now searched in the desk drawers. He looked up and said, "Gobi!" then shot him with his forefinger and said, "Bang." Gobi lay down, then Mitch waved his arm around in the air (why this step was important given that Gobi's eyes were closed I don't know) and said, "Rise, and, walk!" at which time Gobi got up front legs first and walked around in a circle. He stared at Mitch and, without further instruction, lay back down but kept his eyes open.

"Cool, alright, see you in the morning then Mitch."

"Yes, see you in the morning… Ben?"

"Ken." I corrected him.

"Ken. Ken, Ken, Ken. Got it."

I wasn't exactly sure what all was up with Mitch but I knew for sure that he was unorganized. Organization is the plastic thingamajig that holds the six-pack of teaching together; difficult to define yet readily identifiable and deceptively unremarkable at first yet ultimately indispensable, all a direct result of its simplicity. Just as the plastic thingamajig (which I am sure has a proper name although no one seems to know what it is) allows a person to keep five cans on deck while his other hand is occupied with the consumption of one, organization allows a teacher not only to effectively perform more than one task at a time, but also to keep track of how many tasks are completed, in progress, or yet to be started. The tasks are the necessary key elements, but organization allows a person to focus more time on their implementation and less time on their storage.

I knew at that moment that regardless of how much or how little Mitch knew about the Bush or Bush kids, he was in for a rough ride. A class period is a cycle just like the seasons. It has a rhythm; spring (emergence), summer (expansion), autumn (expression), and winter (conclusion). The room of an unorganized teacher will constantly fight this cycle instead of follow it. There will be conclusion when there should be expansion and there will be attempts at emergence when there should be expression, and all along the teacher will say to himself or herself, "But I'm following the curriculum and I was here all weekend getting ready." A farmer does not spread fertilizer over snow or send his tractor out for maintenance in August, yet some teachers try to plant crops that have no chance of taking root and harvest crops that haven't yet sprouted.

Sunday I tried to sleep until my alarm sounded at six a.m., but it was difficult to pace my day through the nearly endless sunlight. As had always been the case, I coaxed myself to finish "just one more lesson" then chided myself when I did not depart at six p.m., promised to push on for "just one more hour" and realized at eight p.m. that that benchmark had long since passed. Finally the last free hour of my last free day slipped from my fingers and the school year began.

# CHAPTER FIVE

The first day of school is the teacher's most optimistic day of the year; every day thereafter, less so. It typically falls on a Monday and begins with some kind of school-wide orientation assembly; part inspirational speech, part lying down of the law (or "expectations" in the colloquialism of the day), and every bit as paradoxically anxious and mundane as waiting for a traffic light to change. Iqsaiqsiq was no different.

Principal Atkinson, adorned with a scarlet tie held in place by gold accessories, introduced the staff and emphasized his enthusiasm for what he called, "Our first and best opportunity for success." Teachers were dismissed with their classes to begin the first period of the day. All of the teachers except me.

Secondary teachers received one full period per day for preparation, whereas elementary teachers had their students excused an hour early. Through a blend of arithmetic and chance my preparatory period fell into the first hour of the day. I returned to my room and closed the door, which I always kept locked after a hard-learned lesson. I could hear the echoes of chairs and bodies up and down the hallway as speech converted to conversation and conversation channeled into monologue. A door would open, a door would close. Another would open then slam shut. There were footsteps in the hallway, some rapid and others sluggish. It was all very customary and routine until Trooper Stan's voice boomed from across the hall.

"I don't want to hurt you, but I'll put you on the ground if I have to," echoed Trooper Stan's even baritone. I opened my classroom door and angled my body so I could see into the majority of the hallway. Principal Atkinson stood just outside Emma's door with his hands down at his sides. I knew that Emma had the seventh grade group first period, which would rotate into my room at the next bell.

Trooper Stan exited the room with a boy, about 5'6" and a little on the pudgy side, wrapped up in a wrist-lock which caused him to scurry on his tiptoes despite his best efforts to plant his feet flat. "Eddie, calm down. Calm down Eddie," Trooper Stan said. Eddie winced and writhed within Trooper Stan's grasp as the two of them, followed by Principal Atkinson, made their way past my door.

I had pondered Roby's words for the last three days as I put my room together and planned my lessons. Was he an accurate and objective observer who offered up guidance, or a bitter and biased victim who wanted to recruit me into his narrative? If the former was true, the application of his advice would be my opportunity to hasten the learning curve and save my students and me months of frustrating trial and error. If the latter was the case, the application would be prejudicial without cause and the results not only detrimental but indefensible.

Between arts and sciences, this question fell into the arts category. It could not be looked at formulaically. It was not given to an algorithm of variables and constants. As I had pondered Thoreau earlier in my journey, now it was time for Frost.

This much was certain; there were two choices and one decision, and the decision was of irrevocable consequence. Beyond those facts certainty evaporated and ambiguity prospered. My standard response would have been to stick to what had worked for me in the past, but my past had not involved being asked in public if I had to poop, a school where the principal had been all but killed for intervening in mischief, or students who had to be forcibly removed from the room ten minutes into the first day. The facts had changed, and so must my opinion.

Ultimately I weighed the perpetuity of Roby's existence in this alien environment as sufficient cause to subvert my instincts and embrace his recommendations, at least until I had enough *a posteriori* knowledge to act upon.

Some say that the first day must be a strict one. A take no prisoners and establish dominance approach. Something told me that would not work here; whether it was Roby's advice, Nick's recollection of the previous year's foibles, my review of the student's previous academic performance, the distractedness and disconnectedness observed during the morning assembly, or Eddie's forced removal halfway through the first period. I decided that today would be a "minimal fail" day in which I would focus on reasons to include, as opposed to exclude, students. It wouldn't be enough just to dissuade negative behavior, I also had to reinforce and highlight models of the rewards for positive behavior to get them to buy in. Despite my positivist approach, I was not guaranteed a positive outcome.

I had a seating chart set out for each student in every class period and names taped to the edges of tables. On five separate two-by-four foot white boards I had the vocabulary word for the day written across the top, followed by the title of and pages in the book for that day's lesson, and a chronological outline of the concepts for the day. My name and the classroom rules were written on the permanent white board. My clock was synchronized with the main office clock which coordinated the dismissal and tardy bells. I had a stack of syllabi (a copy of the classroom rules stapled to each one per Principal Atkinson's instructions) and notebooks as well as my usual stack of mathematical term word searches and a cylinder filled with freshly sharpened pencils. I envisioned Madeline Hunter as she beamed down on me from some post-terrestrial vantage point with pride. My plans and contingencies were as well thought out as D-day and similarly, I would soon discover, still not enough to avert a massive disaster.

The dismissal bell for first period rang and the hallway erupted into a cacophony of sounds, each new one quickly eclipsed by another. I strapped my lips down into a vertical plane, determined to take Roby's Third Law of Bush Teaching to heart. Students began to enter and I nodded and said, "Good morning." Most did not answer, but they all found their assigned seats and sat down. The room was just over half-full when two girls walked in. I recognized them from the yearbook as Rachel Aicia (eye-chaw) and Rosy Aicia.

"We have assigned seats?" Rachel asked. She was plumper, darker, and overall healthier in appearance than Rosy, who was thin-going-on-gaunt and had what almost looked like bleached skin do to its pallor. Rosy also had small, deeply set eye sockets, a dwarfed nose, and a thin upper lip that was almost occluded from view.

"Yes," I said, "they are marked with your name."

"That's baby stuff, for elementary school. Are you sure you're a high school teacher? Do you even know how to teach high school kids?" challenged Rachel.

"Yes, I'm a high school teacher. I even have two pieces of paper that say so, right here," I pointed to my Bachelor's Degree and Alaska Teaching Certificate framed and mounted behind my desk.

"Humph," she said and sat down along with Rosy.

Principal Atkinson walked in with four boys in tow. He saw that I had names marked on the desks and escorted them to their seats. "Mr. Shosatori, these four gentlemen were in need of my guidance this morning. They are once again ready to use this opportunity for success. If they do not use that opportunity, feel free to send them to me for further guidance."

"Thank you Principal Atkinson," I said. The four students were Solomon Aicia (a.k.a. "Mr. Anuq"), Eddie Bowen (a.k.a. "Trooper Stan's personal hall pass"), and two other boys named Daniel Bowen and Derek Bowen.

The bell rang and I pointed to the board. "Good morning, my name is Mr. Shosatori. This is the seventh grade math class…"

"So cheap class, this sucks," Rachel said.

"When I am finished speaking, I will ask for questions. At that time, you may raise your hand and I will answer your question then," I said and continued, "There are two major rules in…"

"How *come?*" Rachel emphasized the word *come* in a way that rolled into a near shout.

"When is the correct time for you to ask a question?" I asked her.

"*Atchu* (at-chew)." She shrugged her shoulders.

"When I am finished speaking, I will ask for questions. At that time, you may raise your hand and I will answer your question then." I began a third time. "There are two rules in this classroom."

"How *come* I gotta wait 'til you're *done?*" Rachel emphasized both "*come*" and "*done*" as if to rhyme them, although I doubted that it was intentional.

I waved my flattened palm at Rachel and continued past her interruption. "Number one; keep your hands and feet to yourself. Hands and feet include anything in or on your hands and feet as well as your other body parts."

Rachel drew attention to herself as she mimicked my flattened palm wave to anyone who would look at her, but she had quit her verbal interruptions, and I continued with my presentation. I counted this as progress.

"Number two, do what you're supposed to do, when and where you are supposed to do it."

Solomon said, "He wants all of us to 'do it,'" which caused a mild stir. I ignored him.

Rachel looked at me and scrunched her mouth in a brutish manner that distorted her cheeks, which distorted her eyes. Some teachers would have flipped out over this, but in my mind I had captured one-hundred-percent of her attention. What should I have done, stopped my presentation to tell her, "Stop looking directly at me and listening to everything I say?"

"A few more things you need to know. I do not allow headphones in my classroom. Not on your ears, not around your neck, not in your pocket. Leave the headphones at home or in your locker. Same with food and drinks, leave it outside. I will provide pencils in this classroom. They are up here on my desk. If you need one, pick it up when you come in. When you leave, please put it back. You get one hall pass per quarter. If you need to go to your locker or use the restroom, do that during the five minutes between classes."

I picked up a stack of word searches. "Every day I will have a word search on this corner of the table. Pick one up when you come in and begin working on it. After the bell rings I will start a sixty second timer. If you are not done at the end of sixty seconds, the remainder is homework. When the timer sounds I expect you to write the word of the day, which is located up here, in your notebook and write a paragraph describing what that word means or how it is used."

"This is a math class, not a writing class. I thought you said you were a high school teacher. I don't even think you're a teacher at all," said Rachel.

I had enough justification to send her from the room at that time, but in the long run I felt it would be more effective to engage her with some verbal judo. "Why don't you think I'm a teacher?"

I had realized since she began that this kid, like many kids, wanted to untie the rope that secured the ship that was the class's attention to the dock that was my presentation. Fortunately, my inquisition had given her enough pause that she had stopped untying. Unfortunately, I had preempted her by basically untying it myself. But I held the rope and I knew how to tie knots quickly.

"*Atchu*," said Rachel.

"You ask questions and say things when you don't even know the reasons for asking or saying them. So from now on, if you (I pointed at her) have something to ask or say to me, you need to write it down and I will read it and answer it later." I realized that this was, in effect, singling out one student just as Terri Bowen-Skeen had advised against. But the elements of Terri's previous argument in favor of cooperation, humility, and tolerance had not played out in the way that she had described. Again, the facts had changed and I chose to adapt to them.

"You can't do that. You can't have one rule for me and one rule for everybody else. That's not fair."

I briefly considered saying, "You're behaving differently than everyone else, therefore you will be treated differently than everyone else," but experience had taught me that once defiance had reached this level, especially on the first day, logic had long since left the room; so I saved the logic for a later date and told Rachel, "Go to the office."

"How *come?*"

"Go to the office. If you have a question you need to write it down. You can do that in the office, I will respond to it later."

"How *come?*"

"Go. To. The. Office."

"How. *Come!?*"

I walked from the front of the classroom to the intercom mounted by the wall.

"Watch out Rachel, he's going to call the po-po on you," said Solomon.

"Go Ahead. I don't care. You *tuniq* (ton-ick)," said Rachel.

I called the office and within seconds Principal Atkinson and Trooper Stan were there. As soon as they opened the door Rachel sprung from her seat, gathered her things, and followed them. As I closed the door behind the trio I tried to reconcile Rachel's behavior with Terri Bowen-Skeen's professed beliefs of cooperation, humility, and tolerance; since Rachel's behavior demonstrated a lack of that skill set.

I asked the class, rhetorically, if anyone would like to review the rules on the board for me. I had no takers, so I read them myself then asked if there were any questions.

Solomon raised his hand and I called on him.

"Are you *gaaay?*" he asked, which sent the room into a tither.

My creative right-brain begged to fire off, "Why, are you looking for a date?" But my logical left-brain (the brain that had so far kept me employed and, for the most part, out of trouble) espoused, "That's not an appropriate question Solomon."

"How *come*? I didn't say faggot. I asked if you were *gaaay*, like Mr. Oosterahn was last year."

"It's still not an appropriate question Solomon."

"How *come*? There isn't anything wrong with being *gaaay*. I'm just curious. How am I supposed to learn if I don't ask questions?"

"If you would like me to explain why it is an inappropriate question I will gladly meet with you, Principal Atkinson, and your parents after school. Should I set that up?"

"No," said Solomon as he sulked just enough to let me relax then added, "I didn't know you were *tho thenthitive* about being gay," and flopped his wrist around in the air.

The response from the class was textbook middle-school and ranged from guarded chuckle to raucous laughter along with, of course, imitation en masse.

"Solomon." I channeled as much of Roby Won Kenobi's never-show-emotion dictum as I could muster. "If you can act appropriately and not be disruptive you can stay here, otherwise you need to go sit in the office with Principal Atkinson."

"Fine, I'll go to the office." With a final limp-wristed wave to us all he got up and walked out the door.

I passed out pencils and word searches. All of the students appeared to work on them. When the timer beeped I asked the students to put their word searches away, which out of cooperation, humility, tolerance, respect, fear, or boredom they all did. Then I passed out the journals and pointed to the word of the day at the top of the portable white board. "Number. Please take the next three minutes to write about what you think the word 'number' means."

Ten heads bent down but only eight pencils scratched away. With a minute left I approached the two non-writers, Daniel and Derek, and asked them quietly what a number was.

*"Atchu,"* said Daniel. Derek put on his hood, turned his head away from me and put it down on the table.

"Well, can you guys maybe write some numbers for me? Do you have a favorite number, or a number of your favorite basketball player?" I asked.

Daniel drew what looked like an L.A. Lakers jersey with the number fifteen on it. Derek did not venture from his withdrawn position.

At the end of three minutes I asked the students to close their notebooks and focus on the board where I had projected some double-digit addition, subtraction, multiplication, and division review problems. I decided to ask for volunteers and, if none presented themselves, would work the problems myself.

With no volunteers I worked through each problem, asked rhetorical questions, "I need six more. Where can I get the six more that I need?" and answered them, "I'll go over here to the tens column and borrow ten to combine with the two I already have." This seemed comically similar to Ben Stein in *Ferris Beuller's Day Off,* but at least I had the boat tied to the dock so to speak and I was sure that something of educational value floated through my room. Also, I felt somewhat vindicated by Bettie Iqaluq's words to the effect that traditionally Inupiat children learned by watching.

I noticed Rosy had her hand up and called on her.

"Is this all we're going to do today? Watch you work problems on the board." She asked.

"I am more than willing to have a student come up here and do them. Would you be willing to do that please?" I responded.

"No," mumbled Rosy, and put her head down on her table.

As I continued I heard the snap of a pencil every time I turned to write on the board. Just one snap, never more. My internal dialogue debated whether this was done; mindlessly out of boredom, intentionally out of destructive impulse, as a distraction to make me stop the lesson, or to provoke a confrontation purely for confrontation's sake. I used my midbrain to perform the rote task of repeated addition and recall the terms "factor" and "product" from my hippocampus as well as coordinate the motor skills required to control my hand as it formed the letters and numbers on the board, all while I focused the resources of my forebrain on finding a productive resolution for this question. I used the four possibilities (a, b, c, and d) as variables and expressed them in formula after formula projected upon the one-and-one-half square meters of my folded cortex. My metaheuristic conclusions suggested a negative linear correlation between the probability of a successful resolution to the behavior and the likelihood of successful completion of the lesson. In other words; despite the less than optimum state that the behavior created in my classroom, the effort to make it better would have only made it worse. A pyrrhic victory at best.

The clock was mercifully near the end of the period and I handed out the homework which consisted of the same eight problems I had worked through on the board. I saw who my pencil snappers most likely were; Daniel and Eddie had their fists tightly clenched. My guess was that Derek would have joined in but he appeared to be asleep. On the return sweep to collect the completed word searches I brought the garbage can with me and made a direct declaration, "Put whatever you have in your hands in here please."

"Nothing," said Daniel while Eddie just sat and stared straight ahead. "I got nothing!"

"I didn't ask what was in your hands. I already know what is in your hands. Now put the broken pencils in the garbage."

"*Azza* (ah-zah)! Such cheap *tuniq* you are." Daniel threw three pencils worth of shattered splinters into the garbage can. Eddie quickly followed Daniel's lead and deposited similar material into the trash can. Eddie, as I would come to find out, was a boy of few words. He stared at me with eyes squeezed shut and a wide, toothless, grin to affirm his acknowledgement.

The bell rang and the classroom cleared of students, most of whom left their homework papers and unfinished word searches behind. I quickly gathered them all into a single pile and put them in a basket on my desk.

The first four students for third period walked in with open cans of Pepsi. I told them, "You have until the bell rings to finish those." The rest of the students walked in, some with Pepsi's some without, and I offered the Pepsi-bearers the same admonishment. Before the bell rang some had finished their Pepsi's and thrown the cans away.

I made the rounds with the garbage can after the bell rang and offered it up to those who still imbibed. They all chugged the remainder and dropped their cans into the waste basket. All except one. A boy I recognized from his yearbook photo as "II Timothy Kala'a" and referred to in his academic record by the moniker "Tim-Tim" sat with a partially consumed can in his left hand. "Time's up, you need to put that in here," I told him.

Tim-Tim licked his lips then shifted his gaze from straight ahead, up to me, out the window, to the Pepsi, and back up to me. "Not finished."

"When you walked in, I told everyone to finish before the bell rang. The bell has rung, so now you are finished whether there is any left in the can or not."

Tim-Tim's eyes retraced their previous steps before he licked his lips a second time and raised the can to them. He took several gulps then deposited the can in the waste basket with a sonorous belch.

The eighth graders graciously let me get through the rules and procedures without interruption. I clarified that the scope was limited to classroom rules and procedures, and asked if there were any questions.

"What if we use our one pass, and then we have to go again?" asked Jenny Iqaluq.

"You can exchange the five minutes of class time that you miss for ten minutes of time before or after school, in here, sharpening pencils."

Tim-Tim raised his hand and I called on him. "How *come* no soda?"

"It causes a distraction."

"What if we're *thir-sty*? It's hard to learn when you're *thir-sty*. I might-could get 'dee hi jaded.'"

I didn't want to begin a seminar on the nutritional and electrolyte content of carbonated versus non-carbonated beverages so I said, "You have time to drink before or after class, you're not going to get dehydrated in fifty-five minutes."

"I *could* (cooo-d)," said Tim-Tim.

"You could... what?"

"I might-could get 'dee hi jaded!' God damn, clear your fuckin' ears out *tuniq*."

"There's nothing wrong with my ears and I'd appreciate it if you did not use the 'f-word' in my classroom."

"I *could*."

"You could, but you're not going to be in this room much longer if you do."

Tim-Tim mumbled something under his breath which I partially heard but ignored before I asked the class if there were any other questions.

Tim-Tim blurted out, "You hear what I said?"

"If you have a question, you need to raise your hand. That's how I know you are asking me a question." I believed this would halt his unproductive nattering.

This massively perplexed Tim-Tim. If he spoke without his hand raised, his remarks did not receive my legitimacy. If he did raise his hand, he would have to acknowledge my legitimacy.

I passed out the word searches and pencils and started the timer. After sixty seconds I passed out journals, introduced the word of the day, "ratio," and set the timer for three minutes. I didn't want to offer the eighth graders the same opportunity to snap pencils that two of the seventh graders had enjoyed, so I collected the pencils and the notebooks at the same time then focused on the review problems.

Mary Iqaluq raised her hand and I called on her. "Can we turn out the lights?"

It had been my experience that a darkened classroom lent itself to lethargy, inattentiveness, clandestine antics, and, if urban legends are to be believed, at least one instance of procreation. The adoption of low glare surfaces had also made the practice largely unnecessary. Besides I wanted to obviate the flight of any objects which might linger in the abyss. Therefore I said, "Thank you for asking Mary, but I don't think it's necessary."

Mary raised her hand again and I called on her again. "Can we vote on it?"

"Tell you what." I reflected on my most recent experience the previous period with the seventh graders and wanted to build some level of rapport. "If someone is willing to come up here and work on a problem, I'll let that person decide whether or not the lights get to be on or off. Any takers?" I looked around the room and saw only vacant stares and perplexed expressions. "No? Let me know if you change your mind." I continued on as head after head drifted down on to the tables. Out in the hallway doors slammed and footsteps fell; sometimes rapid, sometimes measured, but always hard and deliberate.

"*Azza*, this sucks. This teacher sucks. This whole fucking class sucks," said Tim-Tim, and before I could engage him he had already left and punctuated his exit with a hard slam of the door.

I used the intercom to let the office know that he was on the loose and returned to my lesson.

A minute later the handle on my locked door wiggled and then there was a knock. I approached it and, unable to see anyone through the small vertical window, asked who it was.

"Tim-Tim," came the reply.

"Tim-Tim, you left the room without permission so you need to go wait down in the office and see Principal Atkinson. If he brings you back down, you can stay; otherwise we'll try again tomorrow."

Thud. Whack. The door rattled in its frame as Tim-Tim kicked it. "Let me in. Let! Me! Innn!" The door knob wiggled then he kicked it again, and again.

I called back down to the office and explained what was going on. From down the hall I could hear Emma say, "What on earth are you doing? You're not allowed to kick doors like that."

"Fuck you! Fuck all of you! You fuckin' *tuniqs*!" screamed Tim-Tim as he threw his body against the door.

"Why don't you just let him in?" said Josh Aicia. "He never hurt anyone. He just wants in here. You let him get madder."

"Eee, so angry you let him get," said Jenny Iqaluq.

Trooper Stan's leather jump boots slapped the ground as they churned down the hall. "Stop!" he yelled.

Trooper Stan spun Tim-Tim up against the wall and ratcheted his wrists together with chrome. As Trooper Stan half-dragged him down the hall Tim-Tim looked neither angry nor happy, but simply relieved.

"How *come* you never let him in?" asked Jenny Iqaluq.

"Number one, I didn't ask him to leave. He left on his own, without permission. If he wanted to be in here he should have stayed in here. Number two, if I had let him in I would have just sent him right back down to the office for leaving the first time."

"You can't do that. You can't say he can't be in here. This is our school. This is the Iqsaiqsiq School. You just work here." Proclaimed Jenny.

I self-analyzed the condition of my limbic system, the brains turbo boost switch which allows humans to decide if and when they should go postal, and found the safety-seal significantly compromised. I read the internal script I had rehearsed for the question, "Whose school is it?"

I told the class in a highly abbreviated version of the several hundred pages that make up the Alaska Revised Statutes, "We are going to go back to our work, but first I will say this to you. This school is not mine. This school is not yours. This school belongs to the State of Alaska which, through the legislature in Juneau and all of the citizens who vote, decides where to put the schools, who gets to go to them, and who gets to work in them. The State of Alaska put this

school here in Iqsaiqsiq. The State of Alaska says you can to go to
school here. The State of Alaska says that I can work here. And the
State of Alaska says I can make rules for this classroom. If you don't
like the rules I make, write a letter to Juneau, and if the people in
Juneau don't like my rules either, they will make me change them."

"Humph, I never write no letter," said Jenny.

I worked the problems, Ben Stein style, and together we made
it to lunch time. The dismissal bell rang and, once again, I collected the
discarded and abandoned word search and homework papers, and
placed them atop the seventh graders pile. I wasn't a fan of either the
staff room with its stale regurgitations of acerbic pabulum, or school
lunch for the same reason, so I dug out my Clif bars and Nalgene
bottle of pre-mixed Gatorade as I filled out the referral forms for
Solomon, Rachel, and Tim-Tim.

# CHAPTER SIX

There was a knock at my door and through the window I could see the upper half of Cornell's bespectacled face. I opened the door and he helped himself to a seat.

"Good Loh-ord, what was wrong with Tim-Tim this morning. You kick him outta class or something?" Cornell asked.

"I should have, but he got up and left on his own. I always keep my door locked so when he came back I just let him stay out there while I called the office." I told him.

"He's a handful alright. Older brother Tim is even worse though. You know the two I can't stand are that Daniel and Derek. Last year Trooper Stan spent half the year roundin' Daniel up and bringin'm to school, and the other half chasin'm back ow-uht. And Derek, he likes to huff gas. Belle and I were walkin' home last fall and saw him passed out next to a snowmachine with the gas cap missin'."

With his next comment Cornell tipped his hand a little too far. "You been keepin' on top of these kids with their headphones and soda? I know that's most of what Emma has done her write-ups for so far. I think if we can stick to that this first week it'll pay off."

"I had some tension with Tim-Tim over that, it may be what made him leave third period."

"Same way last year. First period, no sodas. Second period, no sodas. Third period, every kid's got a soda. Fourth period, after lunch, same thing, every kid's got a soda. You know why? Store opens at ten, parents go in there and buy it for'em, drop it off here at the office. That eleven o'clock break between second and third period, that's when they all get at it. That's why I was hopin' this guy would say, 'No soda in school,' but he doesn't want to. So… oh well." Cornell braced himself against the table as he stood up. "Hey, you hang in there Bud, I'll catch up with you later."

Cornell left and I returned to my disciplinary reports and Clif bar. The post lunch bell rang and I opened my door ready to greet the afternoon. Just as I had done with the eighth graders I met my algebra one students at the door and gave them my admonition about soda. When the bell rang I turned to close the door and paused while the last few students scurried through the door.

Before my presentation on rules and procedures I held up the timer, set at sixty seconds, and tried a different approach to the soda; one I hoped would lead to less conflict. "Normally, when you come in I will have word searches on the corner of this table and you'll have sixty seconds to finish them before this timer goes off. Today only, since soda is not allowed in this classroom, I will give you sixty seconds to finish a soda if you still have one, and then I will bring the wastebasket around for your cans." I started the timer.

As with the eighth graders, most had finished before the bell and the remainder quickly finished, except one: "I Timothy Kala'a" who went by Tim, a healthy and robust sixteen year-old that at 5'9" and about 160 pounds would have been the envy of any high school football coach in need of a halfback or strong safety, and also Tim-Tim's older brother.

I approached Tim and his open can that sat on the table. "Put your can in here please," I said.

"I won't drink it. I'm just saving it until class is over."

"That's not how it works. There is no soda allowed in this room, so if it isn't finished it needs to be thrown away."

Tim looked up at me indifferently. "You can't bully us around like you bullied those middle school kids. You better watch yourself or somebody might-could *kick, your, ass.*"

Perhaps my patience been worn thin by the seventh and eighth graders in the morning, or maybe it was the vague and indirect threat. In any case, Tim had no justification for his actions other than being obstinate. I knew he wouldn't go without assistance and I didn't want to begin this class, as I had the other two, with a call down to the office. If this went poorly I was concerned I might be brought before the school board but physically Tim didn't scare me, especially since there weren't any fire extinguishers in the room. I swiped the can off the table and dropped it in the waste basket.

Tim sprang to his feet. "*Hey!* I told you I was saving that!"

"Have a seat please Tim. Class has started."

"How *come* you take my Pepsi!? You owe me a Pepsi, bitch!"

"The Pepsi is gone Tim. Class has started. If you want to be a part of it, sit down. If you don't, then go to the office."

"I'm gonna go. I'm gonna go get myself another Pepsi, and bring it back in here." Tim walked toward the door. "And this fucking door better not be locked when I get back. You hear me bitch?!"

Tim flung the door open and it slammed against the filing cabinet. He stared me down hard and still had his head turned when he stepped directly into Trooper Stan's Kevlar-and-nylon ensconced torso. Whether out of rage or reflex Tim immediately jumped back into the room, his right hand pulled back and curled into a fist, directly aligned with Trooper Stan's face. Trooper Stan's right hand was also pulled back, and curled around a four-ounce can of Magnum Red Pepper Spray directly aligned with Tim's face. As they say in poker, Trooper Stan had the better hand as he painted Tim's shaved head like a Jack-O-Lantern.

Tim staggered across the room and groped the air with outstretched arms. When Trooper Stan grabbed him by the elbow to escort him from the room Tim stiffened and quickly found himself in the same wrist-lock applied to Eddie earlier in the day.

The room had the pungent aroma of a fresh Tabasco monsoon and I knew a change of venue was in order. I grabbed my portable white board along with the word searches, notebooks, pencils, and homework, and we went into the library. We made it through the rules and expectations without incident, except for the solution to the, "What if I've used my pass and I still need to use the restroom?" question.

As I moved from the journal, on the topic of operation, to the review problems I actually had one student volunteer to work a problem on the board, Suzette Bowen. After two problems and no other volunteers she sat down and I finished the rest of the set. Again, homework and word searches were left behind.

I returned to the classroom with all of the boards, notebooks, and work sheets in tow and saw a short, thin boy I recognized as Jedidiah "Jay-Boy" Bowen by the door. He wore a Seattle Seahawks jersey and a pair of extra-extra-large shorts all eclipsed under a Portland

Trailblazers Starter jacket. He was the only student that wore glasses. He offered to hold my things as I unlocked the door. We stepped into the room and Jay-Boy sniffed the air. "How *come* it smell like tacos in here?" he asked.

"Previous tenant," I said as I allowed just one piece of snarkiness to slip into my day.

"Whose pee-vee-us tent ant?"

"Never mind. I'm sorry. It was a joke."

"Oh," Jay-Boy chuckled, "You jokes! I jokes sometimes too, wanna hear one of my jokes?"

"It's not dirty is it?"

"No. Here. Ready? What state is like a little can of pop?"

I took my best guess. "New York Seltzer?"

"Nope. Minnesota. Get it? Mini. Soda."

"Good one Jay-Boy." I rearranged the supplies on my desk.

More students entered, some, of course, with pop cans. I offered up my same admonition for the fourth time, somewhat relieved that whatever the response was this time it could be no worse than the previous one.

The bell rang and I finally made it through a waste basket pass without being challenged. I reviewed the rules and procedures. A girl, Midian "Middy" Iqaluq, raised her hand. "How *come* we can't have soda? It never cause problems."

I thanked Middy for her input and said that, in light of her polite request, perhaps we as teachers would discuss a change to that policy, but for the near future it would remain in place.

Jay-Boy raised his hand. "What is 'near future'?"

"It means soon, like tomorrow. So tomorrow soda will still be banned."

"Oh, okay. Hey, I got another joke," said Jay-Boy.

The class let out a collective groan.

"Let's hear it," I said.

"What kind cheese can you never have?"

"I don't know."

"Nacho cheese. Get it? It's not, yo's. Not yo cheese."

"Thank you Jay-Boy, you brightened my day."

"I got anoth…"

"That's okay, let's save some for tomorrow."

I managed to get through the word search and the journal topic, "parenthesis," and on to the review problems. Back to the norm with no takers for the solutions I solved them Ben Stein style and handed out the homework, the majority of which got left behind as with the previous classes.

I was only one period away from the end of my first day. My last class period, Geometry, had only one student enrolled: Lewis Tiqiqiq (Tick-ick-ick). Lewis was the only true senior and would be the only graduate that year. He had already passed the "all-important" High School Graduation Qualification Exam and completed both of the required algebra courses for a diploma. In effect this class was an elective for him. The district was under pressure to offer more than just the required minimum of core academic courses and had been criticized recently because it offered only second-rate electives. When Lewis requested to take, "Whatever math class come after algebra," our schedules serendipitously intertwined.

Lewis appeared at my door. Massive headphones rested around his neck and his hand held a can of Pepsi. "This cool in here?" He raised his can as if to a toast.

"No. Finish it before the bell rings please, and put the headphones in your locker."

"They might-could get stolen. You keep them?" Lewis asked as he leaned against the wall and nonchalantly sipped his way to the bottom of the can.

"Sure." I placed them in my filing cabinet and locked it.

As the bell rang he let the can drop from his hand into the waste basket and found his assigned seat. I gave him a copy of the syllabus and read the rules and procedures. He finished his word search and began on his journal topic; angle.

I began the review problems, which focused on identifying lines, points, segments, rays, angles, vertices, and planes. Being that it was just he and I, and therefore not a detriment to anyone else if he decided to shut down or spout off, I prompted more often and let the questions hang longer in the air.

"Can you tell me which of these angles is acute?" I asked.

"*Atchu?*" He shrugged his shoulders.

I wrote the degrees of each angle and labeled them as acute or obtuse based on their value being either greater than or less than ninety.

I began on another, only this time after I wrote the degrees and instead of asking I stated, "This is an acute…?" destined to let that hangout there until 3:30 if necessary.

"Angle," said Lewis

I lengthened the words in the response and coaxed out more and more in Lewis' response. "This is an…?"

"Acute angle."

"This is…?"

"An acute angle."

Now I had the tempo set. I tapped the dry erase marker around random vertices. "This?"

"Is an acute angle."

Tap. "This?"

"Is an obtuse angle."

Tap. "This?"

"Is an right angle."

"*A* right angle," I corrected him, "Good."

Tap. "This?"

Lewis pulled his arms under the table until basically only his head and neck were still above it.

Tap, tap, tap. "This is a, right…?"

Lewis looked up at me and glanced all around the now streaked board of intersected rays and segments. "Ain, gull," he mouthed softly, and his jaw raised his head off the table where his chin rested.

Tap. "This is an ob…"

"Obtuse angle," Lewis fired out at me enthusiastically.

Tap. "This is an….?"

"Acute angle."

Lewis' body language showed that he had more anxiety than a long-tailed cat in a room full of rocking chairs. I wondered if it was from being wrong generally, or if it was from being wrong about the use of definite articles specifically? What was the solution? Should I not correct his improper usage? Should I take time out from math to teach him language? Should I adapt my lesson so as to avoid the use of definite articles? Would any of these options have a detrimental effect on the ultimate goal? Was the ultimate goal more or less important than confronting this new challenge? All of these thoughts slid up and down the docosahexaenoic-acid-infused myelin sheathes inside my head as I erased the board. I decided to model instead.

"Hey Lewis, I'll tell you what. Why don't you draw some intersecting rays, point to the angles, and I'll tell you if they are acute, right, or obtuse? You want to come up here to the board or use a portable board at your table?"

"I'll sit here," said Lewis, his arms now above the table again.

I wiped the fifth period schedule off the board and handed it to Lewis along with a marker and a ruler. He drew several rays and tapped the marker just as I had done. "This?" asked Lewis.

"Is an obtuse angle." I said

Tap. "This?"

"Is an acute angle."

Tap. "This?"

"Is a right angle."

Tap. "This?"

"Is an acute angle."

After about twenty angles I suggested we switch.

Tap. "This?" I asked.

"Is an obtuse angle," replied Lewis.

Tap. "This?"

"Is an right angle."

Tap. "This?"

"Is an right angle."

Oh well, Rome wasn't burned in a day. With ten minutes left I decided to go over Lewis' journal entry with him. I read it through just as I would have had it been after school:

Angle                          Lewis Tiqiqiq

There are angles everywhere. A house has angles. Its roof its windoes its dores its waals. There are angles on anything that is square. Round things dont have angles. A basketball dont have no angles but a basketball coret does. Sometimes when I cood go play basketball the coret is confuseing because it has so many lines makeing angles. Are basketball coret has a lot more lines because it is also the volleyball coret in the fol time. We play volleyball and basketball but I like basketball better. I mite cood play basketball for a job some day like Ron Artest. Playing basketball wood be a fun job.

"You did a good job of identifying angles in real life Lewis. Thinking about what we did today, are the lines on a basketball court really lines in the way we talk about geometry?" I asked.

67

"*Atchu.*" Lewis shrugged.

"Think about the lines on a basketball court." I drew a rough rectangle. "In geometry a line goes on forever. Do these lines go on forever?"

"*Atchu.*"

"What does 'at chew' mean? Is that yes or no."

"I don't know." Lewis clarified, "*Atchu* means I don't know. That's my answer. 'I don't know,' is my answer."

"How about if I do this." I drew a dot at each corner.

"The line stops at the dot."

"What are the dots called?"

"Segments."

"This part *between* the dots is called the segment, what do we call the dots? Remember this is a basketball court, which word up here makes you think of basketball?"

Lewis stared hard at the board and went through a process of elimination for each term. "Point?" he half-said.

"Right. A dot on a segment is a point. A dot where two segments join, like this, is a special kind of point called a vertex." I labeled the line segments and vertices.

I handed Lewis his homework, which he actually took with him when he left after the bell rang. A certain level of euphoria set upon me as I gathered up another discipline report and headed to the staff meeting.

I staked out the same table at the back of the library I had used for the in-service and filled out the disciplinary report for I Timothy Kala'a.

Principal Atkinson entered then closed and locked both of the doors to the library. I wondered if this had always been his practice or if it was a new habit inaugurated today. He looked around the room and said, "Has anyone seen Mr. Forman?" After he received no response he said, "Mrs. Stanisauvlauvski, can you go find Mr. Forman please. I was with him in the gym five minutes ago, start there."

As Miss Jenn left the room, Principal Atkinson gripped the podium with both hands and tapped it with his thumbs. He took in a deep breath. "The word *tuniq* is a caustic pejorative and beginning tomorrow I will no longer allow its use in this school without consequence. If a student uses the word either towards you or even in your presence, follow the protocol I outlined on Friday."

There were questions about morning hall supervision, lunchroom procedures, when certain after school activities would start or if they would be done at all this year, and of course if/when/how the water and electricity would be restored at the quad-plex. Somewhere in all of this Mitch came in escorted by Miss Jenn. Just before the elementary teachers were dismissed Principal Atkinson said, "We are here to help these students become successful. If they already were successful, or if they could achieve success on their own, we would not be here. Our job is to guide, orchestrate, encourage, and reward success. Keep that in mind as we continue through this week and through this year."

Principal Atkinson asked the secondary teachers to stay. "I suspended one student, Mr. Timothy Kala'a (Kuh-lah-ah), for the remainder of the week. I sent three other students home for the remainder of the day; Miss Olivia Aicia, Mr. Rocky Aicia, and Mr. Tim-Tim Kala'a. I would ask though that if at all possible you keep a student in your room. I don't want the office to become a revolving door. I want to be sparing with my detentions and suspensions, because if they become common place they lose their effect. They become seen as a regular part of the day or the week and I do not want that, I want the detention or suspension to be an event of notice and a time for reflection."

We were dismissed from the library. Mitch turned left and exited the building into the brilliant August afternoon. Emma, Cornell, and I turned to the right and the natural gravity of a cathartic urge drew us into Cornell's room.

"I sent Olivia and Rocky out first period," said Cornell. "Thuh-at Olivia is the *foul*-est mouthed kid in this whole school. Half the time what she says doesn't even muh-ake sense. Then she spits at you. The principal we had last year was useless as tits on a boar and would never do anything with Olivia. She's also the only kid I know've ever hit a teacher. There was this sweet little third'n fourth grade teacher named Amy, and Olivia made it a point to always go off on her whenever she was in the hall. In February I guess it was, Amy decides just once she's gonna confront Olivia 'bout it. Tells her, 'If you had any self-respect you wouldn't talk to people that way.' Olivia wrestled her down right then and there and started punchin' her in the face while all those little ones watched. John pulled Olivia off Amy and Olivia still didn't get suspended. Amy filed charges and Trooper Stan took Olivia to the Fairbanks Youth Facility. Amy stuck out the year, but she was pretty much done after that.

"Rocky, thuh-at kid leaves people alone, don't swear more than any of the rest, but he breaks stuff. We used to have these chairs, and if you leaned hard to one side the legs would bend. If'n he got ticked off, he'd go from room to room and just bend down chair after chair. I tried sayin' he had to sit on a box 'cause he bent so many uh' the chairs in my room. Word uh that got 'round to the village and next thing I know the mayor, David, is in here saying I'm a racist, and the principal made me give him a regular chair. A week later he got ticked again and bent it down to the ground too."

Nick Dowe entered fresh from the first detention session of the year. "Well, I gotta say this for the guy, at least he's not afraid to throw the hammer. Typically these principals start out all, 'Oh, yeah, I'm sure you didn't mean to, so just promise and try harder next time.' I was expecting Olivia, Rocky, and Tim in there today and they weren't even on the list."

"I was just tellin' these two about them. I sent Olivia and Rocky out of first period 'cause they both just flat-out refused to sit down at all, I don't have Tim until the end of the day so I didn't see him, but it sounds like he weeded himself out," drawled Cornell.

Nick poured out his admiration for Amy. "Amy was great, lots of energy and the patience of a saint. I expected her to leave any day before Christmas, but she stuck it out. When she was still here after Christmas break I thought she would become a lifer like Joanne. But once Olivia got on top of her that day she lost her spirit." Nick shook his head. "What happened with Tim?"

Emma shared her story. "Everyone came in. The bell rang. Tim and two others were sitting on the couch, so I asked them to sit in chairs. They started to argue, 'How come, I like it here, I never sit in a chair, I never have to,' I told them they needed to go to the office, the other two debated it for a while then walked out, but Tim stayed on the couch. I told him to leave. Tim says…Tim says, 'You fuck on this couch? That how come…'"

Emma had to make a conscious effort to breathe, "'That how come you never want me sitting here. You might-could get fucked on this couch?'" Emma cleared her throat. "I called the office and before anybody got there, he walked out."

No one wanted to make eye contact after that so I relayed my experience, which began with the extra sixty seconds to finish their sodas and ended with the migration to gym until the pepper spray dissipated.

"You wanna know the sad part?" said Nick. "Right now half of the village is probably talking about what a victim Tim is. Nobody will admit that the expectations were clearly set ahead of time and Tim made a deliberate effort to thwart them. But instead of telling him, 'Get your act together kid,' he will be told, 'Those teachers don't know what they are doing because they don't understand how unique you are,' or, 'Those teachers are trying to make life difficult for you because they don't like you.'"

Heads nodded and there was some small talk, the occasional joke, and a funny story. Before I left I asked Nick, "What does *tuniq* mean?"

Nick's face turned to a grimace. "Nigger. White nigger. The cultural types will tell you it means 'a white person,' or maybe, 'whitey,' but that's as accurate as saying that 'kike' is the same as Jewish or 'chink' is the same as Chinese. It's like that and it's totally unacceptable."

I looked at the word searches for the day. Most had been partially finished to some degree, but only half of them had names. Some had random sets of letters circled, while a few merely had lines drawn across them in heavy, dark, pencil marks. Eddie Bowen (Trooper Stan's personal hall pass) had actually finished his, accurately. Another had the name "Zippy" written all the way down the margins on both sides. I would not know until the next day how many of the unaccounted for papers would be returned.

The journals were not nearly as charitable. I had written the names on the front covers before I distributed them so I knew who had completed them and who had not. Zipporah "Zippy" Bowen had written the word "ratio" over and over again on each line for several pages. Amos-Ben Iqaluq and Joel-Ben Iqaluq had made some modest attempts at forming their letters and staying somewhat on topic with sentences like:

> here are some numbers i know soda is a 1 dollar candy bar is a 1 dollar chips is 5 dollars 9 is scool tim 12 is lunch tim june 6 is my burthda my favrit game is xbox 360

A few had random words (some profane) and pictures (again some profane) in them while the majority were blank. In each case I wrote a response. Eighth grader Sharay Kala'a had the best entry:

> The word ratio is pronounced ray-show. Ray rhymes with Jay, like in Jay-Boy, and show rhymes with no. A ratio is something to do with numbers. Like if there are 4 squares and 1 is black and the other 3 is white the ratio would be 1 black to 4 squares or 3 white to 4 squares. That is all I know about ratio. I hope tomorrow I know more about ratio and other stuff.

The final three all belonged to girls; eighth grader Jenny Iqaluq, freshman Mary Katherine "MKay" Bowen, and sophomore Joanne Christine "JCee" Bowen. All three shared a common theme:

> I fucking hate the tuniqs especially fucking stinky tuniqs like you you tuniqs should all fucking go home and let us fucking live our fucking lives like what we god damn want and not tell us what to do how come tuniqs always tell other people what to do with their shity ass shit smell mouths but nobody tells tuniqs what they can and cant do and anytime the tuniqs dont like whats gets done to them they call troopers and god damn piece shit troopers always do whats asshole tuniqs say and never do whats we wants done to tuniqs because tuniqs is bullshit
> Leave us alone tuniq and go back to HELL!!!
> PIECE OF SHIT!!! I HATE YOU AND I HOPE YOU DIE!!!

I took the three journals down to Principal Atkinson's office and knocked on his door.

"Yes Mr. Shosatori, how can I help you this evening?" asked Principal Atkinson.

I showed him the journals and he perused each one, then made copies of each page, and took notes on a yellow legal pad. When he was finished he looked at me with a face so straight I wondered if he was also a member of the Roby fan club and asked, "Have you developed any solutions for addressing this situation yet?"

"It's pretty obvious that we're not in Kansas anymore, so I guess that if the student wants to expend their energy in that way, let them expend it. It's an inappropriate form and forum, but it speaks to their frustration, and I would rather have them write it out in here than scream it at me during class."

"It's not just the form and forum. It's inappropriate period. Mark these in some way that shows they have been reviewed and received zero credit. I will have a conference with the three students during first period tomorrow, and if need be the parents. Are you agreeable to that course of action?"

"Yes."

"Very well. Dismissed."

I returned to my room and realized that Clif bars and Gatorade would not be enough to sustain me for the two-hundred seventy-nine days I was obligated to remain in Iqsaiqsiq. Even augmented with freeze dried dinners and frozen pizza I needed more. I needed some mojo. I needed... *the words*. On an eleven-by-seventeen inch piece of poster board I scribed my anthem in black Sharpie just as I had done on the inside of my Outer Tactical Vest years before.

I rolled up the poster board and stuffed it in my backpack before I made a final restroom stop. Fourteen hours after I had entered, I left the building on an August evening about the same time commentators and pundits started their shows on which they disparage those in the teaching profession for their overly lavish salaries, lucrative health and retirement benefits, unreasonable negotiated agreements, and "summers off."

# CHAPTER SEVEN

I relied on the alarm function of my iPhone to wake me up at 6:00 a.m. My eyes read the words mounted on the ceiling above my bed then I headed to school to shower. Joanne was on the spin bike again as I walked to my room.

Before I went back to work on vocabulary terms and formula posters I sat at each of the tables. I tried to imagine, "What does it look like from here? What's it like to sit in this seat for fifty-five minutes? If I was so-and-so, with so-and-so beside me, how would I behave in class?"

Shortly after the first bell rang I heard Emma in the hallway. "Daniel. Daniel! Daniel, come back here!" she shouted.

I opened my door and saw Daniel, one of the pencil snappers from the previous day, walk down the hallway. "Tomorrow," he said, "I might-could tomorrow."

Emma yelled something to the effect of, "You can't do it tomorrow! It needs to be done, today! There will be a different assignment tomorrow!"

Daniel didn't even look behind him as he said, "Tomorrow. Not now, tomorrow."

Solomon, Eddie, and Rachel all made their way down the hall at some point, one-way to the office. Trooper Stan and Principal Atkinson, with an aqua-marine tie, came down and walked out with Derek, hands free and under his own power. Later they returned and walked out with Alex Aicia, although I didn't know what he was doing in that class since he was a sophomore.

At other times I heard students maybe in Cornell's room or Nick's argue about soda or headphones, along with no less than a dozen utterances of the word, *"Tuniq,"* and of course doors being slammed. Sometimes slammed open, sometimes slammed shut, but always slammed nonetheless.

First period ended and about half of the students picked up their word search as they entered. Solomon, Eddie, Derek, and Rachel were all escorted in by Principal Atkinson. After the bell rang I started the timer and passed word searches out to students who had not picked one up. Most of them just stared at theirs, Solomon and Rachel slid theirs off on to the floor. I asked the two of them to pick their papers up.

"Shut, up." Solomon said slowly.

"Solomon, do you think that's an appropriate thing to say?"

"So what?"

"Do you think Principal Atkinson would approve of that?"

Solomon stretched out across the table. I warned both he and Rachel that they would be headed to the office if they didn't get to work.

"You want me go office?" asked Rachel.

"No, I want you to do your work. But if you're not going to do your work, then you may as well go to the office."

Rachel put her head back down on the table.

The timer went off and I explained that I would like a response to the comments I left for the previous day's word. I distributed the journals and highlighted the word for the day, integer, then reset the timer for three minutes. With the three minutes nearly finished, the papers on the floor, and nothing written in their journals, I sent Solomon and Rachel down to the office.

I asked to collect homework and didn't receive any. I handed out books and did a ten minute introduction on the topic of natural numbers, integers, rational numbers, and real numbers. Then I circulated around the room. None of the students worked. I retreated to the board and modeled the first problem as some copied, some watched, and others did nothing. The bell rang, I handed out homework, and students left the room. I collected the books and abandoned word searches as the eighth graders came in.

I had to offer the admonishment again about soda. Most of the students politely finished theirs out in the hall, made an effort to cajole the last drops as the bell rang, and scurried in. A few needed to have word searches handed to them, then I started the timer. As the timer clicked from :59 to :58, Tim-Tim produced a Pepsi from his coat pocket and cracked it open.

"Everyone was told yesterday and today, and it's posted on the door, that soda is not allowed in this classroom. Tim-Tim, you need to throw that away," I said.

"No. I don't." Tim-Tim took another sip.

"Tim-Tim, you need to throw that away, or I am going to send you to the office."

"I'll finish it in the office." Tim-Tim got up and walked toward the door. He swung the door open hard, just as Tim had done the day before, said, "No, I think I'll finish it here," and raised the can back to his mouth. In one smooth motion he swung the can from his lips straight at my chest, and said, "You can keep it," then ran down the hallway.

I called down to the office, introduced the topic, "percent," then asked students to read the comments I had put in their journals, and reset the timer for three minutes before I sopped up the Pepsi from my shirt. Fortunately, since I showered at the school, I had extra shirts in my filing cabinet that I could change into at lunch time. Unfortunately, since Tim-Tim was an optimist, the can had been half-full when he threw it. In some macabre way I thought, "For a kid who is so big into his Pepsi, throwing it is really kind of a waste."

I asked again for homework and received only blank stares. I did my introduction and handed out math books. There were a few eighth graders who were actively interested in the lesson. Sharay Kala'a started independently and occasionally asked me to read a word or explain a term. Josh Aicia and Mary Iqaluq were engaged as long as I led the way, while a few others followed along for a problem or two, then put their heads down or doodled on their papers.

The period ended. I handed homework out and collected books then grabbed a clean shirt to take down to the locker room with me.

I passed Cornell in the hall. "What happened to your shirt, Bud?"

"Non-verbal protest against the regime." I told him.

I changed my shirt and headed back to my room. In the foyer I passed three elderly Native gentlemen as they sat on one of the benches. They each waved and greeted me as I past. "Good afternoon, good afternoon," said the first one. "Good afternoon, good afternoon," said the second one. "Good afternoon, good afternoon," said the third one.

"Good afternoon," I said and waved back.

The bell rang to begin fourth period and, like the eighth graders, the algebra one students gathered just outside the door and guzzled away down to the last chime. Rocky Aicia, who had been absent the previous day, did not have a soda, but he did have a large bag of Doritos. A few of the students actually picked up their word searches on the way in. I started the timer and delivered word searches to those who had not picked them up. Much to my surprise and pleasure about half of them got to work quickly. I asked Rocky to come up to the board, which he did without protest.

Rocky had the same gaunt, pale look with small, sunken rabbit-like features and thin upper-lip as the eighth grader Rosy Aicia. I later found out that they were siblings. I handed Rocky a copy of the rules and syllabus. "I know you weren't here yesterday, but food and drinks are not allowed in this classroom. You can put your chips in the drawer and take them with you when you leave, okay?"

"It's not a soda," said Rocky.

"I know it's not a soda, but no food or drinks are allowed in this classroom at all. So you need to put that away." The timer went off and I left Rocky by my desk while I handed out journals and introduced the word for the day, variable, then set the timer for three minutes.

I returned to the front of the room where Rocky still held the syllabus. He looked up at me. "They're chips, not a soda."

"Rocky, put them away please, you can get them back after class, okay?"

Rocky went back to his chair and stared at his journal for a while. Then he ate a chip, and then another. The timer sounded and I decided that it was better for the class as a whole to maintain momentum than it was to bring it to an abrupt halt just to deal with one student. I introduced the lesson for the day and handed out books. Before I took any questions I walked past Rocky's table and told him, "I'm going to put these in the drawer for you," then picked up the bag of chips and put them in the filing cabinet.

It wasn't my desire or intent, but I half expected Rocky to go get the chips out of the drawer and precipitate yet another Tabasco monsoon that would exile us to the gym once again. Rocky just sat there while all of the other students gave an honest effort. I worked in a clockwise circuit to answer all of their questions. For about a minute and a half I was in my zone. I thought, "Yes, this is it. This is why I left the creature comforts of Seattle. This is what my friend Dan was talking about. Those seventh and eighth graders may be rough, but this is worth it, this is the reward. What a great day, what a great class, what could go wrong, what…? What is Rocky doing?"

Rocky got up and walked over to the filing cabinet. He put his hand on the handle, but he didn't open it,. He *opened* it. He yanked it so hard that I thought the whole thing would fall over. The drawer didn't come all the way out so he slammed it shut and yanked it open again and again. Crash, slam. Crash, slam. Crash, slam. It was like a front row seat at *Stomp*. The handle broke off and the drawer was locked shut, there was a pause in the action then Rocky kicked the filing cabinet until Principal Atkinson and Trooper Stan came in. Trooper Stan didn't have the pepper spray though, he had the Taser. I thought to myself, "Yesterday was a monsoon and today will be a lighting storm."

Rocky looked at them both and got the same relieved look that Tim-Tim had on Monday. He panted and his shoulders went limp.

Principal Atkinson said, "Rocky, come outside with us."

Rocky nodded his head and I, again, half expected him to hurl a *"tuniq"* or "motherfucker" or "kick your ass" my way, but he didn't. He just nodded his head and walked out with Principal Atkinson behind him. Trooper Stan closed the door and I was prepared for the class to barrage me with, "How *come* you let him get so mad?" and, "You shouldn't have done what you did." But they just went back about their business and thirty seconds later it was, "I don't understand this," and "Mr. Shosatori come here."

Fourth period exchanged for fifth period and not a single food or drink related issue arose. Before the bell rang Jay-Boy shared his joke of the day.

"Knock, knock," said Jay-Boy.

"Who's there?" I asked.

"Gorilla."

"Gorilla who?"

"I'm gonna Gorilla hamburger on the stove. You want me to Gorilla one for you too?"

Some word searches had been retrieved independently while others had to be offered. I handed out the journals, introduced the word of the day, monomial, and started the timer. When the three minutes were up, I collected the journals and began the introduction.

Olivia Aicia had gotten suspended the previous day before fifth period so today was our first opportunity for dialogue. She opened it with, "Where's our *books!?*"

"I will be handing them out as soon as I am done explaining the lesson." I told her as we evaluated 6 + X = 10.

"Where's our *books!?*"

"Subtract six from both sides of the equation to isolate the variable. They're over on my desk. We'll get to them, don't worry."

"Where's our *books, tuniq!?*"

"X equals four... Olivia, I don't know if..."

"Where's our books!!! Where's our books!!!"

I reached way, way, way back in my old camp counselor training from more than a decade past and simply put my marker down while the room fell silent.

"What?" Olivia asked.

"Are you finished?"

"For what!" (A term that befuddled me.)

"Are you finished?"

"I can't be finished. I can't never start. Cause you never give me no *book!*"

"When did I say..."

"Oh shut up. Shut up! Just close your stinky cunt hole and shut the fuck up before I slap you so fuck fuckin' hard your fuck fuckin' motherfuckin' cock suckin' grandmother feels it, *tuniq! Tuniq! Tuniq!!!*"

"Go to the office."

"Make me ass wipe. Wipe my ass! Kiss ass suck! Bitch, bitch. Bitch... ass, suck!"

I moved toward the intercom to call the office and Olivia sprang from her chair then threw it against the wall. "Don't you dare, you cock sucker. Don't! Don't you dare! Don't!!!"

I called the office and Olivia said, "You shouldn't have done that you! You! You!!!" and spat toward me from an ineffective distance.

Olivia went to the door and swung it open hard enough to slam against the filing cabinet. I don't know which company makes them, but they're really well built doors.

She stepped into the hallway and Principal Atkinson called to her from the left, "Olivia, walk down here."

"Lick my balls bitch!" Olivia hollered back. Then *she* turned to *her* right and walked to the end of the hall where a fire door led outside.

*She* left the building and walked through the middle of the village as *she* screamed, "Lick my balls, lick my balls! Fucking *tuniq*, lick my balls!"

I finished the introduction and handed out the books. I went from student to student, but this group was not the, "I don't understand this, Mr. Shosatori come here," group. This was the stare blankly at the page group.

"What are you going to do here?" I asked Desiree Kala'a.

"*Atchu?*" she said.

"Let's get all of the variables on the left side and all of the numerals on the right side, okay."

Desiree performed that task, but then stared at her book until I made the next round and said, "Combine the like-terms together on the left side, combine all of the numerals together on the right side."

There the students would sit, not one asked for help but not one rejected it when it was offered. When the bell rang I dispensed the homework and collected the books.

Lewis came in, soda-less, and handed me his iPod with the headphone cord wrapped around it. He did the word search and the journal, then we measured angles with a protractor and found the unknown angle of a triangle when given the other two. We talked a lot about basketball, especially the distances from various places on the court to the basket.

As we drew up a court on one of the portable whiteboards, I heard an engine roar up to the school and four locked tires scoured the ground.

Someone shouted and a door slammed. A moment later I could hear the same voice yell again, briefly, and another slam. Finally I heard the voice in what I was sure was Nick's room, and Nick said, "Get out. Get! Out!"

The voice replied briefly and another door slammed. I heard Trooper Stan's baritone in the hall, but could not ascertain his words. Then I heard the female voice clearly howl, "Where's that *tuniq* bitch? She never know how teach my kids… get some Native teachers in this fucking school what know… Native kids and don't treat our kids like junk… blond bimbo says… disruptive. Bullshit! *Tuniqs* is disruptive… disrupt everybody… keep they mouths shut! Never care! …not a real teacher… just teaches fucking Kindergarten."

It sounded like someone kicked or punched a wall several times, then it ended.

With ten minutes left in the class, Lewis said, "Can I go on computer?"

"Next week, when we start graphing, you can use the computer then, okay?"

Lewis seemed amicable to that and went back to work.

When school was over I read the journals and the completed word searches with about the same results as the previous day except that Jenny and MKay left their journals blank whereas JCee had simply written:

I never rite nothing in here no more cause I always get in trouble when ever times I rite in here

I boiled some water in the work room microwave for my freeze dried dinner and while it steeped I gathered wire and duct tape along with my Leatherman in an attempt to repair my embattled filing cabinet.

Cornell came in and I asked him, "What up, G?" "Whu-uht?" said Cornell. "How was your day?"

"Miserable, as usual, but at least it's over. Eighty students contact days left until Christmas break. That's all I can think of. Eighty days of that little Solomon fella asking me how many times I've changed my Depends today."

"Speaking of Solomon, who was Mr. Oosterahn?"

"A teacher here last year. Good with the kids. Got along with the staff. Lived in the apartment across from yours. Over Christmas somebody broke into all the apartments over there, made a big mess, took some things, ate whatever they wanted." Cornell helped himself over to a chair.

"Mr. Oosterahn apparently had some," Cornell swallowed, "Moo-vies, and some 'mag-u-zeeenz' with naked men, only naked men, in the pictures. We came back from Christmas break and the whole village knew about it. Well, shoot, you could be the greatest rock-super-star that ever lived and these kids would never cut you a break. But it gets around that you're a," Cornell tilted his flattened palm, "That's the end there Bud."

Cornell switched topics as I looped a wire around the latch on the inside of the drawer. "These kids ever talk about Mitch in your class?" he asked.

"Nope."

"Wuh-ell, I probably shouldn't say this just yet, but I stopped by this morning during my prep when he's supposed to have technology stuff going on, web pages, school newsletter, that sort of thing. They're just plinkin' 'round on the internet though. I tell you what, Bud. The end of the quarter comes and there's no newsletter, that boys in trouble. And that middle school PE program sixth hour, hell, half of those kids aren't even in the gym, they're out in the hall drinking sodas at their lockers."

I had the latch lassoed but couldn't get it to move in the direction I needed so I put more slack into it to see if I could catch an anchor to leverage against.

"Emma's havin' just the opposite problem," Cornell began. "God bless her she is making these kids toe the line on the headphones. I think almost all of the kids show up in her class with them and she takes them away every day. Keeps 'em all day too. I usually just give 'em back at the end of the class period. You know I can hear her through the wall, and she spends way too much time chasing kids off of that couch. If I was her I'd just take the darn thing out. There's no need for it." Cornell's comment explained why I had had so few incidences with the middle school students and headphones. Soda was another issue.

I got the latch pulled back against the spring and just enough of the handle remained that I could pinch it with the pliers on my Leatherman. I pulled the drawer open and used the pliers to pull the latch all of the way off, then looped wire through the two holes where the screws had held the handle on and covered them with duct tape.

"In the end we each gotta do what suits us best I guess. I'll get outta your hair here and let you finish Bud." Cornell let out a sigh as he stood up and headed for the door.

"Who was that yelling in the foyer sixth hour?" I asked him.

"Oh, that." Cornell's tone made it seem as if this was something of a routine occurrence. "That's Bertha Bowen. She's got three kids in the elle-uh-men-tree. Belle says she can't get her in for a conference or even to say, 'Hi,' to save her life; but once she's drunk she'll let everybody know what's been on her mind for the last couple uh months. Don't worry though Bud, she only yells at the women, even when it's something that a man did to tick her off."

Cornell paused to look at my repair job then spotted the bag of chips in the drawer and said, "Say, are those Cool Ranch?" before he took a handful and headed out the door.

I ate my reconstituted spaghetti and reflected on the last time I had experienced constant verbal abuse and complete disregard for my value as a human being in a chaotic environment without access to family or peer support; the twelve weeks of boot camp at Marine Corps Recruit Depot San Diego. Eighty-four days was my baseline, with two days already credited, and I committed to making it at least that long in Iqsaiqsiq. I headed home after a mere eleven hour day then dug back into my Michener novel. The "kaputtputt-putt" of Honda's barely roused me enough to slide my window closed.

The raucous behavior remained at a fever-pitch right through Friday afternoon. About half of the seventh graders were absent from, removed from, or sent out of Emma's room each day. Solomon finished out the week by asking me if I was: "A Jew," circumcised (possibly a follow up to the previous days question), and a meth addict. Each time I told him that was inappropriate. The seventh and eighth graders continued to be ornerier than the high school students. Every day at lunch I passed the three elders who greeted me with, "Good afternoon, good afternoon." Tim was still out from Monday's melt down and Tim-Tim was suspended through Friday for his one-man Pepsi Rebellion, so I was spared that misery, but Rocky and Olivia returned from their suspensions on Thursday. By lunch Principal Atkinson had dismissed Olivia early for a three and a half day weekend. On Friday morning Emma and I received an email from Principal Atkinson stating that we would be meeting in the library at 3:40 with the parents of Tim Kala'a.

Emma suggested that we meet in my room, then both go to the library together. Since she had more experience, especially Bush experience, I supported the idea. The two of us walked into the library where Principal Atkinson (in white shirt, black tie, and black trousers) and both of Tim's parents sat around one of the absurdly small tables. Principal Atkinson showed everyone a tape recorder and began recording. He stated the date, the names of the people present, the fact that it was being recorded, and the nature of the conversation, then concluded with, "...the behavior of Timothy Kala'a."

"That not my boys name," said Mr. Kala'a, "It's I (he pronounced it "eye") Timothy Kala'a, like in the bible. That's my boy's name. Now fix it."

Principal Atkinson graciously apologized and corrected the name. "I believe Tim has the ability to be successful at school. He has had some limited success in the past which demonstrates that he can function independently in the school setting. His academic abilities are below grade level, but he demonstrates a level of proficiency which would indicate..." and on Principal Atkinson went

When Principal Atkinson was done Mr. Kala'a looked at him and said, "What are you going to do about it?"

Principal Atkinson reiterated that this was a group effort between the school, the parents, and Tim himself. He explained that the school was set up to help Tim be successful; the teachers were trained and certified, the curriculum was being followed, there was a discipline policy in place and all that was left was for Tim to step into it and follow it.

"What are they going to do about it?" asked Mr. Kala'a.

Principal Atkinson explained that the teachers at the school were already following the expectations and that Tim was the one who was not following them.

"He's the problem." Mr. Kala'a pointed at me. "You shouldn't hire such big teachers. That big teacher is a bully. All big teachers are bullies. He makes kids listen to him because he is big. If he weren't so big the kids wouldn't listen to him and there wouldn't be problems for my boy."

When I was eleven, I walked through a fifty foot tunnel at an amusement park. The floor stayed in one place, but the top and sides were part of a cylinder that rotated. It looked utterly simple from the outside, but became exponentially more difficult with each step; the first four steps were perfect, the next four I had to put my arms out for balance, four more and I couldn't even stand much less walk. It completely disoriented me and I began to feel nauseous. I had to crawl the rest of the way to the end with my eyes focused only twelve inches in front of me. Mr. Kala'a's comment made me feel like I was between the fourth and fifth step in that tunnel.

Did he just say that I bullied his child? I had felt much more bullied than bully for the last five days. Bullies generally aren't the ones who end up with soda on their shirts. Did he just say that all big teachers are bullies? Okay, I've been known to generalize as well; I gave him a Mulligan on that one. Did he just say I made kids listen? Outside of marionettes, no one is made to do anything. Did he just say it was because I was big? I had assumed it was out of respect, cooperation, self-interest, and understanding; perhaps with a little humility and tolerance on the side. Did he just say that his son listened to me? Quite the opposite was true, the result being this meeting. Did he just say that if I had failed to appropriately and professionally administer the discipline policy his son wouldn't misbehave? Did he just say that if the teachers were smaller, the students would not listen to them, would not follow directions, and therefore would be better off? On top of everything else, what did my physical size have to do with Tim's inquiry into Emma's use of furniture for reproductive purposes? Even though I had remained seated through all of this, I was already a little nauseous.

Principal Atkinson did his best to stay on both feet as well. He said, "What I understand your point to be is that you are unhappy that Mr. Shosatori is larger than most people, is that correct?"

"Correct."

"And you feel he uses his larger size to intimidate the students into complying with his requests?"

"Correct."

"Do you feel that the students would comply with his requests if he were smaller?"

"No, if he were smaller, no kids would listen to him. Or he would keep his mouth shut. The kids do what they want. The kids say what they want. The kids drink their soda. Nobody gets sent home, and there's no problems."

Principal Atkinson went through several scenarios until all involved understood that Mr. Kala'a was of the firm belief that, if all of the school teachers were of smaller physical stature than the students, either the students would be less likely to accept the teachers authority or the teachers would be less likely to assert their own authority. In the end this would result in fewer students being disciplined and fewer students following the rules, making the school a better place for the students and result in them not being sent home.

Principal Atkinson maintained his command presence. He may have nauseously crawled twelve inches at a time right along with the rest of us, but his stern bearing never betrayed it. He pointed out that he had never personally met any of the teachers before they were hired and therefore it was impossible that their appearance was a factor, and that in any case the logic Mr. Kala'a applied was inconsistent with Emma's actions and Tim's behavior toward her. In the end Principal Atkinson basically said; here are the rules, Tim will follow them or Tim will no longer be in school.

Mr. Kala'a asked, "How *come* my boy can't have no soda at school? They had soda last year. They had soda when I was in school. How *come* no soda now?"

Principal Atkinson explained why he supported it the policy.

"So this one teacher, Forman, what let kids drink soda in his class. You saying no kids learn in that class since they got sodas in there? How *come* you let him let kids have sodas if they can't learn with sodas? You want our kids be stupid?"

This was a tougher one for Principal Atkinson, especially since this whole exchange was being recorded. He deflected it using just a little bit of his own amusement park tunnel logic, although I could see that doing so had made him uncomfortable. Emma and I were dismissed while Principal Atkinson stayed in the library with Mr. and Mrs. Kala'a.

I boiled water in the work room microwave again and added it to my freeze dried dinner. It steeped while I looked through journals and updated my grade book. I finished off the beef and macaroni and washed it down with lemon-lime Gatorade then headed home just a tick before 6:00 p.m. I still had vocabulary terms and formulas to work on but I would finish them when I returned on Saturday or Sunday to shower. At home I chose one of the F. Scott Fitzgerald audiobooks on my iPhone and let Tim Robbins' even, resonant tenor lull me to sleep.

# CHAPTER EIGHT

I woke up around 7:30 a.m., rolled over, and went right back to sleep. At about 9:00 a.m. I put on my running gear and headphones, grabbed my empty Camelbak, and sprinted to the school. After I emptied my body and filled my Camelbak I took a jog around the village. Its flat, even, symmetrical roads lent themselves perfectly to a well-paced stride.

I headed north from the school and came to a fenced in area where the shipping containers I had seen from the air were kept. They were eight feet wide by nine feet tall and between forty and sixty feet long. "Sea-Land" was written on the side and I had heard people refer to similar containers as a "Conex." There were also some fifty-five gallon drums filled with god-knows-what kind of leftover chemicals. I reversed direction, headed south, and passed by the airport where Trooper Stan was parked in his truck with a passenger.

A blue and white Cessna 207 with wings labeled STATE and TROOPER approached and landed. A few minutes later Trooper Stan pulled alongside me and said, "Coffee, tea, or Pepsi?"

"Are you offering drinks or asking about projectiles?" I inquired.

"Drinks. At least for today."

Trooper Stan stopped the truck and I hopped in. "Beautiful morning for a run," he said.

"Running and a day off, this has been the best twenty minutes of my week."

"Mine too."

He asked how I had come to Alaska and I told him. He said that he had retired from the Army at age thirty-eight and been in Alaska for the last sixteen years. He had a story similar to Mitch's in that it spanned a litany of places from Sitka to Dutch Harbor, and similar to Emma's in that it expressed some genuine fondness for a few of them. He finished with, "But Iqsaiqsiq isn't one of those types of places."

Trooper Stan's house was indistinguishable from the rest except that it was free of debris and had a garage. We walked into the little porch that covered the front door and as he bent down to remove his black leather jump boots he said, "Welcome to my new and improved *quniciuq* (cunn-ee-chuck)." The plywood walls of the porch, or *quniciuq*, had been freshly painted white and faux-stone twelve-by-twelve inch vinyl squares covered the floor. One wall had a bench built into it with a row of wooden pegs above.

I slipped off my Asics Gels and slid them next to the two pairs of XtraTufs under the bench, then hung my Camelbak on a peg.

We walked into the house and I was relieved to see that it did not contain the same standard issue table and chairs or couch as my apartment. It had four large leather chairs draped with Pendleton wool blankets organized around an oak coffee table and oriented toward a large television in the living room. The floor was covered with rugs and the walls held framed photographs and paintings. The kitchen had a counter height table in deep walnut with six bar stools. There were curios aplenty. The furniture alone must have cost $10,000 in Seattle or Anchorage, and probably half again as much to have it flown in.

"Nice place," I said.

"Thanks. People who come out to work in villages fall into two categories; campers and dwellers. Jenn and I decided early on that we would be dwellers."

Trooper Stan led me to the kitchen and as I pulled out a chair, a cat scurried out from under the table. Trooper Stan said, "There goes Miss Annie, eleven pounds of claws and curiosity."

Jenn brought us plates covered with poached eggs and patties of flattened mashed potatoes. "Thank you Jenn," I said.

"You're welcome," she replied as she dispensed silverware.

"I caught Ken training for the Iqsaiqsiq seven hundred. I don't know if he has any plans to enter just yet, but he'll win it if he does."

"What's the Iqsaiqsiq seven hundred?" I asked naively.

"It's the seven hundred yards from the front door of the school to the airport. Some people take a permanent practice run mid-semester, but traditionally it's done on the last day of school before Christmas break. Some years there's not much competition, but if there are fewer seats on the plane than there are people who want to leave it becomes a blood sport." Trooper Stan paused to see my reaction then added, "Always fun to watch. Just like a bar fight; terrible to be involved in, but always fun to watch."

My experience with Bush teaching fell into a similar category, although I hadn't had time to reflect on whether it was fun to watch or not.

"Did you take your pill, Stan?" Jenn asked as she headed out of the kitchen and disappeared down the hallway.

"Oh! Thanks babe." Stan fetched a bottle from the cupboard and opened it. "But you won't be making any permanent practice runs Ken, I can tell. I haven't heard you raise your voice, or seen you wringing your hands wondering what to do. If you have a problem you put your energy into a solution, not a justification. You stand up to people but you don't stand over them."

Stan held the pill on his tongue and poured a glass of water from a Brita pitcher. "No one likes to be told, 'No,' and every time you tell one of these kids, 'No,' they will tell you to suck it. That's unavoidable. But when you say, 'No,' to someone in a classroom it's not just that one kid that hears you, it's everybody in the room and each of them will make a judgment as to whether or not it is legitimate. If it is legitimate, then one kid thinks you're an asshole. If it isn't, then all of them think you're an asshole. And all of them will let you know it."

After he washed down the pill, Stan returned to the table. "Can you hold something in confidence Ken?" Stan asked.

"That depends," I asked, as I cut a potato patty with my fork, "Does it involve violence?"

"No."

"Drugs?"

"No."

"Theft?"

"No."

"Lying?"

"No."

"Sex?"

"No."

"Too bad because I was really holding out that there would be some sex involved in here somewhere. Okay, I can keep it under my hat. What is it?"

Stan laughed and went into an explanation that included his signature air judo chop hand gestures. "See, that's it right there. That's what I'm talking about. You've got a good sense of right and wrong, you think things through, you don't act before you have all of the facts, and in the end you don't get all uptight about stuff."

Stan wiped egg from the corner of his mouth and I could tell I had broken the dramatic tone which he had intended to set. "There are two species of teachers that always fail in Iqsaiqsiq, if not everywhere in the Bush, and there's one of each on your staff. They will both be gone before Christmas, if not sooner. The first is the Bulldog, the second is the Albophobe.

"Bulldogs are Mr. or Mrs., 'My way or the highway.' They push in one direction because they only know one direction. They're oblivious to the other 359 degrees, to use a math analogy. They can be conservative or liberal, cruel or kind, passive or aggressive. They only know one way to skin a cat and that's the way they will skin it, even if what they are skinning is actually a dog. Sometimes Bulldogs get lucky and the first village they land in moves in the same direction they happen to push or maybe, since it's their first village, they are more open to change. They will have success in village X, but not in village Y, and they walk away saying, 'There's something wrong with those people in village Y.' Then they go to village Z and experience the same thing until they either find another village X or just give up looking."

"Emma." Stan caught a bit of too crispy mashed potato in his throat and coughed. "Excuse me. Emma is a Bulldog. Either Vitus Cove fit her like a glove from day one, or she, 'When in Rome-ed,' her way through the first couple of years and now accepts Vitus Cove as the standard. In any case, it's village X and this is village Y. It's only a matter of time until Emma goes looking for another Vitus Cove. The good news is that the Vitus Coves of the world do exist, they just don't prepare people for Iqsaiqsiq at all. In fact they are kind of a handicap."

"You wanna take a guess what an Albophobe is?" Stan asked.

"Phobe is fear, so it's a fear of something. Albo is from the Latin *albus*, which is the first name of Professor Dumbledore in Harry Potter. Ergo, it is a fear of professorial wizards."

"First part's right, but it's got nothing to do with *Hairy Pooter and the Saucy Hard Bone*."

"Okay. The Latin root *albus* means white, so it's a fear of white. But I'm not a big fan of white either, it's too hard to keep clean. I prefer cream, beige, or gray myself." I knew he meant white as in Caucasian, but since all of the teachers fit that description I couldn't think of any of them who would be afraid of white people.

"Fear of whiteness, in the broader cultural sense." Stan put our plates in the sink then led me to one of the chairs and turned on the TV which by chance or design just happened to be set to an NFL preseason game.

"Albophobes are Mr. or Mrs., 'I love all these people here.' But that's only half true at best. What they really mean is, 'I hate all those people everywhere else.' They don't come *to* the village as much as they come *from* someplace else. They are liberal, kind, and passive-aggressive. They are typically white themselves, but white mainstream America has not been kind to them, so they seek a new identity in the Native community. A few communities will treat them like a prodigal child, but usually the response is, 'I'm struggling here enough myself, I don't need your insecurities and baggage.'"

"Albophobes will lend money, fix houses, give away clothes, and take in stray animals. It sounds charitable and neighborly at first but they don't set any boundaries, and their motives are not altruistic. Eventually they are broke and worn out, with little reciprocity. That's when Albophobes' passive-aggressive switches get tripped and they shut down or retaliate and eventually leave. Their legacy is, 'Albophobes said they liked us and were our friends. They did all this stuff so we would like them. Then they quit doing stuff for us and left all of a sudden.'"

Stan got up and fixed a tray with some Doritos and Pepsi. As he returned to the living room, he said, "Incoming," and tossed me a can.

"What are you trying to do, induce my PTSD?" I asked.

"Post Traumatic School Disorder?" said Stan.

"Nope, Post Traumatic Soda Disorder."

"Hey man, blame the finger, not the trigger."

"If sodas are outlawed, only outlaws will have soda."

"You can have my soda when you pry it from my cold, dead, hand."

"My soda, my choice. Sorry, I'm running out of bumper stickers to parody here."

"That's okay, I was about to go with, 'Earth first, we can soda-ize the other planets later.'"

"Soda-ize?" I asked. "How about soda-mize?"

Stan spewed Pepsi and Doritos through his nose and created a Jackson Pollock on the front of his shirt. He coughed, snorted, and chuckled. "Never heard that one."

Stan went to change his shirt then let the conversation lull until a commercial. "I knew Mitch Forman was a textbook Albophobe the first time I met him. Less than two days after he got here he said, 'They love me…' not, 'I love them,' but, 'They love me.' He has tried to insert himself into this community in every conceivable way. Or at least, every way that doesn't involve doing his job teaching at the school. He is going to set all of you up for failure."

Stan took a deep pull of Pepsi, looked at the can, shook his head, smiled, and said, "soda-mize," then resumed his solemn tone. "Mitch is going to lavish gifts and gratuitous praise on this community for the next month or more and everybody is going to expect the rest of you to compete with it. When you don't, you will be called cheap, stingy, and abrasive because you are not a giver like him. When he leaves he will make a statement that amounts to, 'I tried to help all of you, but you didn't want it,' and then the community will turn against the rest of you because they will assume that you are all one step away from doing the same thing."

I didn't know Stan past the three or four times he had been in my room. On the one hand he did not seem like a person with a prejudicial disposition, he certainly hadn't said anything derogatory about the Native population, but he did seem to have been pretty judgmental toward Emma and Mitch after less than two weeks.

Then again, his description of Albophobes matched up with what I already knew about Mitch; he bailed from the staff lunch, he bailed right after the staff meeting on the first day of school, he wore an Iqsaiqsiq sweatshirt, he self-referenced an inability to teach in 'civilization,' and finally his comment about, 'kindred spirits.'

I had had three "mentors," for lack of a better term; Roby, Terri Bowen-Skeen, and now Stan. Roby's advice had been accurate, even if understated; it had not made me impervious to failure but it had inoculated me to a high degree. Terri Bowen-Skeen's advice was marginal at best, it appeared sound in theory but I had not observed a single instance of it in practice. In fact, the cultural map Terri had drawn for all of us at in-service bore little resemblance to the landscape of Iqsaiqsiq. Stan hadn't really asked me to take any action, he just informed me of what his experience had been. I guess I would call it one win, one loss, and one tie.

The football game ended and an infomercial came on. Somewhere between "stainless steel design" and "recirculating action" I dozed off.

"Rrrrawnnnk! Rawnk, rawnk, rawnk. Rrrrawnnnk!"

I found myself cradled in the oversized, overstuffed leather chair. Directly across from me Stan reclined, mouth agape, and the sun reflected off of his forehead like a huge luminescent eye. His left hand still held the remote and his right hand tenuously pinched a Pepsi can.

Jenn came out of a back room and gently pried the remote out of his hand. When she reached for the can he startled awake and said, "Was I snoring?"

Jenn rolled her eyes and carried all of the cans and the tray of chips into the kitchen. "Stan, are you going to the dump today?"

Stan looked at his watch, rubbed his face and said, "Yep," then turned to me and said, "You ready to go?"

If the train was ready to leave the station I was hopping on it. "Sure," I said. I thanked Jenn for breakfast and followed Stan out to the *quniciuq*. We donned our footwear and I grabbed my Camelbak before we went over to the garage. Inside, I could see an eight-by-twelve foot box similar to a garden shed jammed into one corner, but instead of aluminum or fiberglass it was made of plate steel and had two steel mesh doors. The garage also had three snowmobiles, or snowmachines as I had learned they were called; one large blue model with the Alaska State Troopers logo on the hood and two smaller green ones. There were four large Hefty trash bags in the corner. Stan and I each grabbed two and threw them into the back of the pickup then climbed into the cab.

"Where would you like me to drop you off?" asked Stan.

I felt better than I had in ten days I decided to try and spin a little freestyle:

Here I am, and here's the plan.
Rolling down the road with Trooper Stan.
He gonna ask me where to go.
But truth is… I don't even know.

I don't want, to be a chump.
Maybe I'll go, to the dump.
But before we go there with the truck.
Better stop at school so I can *aaa-nuq!*

Stan laughed so hard his lower bridge popped halfway out of his mouth. He stuffed it back and asked, "Where did you learn to do that?"

"Sir, in the Marines sir."

"Outstanding!"

Caught up in the moment I picked up the box of wet wipes from dashboard, said, "Tissue?" and threw it at him.

Stan bellowed in his natural rolling baritone, "Knock it off you Jack-wagon! I'm gonna PT you until your ass churns buttermilk!"

We laughed ourselves all the way down until Stan stopped in front of the school, a.k.a. the starting line for the Iqsaiqsiq 700. In the late afternoon shade of the school we each tried to speak but neither of us could get more than two words out before we cracked up. Finally I just opened the door, grabbed my Camelbak, and slid down off the seat.

With the door still open Stan said, "See if you can work that into your class, the kids will love it. Tim and Solomon will still give you a hard time, but you might pull in some of the borderline kids because it's not about getting *all* of their respect *all* of the time, it's about getting *more* of their respect *more* of the time."

"Naw," I shook my head, "It's kinda my thing and I don't want some little punk shitting all over it for me."

"Fair enough. Stop by anytime, okay?"

"See you later Stan."

"Take it easy M.C. Ken."

I slammed the door and jogged up the stairs to the school which was abuzz with activity. All of the teachers except for Cornell and his wife Belle were there. Even Mitch was in his room, along with Gobi.

I showered and went to my room to check my email, then sent out a form email to all of my contacts in the lower 48 that began, "Rays of sunlight shot across the ridge of the Chugach Mountains...." I wrote an email to Roby at Aciq School and asked his opinion on putting more rap into my rapport. I didn't want to take a chance on an interrogation at the store or a bemoan-a-palooza between staff that might ruin my best day in weeks, so I planned a hasty retreat. Then Emma knocked on my door.

"Hi Ken. I was wondering if you had ever read this book?" She held up a copy of *I Heard the Owl Call my Name* by Margaret Craven.

"No, I haven't."

"Well it's really good. It's an insight into the realities of village life and the experiences of these children. I think it might help you develop a Bush-specific pedagogy."

Maybe it was because I had already begun a magnificently wonderful day, or maybe it was because I had started to resent that I couldn't be in my classroom without somebody venting to me, perhaps even something Stan had slipped into my sub-conscious, but mostly I think it was the fact that Emma seemed to have an even more difficult time than I; in any case it annoyed me when she used the term, "...develop a Bush-specific pedagogy." She mentioned something about dinner plans and I declined the whole offer. As I headed for the front door I heard her rant to Nick about Gobi.

I didn't know what Roby's response would be to my inquiry about rapping part of my lesson but I had so much flow to spin I wanted to get it down before it evaporated. I set up Garage Band on my laptop and shuffled through the 136 vocabulary terms for ones that matched phonetically as well as conceptually. By 10:00 p.m. I had all of Monday's lessons potentially covered.

Sunday morning I jogged to school, deposited and replenished fluids, took my run around the village and hid out in my classroom until the rest of the school began to fill with footsteps and greetings. I checked my email about noon just before I left and saw that Roby had sent me a response:

Ken,

Glad to see you're hanging tough and innovating. When we spoke at the airport I told you about consistency and routine. Whether you do it or not is your call but my greatest caution is:

If you are going to do this, you need to do it every day.

Not most weeks, not most days; but every single day for the rest of the year. Sick, tired, sad, angry, busy, whatever; either commit or walk away altogether. Don't use it as an incentive and never withhold it as a punishment. Do not do this for your own benefit. If it is beneficial for the students, disregard their ridicule. If it is not beneficial for the students, disregard their praise.

Good luck,

Principal Roby Beveraux, PhD
Arctic Circle School District
Aciq, Alaska

I went home and read *I Heard the Owl Call my Name*. The cultural map it presented was also out of delineation with Iqsaiqsiq; although in its defense it was set in the Canadian coastal forest as opposed to the American arctic tundra, and had been written thirty years earlier.

When my eyes became heavy I switched to the F. Scott Fitzgerald audio. I awoke a couple times during the night and since sunlight streamed in through my window I stared up at my anthem and read, "Out of the dark that covers me…" as I pondered the paradox that The Land of the Midnight Sun could be more opaque than any trogmai in the Hindu Kush.

# CHAPTER NINE

Still without water or electricity after more than a week I showered at the school and brought in a load of laundry. Joanne was fully involved on the spin bike, headed nowhere fast.

After the first bell rang I decided to take a stroll around the building to observe my coworkers.

Cornell tried to coax the sophomores and juniors to revise some rather bland sentences with adverbs and adjectives. I could see where he had already modeled a few examples. He had a sample sentence that read, "Jane picked up the hot pan and dropped it, causing a noise."

I believe he wanted to elicit a response of, "boiling," "burning," or "sizzling" as a synonym to replace "hot," but all he got was resistance in the form of, "fucking," "god damn," and, at least this wasn't a swear word, "stupid." Every time he received an intentionally, offensively, incorrect answer he warned the student with a threatened trip to the office to which they responded, "You suck," or, "So cheap," which resulted in another threat of being sent to the office. Eventually he filled in the term himself with, "steaming" and moved on to an adverb for "dropped."

"Fucking," said Daniel-Ben Iqaluq. Cornell reminded him that he had already been warned about using that term and the next time he used it he would be sent to the office.

Finally JCee Bowen made a semi-legitimate attempt with, "she." Cornell explained that while the sentence sounded and was grammatically correct, "she" was a pronoun and not an adverb. "Uhhh! So mad you let me get *tuniq*," replied JCee.

Having apparently been warned about using the word *tuniq* previously, Cornell told JCee to go to the office. "Fine. I don't want to be in your stupid class anyway *tuniq*," she said.

I wanted to spare myself the annoyance of being the second *tuniq* to be called a *tuniq*, so I headed toward Emma's room.

Emma flipped between two maps of Africa. The first showed population density. The second showed major waterways. I believe she wanted the students to draw a conclusion between the availability of water and to the amount of human settlement. More than that though, she really wanted them to stay off of the couch.

"Rachel. Rachel! Get off of the couch and sit at your desk. Now. Now!" said Emma.

"*Azza*, how *come?*" replied Rachel groggily.

"Rachel. Do you need to go to the office?"

"How *come?* You never go office."

"Rachel, I don't need to go to the office, you need to sit in at your desk. I'm going to start counting. Three, two…"

Rachel rolled off of the couch and headed to her desk. Emma got off the sentence, "What are some things that all humans need to live?"

"*Anuq*," said Solomon, and sent the class into a tither.

"Solomon, what did I say about using that term in my classroom?"

"What? There's nothing wrong with *anuq*," this sent the room into a tither a second time, "Everybody does it. Everybody needs to do it. If you don't *anuq*," this sent the room into a tither a third time, "You might-could get bladder infection."

"Solomon, that's inappropriate. Do you need to go to the office?"

"You need to calm down. *Azza*. Go smoke some cock." This sent the class into a full-on chortle.

"Solomon! To the office!"

"Miss Rudd! To the office!" Solomon mockingly shook his head from side to side.

Emma got up to use the intercom and Solomon got up to go lay on the couch. Emma told the office that Solomon was being disruptive, had been warned, and now would not leave. Solomon meanwhile reclined on the couch and rested his head on his hands.

I thought I might pop in and offer to escort Solomon down, but experience told me he would not budge and I would only add to the Opsis. I knew what the unalterable end to this tragedy would be so I retreated to my own room and waited until Principal Atkinson, his emerald tie again held down by a silver pin and pearl dot, walked by along with Stan.

Like a channel surfer I decided to see what Mitch was up to in the computer lab. Mitch had all of the eighth graders and a few of the ninth graders. The students sat at monitors with headphones plugged in. The boys seemed to look at pictures of snowmachines while the girls looked at pictures of singers or actors. Most of the students dug their hands into the large front pockets of their over-sized hooded sweatshirts to retrieve something which they then put in their mouths.

Mitch went from student to student and asked them what they were looking at. Most would say, "RMK six-hundred," or, "Avril Lavigne." The tougher cases like Tim-Tim just ignored him. It was actually the most docile room I had seen so far, right up until Henry Bowen dug his hand into the pocket of Josh Aicia's hoody.

"*He-ey!* man," said Josh. "Get your fucking hand out of my sweater."

I expected Mitch to half jump out of his skin, but he just stood there and talked to Sharay Kala'a until Sharay herself looked over to see what had happened.

"What? What, what, what? What's going on over there?" Mitch stammered.

"He try *tiqliq* (tick-lick) from me maaannn." Josh said.

"I never," Henry said.

"Boys, boys, okay boys, let's do some work now, please," Mitch said.

Josh and Henry paused just long enough until Mitch finished then dug into each other with insults. Mitch walked over to step between them and Henry reached past Mitch to shove Josh. I opened the door slowly as if I was unaware of what had happened and walked in. When I entered, all three of them paused and looked at me in silence.

"Do you have any extra printer paper in here Mr. Forman?" I asked casually.

"Pay? Paper? No. No, no, no. Uh…"

I hadn't intended to short-circuit Mitch's brain and it didn't appear as if he would enlist my help so I simply said, "I'll check the work room," and left. I expected to see Principal Atkinson and Stan headed down the hallway to Mitch's room, but they never did.

I checked out Nick's room. His class was parted like the Red Sea; on one side of the room sat seven students with their heads down on their tables, on the other sat five students with notebooks in front of them. At the front of the room Nick labeled the parts of a cell he had drawn on the board. One of the students who took notes was Olivia Aicia. Across the back counter of the room several pairs of headphones were coiled up.

I watched and waited for what I thought would be the inevitable curse, slur, or opposition, but none came. Those that sat and took notes did just that, and those that laid their heads down did just that. There was no third option and there were no opinions vocalized in the room other than Nick's.

I returned to my room and prepared to deliver my didactic sonnet, complete with garage band instrumentals. I had labeled it as "rhyme time" on my schedule, between the journals and the introduction of the lesson.

Rachel, Eddie, and Solomon were the first to arrive; I assumed after having been freshly liberated from Principal Atkinson's custody. The rest of the students came in and most but not all picked up a word search. I started the timer and handed out the remainder out to those who still needed one. When the time was up I introduced the word of the day, prime, and reset the timer. When journal time was over I pushed play on my laptop and let the bass beat and high-hat mingle with my recorded words:

> Three kinds of numbers, talked about in this rhyme
> Special, com-po-site, and prime
> There's only one special, it's the number one
> That's the special list, the special list is done
>
> Prime numbers are next on the shelf
> A prime has two factors, one and itself
> Here's some prime numbers; two, three, five, seven
> Want one more? How 'bout eleven
>
> Composite numbers have three factors or more
> Just look at, the number four
> What factors do you see?

Take a look at them with me

One times four, or two times two
Both equal four, you know it's true
So how many factors do you see?
Count them; one, two, three

Let's try six, it's composite also
But it's got four, factors though
One times six, or two times three
Count them, along with me

How 'bout seven, is it prime or composite?
It's time to play this game and not to pause it
Multiply one and seven, and only one time
Therefore seven, has got to be prime

Where does eight belong, with composites or primes?
What numbers make eight when you use times?
One times eight and two times four
That's four factors and no more

Looking for a prime, nine is not-it
One times nine and three times three, got-it?
How many factors that make up nine, let's see
One, three, nine; that's three, G!

What makes a number composite or prime
I'll tell you this any time
If it only has two factors, one and itself
It belongs on the prime shelf

Composites have more than two factors
Don't listen, to the detractors
If it's greater than two, and it's even
It's composite, that's what I'm believin'

Open up your brain, I've got six words to deposit
Odd, even, factor, special, prime, composite
This is the end of my spin and flow

And it's all true, that's foh-shoh

I didn't know exactly what I had expected, but I hadn't expected all eleven of them to just sit and stare. I received no confirmation whatsoever so I moved on to my lecture. I asked if anyone knew what a factor was. Van Aicia raised his hand.

"Can we listen to that again?" Van asked.

I pondered Roby's words about consistency and realized that if I repeated it today I would be locked into repeating it every day. I also pondered the student's words from the previous week and realized I was almost ten minutes into the class period and had yet to be sworn at, challenged, argued with, threatened, or targeted. I played it a second time and when it was over I asked again if anyone knew what a factor was. This time Alicia Iqaluq raised her hand.

"Who is that?" Alicia asked.

"On the laptop? That's me." I said.

"Phhhttt," said Solomon, "Yeah right. That's not you, that's not no teacher. No teacher never rap like that."

"Why do you say that Solomon?" I asked.

"Cause, cause, teachers can't rap. They can't, they just can't. They're..." He paused and he thought. No, he did more than that that. He deliberated. He cogitated. I could tell he was thinking more about his answer to this question than he had thought about everything he had said and done over the course of the last month. The tension in the room was palpable and finally he said, "They're white!"

The class sat in complete shock for about half a second not knowing what would happen next or how they would be affected by it, then the faces of twin brothers Amos-Ben Iqaluq and Joel-Ben Iqaluq broke from stoic to muffled grin until their mouths burst open with laughter, a crack that eventually breached the levee and flooded the whole classroom.

When things settled back down I thought that I ought to pursue an objective homily on baseless racial stereotypes and the detrimental consequences they exert on the harmonious discourse between disparate groups, but experience suggested it would just devolve to the point where either my door got slammed or my filing cabinet got kicked so I let it drop.

I asked the question about the definition of a factor for the third time and Solomon raised his hand.

"Solomon," I said, "I am asking if anyone can tell me what a factor is and if I call on you I expect you to answer that question. Are you going to answer that question?"

"No." Solomon lowered his hand.

I never did get anyone to tell me what a factor was so, like Ben Stein, I explained it rhetorically. I sought out examples of odd and even numbers and Solomon blurted out, "Do you smoke cock?"

"How do you think I'm going to answer that Solomon?" I asked.

"*Atchu.*" Solomon shrugged his shoulders.

"I am going to tell you that that is an inappropriate question, and also that you need to raise your hand. If you ask it a second time, or ask another question without raising your hand, I will tell you again that it is an inappropriate question, or that you need to raise your hand, and warn you that I am going to send you to the office. If it happens a third time, I will send you to the office. That's the way it works for you, and that's the way it works for every other student, and that's the way it has worked in here since the first day."

I went back to odd and even numbers and had just finished demonstrating how every even number greater than two was a composite number when Solomon blurted out, "You know what cock is?"

I held up two fingers. "If you speak about that again or ask a question without raising your hand again, you are going to the office."

"What's gonna happen there?" Solomon asked, even though he hadn't raised his hand.

In a moment of greater snarkiness than I would like to admit I wrote on the board:

$$\begin{array}{r} 1 \\ 1 \\ +\ \underline{1} \\ 3 \end{array}$$

If x=3, then go to the office.

"For what?" asked Solomon.

"Solomon, I explained that you had three chances. Now go to the office."

"No, it was only two chances. I still got one chance."

I didn't think Solomon was necessarily averse to the idea, it was just more enjoyable for him to debate me than to listen to the lesson. I said, "Solomon, go to the office."

"Mr. Shosatori, go to the office." Solomon mocked me as Rachel had done to Emma. Instead of following Solomon down the rabbit hole the rest of the students just stared at him as if to say, "Dude, you are being such an ass clown right now."

"Solomon, does Principal Atkinson have to come down here to get you?" I asked.

"Fine, I'll go, you can stay here with everybody else to smoke cock." This drew him some empathetic smirks from a few of the students, especially Rachel, although at the time I didn't understand why.

Solomon went to the door and toyed with it a few times before he opened it. As he stepped into the hallway he grabbed the handle with both hands and slammed it shut as hard as he could. As I have said before, those are really well built doors.

After I finished the lecture and handed out books Alicia Iqaluq asked if they could listen to the rap song one more time. I said that if somebody reminded me in the last five minutes I would play it for them again. The students had such a weak grasp of multiplication, many still modeled it through repeated addition, that it took forever to find the factors of a number. With a few minutes left, I pushed play on my laptop again and not a word was spoken until it was finished.

The bell rang and the seventh graders ebbed while the eighth graders flowed and once again I had to offer admonishments about soda.

I timed the word searches, I timed the journal writing, and finally I hit play and let the laptop play a rap about decimals and place value.

Wanting to stay as consistent as possible I played it a second time, as I would continue to do for every class for the rest of the year. When it was through, I lectured about place value. Eventually Tim-Tim's hand went up and I called on him.

"Who's that what's singing?" he asked.

I told him it was me.

Tim-Tim chortled, "No, who's it really?"

I told him again that it was me.

Tim-Tim looked around at the rest of the class and said, "He never know who it is, that's why he never tell us and try tell us it's him." Then he laughed and drew a few others into it with him.

I'm pretty sure Roby would say that I should have just let it go and ignored it, but I wanted to put an end to it without playing twenty questions as I had with Solomon so I said:

You want to know who wrote it, you wanna know Tim-Tim
I'm the one that wrote it, I'm him-him
So you can believe it, or maybe not
But that's not the only game, that I've got

You may be a little bit in disbelief
The first of five, stages of grief
Now you'll have to admit that it's true
I can be white and a teacher and a rapper too

I got many blank stares.
Beth Aicia, Zippy Bowen, and Sharay Kala'a actually clapped.
Tim-Tim said, "So cheap. So junk rapper you are."
I shrugged my shoulders and said, "Well Tim-Tim, tomorrow you can bring in a rap, and as long as it's not offensive you can spin it."

"So junk. I never write no rap. I let you write so stupid raps if you want."

I demonstrated place value, then handed out the books, went around the room, and offered help to those who would take it. With a few minutes left I offered to play the rap again as I had for the seventh graders.

Nobody seemed to offer an opinion.

Zippy Bowen looked over both shoulders then said, "Yeah. Yeah, play it again."

Most of the students sat immersed in the garage band rhythms and a few even tapped their fingers on the tables, somewhat in tune. Tim-Tim of course had to openly mock it and, out of either nervousness or in an effort to make me feel disconcerted, he giggled and chuckled. The rest of the students stared at him, as the seventh graders had with Solomon, as if to say, "Dude, you are being such an ass clown right now."

The bell rang and the students fled. I gave the hallways a few minutes to settle down then went to the work room to run off a few copies. I passed the three Elders on the bench in the foyer.

"Good afternoon, good afternoon," said the first one.

"Good afternoon, good afternoon," said the second one.

"Good afternoon, good afternoon," said the third one.

I greeted them in kind and returned to my room.

Fifth period started and the whole class was there; Tim, Rocky, and a student who had missed the entire first week, Arnold Tiqiqiq.

Most of the students gathered at the front door and finished their sodas or whatever else they had and most of them, even Tim and Rocky, picked up their word search on their way in as the bell rang.

Arnold did not sit in his assigned seat as it was marked, nor did he have a word search. As the other students did theirs, I asked him to come up and speak with me.

"How *come?*" he said.

"Because I have some things to tell you about this class."

"You can tell me right here."

Arnold had a rabbit-like face with sunken eyes, thin upper lip, slight build, and shallow pallor similar to Rocky and Rosy, but his eyes were perkier and he seemed to track my words more quickly.

I handed out journals, introduced the word for the day, and reset the timer for three minutes. Eventually I gave Arnold his three warnings and when he refused to leave, I called the office. Principal Atkinson and Stan came down to get him and, since Stan held the door, Arnold abused the posters and the wall next to it instead. I left that section of wall empty, as it became a magnet for retribution.

Before I had a chance to transition from journals to the rhyme time, Tim chimed in with, "You better watch yourself for Arnold now, he gonna get you out of school."

I looked at Tim and said, "So be it."

"What that mean?"

"You can come by after school and I'll tell you."

"Bullshit! You tell me now *tuniq!*"

I began the rap and Tim argued with me all the way through it until he got a complimentary pass to the office. He left voluntarily, after he vented his frustrations on the door of course.

After the second play through I began the lecture on different ways to express the operations of multiplication and division. I moved to the lesson in the book and things clicked along pretty well. I played the rap for them again at the end of class.

Jay-Boy was outside the door almost the instant after the bell rang with a soda in hand. I noticed that he quickly finished the first one and immediately produced a second from the left pocket of his Starter jacket. He finished that one also and began on a third from the right pocket.

I asked him why he didn't save some of those until after school.

He just shrugged his shoulders and said, "*Atchu.*"

The bell rang and students took their seats, along with their word searches. I asked Jay-Boy if he had a joke, which he did.

"What hold Eskimo house together?"

"Uh... duct tape?"

"Nope. Eee-glue."

Word searches, journal, rap song.

"I like that. You rap again tomorrow?" asked Jay-Boy.

"Yes." I said.

"Oh. Cool."

Rap song again, lecture, hand out books, poke and prod to work, poke and prod some more, rap song again, and dismissed.

Lewis arrived and handed me his headphones. Ben from the elementary wing also came in and disconnected one of the computers. "Sorry Mr. Shosatori, I've got to move one of these down to the computer lab. A monitor got broken this morning."

"When?" I asked.

"First period, Mr. Forman said a student accidentally got a cord wrapped around a chair leg and pulled it off of the desk."

I wanted to ask Ben how probable he thought that was since all of the cords ran behind the computers next to the wall.

Word search, journal, rap song, rap song again, lecture, practice with the graphing calculator, rap song again. Return headphones and dismissed.

Since it was Monday we had a staff meeting. I took my spot at the rear-most table along with referral forms for Arnold and Tim. As the clock ticked to 3:40 Principal Atkinson said, "Miss..." and Jenn was on her feet and out the door in search of Mitch.

Principal Atkinson had a little pep talk, reminded everyone of the disciplinary protocol he had outlined on the Friday before school started and said that in the future he would return students to class immediately if he felt that protocol had not been followed. We went over a schedule for detention and hall duty, and talked about the power and water situation at the quad-plex. At the end Principal Atkinson asked the high school teachers to stay.

Jenn returned with Mitch about the same time all of the elementary school teachers were dismissed. Since the four of them were headed out the door Mitch apparently thought the meeting was over and headed back out also.

"Mr. Forman. The high school teachers are going to stay and meet," said Principal Atkinson.

Principal Atkinson ushered all of us up to one of the front tables and began. "When Mr. Coalman asked about banning soda pop and headphones from the classroom I said that I did not see them as pertinent to any educational purpose and thus would support any single teacher, or group of teachers, who banned them from their classroom. I now feel, after some parental input, that it would be best for students if there were a single policy across the school for dealing with them. I would like for the five of you, as secondary teachers, to develop and commit to a single policy."

I remembered that Principal Atkinson had initially stated that he would not make a blanket policy unless it hampered his ability to function as principal. After our meeting with Tim's parents, in which Mr. Kala'a had pointed out the uneven application of the policy, apparently now the issue was doing just that.

"Wuh-ell," Cornell began, "I suggested last yee-ear, and again this yee-ear, that we just put a sign at the front door: No soda pop. No music players. Fight the battle one time, at the beginning of the day, and be done with it. And don't let these parents bring it in for these kids neither. Good Lord! That's the real problem, the parents, but I could go on about that for duh-ayzzz." Cornell removed his glasses and rubbed the bridge of his nose.

Emma said, "I think there is something deeper here. My issue is not that they bring it in, but that when I ask for it to be put away I get so much resistance about it. It ends up being an interminable argument until they either become abusive and get sent from the room, or go off on a tirade and run out. Ultimately it's a defiance issue. If it isn't pop or headphones it will be hoods or shoes or playing cards. I think the most positive step would be to keep banning them, otherwise it will be viewed as capitulation and every other fight will just be that much harder." She was so disheveled by the day's events that she looked like a Nick Nolte mug shot, strands of hair randomly sprang free from her otherwise tightly coiled bun.

"Thank you Mr. Coalman, Miss Rudd. Next?" asked Principal Atkinson.

Mitch stared into space and Nick chomped on a granola bar so I chimed in. "If my parents had gotten a call about me doing one of these things I wouldn't have heard another song or drank another soda until my eighteenth birthday so this whole, 'You can't whatever, you're just the teacher,' bit has me perplexed. If there is a point or trade-off to be made in favor of dropping it, I'm open to it. Otherwise I intend to maintain a consistent routine and keep going the same direction I have been."

Nick began, "I think the most important part is showing a strong, consistent, unified policy that everyone's aware of and everyone follows and sticks to for the rest of the year, regardless of whether it is pro or con. I think it confuses these kids if one teacher says yes and another says no so I'll go with the group consensus, even if I don't agree with it."

"Mr. Forman?" said Principal Atkinson.

Mitch just stared into the distance.

"Mr. Forman?" Principal Atkinson asked again, "Do you have any input on this?"

Mitch seemed startled back into awareness. "I don't see why you're even asking me. You all have your minds made up already. You don't like pop. You don't like headphones. Since you have all the power you're just going to step in and make it so. Imagine if a bunch of people who looked different than you suddenly showed up and said, 'You can't eat milk and cereal for breakfast anymore,' or, 'You can't read the newspaper anymore.' How cooperative would you be? You people need a reality check. This is their home and we are just visitors. Why don't you ask the kids or their parents what they want before you go making decisions that affect only their lives, but not your own? Maybe if each of you focused more on getting to know these kids and gaining their trust instead of forcing your Western ways on them you wouldn't have these kinds of problems. Make whatever kind of rules you want. I'm not going to sully my reputation further by lending any credence to this kangaroo court."

Mitch liked to fire off his synapses simultaneously. It was like he had ten paragraphs somewhere in his mind. But he didn't evaluate their relevancy and expand on one specific point; he just grabbed all of the topic sentences and delivered them without any of the supporting details or footnotes.

Cornell bit into Mitch's bait. "Hey bud, no decision has been made yet. That's whuh-y we're all talkin' here. You don't want it cause you think it's unfair to the kids, we'll respect your opinion. But you go off luh-ike none'uh the rest'uh us know what the heck we're doin' and you're gonna end up creatin' exactly the kind of situation you say you don't want."

"I just want what's best for these kids," began Mitch, "And I don't see where letting them or not letting them have or not have pop or headphones is going to make the situation any better. It might make it worse, or it may have no effect at all. It's just that we all have been here for, what, one week, and already we are saying this pop and these headphones are a bad thing? We just don't even know what we don't know."

Cornell had sense enough to simply say, "I was here last year and we had the same problem," then let it drop.

It dropped right into Principal Atkinson's lap as five, college-educated, adult heads with nearly 250 years of life experience between them swiveled to face him in the silence. "I prefer that this group find a collaborative resolution," he said.

I, and probably Nick too, had been in enough bleacher seat arguments to realize that we were at a point where resolution might involve a shove to the chest and disparagement of someone's parental lineage, so we remained silent. Emma had checked out sometime after Mitch insulted her with, "...reality check..." and Mitch, well, he always stared blankly at something.

Finally Principal Atkinson said, "I have some ideas, but I think it would be better if ultimately the solution came from within the group."

I internally debated whether further input would prolong or shorten this imbroglio. Finally Nick said, "Alright, let's hear them."

Principal Atkinson proposed scenarios, such as banning items from school altogether as compared to only banning them from classrooms, which were more about the advantages and disadvantages of various options than support for the options themselves. Nick, Cornell, and I parsed our words carefully and limited our input to, "I understand." "How would that work?" and, "What I hear you saying is…." Eventually we (Nick, Cornell, and I) decided to make headphones and soda two separate issues, the five of us would vote on each one. A 5-0 or 4-1 decision meant it was banned, 3-2 or 2-3 would send us back to debate, and 1-4 or 0-5 meant it was allowed in perpetuity.

I had briefly pondered whether to suggest a game of winner-take-all rock-paper-scissors, but that would have been just plain childish.

Headphones were banned 4-1 and soda pop was banned 4-1, although we had decided that the ban would only apply to classrooms.

"Typical," said Mitch, "Just because you all think the same way doesn't mean you're right. For all we know maybe these kids will only do half as well without the stuff then they are now, what if that's true? What will we do then? And still nobody has asked the kids what they think."

"Have *you* asked the kids what they think Mr. Forman?" Emma asked rhetorically, "Or do you just assume that since it is a behavior they exhibit, they do it out of choice. It could be p…"

"Oh, get over yourself Emm…."

Whack! Emma slapped her hand down on the table. "I'm! Speaking!" Emma took a deep breath to compose herself. "It could be peer pressure, or just a lack of other options, or maybe none of them have ever tried living without it. Call it a social norm or a habit. Granted, they probably do enjoy those things. I know most kids do. But don't go spouting off like you have some high minded insight into their intellect when you're just as perplexed as the rest of us."

Principal Atkinson, who lacked only a whistle and zebra-striped shirt at this point, spread his arms across the table and said, "The decision has been reached. It was teacher initiated and therefore up to you as teachers to integrate it. Beginning tomorrow, soda pop and music players are no longer allowed during class. It is now a requirement of your continued employment to integrate this policy. If you do not, you will be in violation of contract and you will be terminated."

I didn't appreciate the way Principal Atkinson espoused neutrality as he brought about a decision that he ultimately championed, yet made the four of us clash with Mitch. In any case, it was done now; water, albeit carbonated water, under the bridge.

# CHAPTER TEN

The introduction of rap songs to my classroom was more a negligible pivot than a U-turn. It didn't reverse the trends of apathy, negativity, defiance, and conflict; but it did deflect them and ease their effects. It brought the class down from reckless autobahn speeds to a merely careless forty-five miles per hour in a residential zone. A lot of red lights and stop signs still got ignored, but at least I had enough control to dodge telephone poles and pedestrians. Some of my cohorts were not so fortunate.

Cornell had found some limited success as he guided students through Daily Oral Language in which he used a template and corrected mistakes in capitalization, spelling, and punctuation. He also found that he could ask a specific question from a textbook, read the paragraph in which the answer was contained, and if he singled out one student to answer the question that student could be coaxed enough to answer verbally. Then he would write the answer on the board and the students would copy it from the board en masse, kind of like choral writing as opposed to choral reading.

Other times he read a book but when he stopped to ask a question about a character or the setting he received only blank stares, shrugged shoulders, and, *"Atchu."* But when it was all said and done at least he kept students in the room and didn't receive too much vehement resistance. Given what seemed like the students antagonistic aversion to either digestion or regurgitation of the written word I would have been hard pressed to do much better.

Emma continued to struggle in two directions.

First she had a hard time getting out of the gate. She didn't have a routine that was self-directed. The first thing she did for every class period was either a monologue or a dialogue, in either case it required that she speak and the students listen, and every class period she had a Solomon or a Jenny or a Tim who quite simply wouldn't let her do that. The first five minutes of class got eaten up as students were told to be quiet, warned that they would be sent to the office, chased off the couch, or had their headphones or soda cans confiscated. By the time that was taken care of the other nine students in her class were off base. The cycle had already passed from spring to summer, but the only thing that had been planted was chaos so that was what flourished.

The second struggle for Emma was that she let the hands of the clock set the tempo for her class. With each orbit of the second hand she had a benchmark to meet, followed by another, and then another. Youthful though I was, even I knew that benchmarks and milestones are great for individuals who are trained, disciplined, and motivated (i.e. factory workers, marathon runners, and doctoral candidates), but meaningless to those who are not. It took a couple of observations and some reflection before I realized Emma didn't instruct students, she administered curriculum. It was as if she masterfully conducted a flawless symphony, to an instrument-less or at least untrained orchestra.

Mitch was the polar opposite of Emma. He insisted on nothing, asked for nothing, and did nothing. But that did not mean that he received nothing. He received every student that got sent out of every other teacher's room, and he did so with metaphorically open arms. He was supposed to have the eighth graders and freshmen first hour, but he also often had any seventh grader, sophomore, or junior that had supposedly been sent to the office. They would come in, typically with soda can still in hand, sit down at one of the computers, magically produce a pair of headphones or earbuds, and search window after window until they saw something they liked. Just before the end of the class period they would head to the office, which meant they missed a good ten minutes of the next class period as well while they met with Principal Atkinson.

In the Schadenfreude alcove of my brain I fantasized about Mitch being unwittingly discovered by Principal Atkinson someday who would be unable to articulate any better response than, "What the fuck is going on in here?"

Nick was kind of the maestro in comparison to all of us. Students didn't eat out of his hand but they didn't bite it either, and there was some transfer of sustenance. There was a clear divide of participants and non-participants, but there were no detractors, no arguments. Any principal or school board member would have been appalled at the scene of so many heads down without consequence. At least they would have until they had checked out Emma or Mitch's room and seen the steady diet of disarray served up in there.

I had some level of camaraderie built up with Nick and I asked him about his style one day.

"Last year it took me four weeks of getting tossed around in the waves and capsizing until I finally realized that I wasn't in a motorboat, I was in a sailboat, and as such there were certain things I could control and certain things I couldn't," Nick said.

"The wind is the main thing I have no control over, and the wind in this village is consistently blowing toward dysfunction. I can't sail against that or any other wind, so what can I do? I can go with the wind, I can drop anchor and stay in one place, or, with just the right blend," Nick twisted his back and rotated his wrist, "of braces and tiller I can close haul across the wind and make some headway then tack back across. It's not expedient, or efficient, but it is effective. If I saw a teacher in San Diego running a class the way I run mine here I would call them a straight up chicken-shit. But if anybody was to criticize me here I would hand them the keys to my classroom and say, 'Knock yourself out,' then jump overboard."

Other than Solomon, Rachel, and Tim-Tim, my morning classes were quite productive. One morning all three of them were absent and it was the first time I made it to lunch without a slur, profanity, or referral. I made a star on my calendar in yellow highlighter to celebrate.

I continued to retreat to my room during lunch. Usually I had disciplinary referrals to complete. Sometimes I corrected papers or prepared the next rap song, other times, especially after a raucous morning, I simply turned off the lights and listened to an NPR podcast. If one of the all-stars had been sent home or was on the verge thereof, Nick or Cornell would poke their head in and give me the update. The three elders continued to greet me with, "Good afternoon, good afternoon," in triplicate, when I passed by and I responded in kind.

Tim had taken to the habit of not sitting down in the classroom. In my room he would stand either behind his assigned seat or right next to the door. Every time he did it he acted like he had never done it before.

"How *come* I gotta sit down?" Tim would ask.

"Because that is the best place for you to be right now." I would say.

"How *come?*"

"If you would like a full explanation, we can meet at 3:30."

"How *come?*"

I would set the timer at sixty seconds and tell him that if he wasn't sitting down when it got to zero he would be sent to the office. Some days he complied but most days he didn't. It was almost completely random, yet with a bias toward non-compliance. One day Stan was out of the village and Principal Atkinson came down alone. Tim refused to go with him and Principal Atkinson asked me to take my class to the gym instead.

I took my class out, books and papers in tow. I don't know what transpired but Tim was out the rest of that week. He came back Monday, got sent out of Emma's class, and was out for another week. After that we had another conference with Tim's parents.

Principal Atkinson explained to Mr. Kala'a why Tim could not stand while the rest of the class sat and Mr. Kala'a said, "Okay. Fine then. My boy will sit down, but I want the teachers to sit down too. No reason they should be standing if my boy has to sit down. That's the way it always is, white people get to stand up while everybody else sits down."

All I could think was, "Has this guy ever heard of Rosa Parks?" as my amusement park tunnel began to spin again.

Principal Atkinson, the consummate professional, explained that it was necessary for teachers to stand as well as sit in the performance of their duties.

"Who says you get to make these rules? Who says that? When do I get to make rules for you?" said Mr. Kala'a

Principal Atkinson explained how school board members are voted on and policies are approved, and the statutes that allow schools to carry out those policies. Then the whole conversation cycled back to the beginning and started over again. Finally Principal Atkinson said, "Tim needs to follow the rules, not insult teachers, not disrupt class, and leave the soda and headphones at home. What assurance do I have from you that that will happen?"

Mr. Kala'a looked at him and said, "None."

Principal Atkinson asked Mr. Kala'a if he felt that it was important for Tim to follow the rules.

Mr. Kala'a said, "Nope. He doesn't follow white man law. He follows Eskimo law."

Principal Atkinson asked how Mr. Kala'a defined that term.

"Respect for yourself. Respect for your elders. Respect for the land. That is all an Eskimo needs."

Principal Atkinson clarified, especially for the denizens of future courtrooms, that it was Mr. Kala'a's absolute belief that he did not feel that the laws of the United States of America and the State of Alaska were of any benefit to his son.

"Correct."

And that it was his belief as a parent that his son, if he followed what Mr. Kala'a described and asserted as Eskimo law, was not in need of a free and appropriate public education.

"Correct."

And that he as a parent would not support the school in its efforts to educate his son.

"Correct."

We were dismissed while Principal Atkinson and the parents stayed. The next day we were informed that Tim would be homeschooled. We were expected to provide books, supplies, and curriculum as well as make ourselves available during our prep time after school to meet with him and/or his parents if requested to provide instruction. The district office also sent out a new laptop computer loaded with software for Tim to use at home.

Jay-Boy showed up with a new joke every day and I let him share it.

"How come cannibals never eat clowns?"

"I don't know Jay-Boy, why?"

"'Cause they taste funny."

At the end of every day I had Lewis to look forward to and without that daily reprieve I might have won the Iqsaiqsiq 700 sometime in mid-September. Lewis never gave me a hard time and as long as he knew I would eventually explain what to do, he would try anything. I wondered how much of his eagerness and achievement was because none of the other students were around to see him succeed or fail, and how much was an innate quality of simply being Lewis.

We typically finished lessons early and split the time that remained. The first half we did some type of writing practice, the second half he was free to use the computer. I used Lewis' internet habits to gather intel on the Iqsaiqsiq teenager; what web sites did he visit, what did he look at when he visited there, which actors or singers or athletes did he follow, what held his interest and what did he click through without so much as a pause.

Sometimes he would run across something and it would prompt him to ask a question. For example, one day he got on to some kind of Hawaii website and he asked, "You ever eat coconut?"

"Yes."

"You like it?"

"Yes."

"Oh."

That was the pattern; question, answer, question, answer, then, "Oh." and never the same topic twice.

"What's a skyscraper?"

"A tall building in a large city."

"You ever go inside one?"

"Yes."

"Oh."

One day he was navigating his way through Wikipedia and came across rifles. A few clicks later he was on automatic weapons.

"You ever shoot machine gun?"

"Yes."

"Where?"

"California, Hawaii, Afghanistan; when I was in the Marine Corps."

"Oh."

Ben started to host a staff movie festival every Friday afternoon. It was held in the cafeteria which, to my surprise, had a magnificent twelve speaker sound system built directly into the walls and a six-by-ten foot projection screen that lowered from the ceiling. The cafeteria was also the only room besides the gym that had absolutely no windows; so it was dark even while the sun stayed up to the wee hours of the morning. Also, there was no chance that we might be observed by the public.

Typically it involved either a series of movies such as *Jaws, Jaws 2, Jaws 3-D,* and *Jaws: The Revenge;* or a complete season of a television show like *30 Rock* or *The X-Files.* We would each bring our office chairs and someone would cook up popcorn or nachos. More than entertainment it was a good chance to vent and share stories from the week.

The elementary teachers had stories of students who had climbed under, inside, or on top of something and had to be commanded or helped up, out, or down. Almost everything that happened in the secondary wing also happened in the elementary wing, only on a smaller scale. Things got broken and thrown and slammed. There was a great deal of lethargy and apathy, and minimal support from home. The greatest difference appeared to be that the elementary students used their mouths less often to swear and more often to bite whereas high school students didn't bite at all, at least not yet. Joanne and Belle commented that it almost seemed as if somewhere between sixth grade and seventh children in the village swapped out their License to Bite for a License to Swear.

I tried to inspire the group with some of Jay-Boy's meek jokes or a comment about something Lewis had said that made me realize just how far removed from the mainstream American experience village life could be at times. If it occurred to me I would also try to pass along some intel on a new slang word or insurgent tactic being employed.

Emma often complained about Principal Atkinson's requirement that she give a student three warning every day before they were sent to the office, and the fact that students kept lying down on the couch. When Joanne asked her why she didn't just have the couch taken out of her room, Emma said, "Why should I have to get rid of it just because they can't follow the rules?"

Mitch never came to any of the movie festivals, nor did Principal Atkinson or Stan. After the first two weeks Emma bailed right at 4:00 and locked herself away in her house, not to be seen again until Monday morning, and I never heard her speak another word about hosting a meal or movie for students. Cornell and Belle stayed for the first half-hour or so, and Ben and Brenda typically left around dinner time. Joanne would stick it out until about seven or eight while Nick, John, and I would stay until we fell asleep. On more than one occasion I woke up alone while the menu screen repeated over and over.

Saturday mornings I got up and went straight to the school to use the restroom and fill my Camelbak. As I ran around the village it was fairly typical to see Stan parked at the airport and for the State Trooper plane to buzz over the village. I did some arithmetic and if the current trend held Stan would probably send out about forty people a year which, for the village of Iqsaiqsiq with its population of just over 300, would make the incarceration rate about twelve or thirteen percent.

On one of my runs Stan pulled up beside me as he had that first Saturday, leaned across the seat, opened the passenger side door and said, "Jenn's got the espresso machine and the waffle iron fired up if you're interested?"

I pushed a set of handlebars and a headlight with about two feet of electrical wire still attached to it over to one side of the floorboard and climbed in. "You got some repairs to tend to?" I asked.

"Nope. That's evidence."

"Of what? Grand theft Honda?"

"Assault. Domestic assault."

Stan described how the headquarters in Aciq received a report of a fight in the street. When he arrived, Mrs. Kala'a wielded the handlebars like an Arctic Samurai to hold Mr. Kala'a at bay while he brandished the headlight nun chucks-style. Mrs. Kala'a dropped the handlebars but Mr. Kala'a continued to swing the headlight at her, so Stan tased him. As soon as Mr. Kala'a was on the ground, Mrs. Kala'a charged Stan, hands empty, but he cartwheeled her down with his baton. They spent the rest of the night in the portable holding cell in Stan's garage where they declared their undaunted love for one another and vowed revenge against the *tuniq* that had put them there.

I asked Stan the question that burned in my mind. "A house full of guns and knives, perhaps baseball bats and boat oars, and they go at each other with spare auto parts?"

Stan said, "I doubt they thought about effectiveness, they just grabbed what was handy when they got pissed off."

Then Stan added, "It usually isn't about causing injury, it's about releasing anger. And abusing alcohol."

"Angst and ale," I said pensively.

Trooper Stan dropped his right eyebrow, lifted his left eyebrow, furrowed his forehead, and glanced over at me. "Angst and ale? What's that, some kind of washed up Seattle grunge band?"

"No," I said, "It's a poem I wrote."

"What is it with you Jarheads? Is it the extra four weeks you spend in boot without getting laid, or that eight-pointed cover you all wear, that turns you all analytical and existential? A bunch of ass-kicking Kierkegaard's going *reductio ad absurdum* between squeezing triggers and running around in the sand."

"A good Marine is a thinking Marine."

"Well, if you thought more *before* you joined the Marines, you would have joined the Army." Trooper Stan chuckled and winked.

"I did think before I joined the Marines, and I thought I had too much self-respect to be anything less."

We removed our footwear in the *quniciuq* and I said, "You want to know why Marines are so introspective? It's all that time disassembling, cleaning, and assembling our rifles. It's such a tedious and mundane task that it gives one's mind a chance to wander and ponder the ways of the universe."

"Possibly, or maybe you just inhale too much of the Cleaner, Lubricant, and Preservative."

"You know the CIA secretly infuses CLP with THC so they can institute mind control?" I raised my eyebrows.

"I read that in the tin foil hat conspiracy blog too. The CIA's secret force of Sasquatch commandos is smoking hybridized marijuana to make them impervious to nuclear radiation when they go fight the aliens. Of course the pharmacological-industrial complex is keeping all of that a secret so we will be slaves to their placebos," Stan said.

We walked straight into the kitchen where Jenn had left me the most exquisite Belgian waffle drizzled with whipped cream and a foam capped latte sprinkled with cocoa.

"Did I tell you what Arnold said about smoking pot?" I said as I cut into the first heavenly wedge.

"You mean kwock?"

"No, not cock," I said with my teeth clenched tightly to confine the waffles sweet and smooth crispiness, "Puh-awe-t; Marijuana, Mary Jane, ganja, reefer, weed, spliff, spice, wacky tabacky, Bob Marley's breakfast burrito. You know, *cannabis sativa*."

"And kwock," said Stan matter-of-factly.

I stiffened myself and straightened a non-existent tie then said in a Principal Atkinson-esque tone, "Mr. Stanisauvlauvski I don't believe it is your place to comment on a student's sexual experiences."

"I'm not. The Inupiat word for 'smoke' is *quaaq* (kwu-ock), it has a hint of a 'wuh' sound after the 'kuh.' It literally means the type of smoke from a fire, but when cigarettes first came to the Arctic they were called *quaaq's*, as in smokes, and later marijuana got the same name. Of course the kids know how easily misinterpreted it is, so they drop the 'wuh' to see how outsiders will react."

"Okay, that explains quite a bit actually." I downed a robust gulp of espresso. "Anyway, Arnold is telling these other kids how much weed his uncle has all the time since he got a medical card because he has cancer. I walked over and said, 'You know it also causes memory loss.' Arnold looks at me, dead serious, and says, 'What does?' and I said, 'That thing you were talking about.' Arnold blankly stared at me like I just asked him to prove how mass turns into energy at the speed of light and finally says, 'Cancer?'

"Had he laughed, or even smiled, I would have known he was messing with me. But he just stared so I said, 'Smoking marijuana causes memory loss.' Arnold said, 'It never. It make you not be sick no more, that how come my uncle smoke, to fix his cancer.' I said, 'It doesn't fix anything, it just lessens the symptoms.' Arnold looks at me, again, dead serious, and says, 'What does?' I just kind of had to let it drop at that point."

I expected Stan to at least crack a smile, but instead he ruminated longer than made me comfortable and stirred a spoonful of Metamucil into his cranberry juice.

I commented on the epicurean quality of the waffle and latte and Stan provided me with another morsel of Bush wisdom. "On the first of every month we call up Fred Meyer's in Fairbanks. They fill a Styrofoam box with milk, eggs, and lettuce, plus anything we might add on like bell peppers or yogurt, then take it over to the airline. We order about $100 worth of stuff, plus $30 to box it up and another $40 for freight. So for $170 we get to live like regular people for a week. I thought it was pure foolishness the first time we did it, but now we'll never give it up."

Stan looked at his watch. "You're welcome to stay and channel surf if you want, but I'm gonna hit the rack."

I rinsed my plate off in the sink. "Let Jenn know I enjoyed breakfast, but I've got a serious following of rap-minions, and if their needs aren't met they have highly detrimental stress responses, so I'm going to get prepared for them. Thanks for the offer just the same."

"See you later M.C. Ken, and if you're ever interested in making twelve bucks an hour guarding prisoners let me know."

"I'll think about it."

I put my shoes back on in the *quniciuq* and grabbed my Camelbak. I stayed at school until it became frenetic with the rest of the staff, then shifted to the less populated quad-plex. The raps took about ten extra hours a week in addition to my standard fifty-hour workweek, but without them I would have vehemently loathed every class period; so it was worth it.

Barely.

# CHAPTER ELEVEN

Solomon continued to ask me all kinds of completely inappropriate questions. Sometimes he would stop at two, other times he would push it to three and get a trip to the office. Occasionally, like all craftsmen, he took a day off. Still he managed to ask me about hemorrhoids, toupee's, and if my, "Porn had arrived, *yet.*"

I spoke with Nick about it one day and he asked me if I watched many movies. I told him, "Not really."

"Start renting some of the comedies over at the store and you will see and hear everything Solomon says and does. The kid is clueless when it comes to social context but he knows when something is embarrassing or disparaging to say, like the Jewish comment or the thing about the toupee. He doesn't know a yarmulke from a Yamaha, but if he heard somebody use it as an insult he will repeat it regardless of whether it actually is one or not."

Rachel would whine, and moan, and complain regardless of the ease or difficulty of the lesson, my only respite was that the other students began to block her out. Like Solomon, some days she would stop at two while others she would pull the hat trick and win a trip to the office.

Tim-Tim began to take more political types of stands and challenged the basis or rationality of a rule instead of merely flaunting or disobeying it openly. My guess was that at home some type of deep theoretical examination of public policy and educational doctrine took place, or maybe his parents just bemoaned everything the school did every time he got suspended, which was once or twice a week.

Headed to lunch one day the three elders greeted me as usual.

"Good afternoon, good afternoon," said the first one.

"Good afternoon, good afternoon," said the second one.

"Good afternoon, Semper Fi Marine," said the third one.

"Good afternoon, Ooh-rah," I responded.

That was the new greeting and it became just as consistent as the old one.

Arnold had become a combination of the lesser parts of Tim, Rocky, and Olivia. Some days he was the defiant instigator, other days he was the frustrated demolisher, and occasionally he was the foul-mouthed objector; albeit a dry, foul-mouthed objector. It seemed to depend on which role was vacant that particular day. I later found out that Nick and I were the only two teachers who had stood up to Tim, which apparently registered with Arnold, and was the reason Arnold had never threatened either of us. But as soon as Tim was out of the picture in Emma and Cornell's rooms, Arnold took over that role in there. Of course, Mitch's room was such a chaotic maelstrom that Arnold couldn't find an established base to push against, so he simply pushed everything and everyone all of the time.

Rocky had the fewest recurrences of any of the high school malefactors, but he still had a couple of meltdowns. The first time was as he kept tempo in Emma's music class with the cowbell while Emma played the keyboard and two other students, mercilessly, attempted to play guitar. Emma halted the ensemble but Rocky whacked away at the cowbell until after three of her shouts he quit and looked up at her, sweating and smiling.

Emma screamed at him, "What is wrong with you that makes you so difficult!?"

Rocky threw the cowbell and drumstick at her, then grabbed one of the guitars and did his own Pete Townshend impersonation before he ran out of the room.

Rocky also had a run-in with Cornell over a reading assignment. Rocky pulled every copy of *Call of the Wild* and *White Fang* (call it a bad day for Jack London) off of the shelf and ripped them in half straight up the spine. Stan and Principal Atkinson were called down and the story was that everyone just stood and watched him do it until he ran out of energy, then he went to the office and was back in school the next day.

Rocky had his greatest challenges in Mitch's physical education class. Generally they involved Rocky being called out of bounds or a point not counting because Rocky had not followed one of the rules. Rocky would throw things, and kick things, then run out of the gym and later be found by either Stan or Principal Atkinson as he sat on a bench. The most egregious act was when he threw a basketball and hit JCee Bowen in the face, which required a trip to the village health clinic.

A few days after that, when Rocky returned to school, I heard him tell JCee, "Sorry." It was the first time I had ever heard anyone from Iqsaiqsiq use that word. A few weeks later Rosy, Rocky's sister, said, "Thank you," and it caught me equally off guard. I heard students say sorry and thank you a few other times, but occurrences were noticeably rare as was the use of the word, "Please."

Olivia really didn't like going to the office. In fact the only thing she hated worse was when Stan or Principal Atkinson led her by the arm to the office. As a result, Olivia's primary *modus operandi* was to obliterate both sides and all four edges of the envelope then, instead of going to the office, storm out through one of the emergency exit doors.

I asked the other teachers about Olivia's non sequitur malapropisms and none of them had any inkling why she used them.

I asked Stan the same question and he said, "Remember the Kala'a's and the junkyard weaponry? Olivia's verbal instead of physical, but it's the same concept; don't think, just grab what's closest and start swinging."

"And spitting." I added.

"Exactly. She spits even if her mouth is dry. If she plotted and planned a little more she would take a drink first and unleash Hurricane Olivia all over the secondary wing, but she never has and probably never will."

One random Wednesday I heard a television on in Emma's apartment. I tried the light switch and voila! The water also worked, even the hot water. I took the honey bucket out to the yellow can for what I hoped was the last time. I added my contribution to the putrid pool and reflected that for all of the threats and lashing out that we had endured at the school, the contents of the yellow can had not ended up on our front door. It would have been the easiest of pranks to pull with opportunity and means immediately available, low cost and untraceable.

About halfway through the quarter the fall whaling season started. All of the teachers received lesson plans via email that focused on some aspect of the whaling culture tied to their subject area. I received one that started with a known quantity, the weight of the whale, and divided it into a given number of portions (X), then multiplied X by factors of .5, 1, 1.5, and 2, to represent the weight of the shares given out to various families. I changed the weight of the whale and/or the number of portions and worked through the formula again. After I had seen how a whale is actually butchered and distributed in the field I realized that the lesson I had been directed to teach all day was totally irrelevant in practice.

A school-wide assembly was held in lieu of sixth period on the Monday before whaling season began. Instead of embracing their traditional heritage, the seventh and eighth graders complained incessantly about not being able to have their regular physical education class until eventually about half of them were either removed or just walked out. The majority of the high school students reclined in the bleachers quietly, eventually a pair of headphones came out and when asked to be removed an argument ensued which drowned out the presentation made over the plasma screen by an elder, whaler, historian, singer, or pastor. The end result was that the elementary school students, who had been held past their regular dismissal time for the cultural benefits of the presentation, became distracted by the argument and lost interest in the presentation. Eventually the elementary students became restless and tussled with one another.

The last presentation was by a Native pastor who prayed for and blessed the fleet of whalers in the Inupiat language while captions in English rolled across the bottom of the screen. Terri Bowen-Skeen, dressed in one of the thin, cotton, floral patterned smocks with lace trim called a *qaspaq* (cuss-puck), thanked all of the presenters and implored the students to take this opportunity to discuss and embrace this unique and treasured tradition.

For a final act, some local members of the Iqsaiqsiq community were supposed to perform traditional Native dancing. The lights were turned on and the plasma screen was rolled out of the way. The dancers claimed that only half of them were present and there was confusion as to the existence and/or location of a drum. The students grew more and more restless and, much to the chagrin of the dancers as they pled for five more minutes until so-and-so arrived, Principal

Atkinson dismissed everyone back to their rooms with twenty minutes left in the day.

From what I had gathered through the presentation, whaling in the Arctic predated Russian and European contact. Inupiat whalers used a wood framed boat, covered in seal skins, called an *umiak* (ooh-me-ack) and wooden paddles to stealthily move between ice floes. The *umiak* was also light enough to be carried from one side of a floe to the other if expediency was required. When a whale surfaced to breathe the whalers threw a series of harpoons into it. The first harpoon had a rope and a floating bag attached to it that was used as a marker. The whalers followed the marker until the whale surfaced again, then pulled up directly beside it and stabbed it with a second harpoon to injure and weaken it. Finally, a third harpoon was used by a whaler who climbed out of the *umiak* and on to the back of the whale. The bareback whaler straddled the whale in the middle of the Arctic Ocean, 500 miles from the nearest Coast Guard helicopter, and drove the final harpoon straight into one of the whale's blowholes which caused the whale to drown in its own blood. If a whale was not killed quickly it might escape under a floe of ice, only to die a slow death, which made it useless to the whalers. Such a loss was considered shameful because it showed the whalers lack of skill, as well as their lack of respect for the value of the whale.

The dead whale was quickly towed to shore where the whole village was enlisted to pull it up on the shore with a rope. If a whale was not butchered quickly the body heat trapped by its adipose outer skin caused the meat to rot even if the outside air temperature was below freezing. Butchering was a non-stop operation that took several hours or even a full day and night. Specific portions were designated to certain members of the community and crew. The majority of the meat and fatty outer skin, or *maqtaq* (muck-tuck), was distributed to all members of the community regardless of age or involvement in the hunt. The baleen, a hair-like membrane which hangs from the sides of its mouth, was divvied up and dried, then used as a surface on which to sketch artwork. Traditionally the large rib bones were used much like lumber for framing and bracing structures, but in recent years were left on the beach.

Over the past 100 years new technologies had been introduced and traditional methods adapted to them but, it was asserted, certain beliefs and practices endured. The whale was often referred to as The Gift. Not *a* gift, but capital T, capital G, The Gift. Its arrival was not happenstance, but destiny. If no whale appeared it was believed to be because those people at that time were not worthy enough to receive it. It was not a conquest by the hunters, but an act of surrender by the whale. A whale may choose to be harpooned or die for a group of whalers out of respect for their skill but no amount of skill could ever *take* a whale. The whale had to *give* itself. Ultimately the belief was that humans, animals, plants, soil, water, and air were all a part of each other and to disgrace or denigrate one part was to disgrace or denigrate every part, including one's own.

Back in the room I asked Lewis his opinions and experiences with whaling. He had very little to say so I shared my experiences hunting for deer and elk in the Pacific Northwest. Lewis said that he hunted geese and ducks, even shot some rabid foxes in the village during the winter, but did not go whaling. I asked him why not.

"No boat," said Lewis.

"Yeah, but there are lots of boats in the village, couldn't you go with somebody else who has a boat?"

"Tiqiqiq's never have boats. Bowen's and Kala'a's have boats. Have to be one of them to go whaling camp."

I switched the topic back to goose and duck hunting since I had hunted ducks as well growing up. Lewis said that he preferred to hunt in the spring because by summer all of the snow melted and transformed the many depressions across the tundra into broad, shallow ponds. Since Lewis did not have the use of a boat or a dog to fetch them, it became problematic if they landed in the water.

"What do you do if one lands in the water?" I asked.

"Tuuqaq (two-cuck) get at it."

I knew that Tuuqaq was Lewis' younger brother who didn't have a boat either. "How does Tuuqaq get it?"

"He wear short pants and old tennis shoes, when duck too far out to reach with stick, he swim out with inner tube, get it, swim back."

"Oh," I said.

I asked Lewis what kind of shotgun he hunted with and he proceeded to tell me about every long gun he owned; brand, caliber, dimensions, age, and most importantly history. He had a 12-guage over/under bequeathed by an incarcerated uncle, a .410 pump purchased with his dividend when he was twelve, and a lever-action .30-.30 that had magically appeared in their *quniciuq* one morning.

I asked him if he had any pistols.

"No." Lewis shook his head. "No good."

"What do you mean?" I asked.

"Only people what cause trouble carry pistol. If I ever see someone with pistol, I walk away."

"Oh."

I later asked Stan about pistols in villages and he concurred. "A pistol packer in the village is a problem child, headed either to prison, from prison, or most likely both. Don't ever be seen with one yourself. It's an equal opportunity prejudice and everyone will think the same of you even though you're white."

As the week wore on Mitch did everything he could to get himself invited to whaling camp, except be patient and wait for an invitation. He helped clean up and straighten gear, carried lines and buoys all over the place, and even bought gas for a few people. He probably spent more time in preparation than any of the actual whalers did. I overheard his conversation with one of the whaling captains, Magnus Kala'a, in front of the post office.

"When are you leaving for camp?" Mitch asked.

"After whales come," said Magnus.

"When do you think that will be?"

"Few days. Maybe."

"I. I, I've got, I can take Friday off if you leave Thursday after school, or if you leave Friday or Saturday I could come... I could, I could come with you then."

"Boat full." Magnus made the slow and measured, left to right, palm down motion with his right hand that gave me flashbacks of Roby at the William's Air Service terminal in Fairbanks. I knew then as I knew now that it meant, "No more."

"If I, if I buy... buy your gas, you could send somebody back Saturday morning and pick me up, alright?"

Magnus rolled his shoulders forward, in, and down; a hard gesture for me to read, but it definitely did not mean, "Great idea Mitch, I'll be sure and do that for you."

"Saturday? Saturday morning?" said Mitch.

Magnus rolled his shoulders forward, in, and down a second time.

"In the morning. Saturday morning. I'll be there," said Mitch.

As soon as Mitch said, "Saturday," Magnus had turned on his heel and walked away. No words. No palm cut. No shrug. Just a hasty one-eighty and straight into his Dodge Quad-Cab.

Mitch hopped from the boardwalk that led to the post office to the road and waved in a manner that reminded me of Forrest Gump on the shrimp boat as Magnus drove away. Then he called for Gobi and Gobi lumbered up from beneath the post office before they both walked toward the quad-plex.

Thursday morning there was an email from Principal Atkinson. It explained that the whaling crews planned to depart that afternoon. It also implied that some negotiation had been made in which teachers and students would attend *briefly* as part of an "education enrichment experience" then return to finish out the school day. Teachers were expected to attend with their students and students were expected to return along with their teachers as soon as the boats had been launched. There was also some mention of school lunch being available to students only, which I dismissed since I never ate the school lunch anyway.

Thursday came and went and not a single boat was launched. There was some talk about not enough fuel, too much fuel, and/or water in fuel lines; the story changed every hour.

Friday the same email was rehashed and redistributed. Ten minutes into third period, as the laptop belted out, *"Like a bird, chomping on worms, fractions are reduced, to simplest terms,"* there was a spike in traffic past the school. Minutes later Principal Atkinson announced over the intercom the expectations for students and staff while they attended the boat launch. We left the room and the school together. By the time we got up to the road half of my students had been spirited away on Hondas or in the open beds of pickups. I thought, "If one of those kids gets hurt, molested, drowned, or goes missing I might as well write 'REVOKED' across my teaching certificate and send it back to Juneau before they even ask me for it."

Emma probably thought the same thing, but she would enclose something else with her certificate; a stack of referrals she wrote up on a clipboard as she propelled herself toward the yet unseen shore. It wasn't even lunch time yet and her hair had already sprung into its Nick Nolte mug shot persona.

At the shore I saw more people than I ever would have guessed lived in Iqsaiqsiq. It was like a giant homecoming rally and Fourth of July parade rolled into one. Pictures were taken and well wishes were written on t-shirts and flags. Just as in days of old each child was given a handful of Tootsie-Rolls and a handful of Jolly Ranchers, more if they were savvy enough to pocket their loot and move on to their auntie, then their grandma, and then their auntie's grandma.

Daniel and Derek (whom I had not seen either of since the first week of school) were up on a mound along with Tim-Tim (who was suspended) and Eddie Bowen (who simply hadn't come to school that day). They each had a dirt clod or two and Tim-Tim seemed to call out targets. Brenda, Belle, and Cornell were the first casualties. I sought out defensive terrain and maneuvered myself as close as possible to the three, "Good afternoon," elders. I greeted them and took up a position on their leeward side. I was nearly a foot taller than any of them so I redeployed from the standing position to a more tactically suitable kneeling position, at which time I became an armrest for the nearest of the three elders. The three of them spoke in Inupiat as they stared into the distance, smoked cigarettes incessantly, wrung their hands often, and farted without hesitation. They reminded me a lot of my own uncles, proof that some things transcend all cultural barriers.

Almost two hours after we arrived the final boat shoved off and the final kiss was blown; then engines cranked, tires spun, and the whole beach vacated except for the teachers and the empty candy wrappers. Eventually the teachers turned toward the wind and headed to the school while the candy wrappers went with the wind and blew northward into the water; a thousand miniature white *umiaks* that chased after their parents.

The area in front of the school was a quagmire of vehicles and feral children.

Just inside the foyer a line, with its genesis somewhere near the gymnasium, ended.

I could see into Principal Atkinson's office where Mayor David Aicia was yelling at him and occasionally shoving papers from his desk. Had I still adhered to Terri Bowen-Skeen's cultural map of Tolerancistan I would have considered that an egregious error on David's part, but I had conceded weeks earlier that those boundaries had long since dissolved and been overrun by the Phuque Province of neighboring I'Kuudistan.

Nick gave me a leftward head twitch so I followed him down to my room. As soon as the door was closed Nick said, "Here's the deal. Any time there is a community function, it's always held at the school. And, any time there is a community function, it's expected that a meal be served. Sometimes the community pitches in and provides the food, sometimes not. In either case, a meal is still expected. A-

Team (a sobriquet we had coined for Principal Atkinson) it turns out, is this hard core by the book guy, and I say good for him, but it is making his life a living hell right now because he is doing *what's right* instead of *what's expected*, i.e. serving the school food to the community. My advice? Hang back, wait until this cools, then pop your head in the cafeteria. If everyone has eaten, help yourself to a plate. If A-Team is directing people or standing watch, don't be seen."

"Thanks Nick."

"See you at movie night."

I waited about twenty minutes and wandered down to the cafeteria. It looked like there had been trays of ten different items including miniature pizzas, but only corn dogs, creamed corn, and pilot bread remained. I took a sample of each and went into the gym where much of the crowd had flowed. I sat on the bleachers with Ben and Brenda as random children of all ages ran to and fro across the gym floor. It appeared as if the older students had all taken the initiative to excuse themselves for the remainder of the day.

Five young men gathered on the stage with David. They all wore simpler, short-hemmed, solid-colored versions of *qaspaqs*. David held a round, flat, skin drum and a short, thin stick. After a conference and much deliberation, David hit the drum with the stick and chanted while the dancers spread out in a line. The children continued to run and chase each other willy-nilly. There was never a "Hey, we're gonna dance now," or a, "Ready; one, two, three, go." It just erupted like a flash mob.

Although the ensemble lacked preparation and organization, it didn't lack accuracy. The movements were either perfectly synchronized or precisely paradoxical, all in tempo with the fluid drum beat. It was on par with the very best Close Order Drills I had ever seen, even at Quantico... and Arlington. Still, I felt uncomfortable amongst all of the students who were effectively unsupervised and showed little interest in the presentation so I returned to my room.

As I graded journals a dark catcher's mitt of a face with a mop head of white, stringy hair popped around the corner. It was one of the three elders from the bench, the one that greeted me with, "Semper Fi Marine." His glassy eyes scanned the room until they locked on mine. "Hey, Mac," said the Elder.

"Hi." I motioned with my hand to come in.

He shuffled in and laid a plate covered in aluminum foil on the table then draped his coat across the back of a chair. "I sit? Okay?"

"Sure." I walked over and extended my hand. "Ken."

"Jerry." He weakly grasped only the end of my fingers.

"When were you in the Corps?" I asked.

"Sixty-seven to sixty-nine at Khe Sahn."

"Third Marines. Fidelity, Valor, Honor," I said.

Jerry raised his eyes at me, the Eskimo equivalent of yes, "You?"

"Ought-three to ought-six with the two-three; Kaneohe Bay, Hawaii. One tour in Afghanistan."

Jerry nodded, then produced a small, single-blade pocket knife and began to clean under his fingernails with it. "You know that show what called MacGyver?"

"Yes."

"I think maybe MacGyver part Eskimo." Jerry passed the knife from his left hand to his right. "MacGyver fix anything with pocket knife." After he had cleaned his nails, Jerry surveyed the pocket knife from all angles. "Every. Eskimo. Need. Pocket knife." He looked up at me. "Got pocket knife?"

"Yes." I nodded. "Would you like to see it?"

Jerry raised his eyebrows at me again.

I dug out my Leatherman Wave and handed it to him.

Jerry surveyed the various implements, especially the pliers. He opened and closed them several times then said in approval, "This. Better than MacGyver. Maybe you part Eskimo?" He threw his head back in an uproarious laugh. "I jokes."

After a few more explorations and examinations Jerry folded it back together and placed it at the edge of the table. Then he stood up, pulled on his coat, and picked up his aluminum foil wrapped plate.

"Nice to meet you Jerry, come back anytime you like, okay?" I said.

Jerry raised his eyebrows *and* nodded at me, the Eskimo equivalent of yes with an exclamation point. Then he shuffled down the hallway.

I checked my email and saw that Principal Atkinson had sent one that stated that all students were to be marked with an excused absence for the remainder of the day and that he would soon distribute a policy that outlined expectations and a supervision schedule for future "educational enrichment experiences."

A minute past four o'clock I went down to the cafeteria. Ben and Nick were the only ones there. As soon as the lights were off and the first movie started, Ben was gone; like the building was toxic or something. While I switched from disc one to disc two of *Sex and the City: Season 6*, Nick took a walk around the school. He returned and said to start without him, then came back about thirty minutes later.

When disc two finished Nick said, "Are you up for some benevolent mischief?"

"Could it get me arrested?"

"No."

"Fired?"

"No, but it could cause a major hassle for us if we get caught, so you can't tell anyone, not even Stan or Jenn, until we've both moved out of the village."

I felt that my inner Tom Sawyer longed to be set free by Nick's unrestricted Huck Finn liberty so I said, "Fuck it, sure."

I followed Nick out of the cafeteria. We walked through all of the hallways and checked every bathroom, office, closet, and open classroom. If a classroom door was locked we knocked on it and tried to look through the narrow window as best we could. It appeared that the school was empty. The last door we ended up at was Emma's, which stood wide open.

Nick walked straight in and lifted up one end of the couch. I spontaneously followed and picked up the other. We carried it down to the storage room where Nick had already carved out a perfect niche beneath a shelf. We draped two boxes worth of old band uniforms over it, then slid it under the shelf and surrounded it with a bunch of Reagan-era computers. For good measure we leaned old chalk boards up against that row of shelves, then blocked off the aisle with media carts.

We cleaned up the cafeteria, stored the equipment, and left. I didn't return to school until Sunday morning, and even then only long enough to print out reports and make photocopies.

Emma went on an epic quest Monday morning and asked anyone and everyone, even the school cook and a few random parents who wandered in, "Have you seen my couch? Have you? How about you? Does anybody know where my couch is? Who took my couch?"

A-Team even sent out an email that requested it be returned, which in reality was probably the last thing he wanted.

I think Emma suspected Mitch, who had wasted the weekend camped out at the beach as he waited endlessly for Magnus Kala'a to pick him up, had taken it to his apartment or given it away. A week later Stan mentioned that he had noticed a twenty-five percent drop in trips to Emma's room.

The successful whalers returned two weeks later and on a Saturday afternoon a feast was held in the gym that consisted of caribou, duck, moose, seal, some type of very oily fish, polar bear, whale meat, *maqtaq*, and of course Pilot Bread crackers along with gallons and gallons of red Kool-Aid; all of which was brought in by the community.

I ate some fish that I was sure had been salted post-mortem like sardines. I also ate some polar bear; it had the texture and appearance of beef but tasted even more like fish than the actual fish did. Then I sampled the *maqtaq*. It was tasteless, like old gum, and released tiny pockets of oil with each compression. It also took forever to break down. I chewed it until I left the gym and finally just spit it out in the waste basket in my room. I wondered why anyone would ever eat *maqtaq*.

Ten minutes later I got the full-on double Hershey bar rush; my heart raced, my skin flushed, my metabolism surged, and I had an insatiable urge to hug something. Then I understood why *maqtaq* was so celebrated.

Thirty minutes later I got the full-on double Hershey bar squirts and rushed to the bathroom. I rode the porcelain Honda and as sweat dripped off of my nose wondered again why anyone would ever eat *maqtaq*. I shit and shit until finally I shit and shit some more. A serious lemon-lime Gatorade bender lay in my near future as the last remnants of sludge dripped from my hinter regions.

I finally de-shit-ified myself, but one short week later the shit really hit the fan. It was dividend season.

# CHAPTER TWELVE

I was a freshman in college the first time I heard the phrase Alaska Permanent Fund Dividend. Two girls from Juneau had just gotten theirs. After they purchased plane tickets for their next trip home, they each bought about $500 worth of clothes, make-up, and CD's; then blew the last hundred to treat the rest of us to an all-nighter of Domino's pizza and Keystone beer. Later that night I had thought, "I really need to get to Alaska sometime and get in on that dividend action," as I urinated behind the humanities building on my way back to the dorm. When I decided to apply to teach in an Alaskan school I dusted off the phrase and asked my friend Dan about it.

"It's only a thousand bucks and you have to live there for two years before you get it," Dan said.

"But it's free money and if I get a check every year and buy a bond with it at six percent interest, after twenty years I'll have over thirty grand when I retire just sitting there in addition to my pension."

"Whatever Ken. Look, people spend their dividend on three things; home entertainment systems, trips to Hawaii, or the Charlie Sheen Experience."

"What's the Charlie Sheen Experience?"

"Steak dinner, box of cigars, bottle of scotch, V.I.P. room at the strip club, and a taxi ride home. Then wait for the next year."

I added the costs in my head and only came to six hundred maximum. "That's not a thousand bucks?"

"It is if you do it right."

The first indication of Permanent Fund Dividend, or simply dividend, season was the chatter of travel by the students. "I go Fairbanks. We go Aciq and see my gram. My mom say we go Anchorage and might-could Chuck E. Cheese."

Then it was chatter of purchases. "I get X-Box. We get bikes from store. My mom might-could bring Hannah Montana costume from Anchorage for Halloween."

The store stacked its shelves high with televisions and DVD players, even chairs and beds. The freezer case was jammed with "value packs;" fifty pound boxes of assorted bacon, beef, bologna, chicken, ham, and turkey all "on sale" for the bargain basement price of $299.

I went to check my post office box and met the postmaster at the front door. He had a large bin filled with letters beside him and dug out my copy of *The Economist*. The interior of the twelve-by-twenty foot building was stacked wall to wall and floor to ceiling with boxes. When he caught my inquisitive glance he simply said, "C.O.D.'s"

It was a Thursday and dividends were to be directly deposited in bank accounts the following Tuesday. For those who did not have bank accounts or chose not to use direct deposit, checks would be sent out on Wednesday and trickle in over the next seven days. Most of the people in Iqsaiqsiq did not have bank accounts so the prevailing wisdom was that we were still a week away from bedlam.

Ka-pow!

The rifle shot hung endlessly in the air around 5:00 that Thursday evening. Although I hadn't heard a weapon discharge since I arrived in Iqsaiqsiq eight weeks prior, it didn't faze me. I had lived around firearms all my life, caribou were often visible from my window, I figured someone was just...

Ka-ka-ka-pow!

Semi-automatic fire at the exact interval it takes to reset ones finger; totally inaccurate, except at extremely close range, and useless for hunting. I stood up to look out my window and saw nothing remarkable; no weapons, no prone bodies, no one in panic. I sat back down with my copy of *The Economist*.

Ka-pow!

Someone yelled, "Muh! Muh-muh. Fuh!"

A different voice, "Fuh, fuh-fuh. Muh! Muh!!!"

Ka-Pow! Ka-pow!

My right-brain and left-brain passed notes back and forth across my corpus callosum like wagers at a horse track window, proposed and analyzed various scenarios, rejected one and moved on to the next. My brain stem meanwhile calmly prompted my legs to move.

Ka-pow!

I retrieved the plastic box from the shelf in my closet and could have debated Greek versus Roman mythology as I unlocked it and removed the contents.

There were more nondescript shouts while some Hondas started and revved.

My thumb slid fifteen rounds into a magazine and my palm seated it into the grip. I racked the slide and turned off the lights as I made my way back to the window and surveyed the village again.

All of the action centered near a yellow house two rows to the east. It was Mayor David Aicia's house. Hondas pulled up within three or four houses, looked for about five seconds, then turned and went around the block to view from the opposite side for about five seconds.

A man in a denim jacket and a green baseball cap came out of the *quniciuq* with a hunting rifle. The man was definitely not David. This man was slightly taller and much, much thinner. He looked a lot like Mr. Kala'a.

Green Hat lit a cigarette and walked south toward the airport. The Hondas to the south scurried like proverbial cockroaches under a hundred-watt bulb. Stan's pickup rolled down the street from the north.

My legs carried me over to my shoes and I slipped them on then sat back down at the window while I tied them. I identified all of the routes that would keep me concealed from Green Hat if I had to move into a position of engagement. Two would allow me to do so within less than one minute. The first was within thirty meters of Green Hat. The second was within ten meters, but would require me to fire from my weak hand. If the need arose I would choose the first position.

Stan exited his pickup, took cover behind the door with his AR-15, and yelled at Green Hat who threw his own rifle down on the ground forcefully as if to say, "See, there, I did it! Are you happy now?" then pointed his finger to David's house, back to himself, and at David's house again.

Green Hat lay down on the road and Stan drove up and handcuffed him, then seat-belted him into the passenger side. Stan ducked in and out of David's *quniciuq* briefly, then drove away. As soon as Stan's truck turned the corner the Hondas converged on David's house from all directions like piranha on an overboard sailor.

I slipped my shoes off, turned the light on, sat down again, and clicked the safety on my Beretta down and back up with my thumb before I exchanged it for *The Economist* beside my chair. When my eyelids grew heavy I picked my Beretta back up and headed for bed. I ran my thumb along the knurled grips and felt comforted by their familiarity. Despite the evening's chaotic crisis, I slept more soundly than I had in weeks.

Emma came by my classroom shortly after 8:00 a.m. and half-invited, half-ordered me to her room for tea along with Belle and Cornell, and Ben and Brenda.

"Are you staying or leaving?" Emma asked me.

"Staying or leaving?" I thought to myself, "Shit lady, you insist that I come down to your room, and then immediately imply that I should leave?" Before I could answer, Emma rambled out a monologue.

"Never," said Emma. "Never in twenty years in Vitus Cove did anything like this ever happen. Never, ever. No one in Vitus Cove would ever do such a thing. Never. This type of thing is just not to be tolerated. I can't believe the people in this village. Never. And still no one has told us what happened. Ugh! Never."

Emma explained how she had hit the floor after the first shot and laid there awake all night, then speculated and conjectured as to who or what might have been involved before she started her rant all over again; much the same way cable news feeds for hours off twenty seconds of shaky cell-phone video.

Meanwhile Ben and Brenda consoled each other next to the piano; his arm draped across the back of her shoulders and her arm wrapped behind his back until her fingers anchored themselves into a belt loop. Belle fidgeted with the large black and white beads of her necklace as Cornell ran his fingers through his thick, gray mane then patted it down flat again.

I gathered that each of them gained comfort from these actions in the same way that I had from the knurled grips and slotted screws of the Beretta, although at that moment the previous night's incident was tangential to me and that indifference disturbed me more than any of Green Hat's actions.

Finally Emma broke her reiteration with, "How much does a charter to Fairbanks cost and how soon can they get here?"

Ben and Brenda shared a glance that said, "To hell with the consequences, we're doing it."

Cornell, normally the most prototypical beta-male, chided her with, "Naw no one's gun'uh go takin' off jus' 'cause someone shot a few rounds off in the ay-uhr last night," and headed for the door with Belle in tow.

I didn't know if Cornell was truly oblivious to even the few details I was privy to, or if he desperately wanted to thwart the first grand exodus of the year at any cost. In either case, Cornell's move toward the door was the most productive action anyone had taken in a good five minutes so I copied it.

When the Bortunds failed to join us in the hall Cornell stuck his head back in and said, "If y'all aren't in your roo-ooms 'fore the kuh-ids show up they'll tear'em tuh pieces 'fore they start in on each other," and waited until they came out. It was neither Cornell's habit nor place to give anyone orders, but he had a patriarchal paunchiness and inhibited gait that let him get away with such things. Had he not done so, the Bortunds may have drowned that morning in Emma's caustic brew.

At the end of second period I overheard some commentary.

"David never share." Alicia shook her head.

"Share what?" asked Amos-Ben.

Alicia quickly popped her shoulders straight up and down.

Joel-Ben bladed his hand to one side of his mouth and silently mouthed, "Juh."

Amos-Ben mimicked his twin and mouthed the word back to him, "Juh."

They both stifled giggles as Alicia looked around nervously then slapped both of them lightly on the arm.

Third period was only about half-full, and both of my major trouble-makers, Tim-Tim and Jenny, were gone. Solomon had been absent second period but I had sent Rachel out, so my chances for another yellow-highlighter star were already dashed. The few students that did show up were more lethargic, disengaged, and glum than usual.

Josh stuck the end of his pencil into the sleeve of his cousin, Beth Aicia's, sweater and pulled on it until the point slipped out. She ignored him or didn't notice the first few times, but eventually she scooted to the far end of their table.

Josh scooted his own chair closer and continued.

Beth was borderline mentally disabled, and not very socially astute, so before she reasserted her discomfort I said, "Josh, quit bothering Beth please."

Everyone's ears perked up.

Josh gave me a very confused look and said, calmly, "I never bother."

"Yes you did Josh, I just saw you. Now stop it." I said.

Beth also gave me a confused look. The rest of the class giggled a little bit.

Josh became visibly agitated. "*I never bother her,*" he said through clenched teeth.

Josh had never challenged me or gone all the way up to the point of being sent from the room. Something was a little off today. I thought it might have something to do with the use of his uncle's house as a shooting range.

There were murmurs and chuckles across the classroom as I prepared to play the final encore of, "*Ratios, Portions, and Percentages.*"

Josh sprung from his seat and hammered the table with his fists. "Shut up! Shut! Up! Fuckers! Motherfuckers! All of you, shut!!! Up!!!" He ran to the door and reached for the handle, then ran back to his table and threw his chair against the wall. He returned to the door and punted the waste basket across the room before he ran out.

Josh's outburst cut short the giggles and murmurs. I pushed play on the laptop, and fully expected to be barraged with, "So mad you let Josh get," but everyone sat through it and left without comment when the bell rang.

A-Team, tieless for the first time ever, came down to my room at lunch and asked what had happened with Josh. I explained exactly how things deteriorated and A-Team asked me if I said anything derogatory to Josh. I told him no. I also mentioned that Josh was a follower and had never given me a hard time about soda, headphones, or any of the dozen other things that most kids made an issue of.

A-Team said Josh's mother had called the school and claimed that I insulted Josh and ridiculed him.

I told A-Team, "All I said was, 'Quit bothering Beth,' and when he said he hadn't, I told him, 'Yes you did, I saw you.' The other students were snickering and Josh lost it."

A-Team's tone and demeanor would tell me nothing beyond his words. I only inferred that a parallax existed between his mother's interpretation of the events and my own; and A-Team had no chart with which to calibrate for the deviation. He surveyed the wall where the chair had hit then left.

I walked past the three elders and we exchanged our, "Good afternoons."

As Arnold sauntered into fourth period he brimmed with glee. First I thought that he was on some type of stimulant, but he was as coherent as ever. He did not pick up a word search and when I placed one in front of him he slid it on to the floor. He did the same with his journal. I set the laptop to play and then repeat, "*Factors and Coefficients, Literal and Numerical,*" and asked Arnold to come to the back of the room. He was not his usual contrarian self for once.

"What happens if you don't do your work?" I asked.

"I get sent to the office, bitch." Arnold began a pattern where he ended every sentence with profanity as verbalized punctuation.

"Is using that word going to get you what you want?"

"I don't care, *tuniq.*"

"You know the rules. You need to follow them. Go back and get to work."

"No way, motherfucker." He didn't raise his voice in the least he just said it matter of factly.

"Go to the office Arnold."

"Whatever you say, bitch." Arnold bopped out of the room without any animosity toward me, or my door.

Jay-Boy had not one, not two, but three jokes ready for fifth period.

"Okay, today is buy two, third one free, okay? Here first one. Knock, knock."

"Who's there?"

"Esther."

"Esther who?"

"Esther bunny. Like Easter bunny, get it? Ready for number two? Okay? Here second one. Knock, knock."

"Who's there?"

"Anna"

"Anna who?"

"Anna-ther Esther bunny."

Jay-Boy took a deep breath in anticipation of his trifecta. "Knock, knock."

"Who's there?"

"Gladys."

"Gladys who?"

"Are you Gladys not Anna-ther Esther bunny?"

I said, "Thank you Jay-Boy," as he smiled gap-toothed and waved both hands in the air like a rock star.

Later something thudded against my window. I looked outside and watched as sixth-grader Larry Iqaluq threw snowballs at all of the classroom windows. Nick stuck his head out the window and told him to stop, but it only encouraged him. A-Team appeared at the fire door and met with the same result. Fifteen minutes later Stan's pickup arrived and Larry ran away.

Lewis came in for sixth period and we worked through transversals. Then I asked him to revise some writing he had done for me, a real minefield of commas and apostrophes. As he clicked around on a game he had found that arranged plane figures into tessellations he began our usual open question period with, "When you go?"

"Go where?" I asked.

"Away."

"I'm not leaving."

"Oh."

I didn't mention that I had checked off 51 of the 84 days on my double-top-secret calendar.

A few clicks later Lewis re-inquired. "Why you come here?"

"Come where, Iqsaiqsiq or Alaska?"

"Iqsaiqsiq."

My first thought was that whatever I said would be broadcast through the village within 48 hours. My second thought was how to explain property taxes, municipal bonds, negotiated agreements, and per capita expenditures to a seventeen year-old who had always; lived in a free house, paid for groceries with a government voucher, and discovered a check for one thousand dollars in his post office box every October. In the end I simply said, "There were too many kids at my old school."

"Oh."

I decided I would try some quid pro quo. I rehearsed my question over and over in my mind until I was sure I had exactly the right tone and syntax for the initial inquiry as well as any necessary codicils. "What happen at David's house?" I asked.

"Jugs."

"What kind jugs?"

"Ron Rico."

I knew how the game worked, so even though I had a dozen follow-ups I simply said, "Oh."

Perhaps it was my sheltered, elitist, collegiate, latte and biscotti, suburban upbringing; or it may have been my xenophobic failure to fully embrace the richness and rarity of the Alaskan Natives' unique culture. In any case, I did not have a clue what a Ron Rico jug was. I Googled it over the school's highly filtered system.

There were results for Captain **Ron**.

There were results for **Rico** Suave.

There were results for milk **jug**.

There were results for, "**Ron** from Puerto **Rico** plays in a **jug** band every other Saturday."

I tried, ron+rico+jug and received:

CONTENT BLOCKED: ALCOHOL

A couple of weeks previous we had all taken up a collection and ordered a stack of Papa Murphy's take and bake pizza's to be flown in, frozen of course, from Fairbanks. The elementary teachers had surreptitiously preheated the ovens and slipped the pizzas in at exactly 3:40.

The pizzas were timed perfectly and we decided to eat and chat before we watched season one of *Lost*. Cornell, Brenda, Ben, Belle, and Nick were all there in addition to the Sledsons and myself. It was the largest crowd in quite a while. Nick kicked off the conversation with, "You hear what happened to A-Team?"

John and Cornell seemed to know, but I was clueless as were all of the elementary teachers.

Nick described how Olivia had "gone off" in Mitch's third period PE class. "Trooper Stan wasn't here so A-Team had to respond solo. He asked her to leave and she refused, so he sent the rest of the class out of the gym. That's when she decided to leave too. A-Team stepped in front of the door and puts his hands up. She grabbed his Hugo Boss fuchsia and magenta masterpiece of a necktie and began to twirl him like a human centrifuge until A-Team slam-dunked her on the court. So, no more Olivia this year."

"And no more ties," added Ben.

We all shared a laugh at A-Team's expense.

Nick also confirmed that it was in fact Mr. Kala'a who had fired the rifle and gotten arrested the night before.

I asked if anyone knew what Ron Rico jugs were.

Ben winced. "Brenda's step-dad loves the stuff, along with Swisher Sweets cigars. It isn't just bottom shelf rum, it's under-the-fucking-shelf rum, in a god-damn plastic bottle." Ben stuck out his tongue for theatrical effect.

John said that the term "jug" was, is, and probably always will be the *nom de plume*, or more accurately *nom de guerre*, for alcohol in rural Alaska. It didn't matter if one spoke of liquor, wine, beer, or some pseudo-synth-improvised-hybrid; nor if it was packaged in a can, bottle, box, pouch, or cask. Whether due to frontier simplicity or lack of sophistication, if it contained alcohol in liquid form it qualified as a jug.

As for variety, John explained that people sometimes drank fortified wine; but Ron Rico had landed on the shores of the Arctic Ocean first, planted his flag to claim adverse possession, and remained interminably.

I also mentioned that Larry Iqaluq had thrown snowballs at the windows and learned that he had been kicked out of Brenda's room after repeatedly asking her if she was, "On the rag," then heaved snowball after snowball at the school for a good forty-five minutes. Not a single window had been spared; apparently Larry was not only crude and agitated, but thorough as well.

We watched the episodes of *Lost* in marathon fashion with no breaks save to swap out discs and I retreated to the quad-plex to sleep off the carb-coma. Less than two inches of snow covered the now frozen tundra and the "kaputtputt-putt" backbeat of Honda's four-stroke bass had incorporated the "brap-brap-braaappp" of snowmachines' two-stroke soprano shrill. The change was not only in tone, but in proximity. Honda's were confined to roads whereas snowmachines traveled between and sometimes right along the edges of houses. Snowmachines also left a distinctive odor of partially combusted oil in their wake.

With water available to wash and flush at the quad-plex, although apparently not village-wide, I had halted my Saturday morning runs. Instead I went to the school to use the spin bike and play a little one-on-none basketball. Saturday night I jail guarded for Stan who finally gave me the whole story of the shoot-out at the O-Kala'a corral.

"You want the straight dope or the various nuanced versions?" Stan asked.

"Straight," I said.

"David is a bootlegger. He fronts the cash and sells the booze but he never brings it in himself, that way if his mule gets pinched his hands are still clean. By the time I know he has a load, it's already been distributed or hidden away. Matt (Mr. Kala'a) had already taken a jug on credit and wanted another, but David wouldn't give it to him. Matt took his rifle over there and threatened to shoot David if he didn't give him another jug. David kept the door locked, so Matt emptied his rifle into it plus another clip. When he ran out of ammo he left."

"And here I thought my classroom door was the most abused one in the village."

"Not even close my friend, not even close."

"What're the nuanced versions?"

"David said he was having dinner like any other normal family man in America when Matt showed up and wanted to shoot Solomon for picking on Tim-Tim, which we all know is bullshit since those two are best buddies. David, 'Feared for his son's life,' so he wouldn't open the door. David claims Matt tried to murder Solomon by shooting through the door." As Stan spoke he gestured with his right hand, which migrated further and further from his torso with each sentence.

"Matt," Stan switched to his left hand, "Either wanted to sell his rifle to David or he owed money to David and was trying to give him the rifle as payment, I heard both stories straight from Matt himself within fifteen minute of each other. David told Matt it was a junk rifle that didn't work. Matt admits he got mad, and shot at the door to quote, 'Show I'm no god damn liar,' and claims he's still mad that David didn't accept the rifle as payment."

"So who's at fault?" I asked.

Stan shot both hands toward the ceiling as if to signal a touchdown. "I am. You are. The rifle is. The door is. Lady Gaga and Barack Obama; everyone and everything except the person who pulled the trigger."

I told Stan what little I knew based on Alicia's comment.

"Yep," said Stan, "There aren't many consistencies in Native culture, but sharing is one that perseveres, usually. If I had to guess, the most popular version probably goes something like this, 'David should have shared his jugs with Matt, then Matt would not have gotten mad and would not have shot up his door.' But bootlegging is a for-profit enterprise, and Matt is an addict. David wasn't going to 'share' his goods when he could sell them, and even if he had given Matt another jug it would have just delayed the inevitable until Friday or Saturday. But that's objective cause-and-effect logic speaking and, as you have since learned Ken, we all left the land of objective cause-and-effect logic the minute we climbed into that Cessna two-oh-seven back in Fairbanks."

I wrote out the next week's raps while I guarded the prisoners. Stan brought a portable VHF radio in so one of the prisoners could contact a family member. When the prisoner couldn't locate the person, Stan left the VHF radio and said I could let the prisoner try later. The prisoner went to sleep instead.

Occasionally the VHF radio would interrupt with, "Good evening, good evening, good evening Iqsaiqsiq." There would be a pause until someone else responded with, "Good evening Carl," or, "Good evening Angela," and then there would be a question about where someone was or what someone was doing, "You know where Johnny?" or, "Got plywoods?" Sometimes a third party would jump in, "Johnny at playground," or, "Magnus got plywoods."

An impaired female voice came over the speaker and offered the customary greeting, but no one responded. After a couple of minutes the voice came on again. "Where, where's everybody? How come nobody never answer me? How come nobody never say good eve-neen? Everybody too good. Everybody too good to talk to Mar… thuh." I assumed it was Martha Iqaluq, mother of Larry (the snowball thrower), Daryl, Gracie, and Athena Iqaluq; all of whom were elementary students.

There was a long pause of between one and two minutes then the voice returned. "Good eve-neen, good eve-neen, good, eve, neen… Iqsa."

A full minute passed before Martha returned. "You what fuck pieces of shit. Never. Ignore me. Never ignore me! Rude what suck fuck pieces of shit you all are in this village. Nobody never say good eve-neen. I gotta Xbox. Anybody want Xbox? It's a good Xbox, I got lots a games for this Xbox. It's. A lotta. Gotta. Fun for, for kids. Make them happy if you buy, this Xbox. Three hundred dollars. Who's wants buy this Xbox for three, hundred, dollars. And games!"

Martha engaged the stagnant audience once again. "How come nobody never wants their kids to be happy? Nobody never say good eve-neen. This village. This village coming apart. Bunch a rude fucks never say, never want, Xbox. Xbox three-sixty and games, lotsa games. Who gonna buy this Xbox for three hundred dollars? Three, hundred, dollars."

A clear Native male voice I did not recognize came on and said, "Go to bed Martha. Go to bed. Stay off radio. Go to bed."

"Who is this?" asked Martha, "Who, is, this? Wanna buy Xbox?"

A cacophony of microphones clicked on and off for a solid minute at the end of which Martha repeated her sales pitch, then dropped the price from $300 to $250, then to $200, and finally $100. Fifteen minutes into the whole quagmire she finally said, "Fuck, fuck-fuck, who wants this god damn Xbox. I give you this Xbox for free. Some, body. Come get this Xbox. Cheap, ass," and then it was over.

A couple hours of silence went by until, "Char-lee! Char-lee!" came an impaired Native male voice. "How *come* you fuck my dog, Charlie? My dog never hurt you. How *come* you fuck my dog?" Three other male voices joined in and talked about Charlie, fucking, dogs, caribou, moose, and seals.

I rode with Stan to the airport to deliver the prisoners in the morning and after the plane left I mentioned the Martha Iqaluq exchange.

"When I was in," Stan said the name of some village I didn't recognize, "People would knock on the door and offer to sell a fur hat or some carved ivory. One week they wanted $100, the next week they wanted $200, then the price dropped back to $100 and a few days later it was up to $300. If you ever want to know the going price for a jug, just see how much people are buying or selling things for. Lots of cash, and lots of buyers, right now and only a moderate supply; $300 sounds about right for a jug. In a couple weeks, when money is tighter and people have brought some more in from town, probably only $200."

Stan scratched his scalp and rubbed his face, which I had come to learn was his stress response. "That's the hardest thing to communicate to people in Anchorage, Juneau, and Outside; judges, attorneys, doctors, counselors, politicians, professors, whomever. They see alcohol like you probably see alcohol Ken, as an intoxicant; often recreational and sometimes addictive. But out here in the Bush it's much more than that. Alcohol is a commodity, a currency, an investment, an icon, and a weapon of coercion. More than anything else alcohol is permission; not just in the user's eyes, but in the eyes of those affected by it and the community as a whole. A jug gets a person what they want, and allows them to do what they want, more effectively and consistently than cash, gold, or elected office; which is why people will give up their snowmachines, guns, furniture, freedom, bodies, children's bodies, and legal rights to get it."

Stan dropped me off at home and I slept all day and all night as well. It seemed like I got tired earlier and earlier in the day, regardless of how much I slept at night.

# CHAPTER THIRTEEN

Monday morning I searched for dry erase markers in the work room while Belle, adorned with triangular saffron earrings and a similar necklace, made photocopies of *Thomas the Tank Engine*. Belle informed me in her gracious southern drawl that she expected pecans in the mail any day and would have me over for pie after they arrived.

We exited the work room into the foyer where most of the students slumped groggily on the benches. Mitch, who had hall duty that week, faced the front door and solicited snowmachine advice from some high school students. Less than twenty feet away Solomon, flanked by Eddie and Tim-Tim, had seven-year-old Croesus, the son of store manager Ty Burnside and the lone non-Native student, corralled into the southeast corner.

"Nigger," said Solomon, "Neee-gurrr. Nigger, nigger, nigger, nigger. Nigger. You're nothing but a nigger, you little nigger."

"Solomon!" I boomed in such a manner that would have made Roby cringe, but did not seem to affect Mitch in the least.

"What?" Solomon said with an indifferent look as he turned and spread his arms out.

Eddie and Tim-Tim both grinned incessantly.

Croesus whimpered as tears streaked down his face.

Belle and I walked over and she extended her hand to Croesus who squeezed between Solomon and Tim-Tim as she said, "Come with me darlin'."

"The three of you," I connected them with an invisible line drawn by my finger, "Go to the office."

"For what?" said Solomon.

By this time all of the attention in the foyer, even Mitch's, had focused on the southeast corner where we stood.

"You were harassing Croesus. Now go." I pointed to the office door.

"I never," said Solomon.

As I said, "Solomon, I saw…" Belle's hand swooped in under Solomon's armpit and boosted his diminutive figure a few extra inches as she led him to the office door ten feet away.

Tim-Tim, apparently a follower of Solomon's in the fundamentalist sense, walked right in behind him. Eddie stood still and shot me his big, silent, closed-eyes grin. When he opened his eyes and saw my Michelangelo-esque finger, he obeyed.

I went into the office with all of them and filled out a discipline referral at Jenn's desk. When I exited the office ten minutes later, Mitch, who still faced the front door with his back toward the benches, had returned to his snowmachine discussion.

"Arctic Cat is more like arctic crap, maaannn, you need Ski-Doo. Ski-Doo is the one what's best, maaannn," Arnold told him.

The levels of door-slams, foot-stomps, and *tuniq*-shouts resurged to their first and second week benchmarks. A-Team was in the hall a few times, but not Stan. I figured he had to either recover from or actively quell other turmoil in the village.

Solomon and Eddie were both in my second period class temporarily before I sent them out. Tim-Tim was absent from third period, as was Josh. Jenny attended and held herself to a two "fuck-off" limit.

None of the, "Good afternoon," elders were on the bench after lunch and it disrupted my intrinsic mojo so much that I poked my head into Jenn's office and said, "Good afternoon," just to feel validated.

After lunch Middy and Rocky were my only students. They were not eager, but they were coherent. Five minutes later Suzette knocked at my door and I let her in. Another five minutes later MKay knocked and I let her in as well. Alex Aicia and Daniel-Ben Iqaluq knocked individually at five minute intervals. Arnold was the last to arrive and his behavior tipped me off. He showed up with headphones and when I told him he had to remove them before he could come in he said, "What, ever, maaannn," in a very disconnected, non-confrontational, and profanity-free manner, then floated back down the hallway.

I had washed dishes and shoveled snow at a resort in British Columbia one winter and based on things I had observed then I deduced that, except for Middy and Rocky, all of them were stoned. I sent an email to A-Team about it.

Fifth period Jay-Boy was my only charge. I asked him to reel off as many clean jokes as he knew, and I provided him with the same. At the end of the period I asked him as tactfully as possible why he did not act in the same way as most other students.

Jay-Boy sang, *"Here's little song I wrote. Might want hear note for note. Don't worry."* Snap, snap, snap. *"Be happy. Don't worry. Be happy now!"* Jay-Boy switched to his regular voice. "I jokes. I never write that song, I hear it. Is good song. I like, 'Don't worry, be happy.' People should try be happy whenever they could."

Lewis was absent sixth period so I worked on report cards, which were due in a little over a week.

The Monday afternoon staff meeting was moderated by our polo shirted leader. The laying on of hands being the divine providence of only certain designated staff members was reiterated, as was a request to keep students in class until their removal was absolutely necessary. After a little "success" pep talk Belle's presence was requested in A-Team's office and the rest of us were dismissed.

A-Team came to my room a few minutes after four o'clock with the policy manual and a yellow legal pad.

I was sure he wanted to discuss the foyer incident.

I was wrong.

He recited the policy that addressed intoxicated students. He then instructed me to inform him immediately the next time such an incident occurred and he would confront and discipline the students at that time, "Based on resources available," but was not going to follow up further on this most recent incident.

A-Team asked me if I understood.

I answered in the positive.

He asked me if I had any further questions or comments.

I answered in the negative.

Then he said, "Very well, dismissed," and wrote notes on a yellow legal pad.

There are three words burned into the Marines psyche; attention, grenade, and dismissed, in that exact order, which is why when A-Team said, "Dismissed," I immediately rose to my feet. I stood there awkwardly for a moment and debated whether to sit or leave then said, "Principal Atkinson, would you like me to leave the room?"

A-Team stared at me befuddled then said, "Pardon me, I misspoke," gathered his materials, and left.

I left the building shortly thereafter and noticed Emma in A-Team's office.

On my way home I passed a post-middle-aged Native woman as she viciously assaulted a Chinese dog. I assumed it was Chinese because that is where most stuffed animals are produced.

She grabbed it around the neck, shook it, and screamed, "Stop following me *kimiq* (kim-ick), *kimiq!*" She threw it on the ground and ran about ten feet away, then turned around and yelled at it again. "*Kii* (key), *kii*, go away *kimiq*, *kii!*"

When the dog failed to obey her bilingual commands she ran up and kicked it, which released white Styrofoam beads across the similarly toned and textured snow. As I approached she incorporated me into her monologue, "*Kii, tuniq, kii!* Go away before I let my *kimiq* bite you *tuniq.*"

Tuesday morning almost all of the seventh and eighth graders, except Josh, were present and in top form. I sent student after student to the office, about half of whom returned to me undeterred. As soon as the last eighth grader cleared the room Nick came in and closed the door behind him.

He tossed his lunch sack on the table and shook his head. "Motherfucker. Motherfucker. Motherfucker."

"Sounds like you're having a three motherfucker day," I responded.

"Yep. Three motherfucker day. You hear what happened to Belle?" Nick explained that Belle had been written up for leading Solomon by the arm.

"How's Belle taking it?" I asked.

"I think she's resigned to sticking it out, married folks like her and Cornell usually do, unless both of them get fed up at the same time. I'd probably endure it myself, just makes a suck ass job even suckier though."

We ate our lunches in silence and when Nick left five minutes before fourth period I followed him out.

Only one of the Elders sat on the bench.

I waved and said, "Good afternoon," but he deliberately stared at the wall.

I thought, "Oh well, that was good while it lasted," followed by, "How many of those eighty-four days do I have left?"

Middy was my only student fourth period and Jay Boy was my only student fifth period.

I asked Jay-Boy where all of the high school students were.

"Crashed out," said Jay-Boy.

I asked what "crashed out" meant and Jay-Boy gave me the quick, straight-up-and-down, shoulder shrug.

Lewis was gone sixth period so I walked around to see what people were up to. Nick had only Middy in his room. Cornell had only Jay-Boy.

Emma was also student-less like me and she used the opportunity to roll up and put away many of her posters. I figured she wanted to shelter them from further harm, or maybe it was just really difficult for her to look at posters that implored, "Reach beyond your grasp," and, "Find the beauty within yourself," while kids constantly yelled things like, "Pull the stick out of your ass!"

Mitch's seventh and eighth grade PE class was totally out of control. It looked as if he had given them free reign to play chase-tackle-take with most of the emphasis placed on tackle. He tried to tell Tim-Tim it was against the rules to scratch.

Tim-Tim said, "Where's your dog, *tuniq*? Go get your fucking dog, I want to see some more tricks," then mimicked masturbation and ejaculation toward Mitch before he horse-collared Mary and threw her to the ground.

Mitch never corrected or challenged Tim-Tim. Rachel slapped and swung at Solomon while Rosy sat on the bleachers and cried. Meanwhile Tim-Tim and Jenny meted out punishment to everyone regardless of whether they had the ball or not.

Mitch's response to everyone and everything was, "Stop that now, please. Be respectful of each other. That's not the right way to play."

My congenital coaching instincts were to burst through the door with a nice thirty-second whistle blast, send everyone to the bleachers, endure the reprise, and send the remainder to the office. But I didn't want to disrupt Mitch's kindred spirit-filled discourse.

Wednesday during lunch Jerry was the only elder on the bench. I said, "Good afternoon," and he waved a single hand, but did not speak. A few minutes later he was at my door.

He came in, hands buried deep in his pockets. I offered him a seat but he refused. Finally he said, "How come, you say, Josh bother Beth?"

I made it a general practice only to discuss student behavior with parents and colleagues, but something intrinsic told me it would be beneficial to suspend that practice in this instance.

"Because he was," I responded.

"Where? Where you see this?" asked Jerry.

"Right here in my classroom."

"Where? Show me."

I showed Jerry where Josh and Beth each sat. Jerry sat in Beth's chair and pointed to Josh's chair. "Sit. Now show me how Josh bother her."

I used a dry erase marker and explained how Josh pulled on Beth's sweater with the tip of his pencil and how, when she moved over, Josh moved over also and continued.

"When Josh bother Beth?" said Jerry.

"On Friday," I said

"Where you see them Friday?"

"Right here, in these chairs."

"What they do Friday?"

I demonstrated again with the dry erase marker and Jerry sat dumbfounded.

"That not bother," said Jerry.

I wanted to keep Jerry as an ally, or at least neutral, since I had enough enemies already. I also felt that I had to assert my perception and the justification for my actions so I asked Jerry, "What would you call it?"

"He pull sweater? I say, 'Josh you not supposed to pull sweater.' But I never say he bother."

"Why not?"

"'Cause bother mean something else."

"What?"

Jerry looked over both shoulders as well as at the door and window as if he was about to slip me a dime bag and said, "Butt. Fuck." Then he straightened and shook his fist, "Buttfuck!"

I told Jerry I had no idea it meant that and that was not my intent, which I think he less than completely believed, and told him I would apologize to Josh as soon as I saw him.

Jerry shook his head. "No good. Only remind people bad thing happen if you say sorry. Person should never say no more. Person should never say sorry. Person should never say bother." Jerry waived his hands in front of him.

Jerry left my room, hands again buried deep in pockets, and the fourth period students trickled in, Arnold included.

"You know how come I'm being such an asshole to you Shosatori?" Arnold asked.

"It's *Mr.* Shosatori, you are now one step closer to going to the office, and my worth as a person is not dependent on your approval," I told him.

"When dividends come, maaannn, I'm outta here. My family's moving to Fairbanks, maaannn."

"Good for you Arnold. I hope you enjoy yourself there."

"Hell yeah I'm gonna enjoy myself. I'm gonna get all gangster in Fairbanks, bitch."

I held up two fingers which my class had learned meant, "Two strikes, next one is a trip to the office."

Arnold feigned effort at the word search and journal, sat through the rap and re-rap then stood up, said, "See you later bitches," and waved both middle fingers in the air as he helped himself out the door.

Attendance was up considerably in fifth period. Jay-Boy recycled a joke and I noticed that with Olivia gone my fifth period operated almost like a normal class, which made it a highly abnormal class for Iqsaiqsiq.

Lewis was in class for the first time on Wednesday. After he finished the regular assignment and an additional writing assignment, he went on the computer. I waited until he was settled and asked, "What's crashed out mean?"

"It's when you never wanna do nothing," Lewis replied, eyes still glued to the screen.

"How *come?*" I inquired in the appropriate regional dialect.

Lewis turned around and checked the exits, just as Jerry had done, then made the universal "smoke" and "drink" gesture with his hands.

"Oh," I said.

Thursday morning I headed to the work room to cut some three-by-five cards into three-by-three cards for a lesson. Mitch sat on the benches in such a way that he could see most of what was going on in the foyer. I thought, "He seems to be catching on."

When I exited the work room Tim-Tim had a can of Pepsi, which was not an offense in and of itself since it was before school. The problem was that he didn't drink it, he held his thumb over the top and shook it. When someone walked past he scooted his thumb back and sprayed them.

I looked at Mitch.

I looked at Tim-Tim.

I debated which inane task I wanted to suffer through, then I stuffed the whole turd sandwich straight into my mouth and walked over to Mitch.

"You see what's going on, right?" I said to Mitch.

"Wha… What, what is going on?"

"Tim-Tim is sitting over there spraying people with Pepsi."

Mitch leaned over to look around me and said, "Tim-Tim, stop spraying people."

"I never," said Tim-Tim, his thumb clasped tightly over the can.

Mitch looked up at me blankly.

There were about a dozen things I wanted to say and do, the first of which was point my forefinger at Mitch and say, "Bang," but since the majority of them would have gotten me fired I just walked away.

Ten minutes later I heard Ben's voice as he squealed, "Get! In! The! Office! Now!!!"

Phone calls and emails were sent out that dividend checks had hit the post office in Aciq, which meant they would hit the rest of the villages tomorrow, Friday.

Arnold stopped by between second and third period to tell me, vulgarly, that he was headed home to pack and he would not be in tomorrow either because his family had plans to fly out on the first plane.

Nick and Cornell visited my room together during lunch. Nick limited himself to one "motherfucker" and Cornell brought individual pudding cups, so all-in-all we had a pretty decent visit.

Nick informed us that Tim-Tim had sprayed Brenda with his Pepsi, unaware that Ben was right behind her and saw it. Tim-Tim denied the whole thing ad infinitum, despite the streak of cola that ran down the back of Brenda's blouse, until Ben lost patience and ordered him into the office. Mitch had sat silently on the bench through the whole thing.

Cornell was pissed off because he felt that if Mitch had done his job in the first place, Belle wouldn't have grabbed Solomon by the arm.

I half, but only half, agreed with him.

In our previous lives Nick had been a Senior Chief and I had been a Corporal so we discussed whether we should take it up the chain-of-command to A-Team or deal with it ourselves. I deferred to Nick's wisdom which was, "Let him be, he'll ensnare himself eventually."

Ben dealt with it *mano a mano* after school. He lectured Mitch on the concepts of pull, head, out, and ass.

Friday morning a battle royal erupted in the foyer amongst the teenage females. The catalyst was a can of Axe deodorant spray randomly applied without consent. In an attempt at mediation A-Team had pushed a few out the front door, pulled a few into the office, and ordered the remainder to class fifteen minutes early. All while Mitch stood and told the students, "Don't you... You, you shouldn't do that. You know that's not, that's not the right thing to do."

A-Team asked me to cover Mitch's first period class while the two of them met. My guess was that at some point a policy manual was opened and a form was filled out.

All three Elders were back Friday and all three greeted me. We were cool from that point on.

Arnold was in fourth period and I reminded him that he had said he would not be there.

"Parents go today. After they get apartment, my sisters and me go. Ha ha ha! *Then I'm gone bitch!!!*" Arnold gave me the two finger salute, one on each hand.

Arnold sat reverently until the end of the re-rap and departed of his own free will.

Lewis informed me that he would be gone for a week to the Alaska Federation of Natives conference in Anchorage along with his brother, sister, mother, and grandmother. It spanned a full week that included both weekends and drew in Indians and Eskimoes alike, from the far southern areas of Ketchikan and Sitka, all the way up to Kotzebue and Barrow. The conference itself was relatively inexpensive. Still, Lewis' family would use their entire dividends for air transportation, taxi cabs, meals, and hotels.

The first thing I had to tell everyone at movie night was the definition of *bother*. Cornell said that he had had a similar experience the previous year but no one had ever enlightened him as to its roots. Joanne immediately went and made a phone call to Stan.

Ben shook his head. "So we've got *anuq*, which means shit. *Tuniq*, which means white nigger. *Atchu*, which means I don't know. Never, which means either can't or don't or won't. Might-could which means possibly. *Could* (he put the elongated emphasis on it), which means, 'Fuck you, I'm gonna go ahead and do whatever the hell I want to anyway,' and now *bother*, which means," he paused, "Anal intercourse."

Belle graciously engaged all of us with her perfect down home drawl, "I'll tell you whu-uht, we could'uh all been saved uh heap uh trouble, if someone had just laid all that out for us on day one. Who in their right mind would ev-uh teach uh child uh word like taw-nick. Course, some uh them use that n-word I'm not gonna repeat, but I never let my children run around and use that word even though almost every adult in town did. I told muh boys, 'When you get too big for paw-paw to hit you with the switch you can say it as often as you like. Until then, it's keep your mouth shut or get hit with the switch.'"

"Then she'd send'em out to go'n cut a suh-witch," Cornell added.

"That's ruh-ight," confirmed Belle, "It didn't stop'em altogeth-uh, but it was uh rath-uh rare occurrence. Same goes for makin' fun of La-tee-nose. I told'em, 'Whu-uht's gonna happen you pick on all them, and some day they're you're boss?' Our neighbors were La-tee-no, and good people too." Belle folded a napkin, placed it in her lap, and rested her hands upon it, which was her sign that she was finished.

I wasn't really in the mood for anthropological analysis so after the nacho's I excused myself from the dual *Toy Story* presentations and jail guarded for Stan. I also discussed *bothering* with him and he said Joanne had asked him to do some investigations based on her students' use of the word. He added that while the term *bothering* was new to him, most villages had some type of euphemism for pedophilia or forced sexual acts and it made investigations difficult because defense attorneys exploited the ambiguity and inconsistent use of such terms.

I made it to the store Saturday morning and passed a group of elementary students in the *quniciuq* as they gorged themselves on Nilla wafers and Hawaiian Punch. I asked them why they weren't at home so they could watch cartoons.

"Everybody crashed out," said third-grader Marcia Kala'a.

"Our house too," added fourth-grader Gracie Iqaluq, accompanied by her sister Athena.

"Those look like some delicious cookies you have there," I said.

"No, they're junk," said Gracie, "but that what all they got left at store."

"Yeah, never get Pepsi and chips 'cause store is stingy," added Athena.

Inside I found the shelves stripped nearly bare. Only a few 12-packs of Diet 7-Up survived in the soda alley and the Weight Watchers Nightmare shelves had been equally decimated, only some bags of pretzels and half a box of Abba-Zabba bars remained. All of the clothing, electronics, tools, and furniture had sold out.

A chasm remained in the locked case behind the counter where the cigarettes had been. Ty silently bagged up my chocolate milk and Eggo waffles but seemed genuinely agitated about something. He asked me where I had grown up and lived and I told him the Pacific Northwest, except for my time in the Corps.

"I don't know about Washington or Oregon, man, but I assume in the military there was some brothers, right?" Ty asked.

I told him there were, along with every other shade of the spectrum.

"And I'm assumin' you probably heard some brothers callin' each other nig'uh, right?"

"Yeah."

"But you knew that it wasn't cool for you to go around doin' that, right?"

I explained I didn't agree with the practice, regardless of background, but I understood his point.

Ty cut to the chase. "Me and my family been called ev'ry derogatory-ass thing since we got here in June. It's worse than Mississippi up in here. And the more I tell people it ain't cool, the more it go down."

I wanted to tell Ty it wasn't all that easy being white in Iqsaiqsiq, but felt it would serve my reputation better to stay as neutral as possible.

As I exited the store I saw the three girls had curbed their appetites and now forced each cookie into their mouths, then took great effort to chew. I asked them why they didn't save any for later and received only shoulder shrugs and, "*Atchu,*" in reply.

Emma's room had been stripped bare to the walls and she told me she had put in her resignation and planned to leave Friday, at the end of the quarter. She claimed it was due to A-Team's lack of support on disciplinary matters, although since everyone else had been able to hang tough I thought that was a pretty weak excuse. She said the district would hold her teaching license for breach of contract and she would probably also receive a one year suspension from the Teaching Standards and Practices Council after that, so it would be two years before she could return to a classroom. She planned to visit her son in California, then tutor and give music lessons in Anchorage.

Stan had been one-hundred percent correct; Emma's extensive experiences in Vitus Cove had been much more of a hindrance than a help in Iqsaiqsiq. It gave me hope that Mitch would soon follow her.

Monday kicked off, literally, another raucous week of door slamming defiance and profanity-filled slurs; all punctuated by garbage cans going airborne. I set my sights on fifth period each day, a tranquil oasis after battle with the seventh graders, eighth graders, and Arnold. As a bonus I had an extra free period since Lewis was at AFN.

That afternoon A-Team informed us that the Superintendent along with other district and community leaders planned to visit the school during our scheduled in-service on Friday.

Nick inquired as to the purpose of the visit.

A-Team said he had not been told the purpose, only to be prepared to meet at 8:00 a.m.

I cornered Joanne and asked her what this meant.

Joanne was unconcerned. "Two years ago, we had a meeting with the Superintendent right after Christmas break and were threatened we would all be fired if we didn't get our collective act together. Last year we met with the Superintendent just before Christmas and he begged all of us to stay for the full year. This is a new Superintendent, so, who knows. I will guarantee one thing; those folks aren't coming out here. At the last minute there will be a so-called emergency and they will fly all of us into Aciq for this, whatever the hell it is."

Stan drove Jenn to school one morning and we chatted about Emma's now public departure and Mitch's general fucked-up-ed-ness. I also mentioned the scheduled summit.

"You realize there's no way in hell they're coming out *here*, don't you?" That was Stan's comment. "I haven't the slightest clue what this is about but mark my words young Skywalker, there will be some miasma which arises and blocks them from coming here yet, strangely, does not block you from going there.

"By the way," Stan added. "It's officially winter now. When you travel, dress like you are going to be outside for a while; hat, jacket, gloves, boots. Long underwear and insulated pants if you've got them. If that plane doesn't make it all the way to Aciq, and sometimes they don't, it will be several hours before anybody even *begins* to look for you. And you're not going to be building igloos or making flint and steel fires if you're sandwiched between the tail rudder and what's left of the cockpit with a broken pelvis."

Wednesday afternoon the staff received an email which stated that, due to Bettie Iqaluq's poor health, it was deemed necessary for the Iqsaiqsiq staff to fly into Aciq. Furthermore, due to the importance of this meeting, it was imperative that it begin promptly at 8:00 a.m. on Friday. School would be dismissed early on Thursday afternoon and the staff would spend the evening in the itinerant quarters at the district office and return Friday afternoon. Meals would be provided.

Arnold made it a point to be in class on Thursday to remind me that he would not be there on Monday, then gave me a profanity-laced send off. Jay-Boy stayed for a few minutes between classes almost as an ersatz Lewis.

"When you come back from Aciq?" asked Jay-Boy.

"Friday night."

"You mean tomorrow night?"

"Correct."

"Oh."

Then Jay-Boy said, "You tell me if you leave, yeah?"

"What do you mean?"

"If you never coming back, you tell me first, yeah?"

I extended my hand to Jay-Boy and he lightly gripped only the ends of my first three fingers, just as Jerry had. I said, "Jay-Boy, I promise not to leave for good without telling you."

Jay-Boy humored me with a smirky, "Okay," but I felt as if my handshake and words meant very little to him.

School was dismissed at 2:30 and a Frontier Flying Service twin-prop like the one I had flown on between Anchorage and Fairbanks waited on the runway.

Once airborne I surveyed the landscape.

A pure blanket of white slipped under a blue inkwell dotted with faintly-bluish flecks, and a yellow-tinged polar bear hopped from one into the murkiness; aimless yet tranquil in the ruffled swell.

My old self would have savored the inimitability of such a moment, but nine weeks in Iqsaiqsiq had left me so languished I merely closed my eyes and slept with my head against the fuselage and my hands buried deep in my pockets.

# CHAPTER FOURTEEN

Gravel kicked up against the underside of the plane as it eased down to the runway then meandered over to a simple, corrugated metal building much like the William's Air Service terminal in Fairbanks.

Various district office personnel met us inside and we filed out the door to a line of black Chevy Tahoes then made our way to the district office where another half-dozen black Chevy Tahoes were parked.

We received an abbreviated tour of the district office, at which time A-Team mysteriously disappeared, en route to a breezeway that led to a series of dorm rooms flanked by a kitchen and dining room on one side. We chose our rooms and sat down to a recently delivered feast of pizza and salad with cases of soda stacked in the fridge.

After the meal, Ben and Brenda walked to the store while Mitch simply walked.

Nick, Cornell, Belle, Joanne, and I strategized.

We concluded that our purpose in Aciq was to receive either a pat on the back or a kick in the butt. Cornell mentioned that maybe they pulled us out so they could sneak another staff in while we were all gone, as was known to happen at mines and on drilling rigs. We talked about how unlikely that was, but if it had happened I doubt we would have fought it.

Joanne added that two years previous the staff was called in for a similar meeting and guilt-tripped until they adopted an entire new curriculum for the remainder of the year, only to revert back the following year under a new Superintendent. "My guess is it will start with how lost the children are and how the school is the last great hope. Don't buy it. It's a set up. What they are saying is that every current failure in the village is the result of what the school did in the past, and every future failure will be the result of what the school is doing now. They are reinforcing their own narrative under the guise of providing enlightenment, all in a way that leaves them devoid of responsibility."

Nick, whom I had come to have a great deal of respect for, added, "We didn't ask for this meeting, they told us to be here. It's not our job to play twenty questions figuring out what they want. Let them outline their reasons for bringing us here first, if they want a solution let them figure out how to manage and pay for it, and before we commit to anything we should meet privately as a staff to discuss it."

I took a moment to perorate Nick's points. "Say nothing until we know what they want. Commit to nothing until after we have discussed it."

The four other heads nodded in agreement.

Ben and Brenda returned from the store, espressos in hand, with tales of four ounce containers of watermelon to be had for a mere $9.00, as well as the availability of bananas and grapes.

Everyone else seemed more interested in sleep so I departed for the store solo.

The Aciq store was twice the size of the Iqsaiqsiq store, with a food court and a produce section. I walked the aisles and noted that the store did in fact sell ice to Eskimoes, for $4.99 a bag. Its clothing section also sported the light, thigh-length, cotton twill and lace trimmed *qaspaqs* that I had seen many adult Native women wear, but none of the shorter men's version. Their prices began in the high $100's and rose to the mid $200's. A couple of Hondas and snowmachines were on display too. I eventually settled on a bag of four half-anemic green bell peppers for $20 and a $7 milkshake.

In addition to the cigarettes, batteries, and other items the Iqsaiqsiq store kept behind the counter; the Aciq store also secured vanilla extract, mouthwash, hair spray, and baker's yeast in a similar manner.

Miniscule pellets of ice wafted about in the air as I sipped my milkshake and walked through three inches of fine, white, powder. Back in the kitchen Nick checked out his son's Facebook page and I asked him how he got on to Facebook using the district wireless.

"The rules don't apply to the rulers," Nick professed.

I pulled out my iPhone and downloaded all of the podcasts I had missed over the last two months and surfed all of the sites I couldn't access in Iqsaiqsiq.

A-Team joined us for Friday morning's breakfast of Tang, coffee, hard-boiled eggs, and the type of big muffins sold at Costco. Free from Iqsaiqsiq's grasp, literally, he had donned a tie for the occasion. After we ate, he led us across the breezeway to a very large and very well appointed conference room. The Superintendent, a male school board member, Bettie Iqaluq, Bettie Iqaluq's interpreter, and Terri Bowen-Skeen were all there.

After introductions, the Superintendent led the charge. "I'm glad we have the opportunity to come together here today, in a spirit of cooperation, and engage in a dialogue about the challenges faced by the children placed in our care. There is much concern within the community and at the board level that the students in Iqsaiqsiq are not being shown the support and patience necessary for them to be successful."

The conversation then flowed around the table to the school board member, Bettie Iqaluq, and finally Terri Bowen-Skeen. They all used different terminology and emphasized different points but their assertion was, "Why can't you get along with the students? Why have two students been completely removed from school, and why are so many students suspended on any given day?"

"Why can't we get along with the students?" I thought. Spirit of cooperation my ass.

Joanne had read Ben and Brenda into the plan so our coterie now stood at seven, and we all adhered to the first step. My guess was that A-Team had already been asked his opinion, and delivered it, in private. That left only Mitch, who sat in a freshly acquired, thigh-length, light and dark blue zigzag patterned *qaspaq* to utter, "Wuh, Well I, I don't send any students out of my room, ever. So I don't, don't know why, why anyone has been suspended."

The Superintendent asked Mitch, "Why don't you send any students from your room?"

"I uh, I don't, they don't do anything that would, would require them to be sent out."

The Superintendent pointed to Belle. "Have you sent any students from your room?"

"Yes."

"Why?"

166

Belle described things thrown or broken and students pushed or bitten, as well as students who ran from or refused to leave the room.

The Superintendent asked Mitch if such things happened in his room and Mitch said, "No." I don't think the Superintendent realized that Belle taught elementary and Mitch taught secondary, or that Mitch was a lying sack of shit. Also Mitch had forgotten to mention that, due largely to his ineffectiveness, there had been a Battle Royal in the foyer while he "supervised" it exactly one week ago, as well as the "accidental" destruction of a computer in his first period class earlier in the year.

The Superintendent moved on to Cornell and Cornell described the soda issue, the headphone issue, doors slammed, garbage cans kicked, profanity, apathy, defiance, destruction of property, and things being thrown at him.

The Superintendent asked Belle if she dealt with such issues and she described some, then he asked Mitch.

Mitch again said, "No."

The Superintendent asked Mitch why he thought other teachers had these problems while he didn't and Mitch said, "I choose my battles more astutely than my colleagues. I don't enforce that draconian policy on soda and headphones."

The Superintendent went around the rest of the room and everyone else matched either Belle's or Cornell's version. Nick went last and added that he felt the majority of students, after some initial resistance, had reigned in their behavior somewhat, and had made more academic progress this year than the previous year. He also clarified that Tim was being homeschooled, while Olivia had been removed only after she assaulted a staff member. Nick said, "It is at Principal Atkinson's request that each student has to receive at least three verbal warnings before being sent from the room." Then he turned to A-Team. "Correct?"

A-Team clarified that the three verbal warnings were a minimum, not an absolute rule, but, yes, each student was given at least verbal three warnings before being sent from the room. He added that typically students were given a detention the first time they were sent to the office and had to be sent to the office twice in a given day before being suspended, which meant that a student received a total of at least six warnings per day before a suspension was enacted.

Then Nick added, "I believe the policy on soda and headphones is school-wide and if a teacher allows them, they are acting outside of policy, correct?"

A-Team said that was a building issue and would be addressed at a later time, and in a different venue.

Nick addressed the command staff. "Kids need consistency and it makes it hard for them when they hear one thing from one source and a different thing from another."

Had Nick been thirty years younger I think he would have added, "Just sayin'."

There was some talk amongst the command staff and Bettie Iqaluq's interpreter said, "Bettie wants to know why you think it's important for students not to drink soda?"

"Really?" I wanted to say, "You fly us in here to talk not about threats, or profanity, or property damage, not even about academic progress, but about soda? Really?" But we had a plan and I thought it was best if we stick to it.

Nick indicated for Cornell to take the lead and he explained the prevalence of consumption over the last two years as well as the many ancillary problems, and also how, now that it had been more or less suppressed, it was less of a day to day issue.

Terri Bowen-Skeen waded in. "Food in our culture is seen differently than in the Western world. For so long, food was not a given or guarantee the way it is now. That is why we do not try to deny, or dissuade, our children from eating or drinking when they are hungry or thirsty."

Cornell highlighted that students were still allowed to eat and drink during breaks, just not in the classrooms. Belle added that the school provided breakfast and lunch to all students free of charge.

Terri Bowen-Skeen made an addendum, "It is also seen as disrespectful not to eat or drink something when it is available. That animal gave up its life, or that berry gave up all the water and sun it had absorbed, so that you could enjoy it and be nourished by it."

Belle, in her Southern manner declared, "That's all well and goo-ood, but we're not talkin' loaves and fishes, were talkin' 'bout soda pop, and *Her*-shey bawr's."

Terri Bowen-Skeen replied, "Food is food, and a meal is a meal, it's about appreciating what you have been provided."

Ben jumped the fence and offered up his description of how Brenda had gotten sprayed with Pepsi.

"That sounds like an isolated incident," said the school board member.

I had the go from Nick and Joanne so I added my story of receiving the better part of Tim-Tim's Pepsi mid-chest. "It doesn't seem very much like appreciation for what he has been given if he is throwing it at someone or spraying people with it," I added.

Everyone else in the coterie seemed to have a story of food, or pseudo-food, being thrown, smeared, or spat, as well as sizable portions of school lunches that had been discarded.

Bettie, who now conveniently did not address the misuse of soda at all even though she had raised it initially, said through her interpreter, "Maybe the kids don't like that kind of food and that's why they throw it away. If the school provided food they like better, then it wouldn't get thrown away. The school should serve more Native foods like whale and caribou, and not all, this… white-type food, like beans and peas."

Joanne waded into the fray. "So which is it? Is all food equal or is there a hierarchy. If there is a hierarchy, what is wrong with saying, 'You can have all the crackers and fruit you like, but not any chocolate or cookies?'"

"We want children to have that option and that opportunity to make those choices as individuals, instead of being bound by only what is available, or allowed," answered Terri.

Mitch piped in with, "It. It doesn't, it shouldn't. Shouldn't. It shouldn't matter if there is a hierarchy or not. It's not our job from the outside, to, for, to, to set policy for," and then Mr. Kindred Spirit himself dropped two of the most divisive words in the human language, "You people."

The school board member sprang from his chair Tim Kala'a style and I think the Superintendent may have shit himself just a little.

I was as close to happy as I had been in weeks because; a) Mitch was about to get punched, and b) I was there to see it.

Mitch had his trademark blank stare going for a while before he realized that he was the subject of dissention, then stammered, "I'm sorry. I'm. No. I meant. I'm sorry I meant that we have no right to tell, tell…"

The school board member sat back down and growled, "Listen! Listen, to, me. Are you listening? We are not, 'you people,' or, 'those people.' We are the Inupiat. Now say, 'We have no right to tell the Inupiat what to do."

Mitch said, "I'm sorry, I didn't mean you people like…"

The school board member leaned forward in his chair and growled again, "Listen! Listen, to, me. Are you listening? I'm not asking you, I am telling you. Now say, 'We have no right to tell the Inupiat what to do.'"

I wished I knew Matt Kala'a's phone number so I could call him and say, "Hey, guess what? There's a bully over here in Aciq. You better get over here and take care of this bully, being that bullying is one of your vital concerns and all." Instead I just watched Mitch try to remember and repeat the eleven words as the school board member had asked.

Mitch began, "I'm sorry I told the Inupiat people what to do," which even the school board member I think realized was about as close as he was going to get.

Belle was the next one to step in the honey-bucket. "Would y'all prefer that we serve whale and caribou instead of…"

"So since we're Native we should only get to eat whale and caribou," roared the school board member.

"That's not what I say-uhd, Bettie was the first one that mentioned serving whale and caribou instead of peas and beans. What concerns me is that the stu-dents should eat at breakfast and luh-nch and not walk around with pockets full uh candy all day-uh." I could tell when Belle finished speaking that she would remain silent because, as she always did, she folded her hands and put them in her lap.

"That's part of our heritage, having, just having it. For so long scarcity was the rule, which is why now we want our children to have, whether it's in their bellies, their mouths, their hands, or their pockets." Terri said.

I knew from my own research that European whalers had introduced an influenza epidemic to the Alaskan Arctic in the 1890's, which brought about severe starvation as a result of most household providers dying off. As a result, I could understand why someone like Bettie would have been raised with the belief of scarcity as a rule. But I thought that a past marked with scarcity led to compulsive conservation such as my grandparents' neighbor, Rabbi Geldberg, practiced. He had survived the Holocaust and ended every meal, even breakfast, with the proclamation, "Save what's left, we'll use it for soup," even though his closets were stacked with canned vegetables and fruit. In any case, Terri and the school board member, not to mention all of the students in Iqsaiqsiq and all of their parents, had come of age as dividend cash, food stamps, and charitable donations poured into the villages. Ultimately something told me that food, and especially soda, was either a smokescreen for, or a symptom of, a larger condition.

Brenda, under the misconception that the ultimate goal was a collaborative discussion in the interest of a productive resolution, took up the flag and ran for a while. "I don't believe this is your intent; but it sounds to me like you're saying is that even though two meals are served at the school every day and the village is awash with Quest cards (food stamps) and dividend cash, you are still afraid that children are going hungry, and you allow this fear to manipulate you into saying that any behavior resulting from or connected to food is justified. So I have to ask, would you approve of teachers not teaching a single thing, as long as the kids could eat whatever and whenever they like?"

"No," said the Superintendent sharply.

"Yes," said Bettie's interpreter as Bettie nodded her head approvingly, as if to say, "Good for you, you understand perfectly."

"Do both. You get paid to do both, not just one, so do both," barked the school board member authoritatively.

"How can they learn without being warm and fed?" asked Terri, not fully addressing the question.

Brenda said, "They are warm and fed, no one is starving at Iqsaiqsiq School. As Belle said, we have lunch and breakfast programs. But the students become pre-occupied with whatever extra food or drink they bring with them, and that becomes their focus instead of the lesson."

Brenda, wisely, took a moment to compose her next volley. "If teachers, parents, or other adults don't dissuade the child from eating when they are hungry, then who or what does dissuade them?"

Terri seemed perplexed; not by the content of the question, but that someone would ask the question at all since the answer was so obvious and fundamental. "No one, nothing, and no one or nothing should. If a child is hungry, then they should eat."

"Always?" asked Brenda.

"Yes, always." Terri nodded her head. The school board member and Bettie also nodded heavily in agreement.

Brenda did her best to clarify. "Always, day or night, regardless of what else is or isn't going on?"

"Yes," said Terri with a smile, "Don't you?"

"No," said Brenda, "I have a schedule because I have other things I need to get done. I plan and stagger my meals throughout the day. I have breakfast, I go to work where I also have lunch, at the end of the day I have a snack then grade papers and make copies until I go home and have dinner."

I think Brenda expected some type of Eureka moment to register on the command staffs faces. When none materialized, she pushed onward. "What keeps them from just eating all of the time?"

"Their bodies, they respond to their bodies. They feel hungry, they eat. They stop eating when they're full." Terri said matter-of-factly.

I couldn't articulate a good counterpoint to Terri's opinion, but something about the time I saw Jay-Boy guzzle three consecutive Pepsis, or the little girls in the store's *quniciuq* force themselves to deliberately chew every last Nilla wafer, made Terri's argument less than cogent.

Apparently Brenda could not articulate a good counterpoint either, so she temporarily conceded and moved to a slightly different topic. "When you say you don't want them to be bound by what is available or allowed, then what are they bound by?"

"Their own preferences, their own desires. They have it, they want to use it or eat it, and they do." Terri added again, "Don't you?"

"No," said Brenda, "I make a rational decision that weighs the costs and benefits, take into account all of the potential outcomes, look at the best option overall, and choose it. I make decisions about food and when and where to eat with my mind, not my stomach."

"So, since you don't do whatever you want all the time, and our kids always get to do what they want, you think that your way is better? That you're a better person than our kids" said the school board member.

Brenda looked a little dumbfounded. "I am no better, or no worse, than the students, but I am capable of making better decisions…"

"She thinks she's better than all of us because she can make better decisions." The school board member said self-righteously.

"You said, 'Kids,' and I said, 'Students,' do not twist this suddenly into, 'All of us.' My point is, I make decisions and I endure the consequences. Sometimes my decisions turn out well, and I repeat those choices. Sometimes my decisions turn out poorly, and I make changes in my behavior. In any case I may not control the circumstances, but I do control the decisions I make under those circumstances."

I hadn't wanted to hug anyone so much since I had eaten the *maqtaq* a few weeks prior.

Bettie made a "shoo-shoo" motion with both of her hands and her interpreter said, "Bettie says get this woman out, out of here, this woman doesn't know what she's talking about. She doesn't want, doesn't want to be with Eskimoes, she's jealous... of our children having so much, so much more than what the teachers have."

The school board member looked at the Superintendent and said, "Yes, get her out of here. We don't need to listen to her put us down, and put our kids down."

The Superintendent looked at A-Team as Brenda stood and grabbed her coat.

A-Team held his hand up to Brenda and said, "Wait," then directed his attention toward the Superintendent, "My entire staff was required to travel here and attend this meeting, not just one individual. If you would like to dismiss my entire staff, you may, but no individual will be singled out."

I wanted to group hug Brenda and A-Team both.

The command staff looked at the Superintendent and the school board member bellowed, "Who's in charge of this thing? You or him?"

A-Team and the Superintendent held a sidebar in the hallway. When they returned the Superintendent told Brenda to leave while A-Team stood silently.

Already across the fence, Ben turned around and pissed on it, fully aware and not at all concerned that it was electrified. He looked directly at Bettie, "Did her words bother you?" and to Terri, "Are you as bothered by it as she is?" and finally to the school board member, "I'm really surprised you're bothered at all, but I guess you must be one of those guys that gets bothered all of the time."

The school board member came out of his chair again and I was ready to throw Mitch in front of Ben as a shield. Terri, Bettie, and Bettie's interpreter all looked appropriately aghast.

The Superintendent hadn't reacted to Ben's remarks but after he saw the command staff's reaction he told Ben, "Get out. We'll talk later!"

Bettie's interpreter said, "Bettie says you are a disgraceful person, that a person should show more respect, and she is, sad, that such, a person such as yourself would be a teacher, person that teaches children without respect…"

The interpreter said "person" but it sounded to me like Bettie said, "Sick cook, *tuniq-siq*, sick-otch cook-otch, *tuniq*, lick luck, *tuniq.*"

Ben paused, just like Solomon would have, and since he was an equal opportunist, took a dig at the Superintendent, "I'm gonna go outside with my wife while she smokes my *quaaq*, you wanna come smoke my *quaaq* too?"

"Leave," the Superintendent sneered forcefully, which almost made me chuckle because within the last three minutes he had shown himself to be the Vienna Boys Choir of leadership.

Ben had absorbed a little too much of the local flavor and slammed the door.

Had I been in charge I would have let everybody have five minutes to go take a walk, grab a smoke, or stare at the wall. Hell, maybe even kick a filing cabinet. But Superintendent Custer of the Vienna Boys Choir brigade pushed us all deeper into the racially tainted and distrustful morass.

The command staff bantered back and forth about how disappointed they were. First, for the original reasons we had all been brought to Aciq. Second, for our disagreement with their assertion that we were unfit and unfair teachers. Third, that Brenda had the unmitigated gall to suggest that their children were anything less than perfect in their organic state. And finally, that Ben was so creepily vulgar, although not a single one of them ever clarified why his use of the word *bother* was inappropriate.

I stared out the window and saw Ben and Brenda pass a cigarette back and forth. In a way Brenda had spoken truth to power, just like Solzhenitsyn, and now stood banished on the tundra, just like Solzhenitsyn. As for Ben, based on his rapid adoption of so many Iqsaiqsiq customs, I wondered how long it would be until he threw a snowball at the window.

Joanne restated Brenda's point more softly about a difference between those who evaluate their circumstances versus those who yield to them, but feathers began to ruffle on both sides so she let it drop.

Mitch jumped in with a few words of support for the command staff's narrative, but in reality he was so isolated from the rest of the staff on a daily basis he couldn't really tell them what any of the rest of us did, or why. Then he randomly mentioned his purchase of a new snowmachine at the Aciq store and inquired if they knew anyone who could ride it out to Iqsaiqsiq for him.

The Superintendent gave him a flummoxed look like, "Are you fucking high?"

After one too many, "All the teachers," generalizations I hopped in with, "You realize not all the teachers are here today?"

There was discussion of the exiled ones. I clarified that it still wasn't the whole list. I told them that Emma Rudd, a veteran bush teacher with almost twenty years of experience, had quit and how a student had asked her on the first day if she, "Fucked on the couch," which I felt was certainly a form of gender-biased harassment some might even construe as a threat of sexual violence.

Terri told me, "We don't consider that a vulgar term, it's just a natural, bodily function. Eat, breath, spit, go to the bathroom, have sex, our culture is much more open about those things than other cultures are."

I told Terri, "The student wasn't talking about himself or some third party; he was addressing a fifty year-old woman directly, and he didn't say, 'Have sex,' he said, 'Fuck.'"

The school board member offered up his suggestion. "Then maybe next time you could ask him not to use that word but use the word 'sex' instead, if it makes you uncomfortable. That's the job of all the teachers, to teach the kids, not just send them away because they make them feel uncomfortable. It's the teachers who should be trying to make the students comfortable, not the way you want it."

I felt the circumstances completely warranted me to expand on Ben's "bothering" monologue, especially since it had now been stated that it was just another thing that people did, but being the master of my fate and not a victim of circumstance I consciously chose not to. Besides, Bettie was about the same age as my own mother and I never could have insulted her in such a vulgar way, but exercising that restraint was part of my own cultural bias.

I decided to make one more statement and let it stand as a concise and honorable epitaph for Emma's career and, as far as I knew, possibly my own. "If a sixteen year-old male student feels it is okay to ask a fifty year-old female teacher about fucking, the remedy for that behavior goes beyond modifying word choice."

One of the secretaries came in and told the Superintendent about lunch and the next outbound flight.

Mitch offered up his opinions, which mirrored exactly what the school board member had said. The command staff prattled, just as Joanne had predicted, about how the school was the backbone of the community and since the teachers weren't doing a very good job the entire community would probably suffer, but completely avoided any mention of parental or community responsibility or involvement.

From there the conversation switched to chairs and seating charts, some talk about locker and computer privileges, and finally to Belle's "egregious" use of force on Solomon, though with no mention of Solomon's nine utterances of the n-word. I chose to hold my tongue and perseverate on the twenty-three days that remained on my calendar.

The secretary came back and the Superintendent announced that we were dismissed for lunch. We had another round of pizza, salad, and soda; which, I began to feel, may have been the highpoint of any Aciq visit. One slice into it the secretary relayed another message about the flight and the Superintendent quickly ushered the Iqsaiqsiq staff, which once again included Ben and Brenda, back into the conference room.

The Superintendent railed against all of us for not, "Cooperating," more with the process he had tried to facilitate.

Mitch feebly inserted that he agreed with what the command staff had proclaimed and the Superintendent snapped, "Next time you're in a meeting like this, don't talk about snowmachines. Got it!"

The Superintendent continued to denigrate us for our poor representation of the district as well as the teaching profession in general and said that he wanted to tell each of us individually about the exact manner in which we had failed to meet his expectations but, unfortunately, he had another important engagement. Apparently the implosion of Iqsaiqsiq School was small potatoes compared to other issues on the Superintendent's schedule. He said A-Team had been given a project for us to complete, then excused himself.

As A-Team explained the task we were to complete I saw the command staff walk to their vehicles in the parking lot, each with a couple of pizza boxes and a 12-pack of soda.

"The task for each of you is to type at least a thousand words describing what you believe the most important points of this morning's conference were as well as how you intend to address those points when you return to Iqsaiqsiq. Do not be flippant or sarcastic;

address legitimate concerns with viable strategies. When you are done email it to me."

The whole thing sounded suspiciously close to the plot line of *The Breakfast Club,* but I kept that opinion to myself.

"Whu-uht time does ow-uhr fuh-light leave?" asked Cornell.

"Nine o'clock," replied A-Team.

Belle checked her watch. "That's awfully luh-ate."

"Nine o'clock, Saturday morning," A-Team clarified.

"So why was the secretary talking about flight times?" asked Joanne.

"The Superintendent is attending a conference in Chicago on Monday, he is leaving today," A-Team said.

"But today is only Friday," Joanne noted.

A-Team didn't verbalize further but the transformation of his normally stolid demeanor already expressed his own level of frustration with the Superintendent.

We retrieved our laptops and gorged on salad, which had barely been touched, while Ben was called in to speak with A-Team.

# CHAPTER FIFTEEN

Friday evening Ben told the coterie how his meeting with A-Team had gone down. "First he wanted to know why I thought the school board member and the three ladies got so upset, I said I had no idea. He doesn't know and I'm not going to tell him. I don't think any of them will ever tell him either. He recognized my use of the Inupiat word for smoke because he had dealt with students for the same reason, but even if I had asked the Superintendent to step out for a smoke it would have been out of line. I had to agree with him there. A-Team says the Superintendent is moving toward firing me and I should contact the union to fight it, but screw it, what's the worst that happens? I get out of Iqsaiqsiq?"

Cornell was glad none of the command staff called Ben out on his use of the word *bother* but wondered why they hadn't since it could have gotten him fired immediately.

Nick answered. "If they admit that it's a euphemism, then they can't hide behind its ambiguity either. I bet if you read all of the transcripts from various school and community meetings they would be filled with references to teachers, Troopers, politicians, and health care workers who bother other people. It's not worth losing all that power just to expel someone they can simply withhold next year's contract from."

After another meal of fresh pizza, fresh salad, and newly acquired soda, I used the phone in the conference room to place a call to Jenn. I told her I didn't know Jay-Boy's phone number or even where he lived but asked her to please try and let him know that I would not be back until Saturday.

Just to humor me, I think, Jenn placed the phone over the speaker of the VHF radio at their house and said, "Good evening, good evening. Good evening Iqsaiqsiq."

A tiny little girls voice came on and said, "Good evening Miss Jenn."

Jenn said, "Good evening Athena, I'm looking for Jay-boy."

An unidentified and unrecognized adult female voice came on and barked, "Who this what's looking for Jay-Boy?"

Jenn responded, "Mr. Shosatori wants to let Jay-Boy know he won't be back until tomorrow."

Jay-Boy's voice came on next, "Good evening Miss Jenn, okay. I copy."

Jenn picked the phone back up and said, "Better than a text message, huh?"

"And equally as cryptic to the uninitiated," I said, "Thank you Jenn, good bye."

"You're welcome Ken, good bye."

Joanne finagled a set of keys for a Tahoe and the Aciq school gym. She and Brenda pounded the treadmills into submission while I tossed four plates on the Olympic bar and Ben kicked a soccer ball against the wall, although I think he envisioned it as something else.

We stopped at the other Aciq store on the way back and bought juice and popsicles. Back in the Tahoe Joanne broke out with, "You may not be impressed with A-Team right now, but he's the only principal I've ever seen not bend over for a Superintendent. At times I feel he is way too lenient on the students, but he is the best Bush principal I've ever worked for and I think it's in our best interest to support him as much as we can."

The only criticism Ben and Brenda had of A-Team was his tolerance of Mitch. Neither of them had any animosity toward A-Team for the actions he had to take that day. "In fact," said Ben, "I would rather work for someone who is overly-rigid, but consistent, than someone who is very compassionate but from whom I don't know what to expect."

"Speaking of consistency," I said, "Are we all in agreement that the Superintendent is a chronically-habitually-gutless-invertebrate who would prostitute his own mother to save himself even the slightest bit of ridicule?"

We cast our votes through a series of whoops, claps, fist bumps, and high fives. The decision was unanimous. Joanne also led us into a sacred pact that none of us would ever waste our urine to extinguish the Superintendent were he found to be in a state of combustion

"How about after the flames have subsided?" asked Ben.

"Then let it rip," said Joanne.

Saturday we had another "breakfast" of muffins and hard boiled eggs. We sat at the airport from 8:00 a.m. to 5:00 p.m. and waited for the weather to clear, which it never did, then returned to the dorms but were told we were on our own for dinner. Mitch announced his intent to take in the local Bingo game. We sat around and Cornell made a joke about ordering room service. Eventually we had food delivered from the other restaurant in Aciq, Chinese, which came to almost $30 a person. Out of pure orneriness we retreated back to the conference room and its stitched leather chairs to eat it.

Ben, Brenda, Belle, and Cornell left for another walk, while Nick, Joanne and I reclined in the conference room. I had something I needed to say.

"You know what a drift factor is?" I asked. Nick knew. Joanne did not. "In aviation, it's the amount of variability or irregularity something has. A low drift factor is good, very stable, very consistent. A high drift factor is bad, erratic, unpredictable. Iqsaiqsiq is the epitome of a high drift factor, it leaves no margin of error. That being said, Ben's drift factor is set beyond what I'm comfortable with. I'm afraid someday he may put us all into the deck, hard."

Joanne said she thought I was being a little too critical of Ben, that during her three years at Iqsaiqsiq he was more toward the positive than the negative side overall of teachers she had worked with, and that if anyone had a 'drift factor' it was Mitch.

Nick explained that Mitch actually had a low drift factor because he could be counted on to fuck up, which made him predictable and reliable yet useless. Nick also felt that Ben was far from terrible, he had just had a bad day.

I told them my greatest concern was that I felt Jerry told me about *bothering* to try and help me out, and smooth things over, not so we as teachers could go around and insult other people. I thought that we should try and communicate with one another so we didn't have to reinvent the wheel individually, but I had to trust that Ben wouldn't lose it again and just blurt out shit. Especially shit that might be traced back to me and damage my relationship with Jerry.

Joanne said, "The teaching staff in a Bush village is not the Olympic symbol, it's a hula-hoop. There is only one circle, one loop, and when you decide who is in or out, including yourself, you need to realize it is binary; there is no third or fourth option. I see your concern, and share it, but we and you are a thousand times better off with Ben in rather than out. Actually, we are god damn lucky to have over half of our staff mostly on the same page; extremely, god damn, lucky."

Nick concurred, but added that in the future if there were things I wanted to keep private or exclusive due to Ben's behavior, he felt it was okay because, "When a fella tells an old woman to go buttfuck herself, he's gotta realize that he's giving up some level of moral authority."

I leaned back and took a nice long stretch. "The Superintendent won't do anything that jeopardizes his current or future six-figure salary. The rest of the command staff won't acknowledge that they, the community, or the parents have any responsibility other than to say, 'We support education.' The students think we're there just to make life miserable for them. A-Team is awesome, but if we openly acknowledge that he loses his appearance of impartiality. I guess it looks like we're it. If anything's going to change or get better it's up to the seven of us, plus maybe whoever comes in to replace Emma, since Mitch is a fuck-up."

"A kindred fuck-up," Nick corrected me and we all laughed.

I told them I was going to make a phone call on the big office phone on the table and they were welcome to listen in. I called Jenn and she passed my message along the VHF until it reached Jay-Boy. Then Joanne stayed and called John while Nick and I retreated to our room.

Joanne came back into the dorms. Nick had a twinkle in his eye and a slip of paper with a phone number on it. He put away his laptop and motioned for me to follow him.

"What's up?" I asked.

"Are you up for some *malicious* mischief?"

"Hell yeah!"

We went back to the conference room. Nick used his calling card, which concealed the source number, called the hotel in Chicago where the conference was being held, and asked to speak to the Superintendent. It was about 10:00 p.m. in Alaska so it was 1:00 a.m. in Chicago. Still the Superintendent took the call.

Nick disguised his voice in the slow, guttural manner of the school board member. "Listen! Listen, to, me. Are you listening? I'm still pretty fucking pissed off about what happened at that meeting today. Are you still pissed off?"

The Superintendent said he was upset, and he understood why the school board member was upset, but wouldn't say that he was, "Pissed off."

"How *come* you're not pissed off? I'm pissed off. You should be pissed off too," Nick bellowed.

Finally the Superintendent relented that he was also, "Pissed off."

Nick ranted on about everything that had pissed him off, then he asked the Superintendent why he, himself, was pissed off. The Superintendent replied that he was pissed off for all of the same reasons as the school board member.

"Hey. *Heeey!* Those are *my* reasons for being pissed off. How *come* you steal my reasons for being pissed off. Go get your own reasons for being pissed off *tuniq!*" Nick grunted.

The Superintendent said that he sincerely wanted to address the school board member's concerns, but perhaps now was not the best time.

"How *come?*" asked Nick, "What are you doing? Are you watching those naked woman movies in your hotel room? Whenever times I go Anchorage I watch those naked woman movies in my hotel room."

The Superintendent said again that he would prefer to continue this conversation at a later time.

"What are you eating?" asked Nick.

"Nothing, I'm not eating anything right now. I was asleep when you called," said the Superintendent.

Nick asked why the Superintendent had been asleep and the Superintendent explained the time difference, that it was late and he was tired, and please could they continue the conversation some other time.

"What did you have to eat tonight?" asked Nick.

"Chicken wings and French fries."

"How *come* you never eat whale or caribou, don't you like Eskimo food?"

"I like Eskimo food very much, they don't serve it at the hotel though."

"How *come* they don't serve it at the hotel? Listen! Listen, to, me. Are you listening? You tell them they need to serve Native food at that hotel. You gonna do that? You do that! You tell them!"

I finally had to give Nick the cut sign and he held up his finger as if for one more minute. Then he said, "Listen! Listen, to, me. Are you listening? This one teacher, Forman, you know Forman? That guy what was wearing that woman's coat today? I don't like any of them other teachers but I like Forman. He and I are kindred spirits. He told me he need his snowmachine in Iqsaiqsiq. You get his snowmachine to Iqsaiqsiq?"

The Superintendent explained that a snowmachine was private property and not educationally relevant and Mitch would have to find a way of getting the snowmachine to Iqsaiqsiq himself.

"Not relevant! Don't you know anything about Eskimoes? Every man needs a snowmachine. How else Forman going to take kids hunting? Listen! Listen, to, me. Are you listening?" Nick motioned for me to cover my ears, "You! Get! Forman's! Snowmachine! To! Iqsaiqsiq! I don't care if you have to ride it there yourself! Forman needs his snowmachine! I call Forman tomorrow to make sure he has his snowmachine. Do it! Or you're fired!"

Nick hung up the phone and we stifled our laughter until we were completely out of that room, then let it burst out interminably. I finally had to sit down on the floor to catch my breath. I told Nick, "You realize if the Superintendent follows through and sends it out there we have just inadvertently done Mitch the biggest favor of his life?"

Nick shook his head. "The Superintendent isn't going to send Mitch's snowmachine out there. It would cost a thousand dollars on the regular cargo flight and probably three thousand to have it sent by itself immediately. The Superintendent isn't going to front that kind of cash out of his own pocket; and if he spends district money, it's criminal. But he is going to be up half the night worrying about what to do, how to do it, and what the repercussions will be. And then he is going to be on Mitch's ass twice as much because of it. If anything, he will find a way to sink Mitch ASAP so he doesn't have to deal with this shit anymore."

Sunday morning. More muffins. No hard boiled eggs left. We went to the airport at 8:00 a.m. and sat and waited. A twin-prop plane was on the runway, but it was a cargo plane without any windows, just a wide double door on one side. About 10:00 the agent took a call and handed the phone to A-Team. A-Team still had a Tahoe parked outside and he left with Mitch for about thirty minutes. At 11:00 a truck arrived with a snowmachine on the back. The snowmachine was lifted off of the truck and into the cargo plane. A little after 1:00 p.m. the Frontier Flying Service plane arrived and we all got on board.

The cargo plane landed in Iqsaiqsiq right after we did and Mitch rode away on the snowmachine.

I walked to school and scrambled to get just enough rap material ready for Monday, then stopped by Emma's room to meet the new guy. His name was Pat Scheue and he had retired from teaching a few years earlier. He looked relatively healthy for a man in his late fifties and confessed that he used to work as a river guide in the summer, but had since reinvented himself as an avid gardener and model railroad builder.

I didn't know exactly how to wedge in what little wisdom I had gained over the past nine weeks so I just parted my lips and disgorged it all over the table. "I am not trying to scare or discourage you, but I would bet that tomorrow you have something thrown at you, get challenged to a fight, and get cussed out and disparaged. I don't know how to put it any more delicately because there just isn't anything delicate about this place."

"I know," Pat said with little affect. "When I was contacted to take this job, the phrase 'challenging environment' kept popping up and it made me want to laugh because when I was a special education teacher that was the phrase I always substituted for 'miserable fiasco.' Another thing I know is that people only leave mid-year for two reasons, they're fired or they just can't hack it. This woman was not fired because, had she been, she would have left this place a mess. Instead, it is impeccable. She made a deliberate, well-planned, effort to leave here and it was neither hasty nor out of spite. It's obvious to me that this woman had some real skill, and still got chased off."

"Dude, you're like a detective. I'm gonna call you CSI Iqsaiqsiq."

"Cool, when do Marg Helgenberger and Emily Procter show up?"

I had to laugh. "They don't, that's part of what makes it Iqsaiqsiq."

I swung into the gym for a spin-bike session where Ben took shots on a goal that always rejected them.

We made some small talk about the phonetic similarity of our names and I suggested that someday we could hit the road as, "Ben, Ken, and the search for Zen."

Ben half-chuckled, then shook his head, and fell solemn.

By the time he spoke again his voice had lost all sentiment, like he wanted to stifle a laugh, or maybe tears. "I'm in way over my head here. I never intended to be a teacher. When Brenda got hired I applied to be a cook or maybe a janitor, but since I had a degree I was offered that program to get certified. Now I don't know who the bigger fool was; them for offering, or me for accepting. I lost it in Aciq, but if I hadn't of gone off I would still feel like shit for keeping my mouth shut. It's like an endless string of, 'Damned if you do, damned if you don't,' situations and the worst part is we all have to face it stone-cold sober while the locals drink themselves stupid."

I would have been willing to place a wager on what Ben would say next and, as it turned out, I would have been correct.

"Brenda and I are out of here at Christmas. We'll have our mortgage deficit covered and then we can move in with her folks. I don't care if we both have to work eighty hours a week at fuckin' Target." Ben fumed out a sigh.

I didn't know if Ben wanted support or sympathy, but with twenty-one days until my own potential exodus I couldn't offer either. I was about to pass off my standard line of, "I can respect that," but reconsidered and said, "You ever see on *The Flintstones* where somebody stubs their toe, and for some reason they don't want to scream so they stick their head in a mailbox and it, like, holds the scream in there until the next day when the mailman opens it up?"

Ben was rightfully wary of a grown man who used cartoon metaphors, but nodded his head in the affirmative nonetheless.

I rested my hands on the spin-bike. "This spin-bike is my mailbox, and riding it is my way of letting out my frustration in a way that no one hears me. If I tried to carry this frustration day-after-day eventually I would drop some of it and either break down, lash out, or run off. This village seems to embrace two things; watching others suffer, and fabricating excuses that shed responsibility away from themselves. I guess in a way I'm being 'stingy' as the kids would say, because I refuse to provide anyone with either the satisfaction of seeing me suffer or a convenient excuse for their own failures."

Ben tilted his head and said, "That's great for you, but I don't *do* physical. I only started playing soccer because Brenda was on the intramural team, and I come in here and kick around because it has the least likelihood of injury."

"Do you have any kind of hobby?"

"Yeah!" said Ben, "Brewing beer! And drinking it!" Ben went from a righteous laugh to a forced, "Ha, ha, ha," and finally sank back to sorrow. "Neither of which I can do here."

"Anything else?" I asked.

"We've got a bread maker, Brenda's big into that, and TV of course, which we pay out the ass for. I get your point though; model airplanes, stamp collecting."

"Maybe it doesn't have to be physical, but something that you can *lose* yourself in."

A glimmer that had disappeared around Labor Day reappeared in his eye as he made his way to the door.

Monday morning Mitch donned his *qaspaq* and rode his snowmachine the thousand or so feet from the quad-plex to the school but the student's response was not, "Wow Mr. Forman, cool snowmachine!" it was, "Fan cooled? So junk fan cooled snowmachine you got." Other students openly shunned him for his hubristic opulence.

The cafeteria was packed full for breakfast as well as lunch, but attendance dwindled from that point on.

Arnold hung out at the door with the rest of the students before fourth period then said, "My parents called Saturday. When the bank opens today they can get the money to buy our tickets for Fairbanks. I gotta be at home in case they call," and left before the bell rang.

Jay-Boy had a new joke for the new quarter. "Why does tissue dance?"

"Why?" I asked.

"'Cause it's filled with lots of boogies."

Lewis was still gone and Ben came in at 2:30 to help me debug some new software he had installed recently. It took longer than the whole period and after the dismissal bell Jay-Boy stopped by, as had become his habit, to download all of the day's raps to his iPod.

I slipped-up when I told Ben, "Thanks Solzhenitsyn," as we now referred to him and Brenda as the Solzhenitsyn Twins.

Jay-Boy asked, "Who's sewed-our-knees-on?"

Ben looked bewildered because he didn't grasp Jay-Boy's intonation. I said, "He was a guy who went to prison and wrote a book about it."

"Like Tupac Shakur?" asked Jay-Boy.

"Sort of," I said.

"Oh," said Jay-Boy.

After Jay-Boy finished his downloads and left Ben said, "Sewed-our-knees-on, it was more like sawed-our-knees-off."

Lewis returned Tuesday attired in new sneakers, new hoody, and new baseball cap.

"How was AFN?" I asked him.

"Good."

"What was your favorite thing?"

"H2Oasis."

"Oh."

I later found out that H2Oasis was an indoor waterpark in Anchorage mostly avoided by locals but heavily frequented by villagers from all across the state.

Pat had a steady flow of students sent or escorted from his room, but no more than I or anyone else had our first week. He got ridiculed by Solomon, just as I did, defied by Rachel and Tim-Tim, just as I did, and challenged by Arnold. But he never raised his voice unnecessarily or ridiculed them. Interestingly, Rocky never once lost it in Pat's room.

I even noticed a few times when Pat turned out the lights and had all of the students put their heads down on their desks. Initially it was a disaster, but eventually it became an accepted routine. He also had a script that he read before he turned the lights back on. I never caught the whole thing, but it ended with, "…three, two, one, resume."

On Friday I invited Pat to our DVD extravaganza and he offered to be the host so we went to the store together to amass an empty-calorie ensemble. The bulletin board in the *quniciuq* was plastered in a mosaic of handwritten flyers. They all offered something for sale:

For Sale: new rear shock, fits Polaris RMK 600, $750, call Junior VHF 15.

For Sale: new 12-piece Pots and Pans with Lids, $60, call Alice 2543.

For Sale: new Blu-Ray player, $100, call Raymond 2511.

I explained that since village phone numbers had only one prefix, people typically only spoke or listed the last four digits.

As an inside joke for Nick, I persuaded Pat to buy hot wings and curly fries. When we got to the counter I introduced Pat to Ty. After the pleasantries Ty said, "So have y'all heard yet?"

"Heard what?" I asked.

"I told David he need to get his boy in line, stop pickin' on little Croesus every single damn day. He asks me, 'Or what's gonna happen?' I tell him I'm not gonna touch his boy, 'cause he's a child and that's not my place, but if Solomon don't let up I'm gonna open the whoop ass on David. So now David is trying to get me arrested for harassment *and* get me fired since the village is the one what owns this store. All that shit David and his kin heap on everybody else, but first thing he do is go to the Troopers. I don't care no how though. I had enough of this place up in here."

On the way back to the school I explained the politics of David being mayor as well as a bootlegger, along with the shooting three weeks prior, Solomon being a general shithead, or *anuq*head, and how it perplexed me that a community, which benefitted greatly from and so fiercely touted equality and the abolition of racial prejudice and stereotypes, freely denigrated others.

"Don't try to make too much sense out of a senseless situation. Remember; come what may, May will come," said Pat.

"Awe, student you are, of Roby Wan Kenobi, the Jedi Master, I see."

"Or perhaps, Master I am, of all things Jedi."

"Yoda speaking, good yours is, perhaps no girlfriend, you have."

Pat laughed. "Girlfriend, yes, along with two ex-wives and four kids. Why else would I take this job?"

"You mean you're not here for the Arctic mystique and the richness and rarity of experiencing an indigenous culture first-hand?"

"Ken, I'll try and say this without climbing on my soapbox, but what's so god damn wrong with doing this or any other job, and doing it well, just for the money? Why is there this supposition that a person can't or won't be effective unless they have altruistic or pious motives? Why aren't a work ethic and integrity enough? Please don't answer that right now. I don't want to miss any of *Shrek*."

I had dinner with the coterie but as soon as it was over I retreated to the work room to make some copies. The VHF radio had been left on and was abuzz just as the bulletin board had been with offers of things for sale, but they weren't the drawn out ramblings like Martha had done with her Xbox, they were very coherent and concise. Sometimes it evolved into negotiations.

"I gots high chair and stroller, still in box. Asking a hundred dollars each," came the first voice.

"Stroller got plastic or cloth seat?" came the second voice.

"Cloth, blue cloth with yellow stars," replied the first voice.

"You take seventy-five for stroller," replied the second voice.

"Uh, you get both for one-fifty, yeah?" offered the first voice

"I come look," pledged the second voice.

Another voice started in, "I got a bunch of DVDs," then read off a list of about twenty titles.

"How much you want for *Pirates of the Caribbean?*" someone asked.

"I'm selling all of them together. Fifty dollars for all of them together," said the seller.

"I got twelve-gauge shells and sparkplugs, you take those?"

"What kind spark plugs?" said the seller.

"D-R-8-E-S."

"I need *B-R-9-E-S*, you got any *B-R-9-E-S?*" asked the seller.

Eventually an arrangement was made in which the seller sold all twenty DVD's for $50 to a second party. The second party then sold the *Pirates of the Caribbean* DVD individually for $10 and traded the remainder for a nine-inch propeller that would fit a fifteen horsepower outboard motor. The person who had traded away the propeller pieced the rest of the DVD's out variously for a shower curtain, flashlight, set of steak knives, and an extension cord. The flashlight and extension cord were subsequently traded for the twelve-gauge shells and spark plugs, respectively. Somewhere that night Adam Smith's "invisible hand" gave Karl Marx the "invisible finger."

I went back to my room for an hour and when I returned to make more copies a voice sniffled and sobbed over the VHF. "How come. How come, how come." Then shrieked, "Why! Why! Why!"

It sounded like a girl, a teenage girl. I tried to decipher who it might be. Rosy Aicia? Jenny Iqaluq?

"You take, you take my dividend," the voice had started to deepen but then shrilled again, "Give me nothing! Nothing!"

I thought Olivia was still at the Fairbanks Youth Facility. That's the only person I thought it could be.

"Fuck. Fuck you mom and dad."

That's when I nailed it. It was Arnold, as in, "Fuck you, I'm outta here and going to Fairbanks, maaannn," Arnold.

Arnold sobbed on. "Fuck, fucking pieces of shit. Take my dividend! Bring me nothing. Nothing! Told me we were leaving, now we stay, and I never got nothing, no new stuff. No new shits. Everybody else gots sneakers and iPods. But! You! Never! Bring! Me! Nothing! And we're still here! Fuck you." Then he mounted to such banshee like proportions that it almost distorted what he was trying to say. "Fuck!!! You!!!"

I listened as Arnold sniffled and moaned, then I clicked the switch to off. Dividend season may have come in with a bang from Matt Kala'a's rifle, but it went out with Arnold's fifteen year-old, despondent, whimper.

# CHAPTER SIXTEEN

Monday we had our staff meeting and covered guidelines for parent teacher conferences that were scheduled for Wednesday and Thursday. There were edicts from on high that all parents receive specific indicators of; where their students were in regards to past performance, how they ranked according to national standards, and what level of progress they had made toward graduation.

For the majority of my students an honest response would have been; better, poorly, and some sort of forced comic laughter. Only nine of my now forty-two students were even remotely close to average or satisfactory. Maybe five more were within striking distance of the bottom rung of the competency ladder.

Jenn, bless her heart, asked A-Team with a perfectly straight face, "When I call parents to schedule appointments, what kind of food shall I tell them is being served."

A-Team looked perplexed as he leaned his open-collared neck out over the podium. "In what sense, Miss Stanisauvlauvski?"

Jenn explained that in previous years there had been sort of a buffet offered by the school to help draw parents in. She added that there was also a raffle each day with a prize such as a power tool or home appliance.

A-Team asked if those things were donated by the community or brought in by parents and Jenn told him they were provided on some level by the school district. "Coffee and cookies, I'll be sure that those are available. No meals. No door prizes. Parents need to be here because it is an obligation to their children, not because there is some type of incentive for them personally."

Wednesday we dismissed school early and actually got off to a good start. Lewis' grandmother came in and I had little to tell her except that Lewis could actually graduate in December if he wanted to. The matriarch of Amos-Ben, Joel-Ben, and Daniel-Ben Iqaluq came in and told me just exactly how wonderful they all were, although in fairness they were pretty decent as Iqsaiqsiq kids went. The three of them were also within striking distance of being proficient, maybe, some day.

Sharay and Desiree's parents, Magnus and Doreen, came in and I learned that their father, the whaling captain, also worked at the power generation plant. Both girls had scored "proficient" on their state tests the previous spring and completed their coursework satisfactorily. Doreen wanted their daughters to transfer to a public boarding school in Sitka called Mount Edgecumbe, but so far they had not been interested.

Magnus reclined with his arms folded across his chest and said, "I go Edgecumbe, never like that place; too far, too wet, too many mean teachers, too many mean Indians. Never good for kids to go away from they land, from they family, for school. Iqsaiqsiq different then, in the eighties. So much go bad in Iqsaiqsiq, maybe now Edgecumbe better place for kids. Never hear kids at Edgecumbe what crash out all the time or hang they-selves like here in Iqsaiqsiq."

Doreen asked me what I thought of the idea. I said I didn't have enough information to form an opinion on Edgecumbe, but their daughters had a good chance of doing well in either case because they had a solid set of academic skills and lots of parental support.

The few other parents scheduled did not show up. A-Team came by and asked how things had gone, then said that Jenn would call any absent parents and reschedule them for Thursday.

Twenty minutes after the last scheduled block David showed up at my door. He went into a lengthy explanation about how busy he was being the mayor of Iqsaiqsiq, which is why he was late. I later found out that he had waited until appointments were over in order to avoid Ty Burnside. I noted that in this one particular instance David had embraced Terri Bowen-Skeen's asserted Inupiat belief in non-conflict; this one particular instance being an inevitable beat-down by Iqsaiqsiq's resident version of Floyd Mayweather Jr.

David went into all kinds of justifications about why Solomon acted the way he did. He claimed Solomon saw those things on TV and implemented them in an effort to assimilate both his traditional, Native, culture and the ways of the Western world. He added that he encouraged Solomon to emulate what he saw in videos because he would probably have to take over and be the leader of Iqsaiqsiq someday.

Of course, David had some compassion for me. Not because of the abuse I endured; but because I, being white, probably didn't understand what it meant to have a strong connection to my ancestral culture the way he and his family did. All of which, ironically, was mighty white of him.

Since David had introduced the topic of connections to ancestral culture I asked him, "Did you go whaling?"

No, he said he had to stay and tend to city business. Of course, I knew from Lewis that David hadn't gone because he was an Aicia, and his family did not own any boats with which to go.

"Do you go duck or goose hunting?" I asked.

He had, in the past, but no, not anymore. His son Alex did though.

I asked about Caribou hunting, which he claimed he did do. I asked him how many caribou he had gotten the previous year and he said, "Two," which I thought for the average weekend sport hunter in Washington would be pretty good, but seemed to lack a little given that for Natives the season was open year-round and a herd often wandered around the outskirts of the village. Besides, two butchered caribou would yield less than two hundred pounds of usable meat; a lot of steaks and stew meat, but not enough for a family of five to eat year-round, or share with relatives and at community potlucks.

I asked him about fishing and he claimed that he did, but when I asked him about specific species, tackle, and seasons he limited himself to a set-net under the ice in winter for Arctic Char.

I told him I would be interested if Solomon or Alex wanted to share some of their culture with the class sometime and asked what types of cultural activities they liked to do.

David was dumbfounded. Finally he said, "Dancing, Eskimo dancing. They can do Eskimo dancing. You know I'm the drummer for the Eskimo dancers."

I didn't say anything, but I thought it was odd he was the drummer since, though he was there for the feast, that was the vital piece of equipment the group had lacked at the first whaling assembly.

Finally David excused himself and asked why there weren't any "gifts" this year. I said that in my experience gifts weren't usually a part of the parent teacher conferences. David exploited the opportunity to chastise me. "Oh, I see. You know, that's part of the challenge for the school and the community. We're always getting new teachers who don't understand our ways and customs, and that makes things difficult. But now you know, maybe next time you can do better and have gifts, yeah?"

I still thought I might stay after my eighty-four day expiration date so I said, "That would be a good concern for you to take to Principal Atkinson." Had I known for sure that I would leave in two weeks, I would have said, "How about I get a douche bag for your wife? That way, when you carry it through the door it will be like she's getting a matching set."

Thursday afternoon I had only one parent come in; Janice Bowen. She was the mother of MKay, JCee, and Jay-Boy; two of whom were prospective bottom-rung aspirants. I told her Jay-Boy was very affable and usually did well in class, but his weak link was homework or anything beyond the absolute bare minimum. I suggested she and I come up with some kind of chart to monitor his homework and daily progress, that way I could let her know every week exactly which assignments he had missed or concepts he needed to practice.

"No, no. That never be good. I never think Jay-Boy like that. If I remind him he never do good, it make him sad, and I never want let him be sad. I like him happy the way he is," said Ms. Bowen.

I had no doubt that the good intentions Ms. Bowen had just expressed were absolutely sincere, and it helped explain why Iqsaiqsiq's future path was so well paved.

We discussed MKay and JCee, how they also could perform at a higher level if, again, there was anything we could do to get maybe just one more assignment completed or one more hour of practice a week.

Ms. Bowen responded, "Mr. Shosatori, I think you're good teacher to these kids. My kids tell me you never yell or grab hold of them like some other teachers have. But my girls never like you, and when they never like a teacher, they never work in that teacher's class.

Maybe next teacher they have they like, then they work good for that teacher."

It was half compliment, half rejection, and reminded me of something I had read about Native Americans generally; they see time as cyclical, repeating over and over again, as opposed to linear with a formal beginning and a definitive end. In Ms. Bowens mind it was perfectly acceptable for her daughters to sit-out every other year or two because eventually another teacher would come along, and if that meant it took them until they were thirty to graduate, that was fine. In a more contemporaneous sense it sounded like Jimmy Buffett's ditty about island life *No Plane on Sunday* which meant, "It certainly won't happen today, and may or may not happen tomorrow either. So why worry about it."

I tried the old, "Everybody needs a diploma to be successful," approach and was vetoed once again. Ms. Bowen said that most people in the village, herself included, had a high school diploma and that it hadn't made a difference in their lives.

Ms. Bowen and I had not engaged in the formal question, answer, question, answer, "Oh," dialogue but I felt I had probably gotten further than most teachers did on their first attempt, received half a compliment along the way, and would snap the line if I pulled it taut any further. I released the drag and let Ms. Bowen run free.

A-Team came by my room and informed me that while I waited for other parents to arrive I needed to call any parents who had missed their appointment and offer to meet them at home on Friday.

I went down the list and received lots of unanswered rings, disconnected numbers, and, "Lemme check," followed by a distant, "Tell him I go Anchorage." I finally got hold of Rhonda Aicia, mother of Rocky and Rosy.

"When you come?" she asked.

"Tomorrow, Friday, at three-thirty in the afternoon." I told her.

"Rocky not in trouble, right? You not coming to tell me Rocky break something?"

"No. Rocky hasn't gotten sent out of my room for a few weeks now."

"Okay. I never need anybody come tell me Rocky break something. I know Rocky breaks things. Everybody know Rocky breaks things. Never need to come over here just to tell me Rocky break things."

Finally she added, "What you bring? What to eat?"

I told her I would bring some cookies.

"No hot pockets?" she replied, "Last year they bring hot pockets. Got hot pockets?"

I told her I would check.

Friday I arrived at the Aicia resident, one of the twelve Aicia residences spread across Iqsaiqsiq, with half a box of Chips Ahoy under one arm and knocked at the door. Ms. Aicia asked from the inside who I was and why I was there. Then she clarified again that I was not there because Rocky had broken something. Finally she told me to come in.

The floor was littered with any type of container once on a shelf at the store. It was impossible to see the carpet. Or was it vinyl? Plywood? Whatever was originally there had been completely obfuscated by a thick coating of potato chip bags, cereal boxes, soda cans, juice bottles, Pop-Tart wrappers, and TV dinner trays. In five-hundred years it would be the key that helped anthropologists unlock twenty-first century Arctic aboriginal life.

There were chairs pulled up around a kitchen counter, a couch, and a plasma screen TV with just about every type of game and entertainment system plugged into it. At the moment the TV displayed either *Jerry Springer* or *Steve Wilkos*; a tattooed fat guy in a tank-top and a tattooed skinny guy in a tank-top duked it out while three different women in muffin-topped Spandex mini-skirts yelled at each other.

Ms. Aicia lay on the couch. She was not obese, as I had half expected, nor was she intoxicated, as I had fully expected. She simply wasn't "there," the only question was whether her brain cells had deteriorated before or after her teeth, which were half gone.

I handed her Rosy's report card, then Rocky's, and tried to engage her about a plan Rocky could follow that might allow him to graduate only two instead of three years behind his peers. But I could not compete with the hair-weaves being pulled out and swung about on the TV. Maybe I should have prepared a rap.

Finally I left everything on the armrest of the couch, held in place by the box of Chips Ahoy cookies, and excused myself. As I turned toward the door, Ms. Aicia said, "Rocky never break anything, right?"

I told her, "No," and left.

Another week dragged by, the last Honda got traded in for a snowmachine, and then it was Halloween.

In the Neverland that was Iqsaiqsiq - where almost no one ever left home, held a job for more than one pay period, or quit having sex with high school girls - Halloween was an all ages event. Joanne said that she had "always," meaning the three previous years she had taught in Iqsaiqsiq, called a truce with her students for the day of and the day after Halloween; kids could bring their candy to school on those two days, eat as much as they liked, but then it was over and anything that appeared later was fed to a giant frog-shaped garbage can.

The rest of the elementary teachers went along with Joanne and after some discussion we high school teachers succumbed for the sake of unity, although for me it ran counter to Roby's consistency dictum. A-Team caught wind of it and expressly told us that there were to be no Halloween parties. All our students were considered at risk, and our school was on some type of "Top Ten Worst Alaskan Schools" list. We needed to drill, drill, drill-baby-drill these students heads full of everything they hadn't learned in the past five or seven or nine years.

At A-Team's behest I abandoned the party in my room and held two "amnesty municipal" (as opposed to amnesty international) days instead. We talked about the meaning of the word "amnesty" and used graphs and charts as well as ratios to compare the number of people incarcerated worldwide to the total world population. I still did word searches, journals, and the raps but instead of the standard book and online lessons we watched *Locked Up Abroad.* Things got pretty rowdy, but not defiant or violent. I did catch some flak for being "cheap" because I merely allowed them to eat candy but had not supplied them with any.

There were some highlights that came out of Halloween.

The first highlight was Mitch's poor choice in Halloween offerings. Mitch handed out various types of nuts, which meant that for the next couple of days kids walked around asking him about his nuts, "You got anymore nuts, Mitch? You still got your nuts?" and commenting about his nuts, "Mitch's nuts are too small. I don't like Mitch's nuts, his nuts are too hard."

The second highlight was that Mitch purchased the three different types of nuts in bulk, then tried to mix them into smaller paper bags as he handed them out at his door Halloween night. The kids, and adults who trick or treated as well, were already bemused by the poor quality of his proposed offering and were further put off by his audacity to make them wait. As I handed out fun-size Snickers, I heard him say, "I guess I really should have gotten all of this ready yesterday." I decided then and there that if the opportunity arose I would use that line for Mitch's epitaph.

The third highlight was something called *Puqtaluq* (poo-kuh-tuh-loo-kuh). The whole village met at the city hall, as opposed to the school for a change, and there was a highly animated costume contest in which people not only wore costumes but acted out various things as instructed by the audience. Someone would say, "Swim, swim," and the contestants had to lie down on the floor and paddle and kick like they were swimming. Someone else yelled out, "Dance, dance," and they did the Macarena. Of course someone, I suspect I know whom, yelled out, "*Anuq, anuq,*" and they all squatted and even wiped. For the record, no one yelled, "Fuck, fuck," or even, "Have sex, have sex," and I duly noted it for the next time I was harangued by the command staff.

Part of what made *Puqtaluq* so *sui generis* was the costumes, all of which followed similar macabre principles. It was important to completely disguise ones age, gender, height, and weight. First, participants donned super-double-oversized clothes from the Goodwill reject pile; not the stuff that people reject and send to Goodwill, but the stuff Goodwill rejects and sends to the dump. Coveralls and garish dresses that looked like bad trailer-house curtains seemed most popular. Second, they stuffed them with rags and towels to disfigure their bodies. Third, they put on hideous rubber masks. Finally, this was the *coup de gras*, they pulled giant Granny panties over the whole thing; the pinker the better. I believe it was what people referred to as a, "Hootenanny."

The winner was a person who pulled a dead fish out from under his or her costume and threw it into the audience. Then he or she threw another, and another, and another. Somewhere that person had seen Gallagher, and liked it.

On the way home a few spritz of red vapor hung high above and I took them to be the Aurora Borealis, although, just like everything else, they didn't quite live up to the stupendous descriptions provided in books and brochures. Snowmachines "brapbrap-braaaped" through the night, but come morning no one had been shot, arrested, or medevac'd; although thirteen year-old Daniel Bowen was found passed out drunk on the store steps and, since Ty Burnside was the store manager, it was obviously Ty's fault that Daniel had done so. Obviously.

The few kids who showed up at school the next day had what looked like little slices of sunburn on their cheeks and beside their eyes. Stan explained that it was frostbite from riding around in the sub-freezing temperatures at sixty miles an hour with only a sweatshirt hood over their heads. It reminded me of the annual blistering I had subjected my ears to as a teenager during the first weekend of surfing every May; a kind of outdoor enthusiasts rite of passage.

By the Saturday after Halloween I had only one square on my calendar left to cross out. Twelve weeks earlier I had made a deal with myself, and myself alone, that now gave me permission to leave on Monday morning if I liked. I gave credence to the community's ability to organize and execute *Puqtaluq* effectively, even though it may have been a singular occurrence. I also had to admit that had I still faced Tim or Olivia on a daily basis it would have weighed heavily as a factor.

Three sessions of spin-bike later I concluded that I would not leave Monday morning. It took me two more session to decide if I would proceed day-to-day, week-to-week, or strive for the end of the semester. I settled on the end of the semester and spun through another thirty-five minutes to decide if I should stick with my original method of counting every day or adopt Cornell's "student days only" method. I opted for the latter because, much like measuring in kilograms as opposed to pounds, it made it sound like less than what it actually was. Then I spun out a seventh and final session to appease the parts of my body and soul that loathed the decision I had just made.

After I showered, I grieved my decision further with a little retail therapy. I went to the store and dug through the freezer for a pint of AmeriCone Dream, picked up a Hungry-Man fish and chips platter, and snagged a bag of Flaming Hot Cheetos along with a twelve-pack of Mug Root Beer for a grand total of $33.00. I ate in my classroom and went to Cabela's online to purchase Cold-Weather Coveralls, Predator Extreme Pac-Boots, two pairs of Expedition Weight long underwear, and three pairs of Powerstretch Thermal socks. I also picked out a Leatherman to give to Jerry for Christmas. After charging $776 to my Visa card I jumped over to Amazon.com and bought the entire set of Soprano's on DVD for $399. My decision translated to a self-imposed tax of roughly $43.00 for every student day that remained.

A few weeks later Stan invited me out for a snowmachine ride on Thanksgiving Day and even though I had a nasty sinus infection I jumped at the chance. We left at 10:00 a.m., while it was still dark, on his and Jenn's personal F570 Arctic Cat's and headed due east via GPS across the featureless tundra. The gear I had ordered from Cabela's worked flawlessly. A few miles out of the village we came upon a frozen river that was smooth and flat, even if it wasn't straight. A set of animal tracks I couldn't decipher headed to the south and we fervidly pursued them as we vaulted off of hummocks and skimmed across the faces of drifts which suddenly appeared without purpose or catalyst. We started to come across what looked like stumps, eight to twelve inches in diameter and twelve to sixteen inches high. Stan stopped in the midst of them and I pulled alongside him.

We removed our face and neck gear, and tucked it deep beneath our coveralls so it would thaw, then raised our hoods back up. Stan decrypted the landscape as we faced west to keep the easterly wind at our backs.

"There is always snow up in here from October through June, but it never covers all the ground at one time. If it did, the caribou, and eventually the wolves, would starve. In a week, all of these drifts will have eroded and new ones will have built up a thousand yards to either side. A month after that and it will be in a totally different configuration, and so on. These," Stan kicked one of the stumps but it didn't budge, "Are called *tussocks* (tuh-sucks). As the tundra freezes it pops up; especially where the surrounding soil is still soft. They are proof that god doesn't like snowmachines."

Stan dug out a pair of binoculars and scanned the dimly lit horizon. He handed them to me and pointed to the southwest. I could see a herd of something I assumed were caribou but if not for the latitude could have just as easily been antelope or mule deer. Stan stowed the binoculars. We wrapped back up in our neck and face gear and headed southwest.

Forty minutes later we stalled out the machines and dismounted to the lee side from the herd. We lay down on the ground, removed only our goggles, and Stan reached up to retrieve the binoculars. "Reindeer," he said softly.

As I scanned the herd Stan explained that in the scientific community the terms reindeer and caribou were used interchangeably, but that here in the Arctic these formerly domesticated *Rangifer tarandus*, with their spork-shaped as opposed to fork-shaped antlers, were called reindeer. The animals we saw regularly around the village that locals referred to as caribou were actually a sub-species designated as *Rangifer tarandus granti* or Porcupine Caribou.

Stan also explained that these reindeer had been introduced to Alaska from Russia during the late 1800's, in an effort to turn the hunter-gatherer Eskimoes into farmer-rancher Eskimoes, by government officials who ignored the fact that they were called hunter-gatherers for a reason.

Stan pointed south and slightly east where an orange disc hovered just above the horizon. "Take a long look M.C. Ken, it will be the end of January before Ra sails his barge this far north again." I propped my head up on my be-mitted hands and watched the sun reduce to a semi-circle, an arc, a dot, a sub-horizon aura, and finally a memory.

In slightly over an hour the wind had swept away our tracks so we navigated in ten minutes sections by GPS until we reached the frozen waterway, then we indulged the synapses of our Y-chromosome biased ventral striatum as we sent rooster tails into the early afternoon twilight. We returned to Stan's house in complete darkness save for a weak, uninspired green wisp of Aurora Borealis around 3:00 p.m. then deposited two giant heaps of nylon, wool, and Polarfleece in the garage before we sat down along with most of the other teachers for the feast imported from that place the sun had just retreated to.

I spent the remainder of the four-day Thanksgiving weekend buried deep beneath my heather gray sheets and sleeping bag. I exited every couple of hours to blow my nose, hawk-out phlegm, drain my bladder, and ingest Gatorade. I received several invitations to watch football or movies and I declined each time. Sunday I was able to scribble out just enough insipid verse to be ready Monday, and went right back to sleep. I barely rose in time to shower, dress, don my coveralls and accoutrement, and hoof to school in the negative ten degree darkness.

As I mixed and recorded my fourth period intro at 8:51, A-Team appeared at my door and asked me to cover Mitch's class. On the way down to Mitch's room I asked where Mitch was.

"I don't know," said A-Team.

"What lesson is he on?" I asked.

"Check his lesson plans."

"Where are they?"

"I don't know."

"Didn't he email you a copy from last week?"

"No."

I figured Mitch had bailed in uber-Mitchesque fashion; no notice, no goodbye to the students or staff, not even an, "I'm outta here!" scrawled across the whiteboard. As students arrived I gathered that Mitch, along with four students, had snowmachined over to the neighboring village of Ciaciqiq eighty-five miles away on Friday morning. They had to wait until Friday because the fuel station was closed Thursday and no one had thought to buy gas on Wednesday because, "Why buy gas today? We're not leaving until tomorrow." Apparently the same fuel-station-logic snared them forty-eight hours later when they attempted to leave on Sunday. Damn the intransigence of fuel stations. Damn the intransigence of logic.

I had seen enough of Mitch's class to know how it operated so I told them, in my heavily congested state, "Don't hurt anybody. Don't break anything. No food, drinks, or headphones."

"But Mitch lets us have soda and headphones," came a contemptible reply.

"I'm not Mr. Forman, am I," I replied.

"No, you're Mr. Shosatori, or So-Shit-Bore-Me," offered up MKay Bowen.

It was all downhill from there. By 9:15 students from other classes showed up at the door and when I refused them entry I received protests of, "Cheap," "Sucks," "Junk," "You're just being mean because you don't like us," and, "I wish our real teacher Mitch was here." That actually would have pleased both us, I thought.

I didn't know when Mitch was due back but I was pretty sure I could get a snowmachine catapult built before I left for Christmas.

Surprisingly, very little of the vehemence bled over to my regular classroom. The chronic malefactors, like Rachel, were their malevolent selves, but the students who had felt they had free reign in the computer lab self-stabilized. Lewis volunteered that he was glad Mitch was delayed because he had agreed to pay Lewis twenty dollars a day to look after Gobi. I thought it might be the one and only thing Mitch had ever done right.

Monday night I was down in the Coalman's apartment to watch David Letterman on WCBS via satellite. Belle offered me chicken broth that she had raised to medicinal grade with a, "*Lawn yep,*" (little bit) of fresh ground paprika and minced habanero. A snowmachine arrived and someone hauled armload after armload of gear into the common entryway and deposited it just inside the door. The snowmachine restarted and left.

I excused myself and crossed paths with Pat as he left the laundry room. He relayed Solomon's most recent inquiries as a snowmachine pulled up and Mitch entered. In my congested state I didn't have the lung capacity to scream at Mitch as vehemently as I desired so I started up the stairs one head-ponding step at a time.

Pat wasn't officially one of "us" yet, but he did have a sense of right and wrong, or as he would later define it, "Right and bullshit." He also had a fully functional laryngological system. As Mitch gathered his gear, Pat informed him, "The students were pretty upset you weren't here today."

"Yeah. Yeah, yeah, well, not much I could do about that, uh, you know, the gas station was closed yesterday so we had to wait until today to get gas." Mitch defended himself.

Pat didn't comment on Mitch's innate lack of planning skills, but he did address his deviation from policy. "I typically write eight or nine referrals a day spread across five classes, today I had six," Pat held up a full hand plus one finger, "In your class alone, all for either headphones or soda. Why is it that I've been here three weeks and when I tell students they can't have headphones or soda they usually comply, but almost every student in your class looks at me like, 'Who the hell are you?' when I tell them it's not allowed?"

Mitch went into his regular scree about white imperialism and the inherent oppressive nature of a federal education system imposed upon an indigenous people. Then he said he was, "Off the clock," anyway and didn't have to listen to Pat's reprimand.

Pat, generally the epitome of level-headedness and constructive resolution, sarcastically agreed that Mitch was off the clock now, as he had been all day in fact.

Tuesday morning I had to cover Mitch's first period class again, doped up on Thera-Flu and Hall's. As I explained how to save a second version of a document after making an edit to the original, MKay complained that I shouldn't be at school if I was sick. "Gaw-lee, how sick you are. Shouldn't be at school if you're sick, might-could get all us kids sick too." That would have been great except that despite Iqsaiqsiq's forty-percent unemployment rate it was hard enough to find a full-time cook and two full-time aides, much less an extra aide to come in and cover a class.

Mitch, and Gobi, managed to make it in after school was over and Mitch claimed he hadn't been able to get out of bed because his back still hurt from the snowmachine ride. That sounded plausible, although he could have just as easily been trying to avoid or retaliate against Pat.

Wednesday the store was closed because Ty Burnside had packed up his family and headed back south. The village was quite upset with Ty because, since he had left, there was no one to run the store. Just like substitutes for the school, the store went largely unstaffed unless or until someone arrived from Outside. On an entirely random basis, which paradoxically was Iqsaiqsiq's standard operating procedure, David opened the store for an hour or two every other day or so, usually from 1:00 to 3:00, but never after 3:30 and never on Saturday or Sunday.

A few more weeks and it was time for the Holiday Program, an annual anathema for all teachers regardless of latitude. Stan attended and afterward he gave me a ride home.

"You know who Oosterahn was?" asked Stan.

"The guy whose closet got ransacked, literally and figuratively," I said.

"Well put. I may get called out of the village while y'all are gone and the minute I do it will be open season on any unoccupied house. If you want to keep anything valuable at my place you're welcome to. If you have anything embarrassing you don't want the whole world to know about, like Jonas Brother's bobble-heads, take it with you or ditch it. Oosterahn was pretty resilient but that whole mess was more than even he could overcome."

I packed up everything except my bedding and kitchen stuff and hauled it over to Stan's in my duffel bag and suitcase. Jay-Boy asked me on the last Friday if I was coming back after Christmas and I again shook his hand and promised that I would. I also felt, again, that he only half believed me.

Mitch stayed in the village over Christmas break because, he claimed, it was his home. John and Joanne, whose home it actually was, also stayed in the village because as the head of maintenance John couldn't be absent at the same time as the principal. The other eight of us split the $5,000 tab for a charter flight to Anchorage.

The twin-prop whined like a million vuvuzelas as it descended through the murky haze of a half blizzard at 4:00 p.m. on the final Friday and it was one of the most beautiful sounds I had ever heard. By 8:00 p.m. we were in Anchorage.

A-Team and Pat headed for a car while the Margarita's siren song and pheromones from bacon ranch quesadillas at Chile's Too lured us in without comment or discussion.

A few hours later Ben and Brenda went to board their flight for Chicago, while Cornell and Belle caught their red-eye connection through Salt Lake City to New Orleans. Finally I walked down with Nick to see him depart for Maui and headed to gate C5 for my own 2:30 a.m. flight to Seattle. In four hours I would see familiar faces for the first time in five months. In six hours I would see a sunrise for the first time in four weeks.

# CHAPTER SEVENTEEN

In the predawn of the first Friday in January I boarded the Anchorage Marriott shuttle bus and made my way to the Ted Stevens Anchorage International Airport. I checked my single, forty pound bag at the ticket counter and proceeded, again unchallenged by the TSA, to the Frontier Flying Service terminal on the lower level where I found Belle and Cornell along with a few teachers from Ciaciqiq.

The Ciaciqiq teachers had similar stories of absentee and uninvolved parents, kids sleeping in class, low academic performance, the students near addiction to soda, Hondas and now snowmachines being run all night and in all directions, foul language, and the prevalence of alcohol abuse despite the village's "dry" status. Ciaciqiq even had its own shooting story; although, since they didn't have a full time Trooper, they had hunkered down in their houses until the Troopers from Aciq flew in around noon the next day. Where the paths diverged was when the topic turned to physical threats, thrown chairs, and kicked walls.

There was much discussion of the amusement park tunnel metaphor and various other ways people had tried to describe in meticulous yet still inaccurate ways the illogic of village life, most of which centered around the titles of popular books, movies, and television shows; *Groundhog Day, Twilight Zone, A Clockwork Orange, Needful Things,* and *One Flew over the Cuckoo's Nest.*

A man in his fifties offered, "The feds and the state have been pouring in money and programs year after year to get these villages turned around. Once in a while a good crew comes along gets some traction, maybe even some positive yardage, but the powers that be don't want first-downs, they want touchdowns. So the entire program gets scrapped and the next year everybody starts back on their own one yard line. You just don't get support for a program that takes more than a year to complete or makes less than a ten percent difference from the norm. That's why I just rub my neck, take my check, and say, 'Thank you very much.'"

I left it up to the Ciaciqiq staff to either rebuke or validate their co-workers opinion and when they did neither we turned the conversation over to the price of air travel and tips on how to shop for mail-order groceries. At 7:30 a.m. one of the Ciaciqiq veterans spearheaded a pilgrimage to the Starbucks one level above for a final espresso before we departed to Fairbanks.

Denali was shrouded in clouds as we passed above it. Fairbanks and the southern horizon were still dark at 9:00 a.m. We tossed our empty cups in the nearest trash can as we filed into the terminal and produced an inadvertent Starbucks-amid in the process.

Over at the William's Air Service terminal we met up with Ben, Brenda, and Nick who had arrived the night before. Nick's bald head still showed the effects from a sunburn the week before. Ben and Brenda had made it back and looked very well rested, more like the couple in a Cialis ad and less like two people on a Dr. Phil episode about infidelity. There were also some teachers from Aciq and other villages.

Ben stepped outside for a smoke and I joined him since the terminal was so crowded. I asked him if he had found a hobby yet and he shook his pocket, which rattled. "Is that dice, or a miniature maraca?" I asked him.

He reached in and produced a prescription bottle of Xanax.

"Great," I said softly.

"Yeah it is, I... Wait, was that sarcasm? I already popped one and it will be lunch before I can read social cues again."

"Yes, that was sarcasm."

The ticket agent explained that the first flight would depart for Aciq at 10:00 a.m. instead of 2:00 p.m., and then continue on to Iqsaiqsiq. All of the Ciaciqiq teachers would fly in on a second flight at 4:00 p.m. The sky over Fairbanks was still dark as we taxied down the runway, but once airborne I had a glimpse of the sun for about thirty minutes until we crossed the Brooks Range. It would be three weeks before I saw it again.

We landed in Aciq and the Aciq teachers got off along with a dozen Styrofoam boxes of chill, the kind that Stan ordered once a month full of grapes and lettuce. We waited in the terminal while the plane was refueled then took off... without us.

The agent explained that the plane had some type of mechanical issue and had to return to Fairbanks, but another plane was on its way to carry us to Iqsaiqsiq, "In about an hour."

More than an hour after the agent had told us we would leave an hour later than the original, "In about an hour," we were still an hour away from leaving. Against her protest we walked across the street to the, "Laughing Buddha Oriental Cafe," which was operated by a Somali family with a penchant for Hawaiian shirts and mariachi music. We ordered rice bowls with curry chicken and peanut sauce for $18 and sodas, which came in a can complimented by a glass filed with ice, for $4.

We finally landed in Iqsaiqsiq about 7:00 p.m. under the same type of half-blizzard we had taken off in two weeks earlier, except now it was about minus thirty instead of the mere zero degrees it had been when we left in December. Joanne took Nick, Ben, and Brenda in the school Tahoe that A-Team usually drove while John took Belle, Cornell, and I in the school truck.

The quad-plex looked like the first scene from *Animal House*. No less than a dozen snowmachines were parked outside and a handful of people, all under the age of thirty and some of them students, smoked cigarettes on the front porch. I half-expected a keg to fly out of an upstairs window at any moment. Once inside we could see that the door to Mitch's apartment was open and Eminem's voice blared out of it.

Cornell looked confused and Belle looked disgusted while I simply shook my head because it was so typical of Mitch. I helped Belle and Cornell get their things into their apartment.

"Whu-uht in the huh-ell is that boy doin?" asked Cornell.

"Isn't it obvious?" I said, "He's reaching out to the community!"

"He can go reach out at thay-uhr house," said Belle, "I'm gonna call Trooper Stan and put an end to this nonsense."

Cornell talked her out of it and I volunteered that, even though I was in no way a fan of Mitch, it was within his right to have guests. Cornell was concerned some of the smokers were high school kids and we might be liable for contributing to the delinquency of a minor. I told him as long as they weren't our guests and they were in a common area we couldn't be held accountable for them. I didn't tell him Stan probably had bigger fish to fry.

I climbed up to my apartment and through Mitch's open door I could see a tobacco pipe on the kitchen table; a three foot tall, bi-cameral, water-filled, rainbow swirled, ceramic, tobacco pipe. Arnold, Tim, even Lewis, and some high school girls sat around in Mitch's modest apartment, as well as some adults. Those that did not have chairs or couch space sat against the wall. I called Stan and asked if I could come over and pick up my stuff. He volunteered that he knew about the situation and told me to just come over and stay at his place for the night. Then he called Cornell and explained that if there was a noise disturbance, after hours, he could come evict people; but the fact that there were just a lot of people there was a landlord-tenant issue and they would have to contact the district office for that.

Stan presented me with a box wrapped in Christmas paper. I opened it and removed a pair of size 12 XtraTufs. Stan said, "You made it back, you're now an official 'Bushy.'" We watched some *Sopranos* DVD's and about 11:00 p.m. Stan got the call from Belle. He went over and everyone scattered except two local Iqsaiqsiq men and a high school girl from Ciaciqiq, all three of whom he took into custody for public intoxication. Mitch was nowhere to be found, so Stan locked the apartment. Later Cornell said people had shown up at his door all night and asked, "You know where that Mitch guy is? You got key for his house?" and, "You got gas we might-could borrow?" To which Cornell had replied, "I don't even have a ve-huckle, why would I have gaz-o-leen?"

I guarded the prisoners from 4:00 a.m. until 1:00 p.m. and put together my arithmetical jams. The Trooper plane couldn't make it through Saturday so I went back and did a stretch from 9:00 p.m. to 5:00 a.m. Stan explained that between the darkness and his work schedule he pretty much just followed his circadian rhythms which cycled through about seven hours awake and five hour asleep from December through February. Sunday the Trooper plane made it in, along with a Cessna 207 owned by one of A-Team's friends who ferried him and Pat in. There was still no sign of Mitch.

Monday morning Mitch appeared at school but wouldn't tell anyone where he had been. First period Mitch got the story that after we had arrived Friday Stan had come over and kicked everyone out. Later Mitch confronted each of us under the notion that we had immediately called Stan specifically to force his "guests" out into the harsh winter squall because we, "Don't like these Eskimoes," a point he claimed we had made clear during our meeting in Aciq.

I corrected Mitch on his timeline and added that if I have "guests" I usually stay around to see that they are taken care of. I also added that I didn't know how many "guests" he had invited but there were at least twenty people there when we arrived.

Mitch told me, "You just don't know the way of the Eskimo, and you never will know the way of the Eskimo, which is why you'll never be accepted among these people the way I am. I've worked around guys like you all my life. You're just here for the money, you don't appreciate these people the way I do and after you fill your pockets with *their* money you'll be on the first plane headed south in May, if you even make it that long."

I didn't give a shit what Mitch or anyone else would think of me if or when I left. But his words made me realize that I had left with such haste, and so successfully pushed Iqsaiqsiq into the recesses of my mind, that I didn't currently have a milestone to focus on. I needed something that was ambitious yet realistic; shorter than the remainder of the year, but still long enough to be significant. The end of the quarter in mid-March was a bit of a reach so I decided on the last Friday in February, which was the day I would receive the sixth of my twelve paychecks, a sort of economic mid-point. I counted only the student contact days and marked my calendar with the first of thirty-five X's.

I mentioned to Stan that Mitch's presence meant he had been wrong about his Albophobic tendencies. Stan said, "Call it the margin of error, but we still have February to get through, and if anything really crazy is going to happen it will happen in February."

I had read a handful of books about rural Alaska, Michener's included, and the only point they all raised accurately was the consecration of basketball as high art. In Iqsaiqsiq there was one team of eleven boys, one team of seven girls, and one coach to cover them both; Tommy Tiqiqiq, a twenty-two year old former student who was paid $6,000 for the season.

The boys practiced from 3:30 when school got out until 5:30. The girls practiced from 5:30 until 7:30. At 7:30 there was an hour of "open gym" for elementary students, followed by an hour and a half of "community gym" for high school students and adults. Almost all of the high school players returned for community gym time in addition to their regular practice, and most of them were in Mitch's hour long physical education class as well. This came to a total of four and a half hours of basketball a day, in contrast to five hours a day spent in academic pursuits.

In order to be eligible, the state required students to pass a minimum of five of the six classes in which they were enrolled. Nick and Cornell told me that the previous year the then principal had pressured them to, "Not *allow* students to become ineligible." Their advice to me was, "Give the kids the grades they deserve. If someone higher up wants to override it, which they probably will, that's on them."

Basketball even drew Tim back into school, although the laptop he had been provided didn't make the return trip with him. Not that Tim *participated* in school, but he entered the building sometime before lunch. Tim was still rude, crude and obnoxious; but he had lost his, "Watch yourself before somebody might-could kick your ass," swagger. I attributed most of this to the fact that in his absence a lot of stability, or at least regularity, had taken hold within the school. Solomon and Tim-Tim were now the princes of the miscreants, and Rachel was the princess, while Tim was clearly the king. Arnold probably considered himself a knight even though he was clearly the jester.

On Friday I went to the store, now operated by a couple of comfortably shod women; Shelley, heavy-set with freckles and long red hair in her early twenties, and Carol, very thin and prematurely gray in her late forties. Mitch lavished attention on three elementary students in the *quniciuq* as I entered.

"That's a nice parka you have, did your gram make that for you?" Mitch asked Gracie.

"What kind of movies do you like? Have you seen *Madagascar?* Did you like *Madagascar?*" He asked Athena.

"How about you, little guy, did you see *Madagascar?*" He asked Tuuqaq.

They all responded with shrugs, nods, or one-word answers.

When I left the store, Tuuqaq was gone but Mitch was still there with the two girls. A woman in her thirties came in, startled to see Mitch, and inquired, "What are you doing in here with my cousins?" It was a pointed, direct question; a type I had rarely heard a sober adult in Iqsaiqsiq pose.

"Oh, oh hi Leena," said Mitch, "We were just, just chatting," then he turned to Gracie and Athena, "Right? Right girls, we were talking because we're friends."

Gracie and Athena gave the forward, in, and down shoulder shrug I had first seen used by Magnus in front of the post office. I had since learned it meant, "If that's what you want to believe, go ahead and believe it. But you're wrong."

Leena got right up in Mitch's face, another behavior rarely portrayed by sober adults. "My cousin's aren't your friends. You're high school teacher. You need to be with high school kids, or teachers, not little kids. I never like you always being around all these little kids all the time."

Mitch took the same type of, "You don't know what you're talking about so let me explain how Native Culture operates," tone with Leena as he did with the staff, and when Leena didn't embrace Mitch's self-serving narrative he stormed out of the *quniciuq* with, "I've got better things to do than put up with your ignorance."

Saturday there were signs up at the store, post office, and school that advertised a snowmachine for sale with Mitch's contact information and the expressed caveat, "Not for sale to tuniqs."

I got a call from Stan early Sunday morning. "Get your heavy gear on. We're goin' for a ride. The Aurora is out. The *real* Aurora."

I pulled on two layers of polypropylene underwear and two pairs of wool socks before I stepped into my coveralls and tied up my boots. I picked through the basket next to my door to assemble my hand and head gear; thin fleece gloves, thick fleece gloves, double-layer fleece mittens, thin fleece balaclava, thick fleece balaclava, fleece neck gaiter, and double-layer fleece hat. I shoved two extra fleece gaiters into my pocket, and left behind several scarves and hats. Five months in the Arctic had transformed me into the Imelda Marcos of Polarfleece.

Outside the air was dead calm, but so discordantly cold at minus thirty degrees it grated my nostrils. Hoarfrost sprouted in feathery clumps from every edge and bulge; the door knob, the railing, and the screws that held the metal siding and roofing in place. Steam belched from furnaces but flattened into a cloud just above the roofline.

To the northeast the Aurora Borealis blazed. It pumped, pulsed, and shifted in striations of green, blue, and red haze that covered more than half of the sky and very much matched the pictures found in magazines. The green ridge was furthest to the north, rested

212

atop the blue, and they both stretched completely across the horizon in tandem from the genesis in the east to some unseen destination beyond the west. The red band formed the southern edge of the trio, but bent forty-five degrees to the south and broadened into a wispy fan as it passed directly overhead. There were also stars, but no moon.

The snowmachines were ready and we skimmed the fossilized powder eastward as frigid air streamed a pathway along, up, and through any portal it could locate within my clothing. A miniature tempest gnawed at my left ear and a colony of invisible ants scurried around and bit my left leg just above the boot.

With the village bent beneath the horizon at our backs, we stopped and lay down upon the snow which crunched and snapped as we shifted. The engines cooled and their tick-tick-tick set a tempo by which the green and blue ridges popped and locked into position; not a flow as much as a hop from one position to another. The red band in contrast slithered as if adrift on a lofty current. I searched for the words to describe the Aurora's movement and came up short every time. The closest I ever came was: Erratic grace.

With the engines cooled and our bodies still my focus shifted from the sights to the sounds, as there were none. No breezes traversed that moonless night. No birds chirped or flapped. No ungulates bounded. No canines howled. There weren't even any insects or rodents to scurry from burrow to burrow. It was literally a trogmai, a still and moonless night, on the tundra. And it was magnificent.

Stan dug a tripod and a high-end camera out of his pack, then set them up opposite the snowmachines. I sat and braced myself against the handlebars to remain still for the long exposure as the ribbons of green, blue, and red poured over my head and across my shoulders. We also set the timer and took some pictures together then stowed the gear and motored back into Iqsaiqsiq.

It wasn't even 9:00 a.m. and Jenn was still asleep. We mixed up blueberries and yogurt to go with our coffee and toast and I asked Stan, "When you tell Outsiders about Iqsaiqsiq, how do you describe it?"

"Non-un-dysfunctional." Trooper Stan took a long, even swallow of coffee then put the cup down.

I could tell I was in for a sermon and felt it was all the more apropos given that it was a Sunday morning. "At one time this village was functional; not perfect or easy, but functional. Think of it as a floor. Then it became dysfunctional, let's say something got spilled on the floor. Not unique to Iqsaiqsiq, lots of floors in this world and lots

of spills too. Next, this is the messy part, a lot was done to cover up
the dysfunction, kind of like moving furniture to cover up the spill.
Finally, the spill started to smell, but nobody will admit there's a smell
now because then people might find out something was spilled."

Stan vigorously struck the table with his index finger. "To take
it a step further, some people will admit that something smells; but they
blame the furniture, and so they want the furniture gone. Of course
there's a very small group, sort of a Native Illuminati, who know all
about the smell *and* the spill, and they're scared shitless that someday
the furniture actually *will* get taken out of the room, because then they
can't use it as a scapegoat anymore. It's a lot more complicated than
simply being dysfunctional. It's non-un-dysfunctional. It, 'Isn't-not-
not-working,' the way it is supposed to." Stan took another long, even
swallow of coffee then asked, "How did you describe it?"

"Through interpretive dance."

"What did that look like?"

"*Swan Lake* meets *West Side Story*, with Tourette's, except I was
naked and drunk."

"Impressive," Stan raised his coffee mug in a salute, "It takes a
real artist to combine pirouettes, switchblades, and nudity." Then he
added sarcastically, "Some might say what you did was wrong. But
since you were drunk, well, you had permission, and everyone else is
wrong for judging you."

After I had re-bundled myself for the walk home Stan walked
outside with me. He had a mug in his hand. I assumed it was filled with
coffee but when he handed it to me I saw that it was just plain water.
"Toss this out and see what happens," he said.

I threw it straight up and the amorphous blob immediately
dissipated into a thousand droplets, all of which crackled
simultaneously as they formed crystals and drifted back down.

"Pretty cool, huh?" asked Trooper Stan.

"Yep. Thanks for giving me a call and taking me out on the
snowmachines. I owe you a surfing lesson someday if you ever make it
to the Washington Coast."

Stan laughed. "I think I'll pass on that Bubba. How about going
to that place where they throw the fish instead?"

"That's in Seattle, but if that's what you want to see consider it
done." I knew at that moment that the parameters of our friendship
transcended and eclipsed Iqsaiqsiq.

Monday I invited Jay-Boy and Lewis over for dinner. I asked them to come at 6:00. When I got home at 4:55 Jay-Boy was already in the entryway of the quad-plex where he sat on the steps, and jammed to his iPod. We went upstairs and I preheated the oven then put in the pizzas while Jay-Boy sat on the couch, and jammed to his iPod. Lewis wasn't there at 6:30 and I asked Jay-Boy if he knew where he was. He dialed the phone, said, "Ready," and hung up. Five minutes later Lewis was at my door.

We had the pizza along with Pepsi and Ben and Jerry's ice cream. We talked about food and both of them said that Mexican food was about the worst thing ever, which surprised me. Tortilla chips were great, cheese sauce was good, but salsa and most definitely beans were not good. They said Taco Bell was the one restaurant they always avoided. They also liked fish, but pan fried and not the heavily battered kind that came with French fries.

Lewis described a restaurant he had once gone to, "A fancy one, where they bring you lots of different forks and spoons," and ordered a couple of small, round steaks wrapped inside bacon. He said that was his favorite food, and sometimes he did the same thing with caribou because caribou didn't have a lot of fat and the bacon made it juicier. "But I never know what those things called. Those kind steak what's wrapped with bacon."

"Filet mignon," I told him.

"Oh," said Lewis.

We all chewed a few more bites and Jay-Boy said, "What it filled with?"

"What's what filled with?" I asked.

"They call it fill-a-min-yawn, so what they fill it with? Pepperoni, like a hot pocket?" asked Jay-Boy.

"Filet is spelled f-i-l-e-t, it's a French word for a piece of meat. It can also mean to cut meat." I made a motion with the edge of one hand over the palm of the other and they giggled. "What's so funny?"

They exchanged glances as if to say, "Tell him. No, you tell him. No, you." Finally Lewis said, "You move your hands like Trooper Stan," and they both laughed.

Jay-Boy said, "Yeah, maybe he's your *Uppa* (up-puh), *Uppa* Stan."

*Uppa* was the Inupiaq word for grandfather, a term of endearment. I took it as a compliment and believed Stan would have done likewise. Stan was somewhere between fifteen and twenty years older than I; too old to be my brother, too young to be my father, but at precisely the right point on the curve of life to be an excellent friend and guide.

"*Uppa* Stan!" Lewis cackled, then composed himself enough to move his hands in the judo chop fashion indicative of Stan and now, apparently, me as well. "Come here, sit on my lap. Sit on *Uppa* Stan's lap. Let *Uppa* Stan tell you story." Lewis threw his head back, jaw extended to full range, and laughed. That was when I had a revelation.

The woman at William's Air Service, Middy, Zippy, Tim, Tim-Tim, Rachel, Rosy, Rocky, MKay, JCee, even Jay-Boy, fully two-thirds of the village by my estimation; all of their mouths missed several teeth, and contained several more cavities. But not Lewis. Lewis still had all of his teeth, almost ten fillings from what I could see, but all of his teeth nonetheless.

After the two Kilroy's finished their *Mr. Roboto* impersonations and returned to the feast I asked them if they ever went to the dentist.

Lewis raised his eyebrows and Jay-Boy said, "Sometimes, but I never like go dentist. Never like getting shot. You know if you got cav-tees they give you shot so they can drill in there. I never like that." Jay-Boy looked at me. "You? You go dentist?"

"Yeah I go to the dentist, once in the summer and once at Christmas. When do you guys go?" I looked back and forth at each of them.

"Summer time, when clinic girls come and open clinic. One week, all week, everybody go see dentist, doctor, eye doctor, ear doctor. Get school physical," said Lewis.

"Fiss-cal," Jay-Boy snickered, "Turn your head and cough. I get fiss-cal, and eye doctor if I need new glasses. No dentist though man. No shot."

"When was the last time you saw the dentist Jay-Boy?" I asked.

Jay-Boy chewed and scanned his internal disc drive, then looked across the table at Lewis, "When I go dentist? You know, when I got that bike, and you got your four-ten shotgun."

Lewis said, "Seventh grade? I get my four-ten in seventh grade."

"Oh, okay, I'm one year younger, so, sixth grade." Jay-Boy nodded his head. "I go see dentist in sixth grade."

There it was in black teeth and white teeth. A simpleton would find correlation between the white-toothed Lewis, a senior who had passed all three sections of the HSGQE a year earlier, and the yellow going on black going on non-toothed Jay-Boy, a junior who had yet to pass even a single section of the HSGQE, and mistake it for causation; then deduce that a billion dollars spent on dentistry for Natives was the way to raise the graduation rate.

But Lewis' white teeth were an effect of some predicated catalyst, not the cause of his academic or personal-social skills. My guess was that Lewis brushed his teeth most days whether he wanted to or not, went to the dentist every year whether he wanted to or not, and had gotten the needle filled with Novocain shoved into his gums so the dentist could fill his cavities whether he wanted to or not. If that was the stance his mother or grandmother had taken with his teeth it extended to his school work as well as curfew and a dozen other aspects of Lewis' life.

Jay-Boy, in contrast, came from a background where his mother said, "If he never like it, he never need it. Never want to make him sad or unhappy." My guess was that something happened during that final sixth grade visit to the dentist that caused discomfort; physically for Jay-Boy and emotionally for his mother.

Two Digiorno pizza's had been annihilated and Pepsi cans took on the form of a soda-mid. I gave each boy a bowl of ice cream with a spoon. Lewis picked at his, like I did, and dug out the chocolate-covered waffle nuggets. Jay-Boy let Pepsi cascade over his and bubble up to the brim, then slurped the foam. After the froth receded, Jay-Boy squashed the ice cream down into the bowl and made an AmeriCone puree.

"You like it better that way?" I asked Jay-Boy.

Jay-Boy raised his eyebrows.

"How come?" I asked.

"I like it soft. When it's too hard and too cold it hurts my mouth."

"Oh."

Jay-Boy's lack of oral care had diminished his enjoyment of ice cream. In the permissive zeitgeist of Iqsaiqsiq, to take a way a child's ice cream would certainly have been considered a harsh act. After all, Terri Bowen-Skeen had said that children were perfectly able to make their own culinary and dietary choices. But, in my opinion, to take away a kid's enjoyment of ice cream was a greater tragedy. Of course, I had been in Iqsaiqsiq long enough to know that if I ever tried to make that argument the first thing I would have been told is that it wasn't the fault of any person, but of the Pepsi corporation, because it makes

Pepsi that is both corrosive and delicious; and the Ben and Jerry's corporation, because it makes ice cream that is cold. Had I suggested that people brush their teeth more, I would have been called imperious. Had I suggested Pepsi not be allowed in Iqsaiqsiq, I would have been called fascist.

In fact, I already knew then that if I ever said anything in a broad public forum about Iqsaiqsiq other than that it was a happy place where generous and cooperative people happily lived close to the land in harmony with one another and danced to the beat of the skin drum in their *qaspaqs*, I would be called a racist. Then again, I had already been called *tuniq,* fuck, *tuniq*-fuck, fuck head, fucking *Tuniq*-head, fucker, motherfucker, cock, cocksucker, motherfucking cocksucker, cock hole, cunt hole, asshole, punk, bitch, son of a bitch, punk bitch, punk ass bitch, fag, faggot, faggot ass, queer, lesbo (albeit only by Solomon), piece of shit, bullshit, shit, *anuq, anuq* breath, cock breath, cunt breath, dick, dick beater, dick eater, a dozen other things I had efficiently shuttered away in the cellar of my mind; plus, by the villages designated marksman Matt Kala'a, "Bully."

Actually, I could live with being called imperious, fascist, and racist. Those words had an almost civil ring to them.

After dinner I offered the boys the remainder of the second Pepsi twelve-pack to take with them.

"All of it?" asked Lewis.

"Sure, I'm not going to drink it."

They tipped the box on its side and let the cans roll out, all nine of them. Then they put the cans into two piles, one at a time, until there were four and four, with one left by itself. They each claimed a pile and found various pockets to fill, but left the single can on the table. I expected a mild debate over its ownership, perhaps a game of paper-rock-scissors, even an acquiescence of, "You can have that one." But it was just left there as if it didn't exist.

I commented on its desertion. "Either of you gonna take that?"

They both shook their heads.

Somewhere beneath that action was a well-established norm I could not decipher and had only heard articulated by a few kids and Stan as, "Sharing." It was better that it go to waste than for someone to have an amount unequal to the other, even though there was already more than enough for everybody. I also knew that these were kids, and higher functioning kids at that, and this was a can of Pepsi in a white man's house. Ten years from now, if there were village or family politics involved, or if no one was around to watch, or if it were a jug, sadly, it would not play out so amicably.

They both put their shoes back on and stepped out into the hallway. Jay-Boy turned around and said, "I got a joke. It's little gross, but this not school, so okay I tell it, yeah?"

I raised my eyebrows.

"When you go bathroom, what country are you from?"

I popped my shoulders up and down quickly, Eskimo-speak for, "I absolutely know the answer, but I'm going to pretend that I don't."

"Russian on your way there, European inside, then you Finnish."

"Thank you Jay-Boy. That's a good one."

"Yeah, see you," Jay-Boy giggled.

"See you, Mr. Shosatori," said Lewis.

"Adios Muchachos," I said.

Somewhere in the single digits of February Mitch Forman, self-professed master of Bush teaching and avowed friend to all of Iqsaiqsiq, kindred spirited himself and Gobi away. Neither Native nor *tuniq* eyes witnessed their departure; just the footprints and paw prints between the quad-plex and the airport. Within hours, those disappeared as well.

# CHAPTER EIGHTEEN

We were all forced to sacrifice our prep periods for the remainder of one week and another full week before Mitch's replacement arrived, the sun even came back while we waited, but it was worth it.

Curt Jackman, who looked like a buffed out Richie Cunningham with a goatee in a size-too-small V-neck sweater, arrived on Friday with thirty minutes left in the day. A-Team walked him straight down to the gym where the four elementary teachers had collaborated to divide and conquer the middle school PE class; one actively participated in the game as the facilitator, one kept a watchful eye as the referee, one kept order on the penalty bench, and one held detention in the classroom for the most egregious offenders.

At 3:30, A-Team brought Curt around to the secondary wing and after introductions I offered to drive him over to the four-plex.

I noticed three large duffel bags in the back of the Tahoe and asked him, "How much they soak you for at the airline for those?"

"Eighty-noin doll-uhs," Curt said in a Southey accent.

"Highway robbery."

"True dat."

At the apartment we discovered that Mitch had left something to remember him by. The toilet was packed to the rim with feces, at least a week's worth. Maybe only four days if Gobi had been recruited. The shower stall had a single mound, topped with a meringue of Charmin. I suspected further dastardly mischief and pulled the stoppers from the bathroom and kitchen sinks to find 52-ring shit-cigars torpedoed into both.

Curt swore up a storm as he opened the windows to the minus twenty degree weather. Hesitantly I peeked into the refrigerator and the stove where I expected to find a heaping tray of crap crepe's, but was relieved they were both empty, although the bottom of the refrigerator was caked with dried blood and inside the oven gristle coated every surface.

I wanted to provide Curt some compassion, but also some realism, so I said, "Had I walked into an apartment like this when I showed up I might have just left and never looked back. But after six months I feel it's a pretty accurate way of telling someone, 'Welcome to Iqsaiqsiq.'"

"I might get on duh next plane outta here," Curt said as he fumed forcefully like a Keurig, "But first I'm gonna unbolt dat toilet, wraw-p it in plaw-stic, and traw-ck down dis Mitch Forman mawthuh fawkuh just so I can shove half'it up his awss and half'it down his throat 'til I'm faw'nuff in to shake hands with myself."

Based on that one interchange I put good odds that Curt would last at least a full week in Iqsaiqsiq.

I drove Curt to the store so he could buy some supplies and offered to help him clean but he said, "Thanks anyway Bub, but dis is my apawtment and I gotta work through dis ting by my own praw'sis."

Curt's already good odds tripled.

I explained movie night and that it would go until at least 9:00 if he wanted to join us. Curt said he would be over, but just to work on his room and lesson plans. I also offered up my couch for a few nights and he said he'd consider it.

Back at the school Curt was the main topic of discussion. He was from, "Bawstin, Mawss-uh-chewsh-its," had taught a few years in Dorchester, and now bided time between the completion of his master's in psychology and beginning his doctorate in psychiatric medicine. Everyone was fairly impressed and we debated whether he was truly as good as we believed or if he just seemed that way because he was the un-Mitch.

I relayed the toilet situation, and how Curt handled it, which solidified everyone's opinion that he was a stand-up guy. Joanne said, "Emma put forth a great deal of effort, but she focused all of it on changing the paradigm instead of adapting to a way she could function within it."

Brenda made a reference to Emma and her similarity to one of the characters in *Who Moved My Cheese?* We all agreed that Iqsaiqsiq as a whole was long on Hem and Haw, and short on Sniff and Scurry.

Cornell added, "Emma's booo-k would be muh-ore luh-ike *Who Moved My Couch?*"

Nick and I shared coordinated glances to communicate, "You gonna say anything? No, you? No."

Ben gave us his take on how the first ninety-nine phone calls for a sub must have gone. "Sub for the rest of the year? Where at? Iq-what's-iq? Oh, I've got to, uh, take my father to the gynecologist. Click."

We decided it would be best if Curt was brought up to speed on the *real* customs and taboos of Iqsaiqsiq, but didn't hear the same stories over and over again from each of us. We wanted to tell him all of the things that Terri Bowen-Skeen should have disclosed at the first in-service, instead of promoting the idealized version she wished were the case. I volunteered to be the messenger and we came up with five things he really needed to know: a) the fire extinguisher story, b) the history behind the policy on soda and headphones, c) the definition of the words *anuq, atchu, tuniq, quaaq,* and bother, d) Solomon's inquiries and how to deflect them, and e) the fact that A-Team was a strict and even-handed policy hound. We figured he would inquire about the rest in due time. The elementary teachers also offered to split his PE class if need be.

Back at the quad-plex the foyer reeked of Pine-Sol and Curt's couch was wedged against the wall at the top of the stairs. When I left on Saturday morning he was sleeping on it. Later as I pedaled the spin-bike, Curt rolled a TV cart into the gym to do P90X. Eventually we both ended up in my room.

"What's the status on your apartment?" I asked.

"I got duh shit stink out, and the cleaner smell has dropped off quite a bit, but it'll take a while before I can bring myself to wash anything or brush my teeth in doze sinks."

"Putting up once with Mitch's shit, literally, might be easier than putting up with the guy in person day after day."

"Was he like a frawt-boy slack-uh, fresh out uh college, or sumt'in?"

"About as far from that as you can imagine. I'm gonna start talking, you just tell me when to stop." I began with my initial impression of Mitch's disorganization, went through the difficulty we had to get him on board with the headphone and soda policy as well as his behavior in Aciq, and wrapped up with the day Leena confronted him at the store. I managed to wrangle the five points the coterie had agreed upon into the narrative.

"So dis auntie at the store, she t'ink he's a perv or sum'tin?"

"I never got that vibe. But she, and others, didn't care much for him squeezing himself into their lives. He was sort of culturally androgynous." Then I told Curt what a debacle Mitch's classes were, especially the middle school PE, because he never put any consequences behind his directives. I added the elementary teacher's offer to help out.

Curt said, "Naw, if I walk in dare wit' 'noth-uh teacher, dare gonna think I'm some kinda half-retawd dat can't function wit'out a chaperone. Good to know y'all got each other's backs like dis dough."

First period Monday morning the eighth graders and freshman greeted Curt with fangs out until he shut down all of the computers remotely. Then they all sat and did nothing until the bell rang, except for those that got sent out or left *sua sponte*.

I greeted the three elders at lunchtime, then swung by Curt's room. He leaned across his desk as he filled out discipline referrals with one hand and held an icepack to the side of his face with the other.

"What happened?" I asked.

"Failure on my pawt to fully consider all the potential hazawds. Third hour, I was reffin' the game, runnin' up and down the coe-uht, a second basketball appears and..." Curt lowered the icepack to reveal a nice knot just in front of his left ear. "I think it was Alex or Aw-nuld, but can't say for sure. Coulda been worse dough, coulda been a fire extingui-shuh. Back to the wall at all times from now on, Bub, back to the fawkin wall."

Fourth hour my class was all atwitter with Curt Jackman impersonators.

"Hey Suzette, Hey Middy, come oh-vuh heee-uh, come oh-vuh heee-uh," said MKay.

"I don't want to come oh-vuh they-uh, you come oh-vuh hee-uh," replied Suzette.

I only had five squares left to count down on my calendar to self-immolation so I asked, with feigned innocence, "Why are you guys talking like that?"

"We weren't talking to you!" snapped MKay.

"I know you weren't talking *to* me, and I know you weren't talking *about* me. I haven't ever heard you talk like that so I am asking why you are talking like that now."

"None of your god damn business. Leave us alone," said MKay.

Over the course of the last one-hundred eighteen student-contact days it had been well established that between the hours of 8:00 a.m. and 4:00 p.m. anything that happened within the seven-hundred or so square feet of that classroom was totally my business, so I said, "If it isn't any of my business, why are you doing it in my classroom?"

MKay helped herself to the door, threw it open, yelled, "Fuck you *tuniq!*" and helped herself down the hallway.

"God, you're such an asshole," said Tara Iqaluq.

I simply held up one finger.

"Is that what you pick your butt with?"

Undeterred I held up two fingers.

"Is that other one what you…" Tara cut herself short.

Tim laughed. "Tara never want to get bumped from the tournament this weekend, that the only reason how come she not tell you what to do with your fingers Shosatori. That the only reason how come lots of us never get all gangster up in here. Regionals in a few weeks though, then basketball's over and it's gonna be hard time for teachers, all you teachers."

I wanted to say, "And a busy time for Trooper Stan," but stayed classy with, "We'll deal with that when it happens, until then let's get back to work," which they actually did.

Fifth period was a legitimate joy, kicked off with one of Jay-Boy's jokes, as usual.

"What you call boomerang what never come back?" Jay-Boy paused. "A stick."

I had been asked by A-Team to speak with Lewis about post-high school plans.

Lewis had two excellent options; a full-ride scholarship to the University of Alaska Fairbanks, and Job Corps in Palmer. The UAF scholarship was due to his status as the highest ranked graduate, even though he was the only graduate. He also had subsidiary scholarships he could apply toward any school, or piggyback with his UAF scholarship to cover additional expenses. Kids in Tacoma or Bellingham would have killed for that opportunity. Job Corps offered nine to twenty-four month programs that ranged from culinary services to heavy equipment operation, the types of jobs where, in Alaska, a nineteen-year-old could earn $40,000 to $60,000 a year.

I told Lewis, "You and I can go down and visit UAF this spring, meet the professors, eat in the cafeteria, and play ball at the rec center. There's also a reception where you can meet other kids from villages. Then Polar Peoples Native Corporation will pay for your mom to come down with you the week before you start classes in the fall. She can meet these people, help you shop for clothes, and go around Fairbanks with you."

"College is hard, right? I never want to go if I just drop out. Everybody who go there drop out, come back by Christmas."

I couldn't help but notice that the trend for some students in Fairbanks mirrored the trend for some teachers in Iqsaiqsiq. "There are people called tutors who will help you with your work, and if you need to take easier classes for the first year, you can do that."

Lewis just shook his head.

I tried to sell Job Corps, especially a course on information systems, since Lewis was into computers.

Lewis was more comfortable with that idea, but in the end he shook his head, "I like computers and might-could be good at it, but not in Palmer. Palmer too big."

Palmer had a population of less than ten-thousand, and Lewis would have spent most of his time at the Job Corps center campus which was much smaller than a typical urban or suburban high school.

"It's okay if you don't want to answer this Lewis, but I'm curious. You and the other kids talk about how boring Iqsaiqsiq is and how great Anchorage is, but here is a chance to live in Fairbanks or Palmer all of next year, or even longer, and you won't go. Why is that?"

I realized it was a rather delicate question and was prepared for Lewis to say, "*Atchu,*" which really meant, "I might know the answer, but even if I do I'm still not going to tell it to you."

Lewis pondered the question for a long time then said, "I know," and retrieved a piece of paper to make a word web as we had practiced for some of his writing assignments. Fifteen minutes later I looked up and saw that he was finished. We made eye contact and he looked back down at his paper. Optimistically, I half-expected something like *Letter from Birmingham Jail,* but Lewis summarized everything in just six, very profound, words: "I never know what happens there."

I took a moment to decipher what Lewis meant by that. When I had a rough idea, basically that the speed with which life moved and things changed in cities was exponentially quicker, I asked him to clarify.

"When I get on bus, I never know about those people, who they are or where they're going. When I go past houses, I never know who's in there, if they're good or bad people. Things happen all of a sudden, like parades or carnivals, but nobody talks about it until next day and I never know about it when it happen. Right now, no Pepsi at store, only Coke." Lewis snapped his fingers. "Everybody know that. Tomorrow or next day, whenever Pepsi come in." Lewis snapped his fingers again, "Everybody know store gots Pepsi."

I had considered Iqsaiqsiq to be much more mysterious than any large city, but realized that they both had tacit intricacies, the difference was that most of the intricacies of cities were documented; bus schedules, movie schedules, phone books, street signs, city ordinances, news broadcasts, and Facebook pages. Also, cities were much more predictable than Iqsaiqsiq; the store always had Pepsi or milk or lettuce, and the post office always opened even if the postmaster was sick or drunk or couldn't find a babysitter. But Iqsaiqsiq was not big on written documentation, advanced preparation, or regular schedules, all of which made it necessary to keep and update a personal mental log of who, what, and where; an impossible feat in any place that exceeds a couple square miles and a few hundred people.

Lewis' opinion was one of the most well analyzed points of view I had ever had a student express, in either Washington or Iqsaiqsiq. Still, I didn't think he understood the magnitude of this opportunity. It was exactly what the other ninety-nine percent of the world preceded with, "If only I had…"

The next words just rolled out of my mouth and afterwards I thought, "Did I just say that out loud?" because they were completely antithetical to all of the college advice I had previously given to students. "Just go Lewis. Just for a semester. See what it's like. You can watch movies, go to McDonald's, hang out with the kids from Galena and Nulato, play pool at the rec center, and make Youtube videos. The worst that happens is you come back here at Thanksgiving and never leave again, and even if you fail every class you will have learned a great deal about the world."

Lewis would have none of it so we looked at some jobs on the internet. The only one that interested him was being a janitor at a large,

226

remote, gold mine; twelve hours on, twelve hours off, for two weeks straight, then two weeks off. He said that Tommy, the basketball coach, had worked there in the kitchen at one time and told him it was an okay place, "If, you know, somebody like, wants to have job."

I envisioned the mine as a self-contained complex of a hundred or so employees per shift, all with their names clearly embroidered on their matching coveralls. They lived together in the same building and ate the same food, day after day and year after year; very routine, very consistent, and very comfortable for a chronically-apprehensive kid from the village.

We printed out the application and Lewis took it as homework to fill in with his social security number and other information. The plan was to eventually develop references and a letter of introduction, and practice interview skills.

At our Monday staff meeting Curt had a big fake smile plastered across his face until the rest of us half-haggard souls drug ourselves in, then he took on a more stoic demeanor.

The meeting was short and sweet, and afterward Curt's presence was requested in A-Team's office, never a good sign.

We all filed into Cornell's room and waited for Curt to pass by. Cornell invited Curt in but he apologetically cited other obligations so I blurted out an extemporaneous account of Tim's behavior toward the Late Emma Rudd and myself on the first day. Curt let his rigid physique soften and joined us.

Curt decompressed. "Yep, dat Tim. Mawthuh-fawkuh, mawthuh-fawkuh, mawthuh-fawkuh."

"Nick, you and this guy related?" I asked.

"Yeah, we're related." Nick raised his hirsute eyebrows and massaged the top of his bald scalp. "We're, 'kindred spirits.'"

The room roared and after we filled Curt in on the origins of kindred spirits and the three motherfucker day he relayed his Tim story. "Second period I'm talkin' to duh class. He's talkin' to his buddies. I ask him to be quiet. He pipes down fo'bit, stawts talkin' to his buddies again. I ask him to quiet down again, or he'll have to move. He stawts talkin' again, I ask him to move. He says he don't need to, we argue, he says, 'What would happen if somebody came over dare and kicked your ass?' I say, 'Dat would be a poor choice.' He says, 'How come?' I say, 'How come you think?' He says, 'Are you threat'nin' me?' I say, 'Why? Are you threat'nin' me?' He pipes down for a bit, then outta nowhere starts spewin' profanity. I tell him to go to the office. He don't. I call the office. Principal Atkinson and duh Stater come in and he walks out wit'em."

Curt leaned against the counter. "For some reason or 'nuth'uh the principal is really uptight 'bout kids actin' up so much. Said I should try to choose my words bet'uh so they don't seem so confrontational, which kinda pisses me off 'cause if anyone was lookin' to push a confrontation it was Tim. He also said he supported me shuttin' down duh computers and benchin' kids, but eventually I need to get duh kids to woh-uhk."

Pat was one of us, but with an asterisk since he had history with A-Team. For that reason, we used Principal Atkinson's proper address around him, and didn't get too critical of his actions. At the time Curt wasn't privy to any of these particulars so we all threw around some small talk then disbanded.

I told Curt he was welcome to use the kitchen and shower in my apartment whenever he wanted. He asked when I was headed home and I told him about 5:30, since I wanted to stop at the store before it closed.

At 5:20 Curt was at my classroom door, all bundled up in his Sorel boots, RefrigiWear one-piece, wool scarf, and Russian-style bomber hat. I slipped into my own gear and we headed for the store. Curt offered to treat me to a TV dinner and as we sorted through them he spotted the value packs. "What're doze?" he asked.

"Fifty pounds of meat for a few hundred bucks."

Curt levitated toward that part of the freezer. He removed one, read the contents, placed it on the floor and said, "I get two a deez, you help me carry one?"

We took the two boxes and two dinners up to the counter. Curt paid the $718 tab with his Visa card and we stopped in the *quniciuq* to suit up for the walk home. It was only negative five or negative ten degrees and there wasn't any wind so I kept my balaclava and goggles tucked away, pulled my neck gaiter up to my nose, and left my hood three-fourths open. Curt on the other hand had his bomber hat snapped snugly under his chin and a sheep and a half's worth of wool scarf coiled around his face until only a one-inch by six-inch slit remained for his eyes.

As we walked on the ice, each with a box on our shoulder, I noticed that we produced a single reverberation. Even when off-base and in civilian clothes a group of Marines will lock into sync with each other in four steps or less, it requires a conscious effort not to adopt a unified cadence. "You ever been in the service?" I asked Curt.

"Naw," said Curt, "Why d'yuh ask?"

"No reason."

A few harmonized strides later Curt said, "I'm glad day got dis meat at duh store. All I brought wit' me is oatmeal, jerky, and protein bawz."

"Sounds like me. I showed up here with Clif bars, Gatorade powder, and some freeze-dried dinners. I've been ordering canned goods by the case through Span-Alaska since October. I go online, click on what I want, and put in my credit card number; three or four weeks later it shows up at the post office."

Curt took the value packs into his apartment and I took the dinners into mine. A few minutes later Curt came back adorned with a Red Sox cap, Patriots jersey, and Celtics sweatpants.

"No love for the Bruins?" I asked.

"I got me some love for duh Broonz." Curt lifted up his jersey to reveal a tee shirt covered with the trademark circle, spokes, and B. "But duh Broonz need to win duh cup at least wawnce dis century before day get tawp billin'."

We both smothered our trays with Tabasco sauce and dug in.

"Ya know?" said Curt as he cut into the edge of his Salisbury steak with his fork. "Last time I was called a cock sawker dis much in such a short period of time was at Yankee Stadium in oh foe'uh."

I pictured Curt with an overpriced Pabst in one hand as he flipped the bird to a Yankees fan with the other. Then it hit me even harder than Lewis' words had that afternoon. "That's what this is. Emma thought this was about philosophy; that she could reason with these kids until they understood and agreed with her. Mitch thought that this was about passivity; that he could yield to these kids, and show them that he was not a threat, and they would embrace him. But this is a rivalry, like Boston and New York. It doesn't matter which team scores the most points, or which one has the best players, nobody will ever convert or concede. Maybe the best we can hope for is to get to and from our seats without throwing punches."

"Or basketballs, or soda cans, or chay'uhs, or half-eatin' candy bawz..." Curt paused. "What else gets thrown around he-uh?"

"Snowballs, pencils, crayons, rulers, scissors, computers, a cowbell, a guitar, trash cans," I had to correct myself, "scratch trash cans, they actually get kicked, not thrown. A student, Olivia, got taken to the floor by A-Team. More of a heave than a throw, but still arm movement resulting in impact. And of course my dearly beloved door, bearer of Iqsaiqsiq's animosity and agitation."

After dinner we lounged at the table and Curt said, "Rivalry, huh. Hadn't thought uh dat. I'll have to put in some academic rig'uh and see if it holds, like your doe'uh, or disintegrates, like dat gui'taw. I already got one theory I'm workin' on, wanna hear it?"

I caught myself as I subconsciously raised my eyebrows, then nodded my head, and finally said, "Hell yeah."

"When Raw-key tore up duh filing cabinet, he didn't do it to get his chips back diddy? He did it to show he was pissed off dat his chips was in dare. I'd call it iconoclasm; destruction of sacred objects. Duh objection is dat duh objects destroyed awen't sacred. So it's simply destruction of objects, although dare's a link between duh object and what duh object represents. I gotta kick it 'round s'more." Curt shot me a smile. "I mean kick in duh figuh'tive sense."

"May I, professor?" I asked.

Curt bowed and swiped his upturned palm across the table.

"That is why I like the rivalry idea so much. Rivalry isn't about points or wins. Rivalry is about; 'I have a blue shirt, blue shirts are the best, everybody wearing a blue shirt is awesome.' Or, 'You have a red shirt, red shirts are the worst, everybody wearing a red shirt sucks.' The empirical evidence is irrelevant, because regardless of what the numbers add up to it doesn't make my shirt any less blue or your shirt any less red."

Curt said, "Uh kiss cannot overcome uh logical awgument, nor can uh logical awgument overcome uh kiss."

"Thank you Father Zosima," I told Curt in acknowledgement of his *Dostoyevsky* reference.

"*Puzhalsta,*" Curt replied with the Russian word for, "You're welcome."

We discussed affective versus predatory aggression, relativism, and coping mechanisms. Given a case of beer, a campfire, forty-eight hours to work out the details, and the authority to act; we probably could have solved all of Iqsaiqsiq's problems right there. But Iqsaiqsiq was a dry community, on a treeless landscape, and we had to go to work the next morning; all of which were most certainly a deliberate Western-Anglo conspiracy to rob the Inupiat of their prerogative.

Besides, we were just two teachers, which meant, if primetime pundits are to be believed, we had no clue how the real world worked and just bided our time and padded our pensions at the public trough until summer when we would get, "Three months off." (Actually 2.3 months off; but why offer a mathematically substantive heterodox to anyone's putative delusions.)

Tuesday Curt went straight back into the gladiatorial arena, absent both shield and sword, whereupon MKay and JCee hurled several peanut butter smothered Pilot Bread crackers at him like Ninja stars. I let him borrow one of my clean shirts and after school Curt voiced that since I let him use my stove and electricity, he would provide the food; which always consisted of a large piece of random animal flesh and a modicum of beans. From that point on we had dinner together almost every night, whereupon we raucously reenacted or debated the day's events, and sometimes sulked in complete silence over the same.

Friday afternoon we all watched *Austin Powers* and indulged in five different flavors of Orville Redenbacher microwave popcorn. Afterwards, Curt and I bundled ourselves against the subzero weather and pushed against the darkness propelled upon us by a fifty mile an hour southerly wind. Our boots grappled for traction on the glare ice, polished smooth by the three day bluster. More than once one of us went ass-over-tea-kettle and cut down the other like bowling pins in a seven-ten split.

After dinner, a pound of bacon and two cups of beans seasoned with curry, I crossed the thirty-fifth student contact day from my calendar and didn't even set the next pitch. As long as Curt stayed, I would stay. If Curt bailed, I would evaluate the circumstances and set my sights on another target. I could finally see a light at the end of the tunnel, even the amusement park tunnel, despite the lack of light at the end of the day.

# CHAPTER NINETEEN

The first week of March we turned several corners. There was daylight for seven, eight, or nine hours a day; although it depended on cloud cover and how one defined the term daylight. Next year's contracts were offered to each of us, except Ben and Brenda. Third quarter report cards were sent in and, despite several students with multiple failing grades among them, the majority of the boys' basketball team stayed in place under some type of district approved provisional-eligibility-for-academic-progress model. Arnold was an outright casualty while Tim and Alex managed to hold it together just enough to get by, and sometimes even asked between the first and second offense if they still had a strike left. If answered in the affirmative they would say, "Then, suck it bitch," and remain silent for the remainder of the class period. On occasion they were victims of their own hamartia.

The girls' basketball team had effectively been disbanded. Only half of the high school girls had gone out for the team originally. Middy Iqaluq was now pregnant, which dropped the team from seven players to six. The three days MKay and JCee were suspended after they pitched Pilot Bread at Curt pushed them past the ten absences permitted to maintain eligible status, which dropped the team from six to four. There would be no Iqsaiqsiq girls team at regionals that year; a fact all of us, even the elementary teachers, were reminded of at every opportunity by students and parents alike.

The Monday before the regional basketball tournament A-Team reiterated the eligibility model which, to his credit, he adhered to as if it was the protocol for a nuclear missile launch. He also stated that the players were scheduled to leave for Aciq on Wednesday afternoon and absolutely must have homework sent with them. I thought it was odd to make travel homework a major issue when daily homework was mostly ignored, but figured it was one of the many, "Let's-do-this-so-it-looks-like-we're-serious-even-though-we're-not," edicts from the district office.

Wednesday morning Tim made sure he was at school early since A-Team had explicitly stated that a tardy would bar a student from travel to the regional basketball tournament. I was in the staff room and heard him use the phone set up on the table just outside of the office. He insisted that the party on the other end find some sodas that he could take with him to the tournament.

"Bring me some soda! I need soda!" Tim yelled into the receiver.

Had I been on the other end of that phone I would have simply hung up. Pat had hall duty and, as an astute human and responsible staff member, intervened when Tim's behavior escalated to an inappropriate level.

"I know store's closed. Go get me some fucking soda at auntie's house!" Tim knocked the receiver against the table a couple times and yelled into it again, "Get me some sodas bitch!"

I would have said, "Tim, that's not appropriate," or, "Tim, hang up the phone," or even just, "Tim, go to the office." Pat was far more experienced than I and it showed in the way he handled it. Pat said, "Tim, let's try and call again later."

Tim turned to Pat and said, "Mind your own fucking business! I'm not talking to you, I'm talking to my mom."

Pat repeated, "Tim, let's try and call again later."

I ducked into the office where Stan - in jeans and a sweatshirt but with his Glock in a paddleback holster and handcuffs tucked in his back pocket - spoke with Jenn, and motioned for him to come out. A-Team wasn't in the office at the time.

Tim propelled a final profanity-laced monologue into the receiver, slammed it down, and stared around the foyer. It probably would have ended there since neither Stan nor I were directly involved and I don't think Pat was particularly offended when told to mind his own fucking business. Then Tim gathered up the cord and yanked it out of the wall.

Pat said, "Tim, I need you to wait for Principal Atkinson in the office."

Tim had a whole series of, "How *come?*" "I *could,*" and, "For what?!" Eventually Tim walked into the office and sat down on a chair, perhaps more out of boredom than compliance.

I went back to my room and about twenty minutes later Mrs. Kala'a pulled up on a snowmachine. She took two plastic bags filled with cans off of the handlebars and carried them into the school. After second period started I heard the snowmachine drive away.

By lunch all of the students knew that Tim had been suspended and, as a result, would not travel to the tournament. At the end of fifth period there was a short assembly after which the team left for the airport. Since Lewis was my only student, and a member of the team, I drove the Tahoe to the airport and waited with them for the plane. After school the staff learned that Tim had been suspended for property damage, i.e., the phone.

At 8:05 Thursday morning we were all called into the library. A-Team was there in a crisp, white, long-sleeve dress shirt with cuff-links but, of course, no tie; face freshly shaved, as always, and gel-laden hair parted to one side. Stan stood next to him in dark blue utilities and black gloves. His AR-15 hung from a Chalker Sling on his chest. It was *Mad Men* meets *The Hurt Locker.*

Stan stated that headquarters had been called in Aciq Wednesday night because "somebody" was "talking crazy" on the VHF. He had spoken with several people but none disclosed who that person was except that it was a "he" and "he" sounded "drunk." They elaborated that it seemed directed at the school as a result of a student who wasn't allowed to go to the tournament.

Certain people had been eliminated as suspects. Lewis, Jay-Boy, Alex, Rocky, Allen, Daniel-Ben, and Ezekiel were all at the tournament with Coach Tommy. Matt Kala'a was still locked up for the October shooting. David was at the tournament with all expenses paid courtesy of the village since he claimed that it was important to be there as the mayor to represent Iqsaiqsiq. Of course, since the village had chartered a plane and paid for a hotel room anyway, his entire family accompanied him. A few other individuals had flown out on the regular flight or made the day long snowmachine trip to Aciq.

"As soon as the weather has cleared, another Trooper is coming in from Aciq to track down Arnold and Tim, until then I'm going to be either in the school or very close," Trooper Stan stated.

A-Team explicitly stated that these were third-party allegations, and he was not going to set a "precedent" of closing down the school "every time" somebody made an ambiguous threat. After 9:00 the exterior doors would be locked and he asked that we each limit student traffic in the hallway and check the fire exits nearest our rooms regularly to be sure they were secure. I felt like A-Team had gone a little too far into the amusement park tunnel on this one, but he was the skipper and if this was a mistake he was comfortable making that was his right, and his responsibility.

Brenda and Curt were livid; they insisted that school be cancelled. Joanne, Nick, and Pat were concerned; they suggested that perhaps it would be best if school were cancelled. Belle, Cornell, and new-and-improved-Xanax-infused-Ben were illusory; they said that they didn't see what made this day different from any other. I abstained and pondered my choices; stick it out or go pack my bags. I was a survivor, with the guilt to prove it, and there was no way I wanted to live my life with the knowledge that one of my colleagues or students had gotten killed as I chugged Alaskan Amber at the Bush Pilot Bar in Fairbanks.

I went back to my room, jotted an email devoid of any reference to the current situation, attached the picture that Stan had taken of me beneath the Aurora Borealis, closed it with, "Best wishes to you all and for always, Ken," and sent it to everyone on my contacts list. Then I taped another layer of paper over my window, as if the first layer would even make a difference.

The classes were very slight and significantly subdued. I really could have used a spin-bike session after school but didn't want to get shot as I rode it and have my sweaty body travel back to Washington State in only a tee shirt, shorts, and tennis shoes. I had left Afghanistan, but some parts of Afghanistan would never leave me.

Stan ferried us home. Over dinner Curt vented how pissed he was that A-Team hadn't canceled school. I replied that while A-Team had made the wrong call, it was his to make and, based on what he had demonstrated in Aciq, A-team was a person of integrity (a notably rare thing in the arctic, regardless of rank or race) and as such probably didn't take his decision lightly because if things went south he would forever be referred to as; "Emory Atkinson, the principal of Iqsaiqsiq school when it got shot up."

"You got a fawkin screw loose Shosatori," Curt told me.

I told Curt, "It's loose because the threads are stripped."

I didn't completely know what I meant by that, yet I knew that it was completely true.

Curt sliced another chunk off of the turkey we had picked at since Sunday, dipped it in Dijon mustard, and stuffed it into his mouth. We finished dinner in silence and after five straight nights of turkey, jettisoned the carcass. Curt's lone postprandial remark was, "Least tomorr'uhs Friday," before he went across to his apartment.

Later that night Stan saw fresh footprints headed into David's house. He staked it out and late Friday morning Arnold and Tim stumbled out, unarmed, each with a plastic 750ml bottle of Ron Rico stuffed in their coats and another that they passed between them. Stan arrested them and searched the house which, inadvertently, the two boys had removed the final pieces of evidence from.

Neither of them admitted to anything and David wouldn't press charges for burglary, subsequently they were only charged with Minor Consuming Alcohol; a fine but no jail time.

David later said, "I never know where kids might-could get jugs. It's sad 'cause alcohol is one of the great hardships brought upon our community. I'm glad nobody get hurt though, 'cause sometimes Troopers might-could get trigger happy and like to shoot Native people. Call it suicide by cop."

The team returned from the tournament on Sunday morning and the next Friday report cards were turned in. We didn't have a spring break, which allowed us to get out a week earlier in May, so we began fourth quarter the very next Monday. Standards Based Assessments and the High School Graduation Qualifying Exam were set to begin in fourteen days. Superintendent Custer of the Vienna Boys Choir Brigade led a district-wide teleconference that stressed; how important it was that the students do well, how it was our job as teachers to ensure that the students did well, and how it was really important that for the next two weeks we, "Focus and elevate the level of instruction to maximum effectiveness."

The Superintendent's words led me to an epiphany because I had intentionally kept my instruction unfocused and at a mediocre level of effectiveness for the last twenty-nine weeks. Now, due to his inspiration, I would kick it all up a notch. Actually, for the last twenty-nine weeks I had endured daily verbal abuse and tried to decipher the cryptic euphemisms and subtle cues of my students as I kept my classroom from imploding, quite successfully I might add. I had borne an imbecilic coworker, who was also my neighbor, in the most dysfunctional community this side of an HBO sitcom; at times without electricity or running water. To cap it all off, most recently I had stood in my classroom like William-god-damn-fucking-Tell and waited for some mama's boy with an inferiority complex and minimal impulse control to crank rounds through my classroom window. As a result, I was slightly cynical of the term "maximum effectiveness." The only thing his speech really inspired me to do was seriously contemplate an Olivia Aicia impersonation and stomp out the emergency exit.

The piece de resistance was when the Superintendent tried to rally us school by school into a group cheer. "Do you pledge yourselves to excellence for students Aciq elementary school?!" he would yell, and the Aciq elementary teachers would shout, "Yeah!" and clap and cheer and whistle. Then the Superintendent would say, "Thank you Aciq elementary, right on!" As with most things in the Arctic Circle School District, it started with the two schools in Aciq and worked its way toward Iqsaiqsiq, which always seemed to come last. Belle whispered to Joanne, then to Ben and Brenda. Joanne spoke to Nick and Cornell, who scribbled out a note and passed it back to Pat, Curt and I.

Through a series of nods, shakes, finger gestures, and slowly mouthed words two different plans were hatched within twenty seconds. The first was to simply sit silently and not respond when the Superintendent addressed us. The second was to deliver a single, sarcastic remark in unison, most likely, "What do you think?"

Ben, Brenda, and Curt loved the idea. Belle and Cornell favored it. Joanne and Nick were neutral. Pat indicated he would not participate and drifted to the edge of the room. I loved the idea too, but it would embarrass A-Team to an undeserved extent. I gave it a thumbs-down that Nick quickly seconded and Joanne and Curt conceded. Belle and Cornell spotted the trend and backed out while Brenda protested then relented. It looked like Ben still might go rogue.

"How about you Iqsaiqsiq? Do you take the pledge of excellence for your students?!" the Superintendent yelled, as he clapped and jumped like an evangelist at a revival.

Curt yelled, "Hell yaw! Whoop!" which thankfully drowned out whatever Ben tried to say, and the rest of us clapped in appreciation of Curt's clandestine sardonic brio, all of which added to the façade.

The Superintendent caught himself mid-leap, never acknowledged Iqsaiqsiq by name, and said, "Thank you all. Thank you for being here today. Let's have a great fourth quarter." Then all of the sites were disconnected and the screen went dark.

We came up with a special testing schedule to handle the various grade levels, administration requirements, and accommodations students were entitled to. Most patently, high school teachers were banned from administration of the test to students who were enrolled in their regular classes. For testing week, elementary teachers would administer the high school tests and high school teachers would administer the elementary tests. A-Team addressed us with a, "Good of the order," and, "Dismissed."

Testing week arrived on the eve of another dividend. This dividend, however, was not the thousand dollars sent to every long-term resident. This dividend was specifically for shareholders of the Polar Peoples Native Corporation set up under the Alaska Native Claims Settlement Act established in 1971. A full shareholder owned 100 shares, and the disbursement was about $25 per share. If both parents were full shareholders, the household received $5,000. In most cases, one or both parents were only partial shareholders, so the amount was less. A few people had inherited shares, and they received more. People born after 1971, and who had not inherited any shares, received nothing.

It was now light almost twenty hours a day, compounded terrestrially by the snow's albedo, and the temperatures ranged between zero and freezing. The atmospheric phenomenon fueled the body. The dividend provided money; some of which fueled snowmachines and some of which, through bootlegged alcohol, fueled licentious behavior. All of that fuel effectively scorched the students' chances for a focused, motivated environment in which to apply and demonstrate any limited skills they possessed.

I administered the test to third graders. Most were good to go for the first hour, then waned. We would take a break and have another go right up to lunch. After lunch we'd charge back in, another break, another try, a nap, and then a canine and equine exposition in an effort to quell revolt until 2:30. It was in the middle of one such exposition that I remembered the Late Emma Rudd's comment, "Develop a Bush-specific pedagogy."

Rap, read story, write at desks, read another story, math exploration on the carpet, and repeat; all without a single bite mark and only a few tears. That was my Bush-specific pedagogy and unorthodox though it may have been, unlike Emma, I was still there to implement it.

Down on the high school end things did not go as well.

Monday Tim gave Ben a hard time and got sent home. Tuesday Tim was switched over to Brenda's group, gave her a hard time, and got sent home. Wednesday Tim was switched over to Joanne's group, gave her a hard time (which she reciprocated), and got sent home; where he then assaulted his mother. Tim denied any knowledge of how his mother received her injuries and Tim's mother blamed her injuries not on Tim's fist and feet, but on, "That teacher what let Tim get so mad." Tim then became an involuntary resident at the Fairbanks Youth Facility for the remainder of the year where, Tim-Tim said later, he asserted, "It's not fair here. They got so much rules, and you never get to do nothing unless you follow the rules. I wish I was back in Iqsaiqsiq, 'cause Iqsaiqsiq never got no rules."

Later that week Solomon and Rachel got involved in some kind of interpersonal conflict I wasn't privileged to except that at one point Solomon completely removed Rachel's shirt and when Belle stepped between them Rachel pushed Belle to the floor. A-Team's solution was to have only one of the students in the building at a time. Solomon attended only first, second, and third periods; lucky me. Rachel attended only fourth, fifth, and sixth periods; lucky Curt.

Between the end of basketball season, daylight, dividends, testing, fallout from testing, and spring whaling, the remainder of April smoothed itself out quite nicely. The daylight had re-energized me as well and with my truncated classes I found that I actually had energy left at the end of the day. Sometimes Stan and I would go out on the snowmachines. If he was busy, he let Curt and I go. Occasionally I headed out solo. Once, and only once, all three of us went out together.

We left right after school. The air was just below freezing, but any exposed ground quickly absorbed the sun's radiation, melted the snow around at its edges, and formed a soggy depression. These pockets of waterlogged snow were thick like frosting. The engine bogged, chugged, and glugged until I pegged the throttle and shot out on the other side.

A few miles out we parked the snowmachines next to a small, open-ended, plywood A-frame and lifted the hoods up to cool. Stan explained that to the northeast was some wreckage and from the air the two places could be connected by an invisible line along which unscrupulous pilots dropped plastic bottles of Ron Rico or plastic-wrapped bricks of marijuana. As the snow melted it often revealed previously undiscovered items that were useless as evidence but at least could be kept out of the village.

As the engines tick-tick-ticked their way back down to a safe temperature Curt, whose Southey accent had finally started to soften, said, "I understand the addictive personality as well as the physiological effects of chemicals, if you jus' pull out the chemical, a large part of the behavior still persists in an altered form. What I don't understand is why he'uh, the altered form is always negative, aggressive, and self-destructive. You ev'uh seen it translated to a positive action Stan?"

Stan gave Curt his definition of "non-un-dysfunctional" compounded by the multi-dimensional aspect of alcohol in the Bush. He added that there were decent Native people, like Magnus Kala'a, who never got involved in any shenanigans, but weren't quite ready to be the next Native version of Thomas Jefferson or Martin Luther King and get vilified by the likes of David. He ended with, "The higher functioning someone is, the more likely they are to leave Iqsaiqsiq. That's probably why we see so few people like that around."

Curt retorted with his take on non-sacred iconoclasm, a hypothesis he had yet to fully develop.

I threw in the rivalry metaphor that I now conceded was more of an observation of the behavior, than a rational for the behavior itself.

Curt said, "Dat's good you finally observed dat."

"Thanks," I said, "It was a rational conclusion."

We fired up the snowmachines and I led the way with my eyes glued to the GPS, Curt followed and looked to the right of my tracks, while Stan looked to the left. I had my coveralls half-unzipped and shunned my goggles in favor of my Maui Jim's. When my head got cold I ducked beneath the windscreen for a minute then reemerged to the breeze that my entire body seemed to inhale.

We reached the plane wreckage left over from several years before, lifted the hoods up again to cool, and Stan narrated. "There's at least one serious plane crash up here every year, often several; almost always during the winter, and usually due to pilot error. But that wasn't the case here. All three blades on the prop separated in mid-flight, investigators found a manufactures defect, not the pilot's fault at all. The pilot called out a May-Day and glided down right here, text-book perfect, not a scratch on anybody and most of the fuselage was intact. It was February and six hours passed before search and rescue got organized and located them. They were all huddled in the back under some blankets. Search and rescue found one and four; one survivor, four corpses."

"Who survived?" I asked.

"A guy from Maine, he was the pilot. All four passengers were from Iqsaiqsiq. He left the state pretty soon after that because, as you can imagine, everybody blamed him for the deaths even though the investigators said there was no way he could have known about the internal damage. The passengers died from hypothermia," said Stan.

"The four people from Iqsaiqsiq, they lived up here all their lives. They would have had an even greater awareness of the risks, and an even greater skill set from which to draw. They all should have survived and the pilot should have been the first casualty, why did he make it?" I asked.

Stan replied, "The pilot had one of those Himalayan suits climbers wear on Denali. The other four people were just wearing sweatshirts, jeans, and tennis shoes. It doesn't matter how smart you are, or how acclimated you are, you can't stay warm at minus twenty in a sweatshirt. The pilot was prepared, or lucky. Whichever one it was doesn't matter now, because the other four were neither."

Curt said, "It wasn't luck. Dat fawkuh from Maine had what's called a, 'High internal locus of control.' He saw himself as being able to affect an outcome. Since he saw dat he could have an effect on what happened to'im, he made the effort to be prepared. As a result, he was prepared. Basically he took responsibility for himself. Luck had nothing to do with it. People like dat don't believe in luck, or fate, and they don't trust other people to look out for'em."

"I guess you could say he was, 'The master of his fate, and the Captain of his soul.'" Stan said with a wink toward me, and a poetic nod to W. E. Henley.

"Or at least the Corporal," I said.

Stan nodded. "So Curt, if the pilot had a high internal locus of control, then what did the other four have?"

"High external locus of control, even if they had expected the plane was gonna crash, their belief was dat eith'uh; there was nothin' they personally could do to increase or decrease their chance of survival, or someone else had more power ov'uh their situation then they did and it was dat person or entity's responsibility to take care of them." Curt paused and scanned the horizon then said, "I gotta take a wicked piss."

We started the snowmachines back up and backtracked via GPS toward the A-frame, Stan and Curt each on a side. We stopped at the A-frame to lift the hoods up yet again and Curt expanded on the locus of control theory. The more he talked about it, the more it made sense. I wondered why it wasn't already widely identified as the primary explanation of all things Iqsaiqsiq, not to mention Arctic Circle School District in general; direct causes were rarely identified, no individual ever accepted responsibility for an action (although other individuals were often blamed), things were "*let*" (allowed to) happen as opposed to having a definitive catalyst, and situations and outcomes were considered unalterable. The whole concept also explained why teachers like Emma and Mitch failed while Nick and Pat excelled, and it underscored the bewilderment of the command staff at Brenda's example and expectation of conscious choice.

"Tell me if this is right," I said. "People with a high internal locus of control believe that their actions can affect their lives, so they take action, they attempt control, and they try to make some correlation between their own personal actions and the outcome. Then, depending on the outcome, they either consciously repeat the action or consciously alter the action, so that the next outcome will be closer to the desired effect. By contrast, people with a high external locus of control believe that everything *except* their actions can affect their lives, so they *avoid* taking action, they *avoid* control, and as a result they *avoid* responsibility for the outcome. Then regardless of the outcome, they continue to *avoid* taking action because they don't believe that altering their actions will have any effect."

"Fawkin-a right Shosatori," said Curt.

"So how does a person develop a highly internalized locus of control?" I asked Curt.

"Same way as wit' anything else, they need an example, an instructor, or a guide to take them through the phases; modeling, direct instruction, guided practice, independent practice, evaluation, reinforcement, and adjustment," Curt said.

"Alright, now the tough one, ready? Why are there so few people in Iqsaiqsiq with a high internal locus of control?" I just let it hang out there.

Curt looked at Stan and said, "I could propose some clinical reasons, the popular theories, but I think you might have the best perception as it refers to local conditions."

Stan stared contemplatively into the distance long and hard, the way he usually did as he stirred his coffee or smeared a bagel when I asked him other deeply philosophical questions in his kitchen, then said, "Five reasons.

"First, coming across Beringia the people who now identify as Inupiat had to function as a single organism in order to survive. There wasn't a lot of 'individual' anything, it was all collective. The identity of the individual was totally subverted, not for convenience, but by necessity. You can't think as an individual if no such thing as an individual exists in your sphere of reference.

"Second, the Arctic is a very unpredictable environment. Even the best meteorologists with satellites and computer models have a hard time predicting the arrival of storms, or their duration. It would be hard for a person to believe that anyone or anything, especially one human or even a small group of humans, could ever have an effect on anything. Same goes for animals. Elders knew the patterns of months and seasons when a given species would arrive, the 'window' so to speak, but they couldn't pin it down any further than that, and they only knew from past experience what to expect. My guess is that such a high level of unpredictability dissuades a person from attempting to control anything.

"Third, when the first high internal locus of control individuals arrived; namely the whalers, miners, trappers, and missionaries, along with their technology of rifles, stoves, canned food, and maps, they proved that, while life was still unpredictable, a person *could* control some things. Unfortunately, what they showed they could control was the Inupiat. In effect the message at that time was, 'A person can control their own destiny, as long as they are not an Inupiat.' When I talk about the spill on the floor that made Iqsaiqsiq non-un-dysfunctional, that's probably the first half of it right there.

"Fourth, as the money poured in from the military, welfare, ANCSA, oil, heavy metal mining, and commercial fishing, it allowed the Inupiat to access that technology; which removed the majority of the external controls. It gave the Inupiat access to everything the non-Native had, regardless of whether or not they actually wanted it; health care, education, law enforcement, snowmachines, outboard motors, rifles, refrigerators, microwaves, telephones, televisions, soda pop, potato chips, alcohol, drugs, and pornography. All of the things money provided came conglomerated and, relatively, instantaneously; a cascade of cash, delivered by next day air, in the same envelope as a Sears catalog and a summons for jury duty. At that point, the Inupiat were still in their original high external locus of control mode, but now with very few truly external controls. In other words, the natural consequences were removed but never replaced by individual

accountability. That's the second half of the spill on the floor that
made Iqsaiqsiq non-un-dysfunctional right there, and it was also the
first half of the furniture.

"Fifth, there are two groups of people on the Outside. One
sees the dividends, scholarships, free health care, subsidized housing
and, theoretically, subsistence lifestyle, and says, 'How can that
population *not* be successful?' The other sees the alcoholism,
depression, child abuse, domestic violence, and geographic isolation
and says, 'How can that population *ever* be successful?' The Inupiat
aren't deaf, they hear both of those narratives and the cognitive
dissonance between them is the second half of the furniture. It allows a
person to get up Monday morning and say, 'I am the greatest and
nothing can stop me,' which is a lie, and go to bed Friday night saying,
'I am a failure and the whole world is against me,' which is also a lie,
and people on the Outside have just as difficult a time admitting that as
people in the Native community.

"Parts one, two, and the first half of three are either static or
ancient history so they can't be altered. Part four is about money and
modernity, and as much some people may reminisce about the good
old days, nobody truly wants to go back to shivering, starving, and
picking lice out of their hair in the dark; nor should they. The elements
of part four are so intertwined they cannot be separated. You can't
have duct tape, snowmachines, and VHF radios without alcohol,
potato chips, and television. Part four is a package deal, warts and all
you might say. For all intents and purposes, those three and a half parts
truly are in one's *external* locus of control.

"So what does that leave? Which parts are within one's *internal*
locus of control? The second half of part three and all of part five; the
narratives, the stories, call it propaganda even. The Inupiat need to say,
believe, and embrace these three principles: First, life is a participatory,
not a passive, activity and one must actively engage in it. Second, one
cannot *control* what happens, but one can *prepare* for what happens; and
that preparation is worth the effort, even if ultimately it is either
unnecessary or less than completely effective, simply for the influence
it gives one over one's own life. Third, one may not have total control
over one's circumstances, and one may have less control than others in
aggregate, but a person has more control over his or her own life than
any other single individual. While those principals are not traditional
Inupiat beliefs, they could be adopted and enhance instead of erode the
culture. The greatest barrier to that ever happening is the lack of an

organic catalyst." Stan employed his non-verbal stress response where he rubbed his face with his hands, then said, "So Curt, what would the experts say?"

Curt had a totally glazed deer-in-the-headlights look. "I think half uh'dem would worship you like you was the second coming, then go lookin' for the Birkenstocks you just knocked dem out'uh."

Stan chuckled. "And the other half?"

"The other half would go lookin' for their Birkenstocks first, then denigrate you for bein' an ignorant and arrogant pig, before stealin' your idea and writin' a fawkin' Nobel Prize winnin' article 'bout it." Curt still had the glazed look on his face. "Dat's some heavy shit Stater, fawk me."

We started the machines back up and headed for home. It was downright balmy, maybe in the mid-thirties, and I could tell that my face was sunburned. Tomorrow, I was sure, my ears would be blistered.

# CHAPTER TWENTY

On the last Monday of the year, Lewis, his grandmother, A-Team, and I met during sixth period to discuss graduation. Lewis and I had ordered decorations and the Polar Peoples Native Corporation footed the bill for the post-graduation meal as well as a DJ to play music at the dance. A-Team verified and approved Lewis' diploma. On the way to the staff meeting at 3:30 A-Team told me it was my job to organize and recruit staff to cover various duties for graduation, which also included a promotion ceremony for the eighth graders. Back in Seattle I would have juggled report cards for over a hundred students, so I didn't fixate on the added duty. Besides, my psyche was permeated with Curt and Stan's locus of control discussion; and being "volun-told" by A-Team definitely fell into my external locus of control.

At the staff meeting the test scores from SBA's and the HSGQE were released. The previous year twenty-two percent of the students in grades three thru six had passed, this year thirty-four percent had passed. At the seventh through ninth grade level, twenty percent of the students had passed last year, compared to thirty-two percent this year. The intricacies of scoring for students in grades ten through twelve were complex, but basically half-again as many students passed this year compared to the previous year, although more than half of all the students still failed. The increase was staggering, but we were still below even the lowest end of average.

I had invited Lewis and Jay-Boy over for dinner again that night at 6:00 and, just like the previous dinner at my house, at 4:55 I found Jay-Boy as he sat on the steps and jammed to his iPod. When I took the pizza out of the oven around 5:40 I glanced at Jay-Boy and then the phone. Just as he had three months earlier, Jay-Boy dialed the phone, simply said, "Ready," and hung up. And just like the last time, Lewis was at my door within five minutes.

After dinner I said, "I want you to hear this from me first, before anyone else tells you. I'm not going to be teaching here next year."

Jay-Boy said, "Why you tell us first?"

"You were always asking me when I was going to leave or if I was coming back and I didn't want you to feel bad or that I was trying to hide something from you," I told Jay-Boy.

"Oh," said Jay-Boy.

Based on the brevity of his reply, and his overall demeanor, I gathered that Jay-Boy had not been as concerned about my departure as he was with *his knowing about* my departure. If I were ever to give some Roby-esque advice of my own to another teacher it would be this: The kids in Iqsaiqsiq do not like surprises.

Lewis was equally indifferent to my announcement but asked, "When you came here you said there were too many kids at your old school. At your new school, when somebody ask why you left here, what you gonna say?"

What a great question, melded with the answer from the previous question for contextual specificity. There was no way I could Bill Clinton my way out of this. I knew what I would have said to someone outside of Iqsaiqsiq, but what should I say to this kid without coming across like a major-league David Aicia? I said, "I will tell them that it was too far away from what I knew, too far from where I felt comfortable."

Lewis responded, "That will be good for those kids. You never make us feel bad for not being like other kids, always telling us you never like us 'cause were not like those other kids you teach before. That's all most teachers ever do, like Miss Rudd. And you never tell us how awesome we are, and that you want to be our best friend, say you like us and there's no place better than Iqsaiqsiq in the whole world but then leave anyway, like Mitch."

I offered up the remainder of the soda again. This time there were six cans left, so the division worked out to two piles of three with none left over. I asked them, "How long will it take you to drink all of those?"

Each of them pushed his bottom lip up toward his nose, the *true* indication of, "I really don't know, and I haven't the slightest clue."

"Well you're not going to bring them into my class, *are you?*" I asked.

"*Nooo.*" They both chuckled and shook their heads.

Lewis spoke first. "I probably give one to Tuuqaq, then drink the other two. He saw me bring last time and ask me if I bring again."

"I might-could share with my sisters," offered Jay-Boy, although I think his answer was unduly influenced by Lewis' altruism.

"But you're not going to save them until after school tomorrow?" I asked.

Jay-Boy shook his head and burst out, "No way. Somebody might-could *tiqliq,* then I got none. I'm gonna drink all mine before I go bed."

*Tiqliq* was the word for theft. I asked Jay-Boy, "Why don't you sleep with them under your pillow?"

Jay-Boy chuckled. "Somebody might-could *tiqliq* under there too, wake me up. Nope. I share, or drink, then I never got to worry what might-could happen."

Simplicity, that was probably the same reason why the girls in the *quniciuq* that day had shoved cookie after cookie into their mouth during fall dividend time even though they were full and didn't particularly like that kind of cookie. It also added yet another dimension to the Gordian knot that was village alcoholism. It was wrong to waste and mentally taxing to retain, or safeguard, therefore, it was better to just finish it off. The benefits didn't outweigh the costs; especially when the next dividend check or Quest card was right around the corner.

"How about you Lewis, you afraid your Gram or Tuuqaq gonna *tiqliq* yours?" I asked.

Lewis shook his head and smirked. "No, but why keep them until tomorrow. Maybe tomorrow I get more, and then I have too much, or maybe tomorrow..." Lewis' smirk collapsed as he pushed his bottom lip up toward his nose. "I don't know Mr. Shosatori, you know, that's... That's all tomorrow anyway."

I believe that had Lewis paused that sentence with a comma, and not ended it with a period, and evaluated it the same way he had his reason for not leaving Iqsaiqsiq, he would have added, "And I don't have any control over anything that happens tomorrow."

I opened the door while they slipped their shoes back on and as they left we shook hands. Jay-Boy grabbed the ends of my first three fingers, just like before and just like Jerry. Lewis gave me the firm grasp, double-pump, release he and I had practiced as a job skill.

Jay-Boy turned around in the hallway and said, "I got a joke. What you get when you cross snowman with vampire?"

I popped my shoulders up and down quickly.

"Frost. Bite." Jay-Boy accentuated each word with a finger poke in the air, then said it quickly, "Frostbite!" and laughed.

I smiled.

They walked down the stairs and turned for a final wave and, "See you," then walked out the door to the porch. I heard their footfalls on the metal steps, the squish of the pallets against the slush, and the crunch of the gravel as they reached the road. There was a silence, a muffled exchange of, "See you. Yeah, see you," and gravel crunched again.

Students became surlier and surlier as the week progressed. The major all-stars would often lash out during first or second period and get suspended for the rest of the day, only to be suspended again the next day. Joanne said that was the way it always went, so at this point it was a matter of just holding it together until Thursday night.

Thursday afternoon school was dismissed at 2:30 so we could put the final touches on graduation before it began at 5:00. I downed a quart of Gatorade and two Clif bars, then ducked into the locker room to shower and don my khaki Dockers, green twill shirt, Brook Trout necktie, brown belt, and highly-polished formal shoes. A-Team also wore a tie for the first time in Iqsaiqsiq since October. A clip-on tie, but a tie nonetheless.

In the interim, Terri Bowen-Skeen and the Superintendent arrived. I sat down on the bleachers and slouched with my arms spread. Terri, in a pink, yellow, and orange *qaspaq*, came over. "*Qaniq Itpitch*, may I join you?"

I raised my eyebrows.

"I see you learned some Eskimo-speak," she said.

A million thoughts raced through my mind, but I limited my retort to another eyebrow raise.

"Oh," she chuckled, "You're good!" and wagged a finger at me.

I said, "Guess so," because I felt any further non-verbal cues I used would come across as arrogant.

"I understand you're not returning," said Terri. "That's a shame, you really seemed to connect with these kids. May I ask what affected your decision? It couldn't be the money, because the Arctic Circle School District is the highest paying school district in the United States."

"Nope, the money and the benefits were delivered as advertised." I wanted to add that they were the *only* things that were delivered as advertised.

"Sometimes I wish we weren't the highest paying school district in the United States. It can attract the wrong element, you know, people who are only here for the money."

I wanted to echo Pat's sentiments about how many people saw that as a detriment, yet the two least monetarily motivated individuals were the same two who had left during the year. I waited for Terri to exhaust her narrative.

"I'm always surprised at how many people come up here and are unaware of the cold and dark, even though it is what the Arctic is known for. I guess some people don't realize just how cold minus forty is, or what it's like not to see the sun at all for two months out of the year." Terri paused, "Were you surprised by those things?"

"Surprised? No. It was new, and different, and not how I had imagined, but it was interesting. I like meteorology and geography, once I even saw the Aurora Borealis in a state less than one percent of humans ever will, and I could handle the cold and dark as long as I divided into sections."

Terri let a longer pause wander all across the empty gym before she asked, "I know some teachers have difficulty either accepting or finding acceptance from the community, but I don't think you had that problem. You're the 'Repertoired-rapper, raw and awesome, ramming words together, making them rawsome.' Right?"

"True that."

Terri excused herself and I went down to my room to wait for Lewis, his mother and grandmother. A-Team's time was capitalized by the Superintendent, and the rest of the staff did their best to corral and seat visitors, except for the squirmy children under the age of five who, as always, ran and chased and crawled around. Lewis escorted his mother and grandmother to the front seats reserved for them.

The ceremony began with a welcome from A-Team, a prayer by the local non-denominational pastor, and an address by the Superintendent. Nick invited the eighth graders up to the stage and spoke on their behalf before A-Team presented them with certificates. Music played over the loudspeakers and Lewis took the stage in his cap and gown. He read a paper he and I had prepared, then made about a hundred comments and recognitions starting with his Gram and ending with, "It was good seeing all you people who came here today to see me graduate." A-Team and the Superintendent presented Lewis with his diploma, the music played, and Lewis received a standing ovation as he left the gym. The eighth graders were then excused and received a standing ovation as well. A-Team invited everyone to move into the cafeteria where food was set up in a buffet and the crowd filed out.

As was the custom in communal eating, the Elders, which included Cornell and Belle, went first. Stan, Mitch, and Emma had spoken of community leaders and teachers going second in other villages where they had lived, followed by visitors, then children, and finally local adults. But that was not the case in Iqsaiqsiq nor, from what I had heard, in Ciaciqiq or Aciq. Even Magnus Kala'a, whom I had since learned was one of the highest regarded whaling captains of all time, blended his family right into the middle of the crowd along with other families, guests, students, and young adults. A-Team and the Superintendent also blended into the nebulous crowd to get a plate. The Superintendent would be leaving soon, but Terri planned to stay in the village overnight with relatives.

The other teachers and I scurried around the gym to set-up tables and reconfigure chairs while what seemed like fifty unattended children darted about as if our only purpose was to provide a place to crawl under and dash around. Then we went to the cafeteria to survey the remnants.

There had been large trays of pre-assembled hot dogs and pre-assembled hamburgers, but they were all gone as were pans of spaghetti and several different cakes. What remained were several bowls of Jell-O mixed with fruit, about ten bags of chips (out of an original thirty), half of the original stack of caribou ribs, half of the original stack of whale meat, most of the cubed *maqtaq,* and of course boxes of Pilot Bread. At the end of the table there was a coffee maker and several pitchers of red Kool-Aid. I stacked four Pilot Bread crackers on a plate and covered them with potato chips. Curt fixed a plate of three-fourths caribou and one-fourth whale, which made me wonder if he had ever considered staying in Iqsaiqsiq solely for the endless portions of animal protein. We returned to the gym and sat on the upper-deck of the bleachers to eat.

David approached and asked me, "How soon can I start the Eskimo dancing?"

I told him, "Lewis didn't mention anything about it while we were planning and this is the first time you have mentioned anything about it to me. Actually, the DJ is scheduled to start as soon as the meal is over."

"What?" said David. "No Eskimo dancing? We always have Eskimo dancing during graduation. The dancers have been practicing all week. It is our heritage."

I was already a step ahead of David so I said, "Okay, go for it."

"Oh," said David, "Uh, well I have to find my dancers, and go get my drum, and they might-could get their stuffs."

"You don't have your drum? You don't know where the dancers are? Didn't you expect to do Eskimo dancing for Lewis' graduation? Don't you always do Eskimo dancing for every graduation? I thought you had practiced this all week. I think a real leader would have all of those things in place so that no one missed out on experiencing a single minute of their heritage." It took everything in my power to remain solemn and not crack a smile.

David was dumbfounded. Finally he said, "Uh, we'll get our stuffs, by that time you can have the tables and things moved, yeah?"

I rolled my shoulders forward, in, and down.

David kind of tilted his head and said again, "You get things ready, get people and tables moved out so everything ready when we get back." Then pointed to my chest and said, "You do that."

I rolled my shoulders forward, in, and down again.

David's face flashed the look vampires get when they see a crucifix, then he said, "I'll get my dancers. You get the gym ready," and retreated.

As he made his way around the gym he stopped at various tables and said, "I gotta go get my drum (or gloves, or Andrew), that guy didn't know we do Eskimo dancing. But he know now, 'cause I tell him. I tell him how important it is for our heritage."

A few people looked over in my direction and frowned as they gave David a sympathetic nod, most ignored him, and a few shot him a look that said, "Dude, you are being such an ass clown right now."

Curt said, "Well played, Shosatori. Well played," then scraped a caribou rib clean and asked, "What's that shoulder shrug thing? Is it yet another Eskimo way of sayin', 'Fuck you,' without *sayin'*, 'Fuck you?'"

"I first saw Magnus use it with Mitch when Mitch wouldn't take no for an answer. Lewis said it's a nice way of saying, 'If that's what you want to believe, go ahead and believe it. But you're wrong.'"

Then I filled Curt in on a little secret. "Nick said that last year they begged David to do Eskimo dancing, but he refused, so they planned the whole ceremony down to the last detail without it. Just after the principal began speaking David came up and insisted on doing Eskimo dancing, 'Like always,' you know what I'm saying? They told him, 'No,' and he made a spectacle, called everyone racist and insensitive. They let him do it afterward and he still played up the, 'Good-thing-I-was-here-or-these-kids-might-of-missed-out-on-part-of-their-heritage,' card, which is why I knew that flat-out telling him 'No,' would be a losing proposition. In fact, I think he prefers to be told, 'No,' and manipulates the situation that reinforces his narrative. My guess is he has been doing that since he was in high school himself because when you have a closed community and the entire staff turns over within five years, or struggles internally, you can play that game and win it every year, which is fun as hell. But something tells me next year might be a bye."

Curt offered me his crowded knuckles and I matched mine to them.

Time is a very abstract concept, especially from the Native perspective. Generally once something started it went until the next thing started, or until the majority of the group lost interest and returned to their personal focus of importance. At previous banquets, programs, and tournaments earlier in the year getting the room cleared or getting people to move so things could be set up or taken down was always a challenge. It didn't matter what we said or how we said it, we still received blank stares as if, "Why are you telling me this?" or outright declarations of, "No, this thing isn't over. There are still people here. When everyone else is gone, then I'll leave." I believed it was done out of the belief that no future event could possibly be more important than the task one was currently engaged in. For that reason, I was not particularly anxious to tell people they had to stand up so that I and the other teachers could move tables while the crowd milled around and sneered at us for, as they saw it, chasing them off.

I figured if the King Douche Bag of Iqsaiqsiq wanted people moved, he could bare that animosity. Besides, the dancing would take place up on the stage and there was no need for the tables or people to be moved before it could begin. In fact, at the Holiday program David had insisted that he be allowed to use the stage because he claimed that no one could see them unless they were up on the stage, even though it was crowded with props and scenery that had to be removed. I would have bet my plane ticket out of Iqsaiqsiq that David had told me to move the tables just for the satisfaction of telling me what to do, and having me comply, with the added bonus of creating even more animosity between the school and the community. It may have also been David's attempt to monopolize the crowds undivided attention by removing the "distraction" of their meal.

About thirty minutes later David returned with his drum and five dancers in their regalia. I nursed my fourth cup of Kool-Aid while Curt tore into a caribou hock like a Cro-Magnon. David came over and said, "Hey, why aren't the tables moved?"

"You're dancing on the stage right?" I said.

"No, not today, we are dancing out on the gym floor."

Since this beef wasn't going to affect my career or the academic success of the students, or inconvenience my coworkers, I had no problem taking it to the mat. I told him, "You want the floor available? Ask the community to remove themselves and the tables so that you can perform. I'm sure they won't have any problem complying with your request, especially since you're the mayor and it's part of your heritage. Otherwise, do it on the stage just like you did every other time this year."

"No, this is the school. It's your job to tell these people to get up and move. Go do your job."

I told him, "This is a community activity not an academic activity. If this is really all that important, then you put forth the effort to see that it gets done. I am stuck here until midnight anyway, then we are turning out the lights and locking the door."

David made some incomplete insults and underdeveloped threats, then stomped away and told various people god-knows-what about our conversation.

Curt said, "Just so I know, this shit gets thick we bailin' or stayin'?"

"Staying," I said.

"Suh'weet," Curt sputtered out through a mouthful of stringy venison.

Eventually David made his way over to a group of men that included Magnus Kala'a. Shortly after he arrived Magnus walked in our direction. He didn't charge, or stomp, and his face held an expression beyond stolid. He said, "How come you never let people do Eskimo dancing?"

I explained that I had said yes, forty-five minutes ago in fact, even though David had first told me about it today, and that David had to go get his drum because he wasn't prepared. I added that despite having used the stage during the whaling ceremony, and insisting upon it again in December, he now insisted on using the gym floor even though he had previously said that people could only see the dancers if they were up on the stage. I finished with, "Mr. Kala'a I know that you are an important person in this village and if you ask me to move those tables I gladly will because I respect what you do for the people of this village. But I know, and I think you do to, that David only wants the tables moved because he knows that it is a difficult task that will inconvenience everyone and make them mad at the teachers."

Magnus made the slow, left-to-right, palm-down motion and walked back across the gym.

David said something I couldn't hear, but inferred from body language was similar to, "So, what did he say? What about the tables?"

Magnus made the slow, left-to-right, palm-down motion again and said, or at least mouthed, "No."

David spoke about a paragraph that appeared to end with the word, "Mayor."

Magnus, even shorter than David at 5'7" and slightly thinner, faced him and grunted loudly, "I! Am Magnus Kala'a!" his jaw practically unhinged as he spoke in a deep operatic tone, "*Umialik!*" (oom-yawl-ick), which meant Captain, or literally; the man with a boat.

"You!" he raised his arm above both their heads so that his finger was pointing down at David, "Are David Aicia, trouble maker. Stop! Making trouble for the village! Stop! Making trouble for the school! Stop! Making trouble what makes you look important, and always let everybody else always do what's hard work!"

Just like the polar bear that hopped from the iceberg, and the Aurora Borealis' erratic grace in the moonless sky, I was sure that I had just witnessed one of the rarities of the Arctic: indigenous leadership. Not just an imposed title or self-asserted importance; but an informed, principled decision made with a legitimate recognition of the true cause along with the means and desire to affect the outcome in a positive way for the good of the greater community, even if it bore personal risk or went contrary to popular opinion. This decade, leadership. Next decade, accountability. Maybe. I hoped.

The dancers had to practically drag David to the stage and the dancers performed their coordinated movements with precision. After the first dance David handed the drum off to one of the dancers and left. There was a second dance, a discussion, and then the dancers elected to cease.

A-Team took the stage and thanked everyone for coming, then informed them that the dance, as had been planned from the beginning and announced well in advance, was limited to seventh through twelfth graders. There was some protest from the eighteen to twenty-five year old demographic as the other teachers and I stood to confront the unenviable task of chasing off everyone's grandmother.

Before any of us got to the first table, Magnus bellowed, "Tables," then pointed under the stage where they were stored and said, "Away."

The six men beside him sprang into action and were quickly joined by four others. Those seated at the tables meandered out with their foil-wrapped "take-home" plates in tow.

After a cursory clean-up, we dowsed the lights, DJ T-Grizz spun on-the-one-and-on-the-two as bars of laser light shot across the floor, and all of the students magnetized themselves to the bleachers. John, Joanne, Ben, and Brenda partied like it was 1999, and the Coalmans scooted like it was 1965. Occasionally a group of three or four girls, and it was always the girls who initiated, would move on to the floor for a song. If they remained on the floor for a second song, a group of three or four boys would move out and join them. All retreated at the beginning of the third song.

I had prepared two raps for the occasion. The first was a cover of *Paul Revere* by The Beastie Boys that substituted Lewis, Tuuqaq, and Jay-boy for the characters, and Pepsi and harpoons for some of the items. The second was a complete original; not because I wanted it to be, but because there wasn't a rap song that centered around Cessnas, whales, solstices, Hondas, Alaska Permanent Fund Dividends, Pilot Bread, and Polarfleece.

At 11:30 we turned the lights on. All of the students begged for one more song even though the majority of them had participated in maybe four dances all night. I helped A-Team and Nick corral the students to their lockers, past the restrooms, and through the foyer to the front porch where everyone's eyes were shocked into constriction by the sun still on the horizon.

The students mounted up in triplets and quadruplets, and filled the air with the clangy, "Kaputtputt-putt," of their Hondas. I pulled Lewis aside and presented him with the Leatherman Crunch I had ordered from REI a month earlier after I noticed that he looked at it on the internet almost every day.

Lewis surveyed it through the plastic package. "Gaw-lee Mr. Shosatori, this is a *nice* pocket knife, it gots little vice-grips and everything. How come you give me?"

"It's a gift, for graduation."

"But you're not coming back? And this is new. Only time any teacher ever give me stuff is when I do work for them, or when they gonna leave and never want to take it with them."

"Well, you're an Eskimo and somebody once told me that every Eskimo needs a pocket knife."

"Oh," said Lewis, then extended his hand. We shared a grasp, double-pump, release, and then he walked away.

I returned to the gym where decorations were either trashed or stored for the next year. One was a series of curved translucent rods that, when threaded together with illuminated cords, formed a giant rainbow. We coiled the illuminated cords and collapsed the rods into sections. Curt, Nick, A-Team, and I carried the pieces down to the storage room. There were spots open for individual pieces, but A-Team wanted to keep it altogether in one place. Curt saw an open shelf at the end of one aisle that was blocked by media carts and some chalkboards. He rolled away the media carts and slid the chalkboards back to make it easier to walk past. The first thing he said was, "Band uniforms? When did Iqsaiqsiq have a band?" The second thing he said was, "Is dat a couch?"

After we had successfully unwoven the rainbow and stored it, A-Team made a close inspection of the couch and said, "Thanks guys."

Curt said, "No pro-blum." Nick and I remained silent.

With the chalkboards and media cart back in place, we turned out the lights and locked the door. On the way back to the gym, A-Team said again, "Seriously guys, thank you. You did the right thing, for her and the kids."

Curt had a look that was like, "Oh, kay?" while Nick and I were betrayed by our apophasis.

A-Team slung his next words free form. "It's hard enough dealing with children who struggle to manage their own behavior, but my greatest frustration comes from adults, who, knowing that, refuse to adapt, adopt, or modify the environment to one in which those most highly challenged students have the best opportunities for success. Again, thank you. What you did was undoubtedly beneficial."

Curt probably thought that the now-constant daylight had affected A-Teams brain, perhaps pushed him to insomnia, but Nick and I knew the genesis for his thoughts and the gravity of his validating monologue.

A-Team drove Curt, Pat, the Coalmans, and I home; John took the rest of the crew. I hopped into the front seat and saw a plate heaped with untouched whale and caribou on the dashboard. "Yours?" I asked A-Team.

A-Team grimaced. "I believe you are fully aware of unto whom that belongs, Mr. Shosatori."

"I'm sure he regrets that he forgot it. Maybe someone should mail it to him." I looked at A-Team and could tell he was in deep thought, perhaps strategizing.

We waded the fjord that separated the quad-plex from the road, climbed the steps to the porch, and dissipated to our apartments. Even if I had reset my calendar back in February, it wouldn't have mattered now since there were no student contact days left. I had made it. Tomorrow was a work day. Saturday all I had to do was get out of bed and make it to the airport. I opened my window, which allowed cool air to pour in along with the rattle and hum of the Hondas that lulled me to sleep.

# CHAPTER TWENTY-ONE

I awoke shortly after 7:00 a.m.; not to my alarm, Hondas, the sunlight that stabbed down through my window, or even gun shots, but to Belle's shriek of, "Corrr-nelll!!!"

I (in a pair of ratty sweatpants and untied sneakers) met Curt (in a Celtics Jersey and boxers) at the top of the stairs as we exited our apartments. Belle (dressed appropriately and professionally for school, even though it was a staff-only day) braced the door as if it blocked a dozen zombies.

Cornell hobbled out of the apartment as he slipped on his shoes and said, "Whu-uht? Whu-uht is it Belle?"

Belle stepped away and pointed. "Thu-at is dis-gus-ting!"

Curt and I descended the stairs as Pat exited his apartment in a robe and moccasins. Cornell opened the door and I saw four up-ended yellow trash cans. Cornell was shocked when he lifted his eyes from the patina on the porch and saw the entire outside surface of the door varnished in a similar fashion. "Good Loh-urd!" he exclaimed.

Pat calmly said, "We've all seen it, you can close the door now," then withdrew to his apartment to call A-Team, who in turn called John to come over and clean it.

As we made our way back up the stairs Curt shook his head and mumbled, "Shit for a welcome, and shit for a goodbye. What a shitty place."

"Do you feel violated?" I asked sarcastically.

"I have been so be-yawn-d violated for duh last two months, I don't even know what dat word means any mo'uh."

"Would you like a hug?" I spread out my arms.

"We're bros Shosatori, but you try huggin' me and I'll bust you right in the knot sack."

"How about if I put a shirt on?"

Curt laughed. "I don't care if you put your fawkin pawkuh n' mittens on," then fired off, "I'm not'uh hug'uh!" as he stepped into his apartment and closed the door.

Twenty minutes later we gathered in the Coalman's apartment for coffee and cookies as John hosed off and bleached the front porch. Cornell had called around. We were the only target. I wondered if it were happenstance or if I had brought it upon us with my repudiation of David.

I found Terri in my classroom as she checked her email. Apparently, I was the only person who had yet to disconnect the computers and stack them for storage. When she was finished, we talked about some inconsequential idiosyncrasies of village life until she asked, "Have I missed something? You understand the culture, you're satisfied with the salary and benefits, you can endure the climate, you're effective in the classroom (debatable, I thought), and the kids like you (also debatable). What else is there?"

"The first Inupiat word I learned was *Qaniq Itpitch*, which means hello. You know what the next three Inupiat words were that I learned?" I asked.

Terri shook her head.

"*Anuq, tuniq,* and *atchu*. Not good morning or good night, or please or thank you. Shit, white nigger, I don't know; those were the next three Inupiat words I learned after hello. Then later I learned that *atchu* doesn't even really mean, 'I don't know,' instead it means, 'I might know, but I won't admit it if I do.'"

Terri waved her hand. "No, that is not what those words mean. As I said in Aciq, we do not consider *anuq* a vulgar term, it is a bodily function. It is human waste, you don't have to interpret in the way you did."

"Then why do children tell us that we have *anuq*-breath? Poop breath. How is that appropriate?"

Terri pled softly. "They are children and don't know any better."

"I would disagree, for many reasons, but what about fifteen, sixteen, seventeen year-olds? They don't know any better either?"

"The teenagers are very angry because they see the things other teenagers have and do on the Outside and realize that they don't have access to them."

While the unemployment rate in Iqsaiqsiq was about forty percent, the snowmachine ownership rate was about ninety percent. The same was true for flat-screen television ownership, as well as Nike Air Jordan tennis shoe ownership. Of course the iPod and Pepsi ownership rates were at ninety-nine percent. It also ran counter to Bettie Iqaluq's assertion months earlier that Brenda was jealous of what the students had, if in fact "Outsiders" did have more or better things than the local population. I wanted to take at least one element all the way to its origin without retreat from, or surrender to, the amusement park tunnel, so I kept those facts to myself and asked, "And being angry, about those things, is justification for aggression, especially aggression directed at teachers?"

"It's not a justification, it's a cause."

"Lots of kids, in lots of places, don't have everything other people have, or get to do everything they want to do. How is that a legitimate cause?" I wanted to add that Arnold had been denied any benefit from his dividend not by the indulgence of Outsiders but by the selfishness of his own parents. Again, I made a choice to stay on track.

"It isn't legitimate, but it is the cause nonetheless."

"If it isn't legitimate, then why is it tolerated?" I caught myself using Stan's air-Judo chops, and consciously ceased.

"Because we love our children, and we understand their frustration, and we tolerate them instead of punishing them."

"You tolerate? So in other words you allow it?" I had also considered saying enable.

"Yes."

"Then how do they know it's wrong?"

"We tell them. We hear them say it, and we tell them, 'That's not the right thing to say,' or, 'That's not the right word to use.'"

"And then, it would appear, they go right back out and say or do the wrong thing again."

Terri, who had straight white teeth incidentally, smiled and said, "In your adult life, perhaps even this year, have you ever tripped, slipped, or stumbled?"

"Yes, a couple of time this year on the glare ice, and last summer, hiking around Mount Rainier. Not to mention a million other times in the thirty-two years before that."

"So you make mistakes too? You don't intend to, or mean malice by them, but you still make them, right?"

"Yes, but walking on the ice, or climbing on the rocks, with the intention of moving forward on an unstable surface, and physically losing one's grip momentarily is different than calling someone a name, or yelling at them."

"How so?"

"Basically, in physiological terms, speech is a much more advanced and complicated skill than locomotion. Speech requires more thought, and therefore more intention. Maybe what you are saying is that people get tongue-tied and intend to say, 'Ship,' and instead say, 'Shit,' but that is not the case in my classroom."

Terri shook her head sympathetically, "But that is how we see it. Maybe not how you were taught, or how you believe is correct. But that *is* our belief, and that *is* how we operate."

I felt I had tracked back to the origin and wanted to make a clarification. "When you say, 'We,' do you mean all of the Inupiat?"

"Oh, certainly not all. Inupiat are free to raise their children as they see fit, and some prefer to raise their children in a Western-Anglo style, or Asian or even a Middle-Eastern style, and that is okay for them. But a true Inupiat would be raised in the way we just discussed. We are not homogenous, though I would prefer that we were."

"If these children are raised in this highly tolerant, to use your word, environment, then why are they so intolerant themselves?"

Terri asked what I meant and I gave several examples from my classroom, most of which she questioned or minimized, but in the end she said, "Well, do you think you were being tolerant of them? If you told them to put the Pepsi away, that was not tolerance, was it? That was prohibition, or prohibitive."

We followed that question all the way down the rabbit hole until we reached a similar conclusion of, "That is our belief, and that is how we operate."

"But," I said, "When the person goes to Anchorage, or Honolulu, and they have to interface with the Western-Anglo world, they don't know the rules, or at least they are not willing to follow them."

"That is what we mean by 'walking-in-two-worlds.' It's taking off your *muqluq's* in Anchorage and putting on your sandals in Honolulu. Then switching back to *muqluq's* when you get back to Anchorage."

"Let's imagine, in your metaphor, that a person has all the *knowledge* that he or she needs to navigate Honolulu. They still need the self-discipline to act on that knowledge and most, but not all, of the people I have interacted with in Iqsaiqsiq lack that level of self-discipline."

"How do you know?"

I cited everything, emphasized the lack of preparation prior to any type of activity, and specifically mentioned the number of chances Tim was given during basketball season yet still sabotaged himself with the telephone incident.

"Those things may have turned out better if people had exercised more self-discipline, but ultimately everything you just described happened in Iqsaiqsiq and therefore is covered by Iqsaiqsiq-standards, and not Honolulu-standards. If you told me that someone from Iqsaiqsiq went to Honolulu, behaved like that, and ran afoul of those people in that place, I would agree with you that that was wrong."

I honestly did not have an example of a person from Iqsaiqsiq getting locked up in the Honolulu jail. I thought of some of the stories I had read in the Anchorage Daily News of Native people being involved, tragically, with the police in Anchorage or Fairbanks, but I did not have the type of conclusive facts on hand to raise that point effectively, so I didn't.

Terri had mentioned one thing I still wanted to address. "Fair enough, I concede this is not Honolulu. Now, you said that the scenarios I described may have turned out better if the individuals had exerted more self-discipline. So if you believe that, then why don't you promote more self-discipline?"

"It's not that I, or we, don't promote self-discipline, it's that we promote or put a greater emphasis on tolerance, on being tolerant of our children, on having them know that we love and accept them, than we do on creating or promoting self-discipline."

"Okay," I said, "Last question, I promise. Why the big secret? Why not just tell everybody at the job interview, or post it on the website, 'We don't punish our children. We don't enforce limits. You will be called these names, you will have these things thrown at you, or receive these threats, and that is just the way things are because we want them that way. If you are willing to put up with that and still want the job, it's yours; if you don't, then stay in Honolulu, or Houston, or Hartford.'"

Terri said, "If it were completely up to me, or the parents, we would. We truly would. But you and I both know that isn't realistic, or practical. I guess the best answer I can give you is, 'That decision is not my responsibility, it is a decision made by the school board.'"

"Then that is my answer. You ask me why I am leaving and that is my answer. Had somebody just come out and told me all about the aggression, violence, defiance, xenophobia, apathy, and scapegoating, as well as the little intricacies and nuances of facial twitches and shoulder shrugs; I would have been able to help students achieve more, *and* I would have a lot more respect for everyone involved. As it is now, I know what happens and how to handle it better than ninety-nine percent of the teachers in Alaska, but I've already jumped the shark: All my meters are pegged, and I am exhausted from having to second-guess or, no, from having to *triple-guess* everything and everyone."

Terri said, "I sympathize, I really do. It gives me insight into why so many teachers have left, and also why others have stayed so long. There is a term I have heard from my own daughters, and please bear with me if it offends you I apologize, but, 'It is what it is.' Does that... Do you understand that, how I think it is supposed to be understood?"

I had another dozen points to make and questions I would have liked answered, but I figured I had already covered enough ground for two lifetimes, or at least two teaching careers, so I said, "I do understand it, and I am not offended. My only caveat would be, 'It is what it is, but it doesn't have to be.'"

Terri stood, nodded, said, "Perhaps it doesn't," then added, "Perhaps it does," and left.

I inventoried and stored my supplies then took my paperwork down to A-Team for final approval.

A-Team handed me my evaluation along with a letter of reference and said, "You're free to go Mr. Shosatori, but would you indulge one question for me?"

"Sure."

"What do you think you did differently to overcome obstacles that hindered some of your co-workers?"

"I guess, first off, I expected it to be different. It wasn't different in the way that I thought it would be, but I didn't waste any time or energy overcoming my Seattle-philia. I also made benchmarks. Not overly-zealous benchmarks of perfection or excellence, but realistic ones that I knew I could reach because I had reached them before; four weeks, nine weeks, the next pay period, the next trip to Anchorage, that sort of thing. The harder things got, the more important it was that I knew they were within my means to achieve. Finally, I probably turned enough RPM's on that spin-bike to power the village for a week. It gave me a focus that was predictable, impersonal, and unrelated to school where I could lose myself for an hour once a day. That was important."

A-Team nodded. "Sounds like you made a conscious decision to stick it out, and had something to distract you while you did."

"That wasn't my intention initially, but, yeah, I'd say that's right."

"Have you ever read *The 7 Habits of Highly Effective People?*"

"Yes."

"I figured you had. You know, I found myself reviewing it several times this year and thinking how much easier this job, in this place, would be if there was a similar type of book specifically for Bush educators. Problem is it wouldn't have a large enough circulation or a broad enough audience to get published, and it would probably be controversial to say the least. Still it would be great if a person could get some level of insight not just on the challenges, but on successful strategies for resolving those challenges, before they set foot on the airstrip out here." A-Team's face went slightly vacant and he swiveled in his chair to look out the window.

"Like a policy manual?" I half joked.

A-Team continued to stare out the window. "No. Not a manual, something interesting; a narrative of examples, even if it lacked a little clarity or accuracy."

"You mean things like, 'A principal once told me never to smile?'"

A-Team grinned for the first time. "Yes, but you would eventually have to say why that's important."

"And why is it important?" I impelled him.

"Hypothetically, if such a principal did exist, and did say such a thing not only to random teachers but to his fellow principals as well, maybe even the Superintendent if he was willing to listen, it was probably because he had learned, through trial and error, that a straight-face conveys calm. Villages like this are laden with calamity and as a result the one thing that is always in short supply is calm. Calm carries more authority and commands a higher premium than all of the smiles, laughs, friendly compliments, and kindly favors combined. Of course there is an appropriate time to smile and congratulate; but as is always the case, a person has to embrace the larger concept before they can articulate the finer points."

We shook hands and I headed to the gym for a final spin-bike session.

Curt had set up his P90X and I voiced my concern that in retrospect I may not have made a wise choice of battles with the way I handled David's Eskimo dancing situation, and thus brought upon the door decoration at the quad-plex.

Curt said, "Fawk it Shosatori. Fawk him and fawk this place. Iqsaiqsiq and David deserve each other like a cock'n a rub'uh, or better yet, some spooge'n a rub'uh. You did the right thing standin' up to him. Problem is nobody'll know dat 'til next year when he either makes plans in advance or keeps his fawkin' mouth shut. Course, neither us'll be here fo'it, and it'll be two oth'uh schlubs what reap doze rewards, or suff'uh through'm."

I was on the deceleration circuit and Curt was in the middle of the Ab Rippers when the three married couples came by before their flight. We said our good-byes and shook hands, there was some, "Keep in touch," and "Let me know how things turn out," that nobody took seriously, and then they were gone. John would be back in a week while Joanne chased down marathons all summer. Belle and Cornell decided that two Golden Years pockmarked and gouged by Iqsaiqsiq were more than enough, and would begin their retirement in a place with much less prejudice and a better track record of tolerance; the house they had raised their children in on Galvez Street in New Orleans. Ben and Brenda were headed for Brenda's parent's house. The next morning they would wake up jobless and pseudo-homeless; but with $25,000 in the bank, Iqsaiqsiq in their rearview mirror, a lot of resentment in their hearts, and a plastic bottle of her dad's Ron Rico to pass between them.

Curt and I met the other two members of the bachelor squad in the cafeteria and watched *The Big Lebowski* over Velveeta on Pilot Bread crack-wiches, bean stew turned piquant via Heinz 57 sauce, and lemon-lime Gatorade as an Arctic aperitif. I awoke halfway through and found the others asleep. I returned to my room, grabbed my backpack, stepped out into the inescapable sunlight, and thrust my Maui Jims upon my face as my XtraTufs pounded their way down the serrated metal steps.

Remnants of snowdrifts sublimated into an evanescent fog as I crossed the vague boundary between parking lot and road. The shaky thrum of a diesel engine approached me from behind. There were many pickups in Iqsaiqsiq, but only one diesel; the Dodge Quad-Cab of Magnus Kala'a.

It rolled up beside me, the passenger window slid down, and Magnus bellowed in his guttural growl, "Rap-man. (My nickname since Christmas.) Get in."

The majority of my instincts said not to, but, as I had told Terri that morning, all my meters were pegged and unable to provide reliable data; except for my give-a-fuck meter, which contained neither needle nor face. Since my give-a-fuck was not only broken, but absent, I climbed in.

We rode in silence and passed David parked in his pickup and Alex and Solomon astride their Honda along the way. Magnus stopped in front of the quad-plex where a slight person wrapped up in an over-sized coat sat on the steps. It could have been Jay-Boy if he were fifty years older without an iPod or glasses, or maybe it would be Jay-Boy fifty years from now, but tonight it was Jerry.

I slid down from the cab without comment and Magnus drove away.

Jerry stood up. "Good eve-neen, Mac. I visit, okay?"

"Sure," I said.

All I had to offer Jerry was a cup of water, which he accepted as if it were pinot noir. We sat at the kitchen table and, as I knew was the custom, I waited for the Elder to speak. He looked at the cup, looked out the window, looked at the cup again, drank from the cup, and put the cup down; then began, "You know this game, '*Call of Duty?*'"

I raised my eyebrows.

"My grandkids play that game. Think is fun. Ask me, '*Uppa*, what it like in the Marines?' Sometime I ignore them, sometime I say, 'No good,' they want to know how come. I never tell them."

Jerry went through another cycle of look at cup, look out window, look at cup, drink from cup, put cup down, and spoke again. "Kids, think war is like on video game. Think you can lay on couch.

Play. Pretend. Then one day; put on uniform, grab rifle, and go be
Special Forces. All of a sudden. Video game never make nobody real
Marine. Only make, pretend marine, video-game-marine, in they head.
I worry, kids maybe never have life, just video game life. Only make
them video-game-people."

Jerry took just one sip, the last sip, and spoke again. "But you
Mac, you gots real life, and you was real Marine, with your life in god's
hands and your rifle in your hands, and you climb the rocks, and you
get at them what other guys in Aff-can-ee-shan. And, you, know! What
life is! What real is! Life is hard, and real is scary. Then you come
Iqsaiqsiq, and you teacher, real teacher, and you do good; even though
it hard, even though it scary, 'cause you real person."

Jerry wet his gums, then smacked his lips. "Magnus, have real
life too, with his life in god's hands and his harpoon in his hands. He
lean out of boat, shove harpoon in whale and, *boom!!!* He set off the
bomb and *feel* the shock. It hurt his hands and move through his arms,
and sometimes the blood spray out on him. That real. That real
Eskimo. Doing what hard, and scary, but doing. Magnus, tell David
what never do no more. Some think that not okay. Scary for Magnus,
but Magnus do anyway, cause he gots," Jerry punched his palm with his
fist, "Strength, to still do even what make him scared."

"Jerry," he pointed to himself, "Real Marine. Real Eskimo.
Carry *rifle* in my hands, carry *harpoon* in my hands, and both times I got
my life in god's hands." The loose skin below Jerry's jaw wobbled as he
nodded his head vigorously.

"When I's young, life's hard, and I struggle, and I suffer. But I
got," Jerry pointed to his chest, "Strength. We all gots strength then.
We all struggle, and we all suffer, and we all gots strength. I go
Vietnams and gots struggle there too, gots suffer there too, gots," he
pointed to his chest again, "Strength there too."

Jerry looked into the empty cup. I held out my palm and he
placed the cup upon it. I filled it at the sink and returned to the table.
Jerry emptied it in two gulps.

"Never let kids struggle now, 'cause never want them suffer.
Never let them struggle, but that never let them have strength. But still
they suffer, *because* there's no strength. No strength to do what's hard
and scary. No strength, because, no struggle. Can't have strength unless
there's struggle. Nobody never want to hear Jerry say that." Jerry
leaned back in his chair, collapsed his diminutive figure even further,
and let out a gasp.

"Some Marine, only video-game-marine. Some Eskimo, only video-game-eskimo. Never go boat in ocean, just drive around in pickup truck. Never go fish camp. Go Disneyland instead, then buy Spam and fried chicken with Quest card. Wear sealskin mittens and sealskin *muqluqs* so they look like real Eskimo but never know how to hunt seal or skin seal or sew *muqluqs,* and never want to, 'cause is messy and hard. Never gots struggle, never gots strength, only still always let suffer, so do bullshit to hide they suffer, hide they got no strength. Instead of struggle, do what's hard, what's scary, and get strength.

"David, a video-game-eskimo. Pretend to be person, but never know how to be person, never know how to do what hard, or scary, so pretend to do those things, and tell everybody 'bout it. Find someone else to do what's hard, someone else to do what's scary, and never trust in god enough to put himself in god's hands. *No* rifle, *no* harpoon, *no* god, *no* struggle, *no* strength, and sooo scared… so scared… he never ride snowmachine out past the airport lights."

Jerry traced along the grain of the wooden tabletop with his finger and, unlike Mitch, I knew that if I was meant to speak Jerry would tell me to speak. I also knew that if Jerry was finished he would leave. Until either of those two things came to pass I was suspended in limbo. Or rather, I *chose* to be suspended in limbo.

Jerry pushed himself up and headed for the door. After we shook the weak, three-fingered handshake and exchanged a final "Semper Fi" Jerry hobbled down the stairs, out the door, and was gone.

Saturday I awoke early, but lay in bed until 9:30. I packed my clothes, pistol, sleeping bag, and rolled up duffel bag into my suitcase and garment bag, then folded my bed sheets and bath sheets into a bundle. I took one last look around my apartment, which looked exactly as it had when I walked into it for the first time, and walked out for the last time.

I headed for Stan's house where Jenn had prepared the Mother-Of-All-Brunches for those of us still in the village.

"Good morning, good morning, good morning Iqsaiqsiq," I called from the *quniciuq.*

"Good morning Ken," answered Jenn as she thickened the whipped cream with a whisk.

"I brought you my sheets and towels, figured you could use them for any future wayward and orphaned adults."

"Thanks." Jenn wiped her hands with a dish cloth, took the bundle to a back room, and disappeared through the door headed for the breezeway to the garage.

A minute later Stan entered the house. It was odd because I knew that Jenn loathed jail guard duty. Stan took an envelope off of the counter and slid it across the table to me. "That's the address, gate code, and key to our condo in Girdwood. Just send me an email or call to be sure it's available and you can use it anytime you like."

Stan and I were tight, but still a house key with carte blanche privileges after nine months was pretty intense. "Thank you Stan, but I don't know if I'm ever coming back to Alaska."

"You will. Not to the Arctic, maybe not as a teacher, but you will be back. Trust me."

I did trust Stan, far more than anyone else in the Arctic, and as much as anyone else ever in my entire life. I trusted not only his integrity, but his judgment. Everyone else was quick to tell me how they wished it had been in the past or how they hoped it would be in the future. Even Roby's version of the current circumstances was slightly restrained, while Nick and Joanne were known to overstate the negatives at times. But Stan had always told me how it really was and I respected him for it. He would spend at least one and possibly three more years in Iqsaiqsiq being called an *anuq*-breathed-*tuniq*, but nobody could ever call him a video-game-trooper.

Stan returned to guard duty and Jenn returned to concoct espressos. She presented me with a platter of half cheddar cheese omelet, half habanero hashbrowns.

"Who's in the VIP suite?" I asked.

"Lewis' mom. Never let a celebration go to waste, you know."

Curt arrived and Jenn presented him with his favorite original creation; chopped bacon and mashed potatoes pressed and formed in the Belgian waffle maker, then smothered with sausage gravy in lieu of syrup. We had christened it the, "Wicked Arctic Fawker."

Stan went to meet the plane and picked up Pat and Nick on his way back. Curt gave his, "Shit welcome, shit goodbye," thesis to the group and Stan mentioned that one other house had gotten the same treatment; Magnus Kala'a's.

We four bachelors nursed various chocolate, double-chocolate, chocolate mint, and double-chocolate mint creations while we flipped between hockey, baseball, and basketball games. Meanwhile, Stan napped and Jenn scrapbooked.

At 4:30 Curt and I said our goodbyes to Nick, Pat, and Jenn before Stan drove us to the airport. Nick would head out on Monday to connect with a flight to Maui where he would remain until he returned to Iqsaiqsiq in August. Pat would stay in the village another week until A-Team was done with his duties, then they would both fly down in the same Cessna that had brought them back from Christmas break. Pat would never return to Iqsaiqsiq, or any other Arctic Circle School District village. Despite being told after the October meeting that he would not be retained, A-Team received a contract and would return to Iqsaiqsiq in August. Apparently a certain school board member had called the Superintendent and demanded it, or at least that's who the Superintendent thought it was.

The plane stopped in Klaciq and Aciq on our way to Fairbanks where we caught another flight to Anchorage. Curt had a room at the Marriott and after a few beers, over which I told him how Emma's fuck-couch came to be in the storage room, we both used the Jacuzzi before I grabbed the shuttle back to the airport around midnight. In a few days a woman Curt had gone to grad school with would meet him and they planned to travel around Alaska by bus, rail, and ferry until med school started in the fall.

I made my way through security and down to gate C5. Recently arrived passengers bound for early morning flights to the National Parks or fish canneries had already staked out their sleeping spots.

On a row of under-padded mated chairs I sat and reflected that I had certainly lived my life deliberately in the Arctic. In fact, I had lived my life at a level of focus and intention that surpassed my previous definition of deliberate. I had also come to the conclusion that the only alternative to such a deliberate life in the Arctic was to abandon any attempt at order, and any attempt at safeguarding one's Pepsi.

I had failed to front only the essential facts of life. I had fronted all of the facts of life, essential or not, because often one does not know whether a fact is essential or superfluous until after one has not only confronted, but mastered it; and the benefits of mastery are worth the concomitant complexity.

I had also learned several facts about caribou and whales; but I still had no idea how to sew mittens, ride a dogsled, or build an igloo. I had seen the real Aurora Borealis though, once, and had to admit that it was pretty cool, as was the polar bear.

A very young couple, much like Ben and Brenda, settled into the set of mated chairs one-apart from mine. They noticed the collection of William's Air Service tags on my backpack and inquired as to why I had been out in the Bush. I told them and they hadn't heard of Iqsaiqsiq, but they were familiar with the Arctic Circle School District. They volunteered that they had just finished their first year teaching in a village on the Alaska Peninsula.

"Are they really the highest paying school district in the United States?" asked the woman.

"Yes," I said.

"We paid eleven hundred a month for half of a leaky, smelly duplex with paper thin walls that cost another four hundred a month to heat. But ACSD's housing is pretty comfortable and reasonably priced isn't it?" asked the man.

"Yes," I said.

"How were your class sizes? We each had seventeen students, but I heard sometimes in ACSD there are classes with only one student. Is that right? Did you have any classes with only one student?" asked the woman.

"Yes," I said.

"Whenever we go to meetings at the district office we have to sleep on the floor with sleeping bags, or find somebody with an open couch to crash on. I heard ACSD has dorms that you get to stay in at the district office. Do they really have dorms at the district office?" asked the man.

"Yes," I said.

"When do you head back in August?" asked the woman.

"I don't. I'm not. I'm done, and I'm never going back." I said.

"Why not?" they asked in unison.

I described the removal of Eddie from first period on the first day, the unabashed dirt-clod assault at the boat launch, the amusement park tunnel logic professed by Tim's father up until the day he shot up someone's house, the racial slurs piled upon Croesus, the drunk woman who abused the Chinese dog, the daily verbal abuse I endured, the daily physical abuse my door endured, and the threat to turn Iqsaiqsiq into an Arctic Columbine. I outlined the finer points of Terri Bowen-Skeen's, "It's-probably-not-right-but-it's-definitely-not-wrong-either-because-it-is-our-belief-and-it-is-what-it-is," mindset as we shuffled into the line to board.

Just before our tickets got scanned the man said, "It sounds like that school could use a full-time counselor to help the students understand their feelings."

"And after school programs, like wood carving or maybe welding, to engage them in something productive," added the woman.

I faced them both and slowly rolled my shoulders forward, in, and down; then turned and boarded the plane.

CPSIA information can be obtained at www.ICGtesting.com
Printed in the USA
LVOW06s1954110314

376960LV00022B/578/P